Asleep Without Dreaming

Barbara Forte Abate

Halcyon Moon Books

In Memory of Justin E. Till
LCPL, USMC

An American Hero

Also by Barbara Forte Abate

The Secret of Lies

ACKNOWLEDGEMENTS

The sincere depth of gratitude I owe to a treasure trove of family and friends is impossible to convey in a few short lies, but each and every one of you is a beautiful and cherished gift. To my very fine fellow, James, our children Caitlin, Chelsea, Carlyle, Laurel, Timmy, and beautiful new Grandson, Sebastian, my boundless love.

Love and thanks to my mother, Jenny Parsons Masters, for the eternal gift of faith.

Thanks from the heart to my sister, Donna Forte Till, for reading this book when it was still a quivering mess, and especially for allowing me to share Justin's poem.

To Lynda Remus and Carolee Post, my ever dependable early readers, I can only hope you know how much you are appreciated.

Ellen Polacastri Lobb, your kindness and generosity are beyond compare. Truly, it is your wise editing skill that has put the shine on the prize, and my gratitude runs wide, and true, and deep.

Janet J. Lawler, tireless supporter, amazing writer, and BFF, I can't imagine this lifetime road trip without you alternately driving and riding shotgun.

To my tireless hometown literary cheerleaders, you are most supremely loved and appreciated. Likewise my Gold Medal Tribe, Fortes, Abates, and Parsons, whose support and encouragement have been high-test fuel for the journey.

And what can I say, Cate, your talents and vision in putting together the cover design for this book makes my heart sing.

I can do all things in HIM who strengthens me. Philippians 4:13

DECK OF FATE

Falling down a endless, lightless hole
With you, your body, mind, but no soul.
Your soul has departed;
As a card in life, You've been discarded.

Deeper, Darker and colder the hole
becomes
Your teeth clenched so hard it hurts your
gums;

As you await your fate.
Either a hellish Hades or a pearly gate;
Behold God or the Devil, for you they wait.
You have nothing left to fear, for you can
never be late.

J.E.T
Feb. 1996

One

Willa has always expected it to feel like more of an adventure when they finally leave. But maybe the thrill will come later, once they've put enough distance between Hoosick Falls and whatever it is she now feels breathing down a threat to reach out and snatch them back. Because only once they're clear—never-looking-back-gone-forever-clear—can all the lousy crappy things that have happened to her since the day she was born, be tossed into the files of distant memory and shoved off a cliff. And she intends to show no mercy. She wants all of it gone. And for good.

She has no idea of the time, but Willa can tell from the shifting shades of grey light that the night is moving fast. Up until now, she's been purposeful to avoid acknowledging the giddy rhythm waxing and waning behind her rib cage like a million miniature wings, trapped and frantic for release. And yet they've been driving for hours now without incident; no sirens or barricades materialized to block their escape. *Can it really be this simple? So easy to drive away from everything you've ever known? Maybe it is. Maybe they really have.*

A peculiar whine rubs in a complaint against her thoughts. It takes a moment for Willa to comprehend that the sound is coming from the car's engine—a low groan—followed by a long snaky hiss that rides out on a galloping shimmy. And just like that, the adventure is over. *Dead.* Deceased on the shoulder of the two-lane, and not a single road sign anywhere to indicate if they've even made it within spitting distance of the state line.

There's no point in pretending disappointment, since quite honestly, Willa would've been far more surprised if nothing unfortunate happened at all. Because something always does.

"Piece of JUNK! Damn crap car," Stella rumbles, smacking the steering wheel with the flat of her palms, hard enough that an angry red crescent instantly appears in a reprimand across the pale surface of her skin.

"The same damn story—the same lousy crap story. Not one damn thing I can count on but lousy bad luck."

A sharp POP hyphenates the spewing eruption of her immediate rage, thickening wisps of steam now leaking from the seams of the closed hood.

"Perfect—great. DAMN-IT! This is just lousy stinking perfect."

Willa slides back against her seat, shifting sideways to keep from getting caught in the direct line of Stella's careening fury. *So this is it then. The bottom falls out and the whole thing is finished before it's even started.*

After so many hours on the road, it should at least feel as if they've gotten somewhere, earned some distance, only it doesn't. Everything still looks, smells, and tastes, like the place they just left.

For the past hundred miles or more, Willa had made a concentrated effort to doze-off. But sleep had remained stubbornly out of reach, her interior vision filled to overflowing with searing images of the car plunging over the embankment and down into the abyss of some bottomless valley the moment she closed her eyes, tragic victims of Stella's inexpert hands on the wheel. They are scenes so vibrantly alive, that rather then risk sleeping (for what might very well be the last time) Willa had remained wide-eyed in prayerful vigil as the hours blew past.

As the car careened wildly around yet another hairpin turn, Willa stared hard into the darkness crowding their flight, ever hopeful that her devotion would work to avert the threat of gravity, and lessen the shadow of impending doom circling overhead like buzzards in anticipation of a carcass.

Only once the grey murk of fading night gradually melted into daybreak—the dark ribbon of roadway un-kinking, rolling out wide and nearly straight—did Willa breathe a tentative sigh of relief, believing that they'd successfully escaped something; a stray bullet, runaway train, a rain of boulders dropped from the heavens and aimed at their heads.

They didn't talk, and so Willa stared out at the passing scenery for miles. The subtle changes beyond the dust-streaked windshield, a plum shaded panorama of mountains blocking the pink light rising in the east.

The ill shaped piece of cardboard Stella had haphazardly duct-taped over the remnants of the broken rear window days earlier, flapped madly in the wind stirred by the speeding car, and Willa found herself wishing that it would tear off and blow away into oblivion, taking the grating whomp-whomp sound with it.

And it is right at this moment, as Willa silently curses the incessant drone, twisting roads, lousy driver, and now, the broken-down car, that she all at once remembers the cats, and the fact that she's forgotten to leave behind a note for the person who will eventually happen upon the abandoned house. Without her instructions, it seems unlikely anyone will find the bag of cat food pellets she'd hidden behind the shutters stacked against the shed in the back yard.

Stella is still there, posed in front of the car as she has been for nearly twenty minutes—staring under the hood at the workings of an engine she knows nothing about, as though expecting some remarkable mechanical component to speak-up and diagnose the problem for her—when a truck speeds past. The vehicle screeches to a stop just up ahead, raising a cloud of grit as the driver fishtails in reverse along the highway's gravel shoulder.

"Breakdown, Ma'am?" a moon-faced man in grease-stained overalls calls out through his open window.

Willa peers over the front seat, striving for a better look at the Good Samaritan stranger who is gracious or curious enough to pull over; unlike the six motorists previous, who have blown past the stranded car as if it is merely the stalled vapor of a mirage. Grateful as she is of his appearance, she pretends not to notice that the very first thing he says is altogether idiotic.

"Broke down, Miss?"

Maybe people around here do this sort of thing—pull over on the side of the road every once in awhile to have a look at the engine—check to see that everything's still in place and ticking smoothly.

"Oh my, but it certainly is looking that way. I thought if I stared at it long enough and talked nice, the darn thing would be sweet and start up for me," Stella says, turning, smiling as the man opens his door and struts across the low-lying cloud of grit stirred up by his tires.

Willa tilts her face for a better view out the open window, leaning forward to catch the accustomed details of her mother's seamless glide into performance mode. Stella's voice immediately softens to imitate the whispery baby tones of Jackie Kennedy—an impersonation she's been diligently working to parrot (even as she adamantly denies this is anything other than her natural tone, as if Willa hasn't known her mother's authentic voice from birth) ever since Stella's best friend Dee insisted she bore an uncanny resemblance to the handsome new president's beautiful and popular wife. No one's ever asked Willa's opinion, but she has yet to see any such likeness herself. As it is, she finds it impossible to align the two women in her imagination, not even for the sake of a brief comparison.

The man grins and ducks his head under the open hood, his thick hands moving over the engine, fingering wires and tugging on hoses.

Willa only succeeds in catching random snippets of the man's diagnosis, as he runs down a list of visible ailments to Stella. There is something about a split in the radiator hose. And now he is pointing out several of the other hoses coiled against the engine in fat rubber snakes, expounding on his original assessment that they are conspicuously dry-rotted and in imminent danger of bursting. "You might best think about having the whole bunch of 'em changed to be on the safe side. Otherwise you're just lookin' at more trouble down the road."

Willa would like to pretend that the dour forecast coming from a complete stranger is nothing of consequence, but she knows better. Though her own predictions might lack the mechanical details of his, Willa has been growing her own suspicions as to the vehicle's sad condition from the day Stella first showed up stop-jerk-driving the hideous thing into the driveway. The car is painfully worn inside and out, and by all appearances it's been in this pitiful state for more years than not. It wouldn't surprise Willa to learn that it's never been new at all. But, rather, thrown together with an assemblage of old mismatched parts to create the Frankenstein monster of automobiles.

She crosses her arms over the top of the seat and rests her chin in the crook of her elbow as Stella and the man continue talking.

"...you won't be driving this until...get that radiator hose changed...*The Moonglow*...just up the road...her name's Omega Pearl...can call a tow truck out for the car."

Willa feels her insides drop. Apparently they are stranded out here—wherever here is—until the car is fixed; or at least bandaged well enough to limp the rest of the way to California.

That her mother has so confidently specified a destination is as unexpected as it is a relief, especially since the entire context of their getaway flight feels far more random and erratic than it feels sensible or sane. Still, if Willa was to guess where they were headed in the moments before Stella made her pronouncement, she never would've dared hope for a prize as rich and sparkly as California.

"You hungry?" Stella had asked, several hours earlier, reaching for the pack of cigarettes on the dashboard, poking a finger through the opening to retrieve her last one, then crushing the cellophane covered wrapper and tossing it to the floor.

"Starved."

"You could've said something."

"You seem in a hurry to get somewhere," Willa had said, pausing a moment before voicing the question that's been swelling to the dimensions of a land fleet in the span of hours it's gone unasked. "Where exactly are we going anyway?"

"Any damn place we want. The sky's the limit."

"Honestly?" Willa says, her eyes narrowing with the immediate apprehension that promptly bobs to the surface. "Are we leaving because of what happened to the car?"

"Don't be so dramatic, Willa. That was obviously just a bunch of bored kids being stupid. Do you honestly think I'd pack up and walk away from my entire life because of a flat tire and some scratches? I'm not that fragile. We're leaving because it's time to get out. Simple as that."

No, not so simple. Willa could taste the lie in her mother's statement. Could hear it in her attempt at nonchalance. Saw it in her white-knuckled grip on the steering wheel.

"It's just time. It was time years ago. There's nothing for us in that garbage town. Not a damn thing. We don't belong there. It's a dead-end. Just one big, lousy dead-end for anyone stupid or lazy enough to stay around and keep on wasting away."

For the first time in forever, Willa found herself in agreement with Stella on something. Though it still didn't explain why her mother's lousy old car had become such a coveted target for vandals.

"But that stuff with the car ... why would anybody bother with this old thing? As if it doesn't look bad enough," Willa pressed, convinced that there was something far more definitive behind Stella's insistence of an immediate and hasty departure. "Why would anybody care about making crap look any crappier? What's the point in that?"

"How should I know why idiots do what they do? Do I have a magic window looking into the pea brain of every nutcase sneaking past the house with a nail in their pocket or a brick crammed down their pants?"

"I just meant—"

"Well, for cripes sakes. Finally something. It's about damn time," Stella interrupts. "There's a sign for a diner. I'm so damn hungry I'd run over the Pope's granny for a slice of bread and butter."

Willa makes no effort to try and retrieve her unfinished thought. What did she care why they left anyway? Besides which, Stella rarely felt inclined to explain her actions, no matter how much Willa fished and prodded. It was just her mother's way of doing business.

Truth be told, aside from the understandable curiosity anyone would have over being shaken out of bed in the middle of the night, it really made no difference to Willa why they'd left. She was just as eager as Stella to leave behind the dull void of Hoosick Falls. Just as anxious to abandon the suffocating airlessness of infinite boredom and malcontent that had so long colored even the most ordinary days. All too happy to wave goodbye to the bland ugliness of every unwanted and unnecessary possession they'd deserted in the gloomy grey house.

"Where are we?"

"No idea. I haven't seen a marker or a sign for miles. Not that it matters. It all looks the same. Crummy little nothing towns that aren't even worthy of a two-dollar sign."

"Can I look at the map?"

"What map?"

"We don't have a map?"

"What for? A map doesn't *show* what a place looks like, just how to get there. What the hell's the sense in that?"

Willa leaned forward, resting her chin on her arm bent across the top of the seat. Stella didn't seem to care that Willa preferred to sit alone in the backseat. She likely assumed it was because Willa liked to prop her back against the door and stretch out her legs along the seat. But that was only half of it. The truth was Willa felt safer back there. Though only one seat removed from Stella, she thought maybe her chances of survival were better back here. That she might actually have an opportunity to eject herself through the cardboard window if she ever needed to make an immediate exit in order to avoid a horrific crushing death brought on by Stella's terrible driving.

"So we can see where we're headed."

"I already know where we're headed."

"Yeah? Where?"

"I'm thinking California would be nice."

"*California?* Are you serious?"

"Sure, why not? You think we need permission? An audience with the governor?"

"That's not what I mean. It's just that California is so far away. And it's—well, it's *California.*"

"If a person wants to change her life she needs to aim for distance. Otherwise there's really no point."

There's no argument that California is the most exotic place Willa can imagine—as altogether foreign to her old life in Hoosick Falls as snow in July. That alone is enough to make her slam the door on the irritating voice of logic tapping into her thoughts with a reminder of Stella's penchant for propagating fruitless schemes the way other people breathe air.

For now she'll ignore it, if only because she doesn't want to hear it.

She'd leaned back against the seat as Stella began whistling an unfamiliar tune—loud and suspiciously off key—but Willa didn't care. Her mind was all at once buoyant, scrambling to focus on the collage of images she can't clearly see because they are moving so fast. And she'd turned her head to stare out at the range of gradually shrinking mountains, purple and blue, farther away then she'd ever seen them. Feeling the briefest press at her temples as her head began to fill with a brand new set of dreams.

The man places his large hands on the hood and pushes down, closing it with a sharp snap.

"Well, come on now, Willa. This nice man is giving us a ride to a motel down the road," Stella says, continuing in her stolen Jackie Kennedy voice. Soft and breathy in a way that is just fine for the genuine article, but which Willa neither likes nor trusts when she hears it coming from her mother's mouth.

"WILLA," Stella repeats, momentarily compelled to abandon the sweet and gentle tones of her mimicry, lifting her voice an impatient octave when Willa doesn't move, but instead stares back at her mother as if she's converted to speaking Swahili. *They're just leaving the car? Here on the road? Just leaving it to go off with this man who is now watching Stella with an expression Willa definitely doesn't like. As if he's just won a fifty-dollar prize from a scratch-off lottery card he's found on the sidewalk.*

"Come on now and help me with the cases."

But the Good Samaritan is already in motion, hoisting the bloated cases from the trunk of the car; effortlessly grasping a suitcase in each of his big hands and carrying them to his idling truck.

"The Moonglow. What a sweet name. It sounds absolutely charming," Stella says when she spies the green and white sign tucked into the pine trees just up ahead. Yet the breathy tones

of her much-practiced coquetry leave Willa mostly uncertain as to whether her mother truly holds to the opinion coming from her mouth.

"It's decent, but then it's not as if there's another place around here to compare it with either. No ma'am, this is it. Only accommodations you're gonna find out here unless you got relatives in town. I'll tell you what though, it used to be a real nice place back in the 30's—before the war. Folks from the city would come out here in July and August to get away from the heat and the noise, and all us local kids would battle it out for the handful of summer jobs they offered out here, hoping to make a bit of money and maybe meet a pretty girl interested in a little summer romance," he grins in a way that feels like a wink.

"Sounds sweet," Stella says, and now Willa knows for certain it is an act. Stella cares nothing for *sweetness*, not the word or its meaning.

"Oh yeah, those really were some good times. Sad though how things have changed in thirty years. Not just that time flies by so fast, it's the people that are different. Seems they've pretty much lost interest in quiet, laid-back places like this. Spending a couple weeks in the country doesn't appeal like a trip to Europe or the Islands. How Omega stays in business is anybody's guess—though it certainly helps not to have any competition."

Willa listens, despite her disinterest. Mostly she's just relieved to be heading somewhere—anywhere being an improvement over the backseat of the broken down car out on the highway.

The man has assured them that The Moonglow is not far— just down the road—a particular relief in light of the too-close proximity of the three pressed inside the truck's cab. Willa is in the middle, her legs discomfortingly cocked sideways on the pretext of avoiding bumping the gearshift, although she is far more focused on the horrifying possibility of accidental contact with the stranger's heavy thigh or thick shoulder.

She wills herself not to wrinkle her nose against the acrid mixture of sweat, oil, and cigarette smoke absorbed into the man's clothes; turning her face toward Stella in an effort to evade both the man and the cumulation of unpleasant odors permeating the truck's interior. But the effort is in vein, the assault on her senses proves unavoidable.

"I'm sure it'll be fine. We're not planning on staying around long—just until the car's fixed. So, as long as it's clean and vermin free, it'll be fine for us."

"Sorry to say I can't vouch for either one, considering I've never had cause to stay out here myself," he smiles. "Never been invited," he adds, and again there is the weird winking smile.

Willa is horrified by the far too obvious suggestion apparent in his words, and even Stella is momentarily silent.

"Well, then, so where is it you ladies were heading to?" he says, minus the grin, possibly sensing that he's leapt too far too soon.

"Oh—well, we're just on our way back home to California. We drove out for a wedding. My Aunt Sally just got married for the third time. Poor thing's been widowed twice," Stella says easily, her tone unhampered by the lie. *She is always good in choosing her roles. Seamless even, if you don't know her.*

From the corner of her eye Willa detects the brief lifting of the man's eyebrow. "California, is that right? I hope you don't mind my saying so, but you remind me of someone. I just can't put my finger on—"

"Jackie Kennedy. Yes, I know. Everybody tells me that," she smiles as if this alleged resemblance is an astonishing achievement.

Everybody, meaning Dee. Willa can't imagine where Dee gets this from. Anytime Willa looks at Stella all she ever sees is Stella.

She wonders how it is that the man appears so thoroughly convinced of everything Stella is telling him—not that her untruths are any of his business—it just worries Willa when her mother's lies are too conspicuous. So markedly false, when everything from their clothes, their manner of speech— even the license plate on the broken down car— are piled-up together to suggest something else. This is all wrong. So garishly deceptive it leaves Willa feeling criminal, even when there is no need. People, after all, lie all the time.

If first appearances are to be trusted—and Willa sees no reason why they shouldn't be—there is nothing even remotely charming about *The Moonglow*. Nothing alluring or enchanting as the name suggests, both the place and its setting sadly forlorn in the manner of things long time neglected.

The man swings the truck into the dusty lot and their first glimpse is of a dark squat cottage that serves as the front office. Laid out behind it, is the rest—a weary village of ramshackle cottages sprinkled amongst an unruly growth of pine trees. A sorry encampment holding to the untidy shore of what is probably the biggest lake Willa has ever seen— though in truth she hasn't seen all that many.

Despite the bright sunlight and assumed tranquility of the wide stretch of shimmering water, it is a decidedly dreary place; an extinct ghost town that by all appearances has never been anything but. Rather than serving to create a sense of peaceful solitude, the surrounding forest of towering pines instead lends a grievous depth of gloom and loneliness. There is nothing here of color—no flowers, whimsical ornaments, or invitingly placed lawn chairs to break or otherwise soften the dark lines of heavy limbed trees and mud-colored buildings. The remains of a dock are visible at water's edge; one crippled edge jutting skyward, the opposite corner melted into the water.

There are three cars parked in the dusty lot, the presence of which do little to distract from the eerie stillness suggestive of abandonment thickly poured over everything here. And while the day is hot, Willa all at once feels an icy finger trace along her spine and slip beneath the heavy ponytail lying against her neck.

The Good Samaritan makes a final floundering effort at flirtation as he hoists the suitcases from the truck bed and deposits them on the bare wood porch fronting the small building marked by a faded grey sign announcing its significance as the OFFICE. "I'd be happy to carry these to your cabin once you've checked in with Omega. It's not everyday a fellow gets the opportunity to lend a hand to Jackie Kennedy."

"Thank you, but this is fine," Stella returns his smile, though she is clearly distracted by the unanticipated crux of their surroundings—as if only now comprehending the full scope of just how stuck they really are. She makes a move to open her purse, but the man surmises her intention and takes a quick step backward.

"No need, ma'am. It was my pleasure to help out, though I'm sorry the best I could do was give you bad news and a lift out here."

"Well, you certainly didn't have to stop at all and we appreciate that you did," Stella says, snapping shut the clasp on her handbag at the same instant she turns off her smile, having concluded that the gesture is no longer needed.

Willa looks away, at once embarrassed by Stella's obvious change in temperature from warm to thoroughly chilled. She hasn't much liked the man's winking smile or floundering stab at flirtation, but still, it's just like her mother to so quickly forget a good deed. Whatever questionable footnote he might've had tacked to his motives, he did at least get them here.

"Think nothin' of it. Out there stranded on the highway is a dangerous predicament for two pretty ladies—especially with a crack-pot like Norman Hitchcock running around. You'd think folks around here would make an effort to watch out for each other," he says, shaking his head. "At least until they catch him."

"Who's Norman Hitchcock?"

"You mean you haven't heard about our boy Norman? That sure enough proves you're not from around here," he laughs. "I have to say, I'm still a little surprised though. I would've figured it was national news by now. Don't matter either way, you'll hear it all soon enough—everything from his shoe size to his favorite brand of cigarettes. Norman Hitchcock is one of Omega Pearl's favorite subjects and I guarantee she'll be plenty happy to fill you in. Not much that woman appreciates more than a fresh audience."

But already Willa can see Stella's lack of interest in this Norman person. Her mother has in fact always disliked gossip, maybe because she has so often been the head, butt, and feet of so many mean and unflattering rumors. And even before their rescuer has extended a reluctant goodbye and climbed back into the cab of his truck, Willa knows that Stella has already forgotten to care about anything he's told them.

"Not from around here," the woman who moments before has introduced herself as Omega Pearl Bodie says in a way that isn't so much a question, as a definite statement. She is round all over like an over-inflated balloon, suggesting that one jarring move might very well cause her to pop. The shiny marble eyes in her round face watch Stella carefully, barely making note of Willa at all; her lips parting to reveal a disconcerting smear of bright red lipstick across one of her inordinately small front teeth as if a particularly amusing thought has just now sprinted through her head.

Stella sets her purse on the desk, keeping a protective hand gripped around the strap. "That's right. This is actually our first time out this way. We were just driving through when our car broke down," Stella says, the affected Jackie Kennedy baby whisper altogether gone to be replaced by a tight, careful smile Willa recognizes at once—the one assuring that her mother has instantly arrived at a certain and altogether conclusive impression of the woman. Which is to say that Stella has already decided to dislike Omega Pearl Bodie.

"I figured as much when I saw you pull up out front with Bud. With all that's been going on around here for the past few weeks I figure the only way anybody's gonna stay anywhere within sprinting distance of this town is if they're lost—or stranded," Omega snorts. She bends forward, reaching her short sausage fingers to grip the crook of the cane leaning against the wall beside her, using it to balance her weight as she hoists herself from her chair with conspicuous effort, offering a first glimpse of the dingy white cast plastered around one heavy drumstick leg just below the knee.

It is obvious that Omega has planted her statement with the intent of stirring curiosity. Because just as the Good Samaritan assured before leaving, Omega Pearl Bodie is eager to share whatever it is bubbling up below the surface, just as Stella is adamantly determined not to hear it.

"Yes, well, I can't say just how long we'll be needing a room for, but—"

"I don't rent rooms here, they're cottages. I rent cottages."

"*Cottages*," Stella repeats. "Yes, fine, wonderful, a *cottage* then. We'll need a *cottage* for a few days until the car gets fixed."

"I'm assuming Bud would've mentioned that you'll never get anyone out this way until Monday at the earliest. Everything pretty much shuts down around here on the weekends. You might get a tow truck today if Otto happens to be hanging around the garage avoiding his wife—but that's pretty much all there is," Omega says, turning awkwardly, her injured leg sticking out like an artificial limb wrongly attached, shuffling her fingers through the keys hanging from a row of pegs on the wall behind the desk.

"Hum ... lets see ... number five has twin beds, but that'll cost you an extra dollar and a half a night, since that's two sets of sheets that'll need laundering. Or there's number three and number seven—those both have doubles. Number two has—"

"We'll take the twin beds," Stella interrupts, and Willa feels an immediate rush of relief that in this instance at least, her mother hasn't stopped to consider the necessity of conserving funds.

In fourteen years of upside downs and inside outs, they've never had cause to share a bed, and Willa is vastly relieved that this latest dose of dire circumstances won't require them to share one now. Thankfully, what has always been a definite rule between them holds firm—cemented in stone from now till eternity—the essential requirement that they keep to their separate spaces, never trespassing into established boundaries, whether asleep or awake.

And yet, relief aside, Willa is nevertheless baffled. After all, there's no ignoring the fact that they've had to scrape for every crumb since Martin left—more honestly, since before he left—and their ill-prepared flight from Hoosick Falls will only have worsened the situation. *Exactly how, she'd like to know, does Stella intend to pay for a single, a double, or anything else for that matter?*

And even as she stands speculating over the particulars of Stella's potential scheme and purpose, Willa feels a tight ball of heat rolling up from the pit of her stomach. *Is Stella planning to sneak away in the night once the car is fixed—long gone vanished before Omega Pearl Bodie has the chance to realize she's been stiffed?*

"Fine by me," Omega says, the instantaneous arc of her lips betraying her ridiculous pleasure over the prospect of earning an extra dollar-fifty a night. "Course, no offense, but I really have to insist you pay up front considering how you're a stranger from out of town and all," Omega smiles, though the red slash of lipstick still in evidence like a wound across her weird baby-sized teeth renders the expression closer to that of a smirk. "Nothing personal."

Well then, so much for running away like criminals. Apparently Omega Pearl Bodie is a sharper tack then Stella has assessed at first glance.

~ 22 ~

"No, that's fine—perfectly understandable," Stella says, pinching open the clasp on her purse, nothing in her voice to suggest anything other than convivial agreement. "It's sad really, but necessary when you consider the way things have gotten to be in this dishonest world we live in. We'd better watch out for ourselves—especially us girls—or the next thing you know you've been had by some con-artist."

Us girls? It's all Willa can do to keep from howling outright over Stella's blatantly artificial attempt at camaraderie and she drops her gaze, watching as her mother rummages through her purse, curious to see how Stella intends to pull the necessary rabbit out of the hat where none exists.

And she can't quite believe what she is seeing when she glimpses the thick paper sandwich folded inside her mother's droopy brown purse just before she snaps it shut. *Impossible* ... even as an urgent Morse code immediately begins tapping inside her head, assuring that the roll of bills she's seen nested there between Stella's old red wallet and her scratched plastic compact is anything but a mirage.

Two

"Mark my words, as soon as that piece of junk car is fixed we're out of this crap hole and that nosey fatso can eat my dust," Stella swears, collapsing on one of the sagging twin beds and earning an immediate complaint from its creaky frame.

She kicks off her shoes one at a time, letting them fall to the wood floor with a dull thunk as she roots through her purse for her cigarettes.

"I don't think it's so bad," Willa offers. "It's actually kinda neat—sort've like camping out."

"Right, camping out, except I'm paying good money to *sleep in*."

Aside from the twin mattresses with their deep cratered centers, the room is outfitted with a single night table that serves to separate the two beds, a lopsided dresser with five ill-fitting drawers, and a plain wooden chair pushed up near the window; none of which share any particular traits that might constitute a matched set.

Sitting on the bed opposite Stella, Willa traces a finger along the stitching running in pale lines and swirls patterning the top of the faded quilt, anxiously searching for an opening to broach the throbbing question as to the origins of the unexpected wealth tucked inside her mother's purse.

And yet, as she shifts her eyes, discretely watching Stella light another cigarette—her deep drag as the tobacco takes the match, impatiently inhaling and exhaling in order to have the thing gone so she can light another—Willa finds herself hesitating.

"What do you think she was talking about when she said that thing about no one wanting to stay around here because of that Norman guy?" Willa says at length.

"Who knows. She's obviously a busybody looking for an audience so she can spread around her load of horse manure. I'll bet she's on the phone right now yakking to some other blabbermouth about *the suspicious looking strangers* holed up in one of her precious *cottages*," Stella snaps, mashing the stump of her cigarette into the chipped ceramic ashtray perched on the night table.

"Frankly, I could care less. All anybody has to do is take a look at this place to know there's nothing happening around here whatsoever. Probably hasn't been one newsworthy event in the past 100 years, and I sure as hell doubt the town looks any better than this ugly place out here—that's if there even is one. The name alone is ridiculous—*Harriet's Bluff*? Who the hell is Harriet?"

Willa laughs, though she's more then a little curious and altogether willing to hear whatever tale Omega Pearl Bodie is apparently bursting at the seams to share. And she's absolutely certain that if she can manage to sequester Omega Pearl sometime when Stella isn't around—before the car is fixed and they're gone from here—she intends to find out about this Norman person herself.

"DAMN-IT!" Stella slams down the receiver, her fury running unchecked despite the fact that Omega Pearl Bodie is right there sitting in her chair behind the front desk— watching, listening, and mentally recording every snippet in order to repeat it to someone else at the first opportunity.

"Complications?" Omega asks, eyes brightening with a newly lit bulb as she leans forward, reaching for the bottle of cola that by all indications remains perpetually refreshed and at hand throughout her conscious hours.

"That would depend on how a person interprets a statement like *the car is shot.*"

"I'd say it's a complication."

"What do they mean by *shot?*" Willa says, coming through the door in time to catch just enough of the conversation to know that the prognosis is not particularly good.

"Shot. Dead. It means stone-cold dead," Stella snaps, rubbing her temples as if to clear her mind of the immediate flux of exasperation volleying hard against the inside walls of her skull.

"What do they have to do to fix it? How much is it gonna cost?"

"There's no fixing dead, Willa. That's the point."

How are they supposed to get to California without a car? How are they supposed to go anywhere period?

"Then what do we do now?" Willa asks, aware that it's the wrong question at the wrong time, but nevertheless pushing it out past the flood of panic rushing up from the floor of her stomach like a bad stew.

Stella flashes a hard stare toward Omega who promptly shifts back in her chair, her puffy sausage leg in its plaster casing jutting out in front of her like a downed pole when she reaches for the *Heartthrobs* comic book curled on her desk and pretends to read.

"Alright, well it's a little kink in our plans, but we do have some other options," Stella says, turning her face toward Willa, widening her eyes in a silent admonishment that not another word is to be breathed in front of Omega Pearl Bodie, unless they don't care about it being spread out across the whole of Harriet's Bluff like a virus.

"We're screwed, that's what," Stella curses, pacing the cottage from door to window and back.

"But you said there were other options."

"I just made that up for the benefit of Miss Busybody. I sure as hell don't intend to hand feed that gossipy snoop my personal business if I can help it."

"Oh—I figured you were talking about the money," Willa says without thinking.

Stella halts her pacing in mid-step. *"What money?"*

Willa hesitates, her tongue pinned to the floor of her mouth by the piercing points of her mother's stare.

"What money?" Stella repeats.

"I don't know ... Just any money."

The expression on Stella's face instantly hardens, her features turned cold and still as a mask.

"You went through my purse?" The question scratches like nails past the hard line of Stella's lips.

"What? No! I did not."

"Don't you dare lie to me, Willa."

"I'm not. I just thought you had some—I thought I might've seen something when you were paying for the cottage."

It's easy enough to decipher from the glare reflecting off Stella's unblinking stare, that her mother doesn't believe her.

"My purse and anything in it is *my* business. It has nothing to do with you and you have no right to snoop through—"

"I didn't snoop," Willa says, heat rising to her face in a suggestion of guilt, though all she's done is inadvertently see something Stella hasn't wanted her to.

"You'd just better keep your mouth shut. It's nobody's business. Not yours—not anybody's," Stella says, the steely barricade shooting up behind her eyes as much a warning as the words themselves.

Willa makes an effort to return Stella's simmering glare, just so her mother might know how insulted she is by the insinuation. But the gesture is wasted. Stella doesn't appear to care at all.

It's clear that Stella has been increasingly jumpy ever since leaving Hoosick Falls, but it's the dire prognosis from the mechanic at the garage that works to shove her to the edge, threatening to explode her right through her skin should anyone give her the wrong look or say the wrong thing. Worse is that this potential eruption has been percolating for weeks, ever since the morning when Stella went out to her car and found one of the windows shattered; the brick lying on the backseat proving a quick and easy assessment as to how it had come to be that way.

Despite Stella's reactionary barrage of swearing and fist-shaking bravado, in truth, the deliberate nature of the incident had left her visibly and uncharacteristically shaken.

"Damn cops. I've had enough of this baloney. When the hell are they gonna do something?"

For once, Stella wasn't all that far off the mark from what appeared to be justifiable anger. After all, it was the third act of vandalism in as many weeks. The first offense was a flat tire accompanied by a folded slice of paper tucked under the arm of the driver's side windshield wiper. A note Willa hadn't had a chance to read before Stella snatched the offending paper from her fingers and tore it into microscopic bits right there in the yard. A few days later came the appearance of several zigzagging tracks viciously keyed into the car's lusterless paint along the entire length of one side door panel. The assault on the window coming not long after.

"I don't get it. Why does anyone want to bother with us?" Willa said as she stared at the offending brick lying amongst the glittering diamonds of broken glass rained across the back seat, needing to take a step back as the acrid taste of fear and disbelief came rushing at her full throttle, squeezing her chest hard enough to make her gasp.

"How the hell am I supposed to know? You think I have a tap on every nut in the country? That's what the cops are for. It's their job to get a handle on these sickos who like to run around terrorizing innocent people."

Though she hasn't gotten so far as to figure out what it all means, Willa suspects that Stella does in fact know something. Especially since it was that final assault—the not-so-random brick hurtled through the car window—which unequivocally succeeded in launching her mother into the middle-of-the-night flight that landed them here.

Stella throws herself back onto the bed, hard enough to knock the wooden headboard up against the wall, and reaches for her cigarettes, a ritual she's performed several dozen times already in the day and a half they've been here.

"I hate this place. When are we leaving?" Willa says, hearing the whiney brat tone in her voice and not caring.

Stella snorts a laugh conspicuously lacking in amusement. "Oh my, you must've missed the chapter where the piece-of-junk car breaks down and the fleeing damsels are stranded in a dump at the ends of the earth. Not to worry, though, you'll be able to catch it in reruns." She shifts her arm, tapping the ash from her cigarette onto the floor beside the bed.

"Or does this have to do with your fairytale idea that I'm growing money in my purse so all's well in paradise. Well, think again. You're sorely deceiving yourself if you honestly believe a few piddly dollars will get us anywhere other than nowhere. Frankly, Miss Scarlet, we're stuck here for a while so you might just as well get used to the lousy scenery, the lumpy beds, and the busybody ham-hock running this place."

Three

Until now, Hoosick Falls is the only place Willa has ever been—unless of course she counts the drives out to the horse track with Martin—which she doesn't, since the track is only two towns away from Hoosick Falls and they were only ever gone for a few hours before going back home; and she never actually saw anything while she was there. All of which makes this entire broken-down-stranded car situation all the more frustrating, since here she's finally gotten away from the miserable nothingness of her birthplace only to land in an equally dismal place not more than twenty four hours later.

She doesn't doubt that some would likely inform her that her complaints are both idiotic and melodramatic, but Willa's life has been so lousy for so long that she's come to believe, even expect, that it will always be like this—a charter chiseled in stone by the gods.

Sometimes she thinks maybe that's why Martin left—why he had to leave. That maybe it wasn't just about the money. Quite possibly he felt the same way Willa feels now. *Trapped—captive* of a life he wasn't all the crazy about. He'd certainly never gone anywhere. Not to college. No business trips or vacations. From the time he graduated high school, his job at the pencil factory was the only position he'd ever held. A fact Stella felt compelled to remind him of with the regularity of a clock tolling the hour. "You've spent your entire life working in that lousy factory for what? A paycheck so piddling a bum on the street would refuse it."

Still, despite the razor edge slicing through each of Stella's unceasing insults, Willa can never recall her father expressing concern or disappointment over his lack of promotions and non-existent pay raises. Nor had he ever mentioned quitting the factory or looking for something else, as if perfectly satisfied to remain a machine operator—crimping medal banded eraser heads onto glossy yellow no.2 pencils until the end of time and beyond.

From Stella's continual snide remarks and biting comments, Willa understood early on that such disinterest was not especially admirable on his part, though she herself saw nothing particularly wrong with Martin's uninspired choice of career. It seemed a perfectly acceptable occupation for a man like her father who'd never pretended to have any ambition other than earning a regular paycheck.

The unchanging nature of his daily routine assured that his comings and goings remained as nondescript as they were ordinary. Perfectly uneventful in that he left the house every weekday morning at six-thirty and returned home at four-forty-five sharp every afternoon—except on Fridays when he drove to the bank in a neighboring town and cashed his paycheck.

"What the hell's the sense of going all the way over to Ephrata, Martin? You think the tellers here can't count past ten?" Stella sneered, her lips pinched tight over her annoyance; the knobs of her clenched fists pressed into the sharp angles of her slender hipbones as she glared at him.

"People around here know each other—they talk. And I don't appreciate having my personal finances discussed amongst a bunch of magpies."

"*Finances?* Since when does cashing a check once a week constitute finances? You haven't deposited ten cents into an account since I've known you, so if anybody's talking about your finances, it's only to say that you don't have any."

"Only an idiot would trust a bank to hold their money," had been his stony reply and Stella stared at him incredulous, though she might just as easily have laughed had his words not piqued her ire so effectively.

The change when it came was subtle, though maybe Willa would have recognized the slow stirring of Martin's impatience with the chronic sameness of his life, had she known how to diagnose the symptoms: the seldom-voiced remarks pertaining to his daily routine; complaints stronger and louder for the fact that he didn't speak them, but instead wore like a uniform over slouched shoulders that appeared to have lost their framework, buried in the blank void of eyes that stared out at nothing.

Only afterward would Willa look back and see what she's missed—hindsight readily serving up the visible signs of his discontent as it swelled into the proportions of a malignancy. Distinct clues framed within the tightly held silences hovering over the supper table night after night. Obvious inklings in the jokes and amusing anecdotes that failed to come.

It was a gradually shifting pattern of everyday life that felt not so much alarming as expected. *People, places, things change. They just do. The world is like that.* And there was nothing particularly startling or otherwise threatening in days that passed with much the same unchallenged ordinariness as they'd always possessed; nothing remarkable, noteworthy, or especially interesting in what had customarily been mundane. So that despite the weak stirrings of restlessness hovering just below the surface of Martin's innocuous facade, the consistent non-events of family life remained altogether typical of how the daily page had forever been turned.

That Martin had actually wanted something different—that somewhere behind his passive and colorless exterior lived the skeletal remains of some unclaimed dream or ambition—felt no less likely than it did impossible, if only for the fact that he'd never been that sort of man.

Maybe it's too soon to tell for certain, but right now it feels as if their single accomplishment has been to climb out from one mess, only to land head first in the muck of another.

"Oh I know she's cursing this like bad luck hand-delivered straight from the devil, but as far as I'm concerned it's the answer to a prayer, honey. You think you're in a pickle? Well take a look at me—bad enough I have to drag around this thing for the next six months," she taps the plaster cast with her cane, "But then that tramp Lorna just up and quits three days before y'all turned up. Seventeen years old and she's got two kids. No husband, mind you—no ma'am, she just keeps popping out babies like jellybeans. I can't figure if she's gullible, stupid, or both," Omega Pearl says, sliding an ashtray filled with coins across the desk toward Willa.

"Here, hon. Get yourself a bottle of pop from the machine. The soda man was just out to fill it yesterday. Try the grape, it's positively sinful. Oh—and be a doll and grab me a cola while you're out there, would you?"

"Sure, Miss Bodie."

"For Pete's sakes," she smiles and Willa quickly shifts her gaze just off center from Omega's face. She likes the woman well enough, but the sight of those strange pointy baby teeth grinning from the full moon face reminds Willa of wicked gnomes and mutant trolls, disturbing characters from some demented fairy tale she's either read in childhood or simply imagined. "Didn't I tell you to call me Omega Pearl? Miz Bodie sounds like somebody's spinster aunt."

"Yes, Ma'am," Willa nods, helping herself to the coins.

She can't decide whether it's funny, flattering, or just ridiculous that Omega Pearl Bodie would consider a situation as dire as being stranded in this strange and cheerless place as some Divine plan. Because as far as Willa can determine from the months invested in Saint Cecilia's, this is generally not the way she would expect God to operate. Not that she knows all that much about the behaviors of God, considering that her sole experience with The Almighty had been during Stella's whirlwind religious phase back in Hoosick Falls when she all at once decided to give the Catholic Church a spin.

Stella's pronouncement of newfound spirituality had arrived in much the same way as any of her spur-of-the-moment schemes aimed at reinventing herself—which is to say, sudden and unexpected.

"Huh...what're you doing?" Willa rolled over and blinked, staring at Stella, who stood with the sheet she's just whipped from Willa's sleeping form still in her hands.

"You heard me. We're going to noon mass at Saint Cecilia's, so get a move on."

"What're you talking about? We don't go to church. And you can't just do that—go walking into somebody else's church like that."

"It isn't *somebody else's church,* Willa."

"Well, it isn't mine."

"The church, any church, is open to anyone that wants to walk through the door."

"I don't care. I don't like church."

"You've never even been inside one."

"Exactly. Why should I have to go now—I don't even know the rules."

"There are no rules. You just have to follow along with what everyone else is doing."

"Religion is too complicated to just show up."

"You need special training to stand and kneel?"

"Yeah, well, God scares me."

"That's precisely why you're going. A kid your age has no business being scared of God. It's ridiculous—and I'm pretty sure it's a sin too."

"This is stupid. This is just stupid. I'm not going," Willa said, grabbing the edge of the sheet and pulling it back over her prone limbs. She tightened the fabric under her chin like a tourniquet and crossed an arm over her chest in what she hoped was an intimidating barricade.

Stella breathed through her nose slowly, carefully, as if aggressively determined to hold firm to her newly claimed state of grace, and bit back the string of curses and threats that ordinarily punctuated her dialogue.

"You've got ten minutes to comb that rat's nest on your head and get yourself dressed in something decent. If you're not ready when it's time to walk out the door that's fine, too. God doesn't care what you look like in your pajamas—though everyone else sitting in church probably will," Stella said, her voice holding calm and steady, though her eyes held the hard shine of something far from serene.

It was a look Willa easily recognized. One that assured Stella meant business and was not accepting negotiations. Whether erroneously sainted or not, it had never been Stella's habit to sprinkle empty threats. She would have no qualms about dragging Willa up the aisle of Saint Cecilia's wearing her outgrown yellow shortie pajamas if that's what it took to land her at her intended destination in time.

Stella turned to leave, pausing in front of the small pedestal mirror on Willa's dresser. Several days earlier Willa had carelessly knocked it over during a hurried search for a lost barrette and cracked the glass. She held her breath as she watched Stella and waited for the certain eruption. *She'll be furious. Not so much because of a cheap broken mirror, but because Willa had now ushered in seven years of bad luck—something they definitely don't need.*

And yet, nothing. Stella merely tipped her face—an eye and half her nose, lips and one cheek—spliced into sinister reflections running in parallel lines the length of the splintered glass. She ignored Willa as she touched a pinky to the corner of her mouth; correcting a miniscule smear of lipstick wandered from the outline of her carefully painted lips, and repositioning a thick wave of dark hair drifted onto her forehead.

"What am I supposed to wear? I don't even have *church* clothes."

"There's no such thing as church clothes. Jesus wore flip-flops and a sheet so I'm sure you can find something presentable with a little effort."

Willa continued to glare at her mother without moving, holding tight to the sheet she tightly gripped under her chin.

"You're down to seven minutes," Stella said, slanting her wrist for a glance at her watch. "And I sure as hel—heck, don't intend to be late on the first day I show my face over there."

Willa's furious stare followed the defiant line of Stella's back as she passed into the hallway; holding her ground for one last stubborn instant before bobbing upright, tossing the blanket aside, and dropping her legs over the edge of the mattress. *Church! Ridiculous.*

Stella had never so much as expressed a fig of interest in church. And on the handful of occasions Willa could recall someone inviting her mother to attend a church function or participate in anything akin to religious activity, Stella's customary response involved a crude remark or rude joke. Once, when Willa was four or five, they'd been walking past the Elm Street Baptist Church just as Sunday services concluded and a colorful stream of beautifully outfitted men, women, and children, flooded out the open doors and onto the front walk, smiling, chatting, and laughing. The bright colors of the ladies plumed hats and Sunday suits reminded Willa of a flock of exotic tropical birds, and she slowed her steps, turning her head in an effort to catch a glimpse through the open doors into the shadowy innards of the mysterious place they'd alighted from. But then Stella had all at once reached out and grabbed her arm, promptly dragging her along the sidewalk like a misbehaved puppy guilty of soiling the carpet.

"What is that place? Why can't we go inside and see?" Willa implored the back of her mother's head as Stella hurried her steps.

"It's nothing you'd like. It's not for us. Places like that are for other people. Gullible people."

"But it looks nice. All the ladies wear pretty hats."

"Well it's not nice, it's a church. And when you're old enough to know what's going on in there you'll be thanking me seven ways to Sunday that I didn't make you go."

And just as Stella predicted, the time had indeed arrived when Willa was old enough to know something of what was going on—or at least to be just fine with having no part of it.

Willa skulked across the room, tripping over a sneaker partially camouflaged by a pair of shorts she'd dropped on the floor days earlier. *Stupid! This is stupid. Stupid Stella—Queen of the Stupids. Stupid, stupid. A waste of time. All just a stupid waste of time.* She rummaged through the closets and half open drawers, knowing there was nothing appropriate, nothing nice, nothing pretty, not a single garment that wouldn't make her feel like a renegade wart on the perfect nose. Not that it made any difference to Stella. She would make Willa go regardless.

Stella marched up the aisle to an empty pew near the front. Willa sat beside her, round shouldered and slouched forward to chew her nails in angry boredom; but then nearly yelped out loud when Stella discreetly moved her hand to pinch Willa's bare thigh between two fingers.

The warning in Stella's silent reprimand was unmistakable. And while Willa instantly dropped the offending fingers from her mouth, she was deliberate in keeping the glaring scowl firmly planted over her face.

Stella had towed Willa off to Saint Cecelia's every Sunday for nearly a year. And even more startling than her mother's freshly manufactured spiritual state, was her dedicated metamorphosis into First Class Volunteer, poised and ready to cheerlead her way through any assortment of church activities and fundraisers; serving cookies and donuts on hospitality Sundays; arranging flowers on the altar; pulling weeds from the window boxes at the rectory.

Where this generous slice of spirit had originated from puzzled Willa more than any single aspect of Stella's mysteriously inspired interest; so confused her interior warning bells that once they started to chime they never ceased ringing. It was all just one step too many past the acceptable boundaries of change for someone like Stella, who had never been a giver and even less of a volunteer. Even Stella's best friend Dee had been baffled.

"What the hell, Stella? Next thing I know they'll be putting your face on one of those stained glass windows over there."

But Stella had merely smiled. Smiled like a serene Gandhi and said nothing.

But then, just as unexpectedly as it had arrived, the infatuation was all at once finished. Without hint or explanation, the bloom clipped and discarded with Stella's simple declaration that Catholicism required a far greater effort than she was prepared to extend for any substantial length of time.

"Turns out I'm not all that good at religion after all. There's all that business of forgiving and turning the other cheek, and I sure as hell can't see how that type of thinking is supposed to work in modern times when everyone is so selfish and hateful to each other. And let's just be honest, show me the person who isn't holding onto a grudge and praying for the day when they can slap the starch out of some jerk, and I'll show you a liar. It doesn't make all that much sense why someone should have to give that up. What the hell's the difference anyway? Does anybody really care who's mad at who? That's the problem with religion. Everything's just a little too serious."

Willa hadn't expected to feel so genuinely disappointed over Stella's abandonment of their Sunday routine, aware only once her attendance was no longer a requirement just how much she'd come to relish being part of something so big, or drawn to ancient rituals as mysterious as they felt solid and dependable. And then there was Jesus Himself—someone, she was starting to believe, a person might really come to count on.

Not long after they'd stopped going to Mass, there'd been several visits out to the house by various members of Saint Cecelia's; the church secretary, two men Willa recognized as ushers from Sunday services, a group of ladies that volunteered with Stella on the hospitality committee—and once, Father Michael himself. Willa had felt warmed to bursting, joyously touched to see just how sincerely missed she and Stella were by their church family, her secret hope being that her mother would be equally moved. And yet Stella had visibly blanched at each visit, refusing to open the door as she peered from behind the front curtains—watching and waiting until the visitors ceased with their insistent knocking. Remaining hidden until they reluctantly retreated to their waiting cars and slowly pulled away—heads turned to study the outside of the silent house in much the same way that Stella watched from the inside.

"If they think they're gonna accuse me of something, they've got another thing coming," Stella said, steeling her jaw like an animal trap set to spring.

For the next several weeks Stella held to the implication that her floundered spiritual life was simply the byproduct of disillusionment, a moment of truth breaking through to the core of some newly discovered flaw rooted in church dogma. It was a good enough show for someone else maybe, but Willa easily arrived at the conclusion that the thing responsible for snagging Stella's perpetually wandering attentions was something far less profound. Specifically, the advertisement printed on the back page of a previous week's church bulletin, offering an eight-week course in hairstyling.

And it didn't occur to Willa until sometime later that she should've been a good deal more surprised than she was when Stella promptly produced the necessary tuition, despite the rock-bottom state of their finances.

"Thanks honey," Omega says, when Willa returns and hands her the bottle of soda. She sets it on the desk, breathing an exaggerated sigh, wholly obvious in the way of someone anxious to drop some theatrical bomb. "Ah…but I swear, I'm still so darned shook-up after that whole thing that happened out here last month. Scares the hell out of me every time I think about it."

Willa twists the cap from her bottle of grape NeHi, waiting for Omega to elaborate. Somehow, although she knows next to nothing about this woman she's only just met, Willa has the distinct impression that Omega Pearl Bodie possesses the ability to talk straight into tomorrow as long as no one comes along to stop her. It's a trait Willa doesn't especially mind, since she's already gotten the impression that there's no subject Omega Pearl considers taboo. And unlike Stella, Willa isn't disgusted by gossip or scandalous talk, even relishes the occasional tale, particularly those she shouldn't.

"They were this close to getting him," Omega Pearl announces, pinching together a stubby thumb and forefinger. Standing behind the desk, plump arms resting on the pot-marked surface, Omega poses like a news anchor preparing to break a monumental story before the cameras. "They could've had him this time, but the bumbling fools let him get away. Honest to Pete, he was right here under their noses—right there in number seven."

"Who?" Willa tries to recall which of the mournful little cottages in Omega Pearl's lakeside empire is number seven on the chance there is something significant in this detail, but there is no image forthcoming; they all look alike. Equally pitiful and sad.

"*Who?*"

"Yeah—who was in number seven?"

"Are you kidding me? Norman of course," Omega says, leaning forward on her elbows.

"*Norman?*"

"Good Lord! Do not even try and tell me you haven't heard about Norman Hitchcock!" Omega says taking her time over every word. There is a definite shine of excitement glinting in her small bright eyes, twin pink swatches stroked across the top of each round cheek by an invisible brush.

"Well I haven't. We're not from around here, remember?"

Omega waves away the reminder like a pesky gnat. "Doesn't matter where you're from. He's a killer. And you better believe a cold-blooded killer is everybody's business—at least he sure as heck should be," Omega says, shaking her head as if nothing has ever been more incredulous. "If I hadn't heard otherwise I'd think you and your mama just crawled out from under a rock in the desert."

"We don't have a television and Stella doesn't like newspapers. She says you can't trust a reporter to write an honest story when people just want sensational," Willa says, oddly shamed when she catches the disbelieving expression flitting over Omega Pearl's face, as if to suggest that only a full-fledged idiot would carry around such a foolish notion.

"To be honest, I can't imagine such a thing, but I guess maybe you people do things differently out there in California," Omega shrugs, anxious to continue. "So, anyway, as it happened, I not only had an escaped convict living right here on my property, but he popped up right outside my bedroom window three weeks ago Monday."

"An escaped convict?"

Although her announcement has scored a direct bulls-eye, instantly succeeded in capturing Willa's full attention, Omega pauses to take a long swallow of her cola, purposely prolonging the delicious moment of suspense that comes right before full disclosure.

Omega swipes the back of her hand across her moist lips. "You betcha. That's how my leg got broke."

"He broke your leg?"

"Damn right he did. Woke me out of a sound sleep. I could hear him creeping around outside the window, and I just laid there—frozen solid as death. I didn't know what to do and I figured he must've cut the phone lines already—I could feel his cold killer eyes staring at me through the screen. Scared me so bad I fell right out of bed. Being a little chubby, I must've landed wrong when I hit the floor—darn thing snapped like a twig. All I could do was lie there and scream my head off, but at least I made enough noise that he hightailed it right out of here."

"Did you get a look at him?"

"Didn't need to, I know what he looks like."

"No, I mean how can you be sure it was him and not someone else—an animal maybe?"

"Honey, Norman Hitchcock's not your average bonehead criminal. Of course it was him. He figures this is the safest hideout in Harriet's Bluff because they caught him here that first time—just one day after he'd shot those two men in cold blood. He shot them in the head. Both of them—point blank—IN THE HEAD. He figures nobody would expect him to come to the same place again.

"You rented a cottage to a *murderer*?"

"I sure as heck didn't know he was a killer until they came and hauled him away in handcuffs. You can bet he wasn't advertising it on a sign around his neck when he checked-in."

"Gosh, that's so creepy."

"Oh, it's creepy all right, but at least he was paying for his accommodations back then. Things have changed. Not only is he a convicted killer this time around, but the son-of-a-so-and-so is sneaking around taking nice hot showers on my dime, sleeping all comfy in my beds like a bird tucked in a nest, and no doubt watching clips of himself on my TV while half the country's turning itself inside out looking for him. It's sickening, is what it is. If I hadn't started getting suspicious over a few little things here and there who knows what might've happened," Omega says, rubbing her hands together as if an arctic wind has just blown past, chilling her to the bone.

"And he's still on the loose?"

"That's only the half of it. Not just on the loose—on the loose and looking for revenge."

"So where's he now?"

"That, honey, is the million-dollar question," Omega nods her head, smiling her satisfaction that Willa is at last comprehending the levity of the situation. "If anyone knew the answer to that, then he wouldn't be a fugitive, now would he?"

Four

Omega Pearl Bodie is either generous or conniving in offering Stella the recently vacated housekeeping job in exchange for a miniscule salary and free accommodations in the cottage she currently occupies with Willa. And while there is little denial of the sense of relief to be gained from having four walls in their hour of need, the agreement nevertheless fails to provide the one thing they most require—which is money—since the trading of labor for accommodations and just enough cash to cover food and a few essentials, means that Stella will not garner the funds necessary to allow for their ultimate departure anytime soon.

"For cripes sakes, Willa, take the tragic look off your face," Stella says once she's accepted Omega Pearl's proposition. "You've sure as hell known me long enough to get the idea I don't intend to make a career of scrubbing toilets and changing sheets. I never did it in my own house and I damn well don't intend to do it for that gimp-legged blimp. Sure I'll do it for now—but only until I come up with something better and we can blow this dump."

Little more than a week has passed and already Willa knows that Stella is losing patience with her housekeeping duties. All the recognizable signs are there, collected and held within a quietly simmering stare and glum expression that indicates one thing only—the dreaded stirring of Stella's habitual restlessness. It is a dangerous brand of disquiet that will unequivocally lead her headlong into a rash of odd behaviors and strange ideas.

It isn't as though Willa isn't equally anxious to get away from The Moonglow at the very first opportunity. Being here in this largely forgotten ghost town of tumbledown cottages with Omega Pearl Bodie's eyes pinning their every move like insects under glass, is altogether strange and unnerving. But she also understands they can't just grab their suitcases and head down the highway. Unless they intend to risk ending up at another dreary motel in another nothing place, they need to have a plan, or at the very least, the broad outline of one.

It occurs to Willa that she should offer to help out with the roster of daily responsibilities Omega has assigned Stella. Not only because she's several miles beyond bored with sitting around the cabin playing solitaire with the deck of cards she's found in the drawer of the night table (games impossible to finish with any satisfaction, since the queen of hearts, ten of spades, and three of diamonds are missing from the deck), but she's hoping that sharing the load, for a while at least, will settle even a portion of her mother's growing impatience and boredom, long enough even to keep Stella from doing or saying something that will only worsen this mess they're in.

Still, she hesitates to voice the suggestion, since the customary outcome of pitching in to help Stella generally results in Willa ending up doing everything herself. Her mother having a particular way of walking away for a glass of water, a trip to the bathroom, or to answer a ringing telephone, rarely returning until the job in progress is done. Shallow tricks Willa has learned to anticipate through countless seasons of lone leaf raking, snow shoveling, and housecleaning—tasks she starts with Stella and then finishes alone.

For several days Willa continues to consider over the best foolproof approach for volunteering safely, and is in the midst of taking a shower when Stella settles the dilemma for her.

"Just to clear up any of those misconceptions you apparently have—you weren't born a damn princess and I'm not your fairy Godmother," Stella says, yanking back the shower curtain with one quick sweep.

Willa grabs the cheap plastic liner and holds it against herself in a shield, too stunned even to scream. "What are y—"

"You're gonna help out around here, that's what. Apparently you've forgotten you're locked-up in this mess just as tight as I am and there's no reason I should be working my damn tail off while you lie around here like royalty."

Willa bristles at the insinuation, but doesn't bother to leap to her own defense. There's no point in insisting that she's actually been thinking over ways she might help to move things along. She knows Stella would only stare at her—the patented expression of smirking disbelief in place over here face—forever adept at twisting good intentions into the ugliest of designs.

The Moonglow. It is a name as tranquil and soothing as any well-told lie, and Willa makes every effort to persuade herself that the place isn't nearly as dreadful as it most assuredly is. Gathering her determination around her like a shield, she purposely steers her thoughts off to other things, other places, as she changes soiled sheets, scrubs ancient toilets that will never again look especially clean, and vacuums permanently matted squares of hideous avocado green shag carpet, all the while consoling herself with the assurance that each dull and repetitious task is in effect moving her one step closer to the last time she'll ever need to do them again.

They rarely talk while they work, as if holding to some previous agreement where they've mutually stated a preference for solitude; though, in truth, it has never been mentioned. It is simply the way they have always been together, unanimously electing to keep their separate thoughts detached and wandering.

What Willa hasn't expected is to find herself thrust headlong into the curious assortment of inscrutable lives passing through The Moonglow's faded cottages. And while the evidences are undeniably everywhere, Willa is nevertheless startled by Stella's unceremonious divulgence of the true character of The Moonglow's regular clientele.

"Apparently our new bosom buddy, Omega Pearl Bodie, is playing the happy hostess to every cheating husband and closet pervert for a hundred miles."

"What's that supposed to mean? We hardly even see the people that go in and out of here."

"Precisely. It's called *sneaking around*, Willa. The idea is not to be seen. You'd have to be a complete idiot not to figure out what's going on around here."

Willa bristles at the insult. "That's not—"

"Don't get your undies in a twist. I don't mean you. You're just a kid. You're not supposed to know anything. I'm talking about Miss Busybody."

"Right, so wouldn't Omega be the first to know if something was going on around here that she doesn't approve of?" Willa says, recalling Omega Pearl's detailed accounting of her frightening near-face-to-face interlude with Norman Hitchcock.

"You bet she does," Stella smirks as she pulls an armload of rumpled sheets from the bed. "These dumpy rundown places are all the same. If it wasn't for perverts and adulterers this collection of shacks would've turned to dust years ago and she knows it. So she just turns her fat cheek, takes the money, and hands over the keys."

"But isn't that sort of—well, you know—*dirty.*"

"You better believe it's dirty. It's disgusting, is what it is. But there are more people than not who could care less. They think as long as nobody's advertising whatever it is they're doing out here then everything's fine. The key goes in the lock and the door shuts behind them. They step out of the world and perform their sins in private. No harm done if no one ever sees it."

Willa doesn't offer an immediate response, but if she did, it would be to tell Stella that she couldn't be more wrong. There is nothing private about what goes on here. From the start, Willa has found it impossible to dodge the sensation that it is her own eye perpetually pressed against the keyhole, looking in on those alleged *confidential* interludes and putting together the scattered pieces of things she prefers not to see. It is all too ugly, too personal—the evidences of flagrant episodes, marked by the details of whatever props are carelessly left to be cleared away and restored to anonymity; a mattress pulled from its box spring and upended against the wall, its quilted coverlet indecipherably stained; a vibrant smear of crimson lipstick painted across a bathroom mirror, scribbled in jagged lines on the pink tile walls in an illusion of blood violently spilled; a deflated condom tossed behind a chair, another left on the night table like a boastful sportsmen's trophy.

Her initial sense of embarrassed surprise has yet to fade, flaming up with each subsequent discovery, trying hard not to notice those clues that are right here in front of her, pictures that slide into her head like dirty clouds, stubbornly refusing to be pushed away. She reminds herself that it doesn't matter what anyone else is doing in their private world, that either way she could care less. Yet she is still only minimally successful in pretending her mind away from considering over the identity attached to fingers hurrying a key into the lock of some particular cabin—firmly closing the door as they quickly step inside and out of sight.

Willa carelessly swipes the grungy cloth Omega has provided for dusting across the lusterless finish of a veneer-topped bureau, the grey face of a tabletop radio, a night table cratered with shallow cigarette burns. She mindlessly vacuums a path along the length of ugly green carpet running from the front door to the postage stamp confines of the bathroom in back, exchanges damp threadbare towels for dry threadbare towels, replenishes miniature bars of soap and replaces empty rolls of toilet paper. And all the while, she wonders how many of the visitors who inevitably land in this colorless place have actually come without complications.

Have any of them checked into The Moonglow with a simple desire to sleep? Genuine travelers, eyes burning with fatigue and road grit, hearts lifting when they catch sight of the flickering vacancy sign coaxing them away from the dull stretch of desolate highway. A weary sense of relief settling over them when they spy the sprinkling of cottages dotted amongst the trees. Sleeping children, awkwardly lifted from the backseats of cars and carried across the creaky porch boards to be gently deposited into the ditch of a too soft mattress.

Willa figures it must be these once-in-a-blue-moon authentic travelers who actually make a futile effort to decipher the grainy black and white images waving across the screens of the small television sets Omega Pearl has planted in three of her *deluxe* cottages. It's these who leave the bedclothes rumpled, the bath towels damp, but little else of the room disturbed, since they will be gone with the sunrise.

She believes that holding determinedly to these, envisioning the real and non-offending people who come here, will serve to blot out her disgust for all the others. The contemptible ones who slink into The Moonglow carrying their ugly lies and dishonest fabrications that differ even from the distortions they will take home afterward.

Five

The night is too full of sound. Loud in a way that feels like one long, endless screech—split, divided, and multiplied amongst a million insect battalions.

Unlike the descent of twilight in Hoosick Falls, where all summer long Willa could hear occasional shouts slicing though the lengthening dark from several lawns away—followed by a raucous concert of wildly shrieking children, bobbing shafts of light sweeping along hedges and darting beneath shrubs in a spirited game of flashlight tag—the fall of evening over The Moonglow crashes down with an eerie quiet so loud it can still be heard above the mad shrill of incessantly shrieking night creatures.

So far, Willa hasn't decided whether she misses anything at all from her old life—the one she'd had only a few short days ago—although she does know she isn't sorry to be gone. She even thinks that, maybe, if she can find even one thing to like about The Moonglow, she might eventually start to feel something of a connection to the place, at least until they are able to leave it. But so far there is nothing.

The accumulation of days has not softened the air of regret that hangs over everything here. The dark collection of unpainted cottages still look as if they are slowly sinking into the dust and patchy grass they are planted on; the silent lake with its crippled dock and weedy shoreline uninviting to anything other than water snakes and snapping turtles; the thick growing pines rising up at all four corners of Omega

Pearl's stagnant settlement, feeling more like a barricade than a lush, natural landscape.

The last of afternoon light is dwindling on the horizon when Willa comes out to sit on the cabin's crooked front step; the porch it belongs to so misshapen in its delinquency that it appears in the process of leaving the building altogether before long. She stares out toward the highway. *Quiet, so quiet.* She concentrates on drawing her mind to blank as the last of twilight slips away behind the trees, the sky now leaning heavily into full dark. Any moment now, Omega Pearl will flick the switch on the wall adjacent the front desk, and the sign out by the road will blink awake, spelling out MOONGL W OTE , since several bulbs have burned out and are yet to be replaced.

A light winks on in the front room of the cottage opposite. Of the two arrivals that have checked into The Moonglow earlier in the afternoon, Willa guesses that the light belongs to the middle-aged woman traveling with her daughter and not the shaggy-haired man who's apparently come from nowhere, having walked in from the highway carrying a misshapen canvas duffel bag and a heavily scratched wooden box, no vehicle in sight.

She imagines that the woman with the kind face is right now going about the ritual of preparing the little girl for bed, first pulling a soft cotton nightgown from the suitcase. *Pink, she guesses. Embroidered with tumbling pink bears…or maybe, chubby little hippos dressed in ballet slippers and buoyant tutus.* She will comb out the girl's long yellow braid and remind her to brush her teeth before settling her into bed and reading a story from the dog-eared story book she has tucked inside her bag. Stories about charming animals that talk and go on incredible adventures when humans aren't paying attention, well-polished children that live in big houses with pretty toys, perfect pets, and festive parties. The woman's voice falling away only once the girl closes her eyes and drops off to sleep.

Willa attempts to blink away the man, but he will not leave. His grungy, disheveled appearance filling her mouth with the unpleasant taste of neglected and moldering things as he takes a seat directly in the center of her mind. And she can see him sitting on the bed, chain-smoking filter-less cigarettes, dishonest eyes staring twin black holes into the dark.

She wonders if he is one of the *crazies* Omega refers to when stating that with any luck the strange and curious will begin a steady migration to The Moonglow as news of Norman Hitchcock's prison escape continues to spread.

"It's the same thing as when people slow down to stare at a car crash, or rush out to see a train wreck. We're all wired like that. We all have that same impulse—morbid fascination with tragedy. It's there from birth," Omega says. "I heard a doctor talking about it on the radio one time. He even had a name for it, but I don't recall now what it was."

"How about *nuts?* That's what we call it where I come from," Stella smirks, ambling into the office, the bucket of cleaning supplies swinging back and forth in her hand as if she's just returned from a picnic, rather than from scrubbing a toilet.

Omega Pearl responds by throwing Stella a disapproving stare, as if to remind her that this is serious business and nothing to joke about. Of course Willa hasn't the foggiest clue whether Omega's observations concerning inborn instincts and Norman Hitchcock contain even a shred of truth, or if they are simply another of her exaggerated inventions. Either way, Willa insists that she herself can't contemplate for an instant why anyone would want to stare at a car wreck or poke around hoping to catch a glimpse of a runaway murderer, when in truth she has a penchant for both.

Now, sitting here alone in the dark, she thinks that maybe she doesn't actually want a peek at Norman Hitchcock after all, especially when she considers that he could very well walk up behind her right now and grab her by the neck like a goose, easily choking the life from her. And yet, far worse than being strangled dead on her front steps, is the question rapping hard knuckles inside her head, asking whether anyone would notice if she all at once disappeared, simply vanished from the splintered wood step never to be seen again. *Willa Burkett…extinct in a blink of light. Gone. Simply gone. Will anyone notice? Will they care either way?*

She makes a half-hearted attempt to shove away the parade of dismal thoughts creeping into her head, marching in a tight knot behind her eyes, annoyed at her subconscious for allowing them in. She has never been the variety of pessimistic person that Stella is herself, and she wonders what it is about this place that so effortlessly coaxes her mind to race off in search of dark places.

If her mother and father had somehow managed to care for each other, things would've been different…if they'd just tried a little harder back when they still had the chance…or if Stella had been a little less demanding, condescending, and difficult. If Martin had not been so much inside himself—still water running deep and all that. And yet, there's always been a distance of obvious proportion spanned between them, large and echoing to suggest that maybe it was always out of reach regardless. She certainly can't recall a time when they might possibly have loved each other; and if they had, the evidence was dissolved long before she ever had the opportunity to witness it herself.

In truth, their family life had been one of quiet cohabitation. Much like reluctant strangers coerced into sharing a table at a crowded restaurant—minus the politeness—loathly exchanging anything of a personal nature other than the air between them. They were three people separate from each other in every way, collectively averse to extending or receiving even the briefest physical exchange or thoughtful word. Determinedly insulated, excepting for those oddly disturbing occasions when the sounds of her parents lovemaking turned Willa's face to flame in the dark as she tried not to listen, yet heard everything through the thin walls. Late night interludes that, for a time, proved the single glue holding all the drifting parts of their marriage from falling loose and crumbling apart like a fistful of ancient dust.

The darkness grows heavier, pressing hard on Willa's shoulders so that her chin now rests on her bent knees. The night leaks through the window screens, swelling to fill every corner like heavy syrup, melting into the small tight rooms of the quietly resting cottages. She tries to imagine this place long ago, back in the glory days of The Moonglow, the far gone summers the Good Samaritan had mentioned to her and Stella, when families from the city packed up their bathing suits and swim caps, anxious to escape the heat and grit in exchange for several weeks in the country. They must've had high times. Picnics and rowing parties, swimming lessons for kids who had probably never seen a body of water beyond their bathtubs. In the evenings they would've sat out on these very porches, maybe someone bringing out a pitcher of iced tea, another a bowl of sliced watermelon—the kids immediately reaching to grab a bright pink slice because someone had already suggested the idea of a seed-spitting competition.

Maybe this place really wasn't so bad back when it was a living, breathing thing. And maybe that's why Omega stays, because she remembers.

Willa is still here anchored to the steps, head tilted to rest a cheek against her kneecap, when she all at once hears it ... a far-off sound ... a noise that startles her for only the instant it takes to recognize it. She bolts upright, instinctively training her gaze to the distance as though she can actually *see* the sirens splitting the dark. And even as she listens attentively, attempting to determine the destination of the steady wail, Willa contemplates whether she has time to dash to the shed out back and haul out the rusty old bicycle discovered days earlier while searching for a pail to wash floors, now that Stella has added this chore to the list Willa already has.

She stands—unable yet to guess the direction the shrill pulse of sirens is taking. Although she can still hear them, the noise is growing increasingly distant rather than closer, the fleet of fire trucks flying off on a route opposite the highway stretched in front of The Moonglow. And it is only a moment before the darkness closes around the dwindling sound and it is altogether gone.

The night returns to quiet and if Willa hadn't been paying such close attention, she might almost think that she's imagined the brief disturbance. The front office remains dark; the sign out front still winks its faltering light. The cabins lie silent, not a single face peering out through parted curtains. There is only Willa, staring off into the vast and boundless sea of night, infinitely curious as to which particular piece of Harriet's Bluff is right now going up in flames.

Six

She knows better than to admit it out loud, but there's a certain sense of excitement about the fires that keeps Willa from suiting-up in the same wardrobe of fear that nearly everyone else in Harriet's Bluff is now wearing like a shroud. Judging from Omega Pearl Bodie's high-strung reaction to each and every incident, Willa can pretty much imagine the reaction she'll get if she is to tell someone, anyone, about the rush of adrenaline that hits her like a cannon shot every time the alarm sounds, sends her chasing after scenes of terrible destruction; each subsequent blaze thoroughly captivating for the tragic beauty of such devastating ruination.

By late spring there have already been several spectacular blazes. And like several dozen other curiosity seekers in Harriet's Bluff, Willa races to join the audience whenever a fire happens to occur within bike riding distance; the witnesses in attendance wide-eyed and wholly mesmerized, though Willa herself has yet to feel anything resembling of fear.

All attentions remain locked, chained, and bound to the town's notorious, escaped convict; but for Willa the name Norman Hitchcock holds nothing of status or meaning, other than as a bookmark belonging within the pages of irrelevant folklore. What's more, her sentiments toward the mysterious Norman Hitchcock are altogether similar to those she has for everyone else in Harriet's Bluff; which is to say there's no one who holds any particular significance to the grand scheme of her life. She has no connection to any of them, past, present, or future, the town and its inhabitants no more substantial to her interests or affections than a colony of cardboard cutouts.

It's the fires that hold her mesmerized—watching the men in their thick, rubbery uniforms, bulky gear weighted to their backs and shoulders to give the illusion of misshapen space invaders, as they move in and out of view through dense clouds of heavy black smoke belching past the flames. She is captivated, though not especially convinced that she is witnessing anything of notable consequence. They are, after all, just fires.

Whether or not it actually is the hottest summer on record could be argued by anyone possessing a longer memory than Willa, but it's definitely the most blistering she can recall herself.

The heat comes all at once in late April and stubbornly holds on—simmering the earth and all that springs from it with an eternal flame, the brief sprinklings of sporadic rainfall evaporating in midair, long before the droplets chance to dampen the parched earth.

By early June the whole of Harriet's Bluff is so thoroughly deprived of moisture it seems inevitable that the theory of *spontaneous combustion* will be mentioned and collectively accepted as fact amongst the know-it-all regiment of old men who routinely line the long, wooden bench at the bus stop in town (although none intend to go anywhere—not this day or any other); whittling sticks into toothpicks, scratching their privates, and arguing about long past events no one else really cares about or honestly remembers. Their conjecture will rapidly take on momentum after a dozen enormous bales of hay, neatly rolled and aligned like fresh bakery loaves in the fields of Dick Hayes farm, mysteriously catch fire. And for a time, there does seem to be a certain vein of reasonableness in the idea (odd, but not impossible), especially since there have been no other plausible ideas forthcoming, unless anyone seriously considers an earlier suggestion of Martian invasion.

Stella is half propped against the headboard of her unmade bed wearing only a slip and torpedo cone bra, rolling an unopened bottle of pop along her arms, across her chest, up her neck, the condensation speckling the cold glass offering only the briefest relief before the heat of her skin burns it away.

"People around here wouldn't recognize crap on a bun," Stella smirks when Willa repeats this latest hypothesis. "And those ridiculous coots are the biggest clowns of all. They think they're got everything figured out. A real bunch of scientific geniuses—more like masters of ignorance. Spontaneous combustion my ass. Idiots."

Nonetheless, it is a theory that holds on steady, though a degree less convincingly, when the meticulously trimmed row of boxwood hedges lining the side entrance of the Episcopal Church smolders for hours one night while the town struggles to sleep in the hot dark. The quietly simmering nest of embers, altogether unnoticed until all at once bursting into a brilliant wall of live flame, finally alerting Reverend Turant's attention away from the late show gangster movie he'd been watching on the tiny black and white television he kept in his office at the rectory.

It is barely a handful of days after the last of the ruined hedge is dug up and the blackened earth raked over, when a long-abandoned Esso station, left to crumble on a weed strewn lot several blocks from the church, is next to light up the night.

It is this most recent incidence that serves to move the closely linked chain of fiery events from the realm of the curious to something distinctly criminal. The spontaneous combustion theory seriously quaking, then altogether dead, as coincidence comes to a full stop alongside the fact that before Norman Hitchcock's prison break, the volunteer fire company spent more time playing cards than fighting fires. Now they barely have time to shuffle the deck before the sirens are once again screaming and they are off and running.

With the finger turned and pointed at Norman Hitchcock, no one steps forward to disagree or argue on his behalf; no sympathetic voice speaking up to blame a sad childhood, school yard teasing, or a mother who never extended a comforting hug or baked chocolate chip cookies for an afternoon treat when he came home from school. All are in unanimous agreement that he is simply evil for the sake of being evil.

Twice already Omega has attempted to captivate Willa with a dramatic retelling of Norman's escape, but it strikes Willa more as a tale of luck, than of daring. And because it is Willa's immediate impulse to laugh, she bites down hard on her lower lip now quivering on the verge of a smirk, fixing her eyes on the intense frown scribbled over Omega Pearl's brow like furrows plowed across a full moon.

But honestly, how is it that no one at the prison failed to notice when he went on a starvation diet and didn't touch his bread and water, or prison gruel, for all those weeks before the great escape?

"He has always been one of those wiry types, all skin and bones even before they put him away, but apparently he didn't want to take a chance on not fitting through the window when the time came. Once he sawed through that section of bars, he knew he'd have to get his butt out, and quick."

"Did someone bake him a cake?" Willa says, and Omega frowns, clearly missing the joke.

"Hum?"

"A cake—you know, with a file in it."

"Oh, no. They don't let convicts have baked goods from the outside," Omega says, her expression sober. "He made some sort of tool—they all do that. I saw it on a television program once. They make tools and hide them in their mattresses. They're just as sneaky and conniving in jail as they were before they got in there. You can bet Norman was scheming over getting out for months, probably years, planning how he'd come back here and get his revenge on everyone responsible for putting him away. Only it's starting to look like he figures we're all responsible."

Although she's already shown it to Willa several times, Omega once again unfolds the three-month-old edition of the county newspaper she keeps in her desk drawer—a full-page photograph of Norman Hitchcock beneath the bold headline: **ESCAPED**. Quite honestly, Willa doesn't mind seeing it again, will likely not mind seeing it a dozen times more. His image fascinates her in the oddest way—a hideous contradiction that causes her insides to sway and churn, but which holds her eyes regardless. Perhaps it's because the image is precisely what she expects a criminal to look like; a near perfect cliché with his sharply menacing jaw line, heavy dark brows that jut out like a rocky ledge to shadow small, dark eyes—hard, black buttons that remind Willa of a crow's. The narrow line of his lips is pulled taut in an expressionless cord that appears incapable of movement. It's a face that belongs to someone who has never been anything other than bad.

It is this same photo which will be printed at the top left-hand corner on page one of the daily newspaper everyday "for as long as he remains a fugitive," according to the editor. Norman's coldly threatening image accompanied by a brief sentence or two—occasionally a paragraph—speculating over his current whereabouts and the potential location of his next unfortunate target.

"It's a little crazy the way everybody keeps talking about him like he's a movie star. Like they're scared, but proud of him at the same time," Willa says.

"It has nothing to do with crazy, it's human nature. Everybody's a little stupid like that. The more dangerous or bad somebody is, the more interesting they are," Stella says, perched on the edge of the bathtub in cottage number three, weakly scrubbing at a brownish band of soap scum ringing the dull porcelain, as if to exert greater effort will assuredly cause injury.

"But he isn't just *bad*. Omega says he killed people."

"All the more reason to be captivated. If all he ever did was steal a carton of cigarettes or pull away from the gas pump without paying, nobody would give a fig. Nope, this guy's the real thing. A bona fide killer. And it sure as hell doesn't get much better than that."

The blaze at the gas station is visible for miles, drawing the curious like insects hypnotized by the glow of a porch bulb. The thick clouds of smoke trail the acrid odor for miles, reaching even as far as The Moonglow.

Stella is already asleep and snoring softly when Willa first hears the far-off wail of the firehouse alarm. She rolls over in bed without opening her eyes, waiting to see if it's a dream that's shaken her awake or a true summons.

But when the sound is still there several minutes later, drilling a hole through the darkness, Willa sits up and pushes aside the sheet. It would be so much more convenient and appreciated if Norman would attend to this business of revenge in the daylight hours, Willa groans inside her head as she reaches for the shorts and tee-shirt she's pitched onto the single chair beneath the window hours earlier ... carefully ... quietly ... on the chance that even a movement as slight as extending her arm will shift the molecules in the air just enough to wake Stella.

Dressing quickly, she doesn't bother to pause long enough to turn her tee-shirt right-side-out before pulling it over her tangle of hair. She creeps toward the door even as she is tugging up the zipper on her shorts, heedful of every step she softly plants across the bare floor to avoid creaks, then slipping out into the night like poured syrup once she reaches the door.

She holds to the front step for a long moment, wrestling between reason and impulse. The sounds that woke her are still there—distinct and coaxing—and she darts across the grass to retrieve the cranky old bike she's left propped behind the dense tangle of blackberry bushes around back of the cottage. She throws her leg over the seat at the same time she wheels out toward the highway.

Her heartbeat drums a crescendo against her ribs when she catches sight of the blaze in the distance. Peddling furiously to reach the scene, her eyes hold to the brilliant orange and yellow flames shooting upward to melt a glowing crater in the protective firmament curved against the indigo sky.

"Those tanks sure as hell better be dry or this whole place is gonna blow to kingdom come," a voice says behind Willa as she stands in awestruck wonder, her legs straddling Omega Pearl's wobbly old bike between her knees.

"HEY, COME ON—YOU PEOPLE GOTTA MOVE BACK. THIS IS A DANGEROUS AREA HERE," a fireman yells, lifting his hands and pressing the air to motion the crowd back.

Willa ignores his warnings as if none of it has anything to do with her, her limbs declining to comply, even as the crowd reluctantly shuffles backward in a concentrated mass. She remains where she is, captivated by the waves of heat and the smell of dense roiling smoke pouring from the building's shattered windows in a filthy black river.

"HEY, KID," someone shouts and she pretends not to hear. "You better move outta the way."

And still she remains where she is, watching in silence, thoroughly mesmerized by the astonishing beauty of it all.

Seven

His are the sort of looks that people notice right away, that hold the eye for several beats beyond what is considered polite at first glance. And it isn't simply a matter of components nicely packaged—smooth dark hair, soft boyish features already in the process of changing into something sharper, *older*, slim build and long legged stride—it's his eyes that draw a person in. Eyes so dark they appear bottomless. The kind that are impossible to read, and yet which hint at things—uncertain things without absolute description.

"That's Jesse Truman. I hired him last summer to cut the grass, but then I figured as long as he's here I might as well get him to take care of a few other things around the place, too," Omega says once Willa can no longer hold back her curiosity and finally asks about the boy she's occasionally seen rummaging around in the shed out back and fussing over the mower.

"Just keeping the trash picked-up around here is a job for ten. It's disgusting what people throw out their car windows. They act like the world is one big landfill, and then the whole mess ends up blowing down here around my place. You won't believe the junk that turns up," Omega says, taking a bite of her tuna sandwich, chewing as she continues talking past the mouthful. "I mean what kind of animal throws a used tampon out the car window?" Omega shakes her round head.

"Actually, I'm thinking I should probably have him turn the mattresses once in a while, too. Back when my mama ran this place she always made sure they got flipped every so often. It's supposed to make 'em last longer.

"I'll be honest, though, I don't mind admitting it didn't take much to talk myself into the idea of having a handy man around the place, especially now, with Norman running amuck. Makes this ol' gal feel a whole lot safer having a male body around. And it doesn't hurt that he looks like that," she adds with a wink.

This isn't the first time Omega Pearl has attempted to draw Willa into what she refers to as 'girl talk,' nor is it the last time Willa will decline the invitation. She has no intention of sharing her personal thoughts or opinions with Omega Pearl Bodie, and certainly not any having to do with boys. Not that she doesn't appreciate hearing what someone else has to offer in the way of confidential observations, she simply has no desire to share her own. It's too much like showing your hand in the middle of a card game—fine if someone else is fool enough to chance it, but not if you're still trying to win the game.

Besides which, Willa is absolutely not looking to cultivate friendships with boys as Omega routinely suggests. The truth is, Willa hasn't had a real friend, male or female, since grade school, largely because she's wary of the requirements of friendships—the price of sharing what she'd rather keep hidden, and allowing someone within the messy confines of her life.

Nevertheless, even with her longstanding resolve intact, Willa might just as well cannonball off a cliff as ignore the insistent twittering tapping into her senses like Morse code whenever she catches a glimpse of Jesse Truman carrying a ladder around back of one of the cabins; pushing Omega's cranky old mower back and forth across the splotchy stripe of grass separating the dusty parking lot from the highway; or collecting discarded candy wrappers and crumpled cigarette packs from around the cottages where the wind has carried them.

"You got a boyfriend, honey? I'll bet you get plenty of attention with that pretty hair and cute little figure of yours," Omega says one afternoon as Willa returns the ring of keys to the hook on the wall behind the front desk.

"Uh uh. I'm not much interested in boys," she says with her back to Omega, taking a moment to give what she hopes will be the right *change-of-topic* reply.

It strikes her as an odd, out-of-the-blue question, until she turns and follows Omega's gaze out past the wide front window to where Jesse Truman crouches beside the lawnmower in a long rectangle of un-cut grass, the decrepit machine apparently having stalled. "They're mostly just annoying," Willa adds, staring now herself.

They watch as he tilts the machine forward and peers underneath.

"I'm sure that's what you tell your mama, but you don't have to play that game with me, sugar. We girls are born interested in boys. If we weren't they wouldn't have the power to give us such grief. Nothin' we can do about it either. It's natural instinct to go running after a good lookin' man, and it's just a waste of time and effort to try and pretend otherwise. You'd just better take my advice though and watch out for that one," Omega says, tipping her head toward the window.

"What do you mean? What's wrong with him? You're always saying what a big help he is around here. Did you catch him goofing off or something?" And even as she says it, Willa knows that if such an accusation is true, then he is very adept at pretending otherwise, since every time she sees him coming or going he is carrying tools, gathering trash, or pushing the mower over the spotty grass—either finishing a job or in the process of starting another.

"For Pete's sakes, honey, that's not what I'm talking about. I'll be the first to tell anybody how he's fixed things around here that've been busted for ten years," Omega shakes her head as she turns from the window, reaching for the bottle of cola settled on a stack of *Glamour* magazines piled on the desk.

"Uh uh, I'm saying he's the kind that'll break your heart. Maybe not on purpose, but he'll do it either way."

Willa doesn't answer, silently recalling the number of times she's caught Omega staring after him, eyes holding steady like those of a jackal moments away from a meal, a clear suggestion she'd gladly butter him like a slice of bread and swallow him up in one bite should the opportunity ever present itself. Yet here she is sermonizing over broken hearts.

"And God knows that situation with his family is just a mess—a hell of a mess. And that kind of situation just doesn't right itself overnight."

But Willa has stopped listening as her gaze drifts beyond the gently wafting curtains stirring at the open window, watching Jesse Truman as he leans forward and gives a sharp pull on the starter cord. The engine responds with a loud belch before sputtering into a rough idle, the noise altogether effective in drowning out the remainder of Omega's dissertation.

His eyes are nearly too arresting for his face—a blue so vast and deep, that to look into them is to become instantly immersed—rendering Willa momentarily speechless as she paddles furiously in an effort to resurface.

"Omega said to ask you to unlock number seven for me," Jesse says easily, as if he has no idea as to the effect his navy gaze has on ordinary mortals.

"Number seven?" Willa repeats as if he's just quoted a mathematical equation of impossible proportions, her brain scrambling thoughts in an attempt to comprehend his simple request.

"She said something about a broken—"

"Oh, yes—right, that's right—the bed frame. It looks like one of the legs is cracked," Willa says, dropping her gaze as she fishes in the front pocket of her shorts for the keys she's now required to carry since Stella has decided that her workday uniform will be a slim fitting skirt or sundress, *on the chance that someone of interest happens to check into this dump,* neither outfit possessing the necessary accommodations for the ungainly ring. *Not everyone who shows up here is a bum, Willa. You just never know who might pop-up, and it won't do much good if I'm standing around dressed like a rag picker. That's not the way to get someone's attention.*

"People do some crazy things around here. Well …. not that … I mean, of course it could've just broke for no particular reason—because it's old," Willa says, sidestepping past him, horribly aware of her idiotic babble, but unable to recall how to shut herself up as he patiently waits for her to insert the key into the lock and turn the knob.

"Thanks."

Willa turns to leave, then pauses, gathers her nerves before glancing back over her shoulder, "I'm Willa Burkett, by the way."

"I know," he says, smiling for barely an instant before stepping inside.

Certain that no one is watching, Willa quickly ducks beneath the spidery arms of the enormous willow drooping at the edge of the lake. Several days earlier, while wandering at water's edge, she'd discovered this perfect place, the tree's weepy branches providing an ideal hiding spot to eat her lunch in solitude, temporarily removed from Stella's glum moods and growing catalog of complaints.

"Damn well figures I'd end up stuck in a place with a crazy, murdering, escaped-con, firebug running around. And let me not fail to mention the absolute perfection of spending my days scrubbing toilets and changing dirty sheets in this back-road, lunatic colony straight from hell. But of course, that's not nearly degrading enough—because now she wants me to wash the damn sheets and hang them out on a freekin' line," she seethes between impatient drags on her cigarette." I swear, if this was a movie I'd damn well walk out and demand a refund."

And while there are times when Willa can't help but laugh at Stella's penchant for greatly embellished drama, lately her mother's grumblings have succeeded only in getting on her nerves. Especially when Stella continually implies that all of this is only about herself—that *she* is the only one stranded in a 1930's ghost town, that *she* is the only one feeling disappointed and miserable, that *she* is the only one anxious to get away from this dismal place—all of which irritates Willa like a splinter driven so deep the only way to remove it is to hack off a limb.

Stella never asks Willa where she disappears to every afternoon to eat her lunch, but then it has always been this way between them. Stella has always been far too preoccupied with her own doings to concern herself with anything Willa might be up to. Just as it was back in Hoosick Falls, as long as Willa remembers to show herself now and again over the course of the day, Stella is more than happy to leave her to fill her time alone.

Now, anxious to escape the press of heat that has piled up throughout the morning, Willa tucks her paper lunch bag under her elbow and parts the pale green curtain of limp branches with her hands, dipping her head under the drooping canopy at the very moment her eyes land on Jesse Truman sitting with his back against the tree's broad trunk. His eyes are shut, one hand balanced on his bent knee.

Her immediate prayer is to sprout wings and flee unnoticed before he senses her presence, opens his eyes to find her standing before him like a startled animal, paralyzed in a beam of light.

But, "You don't have to go," Jesse Truman says, just as she takes a careful step backwards.

"Oh … sorry. I didn't mean to wake you up. I was just … there's never anyone else here."

"It's all right. I wasn't sleeping."

"I'll just—"

"No, really, it's okay. I need to get back to work in a couple minutes anyway. Omega has a truck coming tomorrow to pump the septic tank so I need to dig out the cover this afternoon."

"But it's so hot. And isn't the guy who comes with the truck supposed to do that?"

Jesse shrugs, tipping his head back against the tree trunk and re-closing his eyes. "She says he'll charge less if it's dug out and ready when he gets here."

Her limbs jerk with the awkward movements of a marionette maneuvered by an inexperienced hand, dropping her to sit on the ground, her lunch bag falling into her lap from nowhere.

She unfolds the bag though her appetite is altogether gone, vanished the instant she ducked under the branches to find him here. Yet it feels necessary that she feign indifference, eats, or at least pretends to.

The obtrusive rustle of paper feels near painful in the quiet, the immediate tingling of self-consciousness pricking fiery pinpoints along the edges of her scalp. Willa shoots a glance at Jesse, relieved to see that his eyes remain closed. She unwraps the peanut butter sandwich, only to stare at it as though she's forgotten what it is and why she now holds it in her hand. She lifts it to her mouth and immediately takes too large a bite, so that she is forced to chew and swallow rapidly in a panicked effort to have it gone. She swallows again, and yet again, in an attempt to move the tasteless paste down her throat.

She shifts panicked eyes for a quick glimpse at Jesse Truman, fully expecting to find him staring in disgusted horror as she gulps her food like an anaconda swallowing an antelope, eternally grateful that his lids remain closed.

The burden of quiet presses the air around them with an intimacy that is impossible to pretend away. The fact is they really don't know each other. The occasional words they've exchanged in passing hold nothing of depth or familiarity. They are one step removed from strangers, and that's all. Not quite acquaintances and certainly not friends. Because if they were, it wouldn't feel so unnatural now, even a bit presumptuous, closeted alone beneath the tree.

Almost as if she's spoken her thoughts out loud, Jesse Truman right then opens his eyes and pulls to his feet with a barely discernable sigh. "I'll see you around," he says, and Willa mumbles something in reply, words she can't recall even two minutes later, disappointed as she is relieved by his leaving.

Stuffing the unfinished sandwich back into the paper bag, Willa stares after him, puzzling as to what it is about Jesse Truman that leaves her feeling as if he's calling her name, even when he hasn't uttered a word.

Eight

The moment she slips outside onto the porch, Willa knows that something is wrong—or at least more wrong than usual. The air is wrapped with the heavy odor of heat and smoke, strange in itself since The Moonglow is just far enough removed from town that the deep-charred odors of fire and ruin do not ordinarily succeed in carrying across the distance. And yet the acrid smell curling out against the night is distinct, and Willa knows it can't conceivably belong to anything other than smoke and flame.

Ordinarily Willa is careful to check whether Stella has fallen asleep before taking off on Omega's bike, but she forfeits the habit now, unwilling to waste potentially valuable time as she slides her feet across the porch boards as though gliding on ice—biting down on her lip when the toe of her sneaker touches the step, and despite her care, induces a low groan from the ancient wood. She holds herself perfectly still, waiting for the incriminating glare of light from a hastily switched on lamp to pin her in her tracks, breathing a fragile sigh when the protective veil of darkness leaking through the cabin's open windows remains undisturbed.

She skitters across the yard in search of Omega's mislaid bicycle. Two nights previous she'd had to pitch it hastily beneath the low hanging limbs of a dense pine tree out front when she'd returned from a fire and detected a light on in Omega's office. She hasn't had a single opportunity since, to retrieve and return it to its customary hiding place; and she worries now, that despite the bike's rusted frame and cracked vinyl seat, someone lacking anything better has found it and simply rode away.

But, thankfully, it is right where Willa recalls dropping it, and she grabs hold of the handlebars and yanks it upright.

She runs alongside the rickety frame and steers toward the highway, swinging her leg over the seat and quickly mounting once she reaches the pavement. And it is right then that she sees it, the reflection in her eyes mirroring the spectacular tongues of brilliant flame lapping against the night sky in the distance. *Incredible! It's right here! Right here in front of her.*

Her legs peddle fast and furious, twin beaters churning the air, ancient rubber tires slapping the uneven pavement in complaint. Her insides roll and crash with incoming waves as she closes the distance. Someone is shouting—then a woman's high-pitched wail—the hysterical squall going on and on until all at once obliterated by the approaching fire engines careening across town from the station several blocks away. The steady bleat of sirens cracks open the night and swallows every other sound.

Willa drops the bicycle on its side, not caring where it falls, her feet dragging lead as she moves closer, eyes wide and staring in an attempt to fully absorb this terrible thing. She sees the regal old house on the corner, its gracious facade melting like wax behind mushrooming clouds of black smoke. And for the first time since becoming a willing witness to Norman Hitchcock's path of vengeful destruction, she feels something other than mesmerized curiosity. Her unblinking eyes pour out her immediate grief and anger in a suffocating tide of overwhelming sadness that threatens to overtake even her breathing. *Why this house? Why couldn't he just leave this one alone? He's gone too far. This time he's gone too far.*

Willa has never been someone drawn to wistful dreams or romantic notions, all of which makes her fixation on the old house all the more inexplicable. Yet remarkably, especially to herself, she has been caught and held by the place at first glance, her imagination churning over the ancient structure like a dream she's had before. Long vacant and crumbling, its one-time grandeur long faded, the monstrous house solidly planted at the end of the block has not only drawn her attention, but proceeded to swallow it whole.

"If it isn't haunted, it sure as heck should be. People *died* in that house. *Murdered.* An entire family," Omega offers, when Willa mentions the house, immediately sticking the miniature brush back into the bottle of bright green nail polish at her elbow, all too happy to forget about the unpolished nails on three of her fingers in favor of sharing the details of this particular tragedy with Willa. "It was just terrible, the way it happened. I was a little girl at the time and my mother of course didn't want me to know about it, so she made a point of hiding the newspapers for weeks afterwards. I was going through a stage at the time, scared of my own shadow and having nightmares, so she must've figured a story like that would've set me off my rocker. She'd shake her head at my father and give him a look if he started to tell her some tidbit about the family he'd picked-up around town, but I heard everything anyway. For months, I heard about it, every time she got on the phone with one of her girlfriends they'd rehash every detail," Omega smiles, swatting at a fly with her moldy green fingertips when the insect chances to land on the lip of her soda bottle.

"I swear, but she honestly believed that as long as I was setting up my little plastic farm animals or sitting with a story book open in front of me, then I couldn't hear a thing—like a kid can't play and hear at the same time."

"You mean that's where it happened? That's where he killed those people?"

"*He?*"

"Norman Hitchcock."

"Oh, goodness no. Not Norman. That was long before his time. No this was something else entirely—there was this man who just lost his mind and killed his whole family except the youngest girl. Nobody knows how she managed it, but she got away and hid in a closet while he went through the house and shot the rest of them—his wife, three sons, and two older daughters. Every one of them—shot in the head. They were all in their beds so they must've been sleeping at the time. The girl probably heard something that scared her and she had a notion to hide. I've always wondered if he went looking for her or what. Can you imagine? Lord, but they would've found me dead of a heart attack long before that lunatic would've had the chance to shoot me."

"Jeez, that's horrible," is all Willa can think to say, though the words don't even begin to cover the sense of horror prickling sharp needles along her hairline. *They were just sleeping in their beds. Sleeping—probably dreaming.*

"He shot himself afterward, so nobody ever knew for sure why he did it. There were no notes or anything left behind. Must've just lost his marbles.

"They boarded up the house and the little girl went to live with a spinster aunt on the other side of town. It was pitiful sad. She was a real pretty little thing, with long red hair and big blue eyes," Omega says, looking down at her fingers, frowning when she notices the smeared polish on her thumb. "They couldn't get her to say a word about what happened. People said she saw the whole thing through the keyhole, but then how did they know any of that if she didn't say so herself?

"She stayed with the aunt for a few years, but then one day she just up and disappeared. It was weeks before they found her—hung herself in the very closet she'd hidden in all those years earlier—poor child. Just terrible. A person just doesn't get over something like that. It was so sad. Just terrible sad.

"There were a few different families who tried to live there over the years. Big place like that going for such a cheap price. It's tempting. But none of them ever stayed long. Live people can't share a house with ghosts.

"You'd do best to keep away from that place, really, honey. I'm not fooling. I know how you kids like all that scary stuff, but that place is evil. A house can't survive violent death. Once something like that happens, that's it—well, it's ruined."

But, it isn't the variety of warning Willa is likely to heed. In fact, she finds it impossible to stay away, if only because she's forever been drawn to things living in the shadow of sadness and tragedy, time and again surrendering to the determined pull of gloom and melancholy, even though her own life has not been so much tragic, as directionless. Although, quite honestly, she does prefer the mournful portrait of a tortured, wandering apparition. She suspects that the marvelous old house has just as likely died for much the same reasoning that everything else in Harriet's Bluff apparently has, drawing its last breath only once an entire population collectively lost interest and abandoned it to stand alone beneath the shroud of its tragic past.

For weeks she has found herself standing on the sidewalk across the street, studying the house at deliberate intervals, just long enough to avoid drawing attention in a town that so obviously thrives on broad suspicions and random curiosities, imagining what is there beyond the skin, within the walls, until it's become something of an obsession. And she wonders if her fixation is somehow linked to that other house—the one she'd loved and lost back in Hoosick Falls.

She remembers that she must've been five, possibly six, when she first noticed it, walking home from the market with Stella and paying little attention as her mother complained about the ridiculous price of cigarettes, a lousy cut of meat she'd consequentially refused to buy, and the fact that the bag boy had stupidly packed all the soup cans in one paper sack and then hadn't even bothered to double bag. As young as she was, Willa had already learned by then that the purpose of her mother's rants weren't so much in anticipation of a response from Willa, as they were intended to pacify the bristled edges of her annoyance with the soothing tonic of her own voice.

Asleep Without Dreaming

Although Stella's immediate tirade would typically slacken by the time they'd covered three or four blocks, there would be some new complaint ready to slide in to fill the space. Some new vexation would chug alongside as they continued the tiresome trek across town, so that by the time they reached the long abandoned house settled at the end of the block from where their own plain and cheerless bungalow resided further down the street, Stella would have built up enough steam to move a locomotive.

And while Stella rekindled her litany of complaints, shifting the troublesome bag on her hip, she would awkwardly root through her purse for a pack of matches to light the cigarette she couldn't possibly postpone until she reached home. Willa would then take the opportunity to slacken her pace— purposely falling behind just long enough to imagine herself onto one of the upper porches trimmed in peeling gingerbread, wondering what it would be like to live in such a grand castle.

But even then, as determinedly as she pulled and twisted her imagination, Willa could never quite succeed in envisioning the elegant parties and festive occasions one would deem as essential in such a place. She could only ever see herself alone. And it was a portrait that didn't so much unnerve or depress her, as it brought a satisfying sense of contentment.

"For cripe sakes, Willa. You wanna step on it before I drop this damn bag right here on the sidewalk."

As the years slipped past, the old house remained unchanging other than to grow shabbier, her own life turned shakier; and the dream itself began to change.

For a time, the fantasies of wishing herself within the walls had been enough and Willa had been content to study the house from the sidewalk, passing slowly as always, staring up at the vacant windows and wondering what might be there behind the glass. But the day inevitably arrived when she knew it was no longer satisfactory to wonder and dream from the outside looking in, her imagination increasingly impatient to wander the rooms and pretend that the future had already come.

She didn't deny knowing the inherent risks involved, should she attempt trespass in an abandoned house in the middle of Hoosick Falls on a brilliant July afternoon; but her lingering childhood fear of the dark remained stronger than the trepidation of being caught red-handed in the act of invasion. Risky as it was to break and enter in daylight, she nevertheless wasn't crazy enough to carry out her crime once darkness settled and all things sinister crawled out from their daytime hiding places.

Even so, it took several aborted attempts over a span of weeks—time and again surrendering to panic, impossibly frozen beneath the candid glare of a sun that hid nothing—before Willa was finally successful in convincing herself that her fears of being caught were unfounded, that there was no one watching, no eyes peeking out from behind parted curtains with one hand on the phone ready to dial the police.

It was a dull and rainy morning late in August when Willa gathered together the necessary fortitude to complete her plan.

She was deliberate in avoiding even a sideways glance at the house as she walked past, watching her dirty white sneakers take one determined footstep after another, breaking stride only once she reached the thick hedge of privet bordering the side yard. Darting around to a porch she'd selected on previous surveillance missions because of the line of towering hollies sheltering it from view of the sidewalk, her nervous eyes scanned the length of first floor windows for a broken latch or loose screen fallen from its track. And yet the derelict place stared back with the smug assurance of a fortress, no pinhole or crevice that might have allowed a quick and painless entry.

She skulked back and forth, being careful to keep out of sight behind the hollies—intermittently directing her eyes to the line of locked windows as she trolled her thoughts for the missing genius idea.

"QUEENIE!" a voice called just on the other side of the holly bushes.

Willa froze, holding her breath or forgetting how to breathe, she wasn't certain of which.

"Get out of there you bad dog. You go and get yourself bit by another snake and that's it. I'm done taking you to the vet – stupid dog."

Willa stared at the section of greenery where the woman's voice had filtered through, waiting, pasting together an immediate explanation as to what she was doing there crouched behind the bushes—*a cat... her cat was hit by a car and ran over here ... no, a cat wasn't likely to be running after it was hit by a car ... the cat saw Queenie the dog and took off in this direction.*

"Damn it, Queenie, get over here," the voice says, a little further along the hedge now. "You're a bad dog, a bad, bad dog."

Willa remained crouched between the porch and the hollies, pinching her elbows in an effort to ignore the aching in her legs, then kneeling on the ground when the burning in her thighs and calves became too much to ignore. She felt something pressing hard against her kneecap, and she shifted back onto her haunches, looking down to see the broken piece of a rusty hinge molded into the damp clay edging the foundation of the house. She attempted to pry it loose, but the thing was too firmly planted in the earth. Standing, she stubbornly kicked at the metal with the toe of her sneaker, eventually dislodging it just enough to wedge her fingers underneath and pull it free.

It proved the perfect tool for prying a basement pane from its casement, just wide enough to allow her to slip inside. The dimness within was suffocatingly thick with ancient odors and unknown objects left to decay over time, and for a long moment Willa hovered close to her port of entry, her heartbeat slamming inside her chest as she frantically swatted at cobwebs immediately netting her hair, listening for sounds of the unfamiliar, but hearing nothing beyond the quiet. As her vision gradually adjusted to the opaque shades of gloom, she forced her thoughts to focus on the logical—the location of the stairs climbing to the rooms above and whether she in fact possessed the fortitude to use them, rather than allowing her mind to quaver over the pasty, flesh drooping zombies potentially creeping toward her, perfectly noiseless movements that only monsters are capable of executing.

And yet for all her uncertainty, Willa understood there was no going back: Despite the prickling sensation of fear squeezing hard at the back of her neck with icy fingers, she would not leave until she'd ascended the stairs to the waiting house above.

For the remainder of that summer the house was hers—the maze of hollow rooms with their desolate echoes.

Oftentimes she would bring along one of the books that sat unread on the dusty bookcase in the living room at home, neglected and unread from the time it had first arrived crisp and new from the Readers Digest book club (ordered by Stella, not to read, but for the collection's attractive uniformity on a shelf, and because she insisted that a bookcase without a single book made it look like the house was inhabited by ignoramuses). Other times, she would sit quietly … thinking about the complications that had come to settle now that Martin was gone, and by all appearances wasn't coming back. She stumbled through the confused myriad of possibilities forever crowding her head, images jostled together, pushing and shoving against one another in an attempt to secure her attention.

Time passed slowly within the space of her solitude. After a while, even a thing as uncomplicated as random thought felt too great a labor. And Willa would lie on her back, spine pinned flat against a rectangle of pale yellow sunlight streaming onto the dark hardwood floor, the thick mass of her honey colored hair bundled into a pillow to cushion her head, lulled away from consciousness by the sun's golden warmth leaking over her skin.

And she'd slept. Sometimes for hours. Waking only after some sharp noise from the outside poked a hole through the bubble of her subconscious, her dreams immediately draining away through the gaping void, eyes snapping open to the diminished light of late afternoon.

Before long the cold months had settled in, turning the old house unbearably arctic. It was impossible to sustain even the briefest of visits then, and Willa had eventually stopped going altogether.

It wasn't until late the following spring when she again crawled through the basement window, only to discover certain peculiarities which hadn't existed before. Several threadbare blankets lay rumpled across a mattress someone had been dragged downstairs from a second-floor bedroom; empty beer and soda cans had been stacked into a pyramid in the center of the room; newspapers and empty food wrappers were strewn across hardwood floors now stained and pock-marked from burning cigarettes. An impossibly voluptuous nude pouted from the glossy centerfold of a magazine which lay open on the blue stripe ticking of the dirty mattress, prompting Willa to kick the pages shut with the toe of her sneaker.

It was an easy enough scene to decipher, nothing of what she'd found there that she didn't understand or hadn't in some part known to expect. She had in fact surmised from the moment of her own trespass that it was only a matter of time before some other neighborhood kid did the very thing she had done—found a way inside and staked a claim on territory she'd erroneously coveted as her own.

And then one day the place was simply gone. A demolition crew came late one spring and stripped the house to its foundation; taking away the remains in enormous sections, leaving nothing to prove its former grand existence other than the gaping cellar hole.

Willa mourned the loss, as if for a dead relative, even while knowing that the sentiment was ill placed and thoroughly ridiculous. She heard the voice of logic in her head reminding her that it was *just a building for heaven's sake. Wood, mortar, and stone. Nothing more.* It hadn't represented any tangible dream, nor did it hold any real promise of holding a place in her future. It was just a house. Someone else's and not her own. She knew this, and yet, still, she didn't quite believe it.

Willa watches the building burn, reminding herself that unlike the house back in Hoosick Falls, which had been opulently furnished with her expectations, she has no ties to this particular place, and any misplaced predilections she's invented are merely based on similarities in architecture, the logic of which makes her heightened flux of emotion feel both unearned and foolish. It's true she's bumped into the occasional roaming curiosity passing through her head, wondering about the forlorn house from her first sighting weeks ago. But she knows it was surely Omega Pearl's crazy story that worked so effectively to water the sponge of her own imagination to saturation. Otherwise, Willa would say it's only because the place reminds her of something that's been gone for years that her interest has been piqued at all. She certainly hasn't been harboring any plan to pry open a window and sneak inside, wander the rooms in search of another temporary hiding place to secret herself from the world.

For several days after the blaze, the charred carcass rising up from the Victorian's stone foundation continues to smolder. And just as she'd done before the fire, Willa pauses briefly on her way past, except that now it is in mourning of the ruined place, newly enraged by the senseless destruction with each viewing.

She knows, from watching the aftermath of the other fires, that it won't be long before the clean-up crews begin the work of clearing away the burnt remains, hauling away all things portable, leaving only the massive sections of foundation to be razed sometime later—the stately stone buttresses blackened by ash and soot, but nevertheless standing.

Whether foolish or ridiculous, Willa easily comes to the determination that she must have something of this lost castle for herself. A memorable piece of what is gone. She doesn't so much care if it's a scrap of decorative molding, a square of colored glass from one of the magnificent stained glass windows, a carved brass doorknob or fancy latch from a kitchen cabinet. All she wants is some tangible thing that will enable her to recall what once stood here, should she ever care to remember, years from now when she's living far away in California with Stella.

She knows it's impossible, but even so, Willa swears that the color of night in Harriet's Bluff has changed. And it is consistently darker now than it had been at the beginning of the summer. It is almost as if Norman Hitchcock's ambition to burn down the town, building by building, has in effect stolen the light and lengthened the shadows that run ever deeper and darker in a bold threat to eclipse every last glimmer of dwindling light.

Stella's been restless all evening, smoking a nauseating string of cigarettes, slapping out cards on her rumpled bedspread as if attempting to hurt them rather than simply lay out another game of solitaire she will never finish before losing interest. Willa is immersed in drawing stick figure cartoons in the Big Chief Tablet she keeps under her mattress and doesn't immediately notice when Stella's head slants sideways on her pillow and she drops off into a fidgety sleep.

Willa studies her warily, attempting to judge from her mother's breathing if she has yet landed into full asleep, or is merely grazing on the surface of subconscious. She counts the short puffs of air wheezing from Stella's nostrils—*one in, two out, one ... two in, one out*—listening for a definite rhythm to indicate that Stella has reached knocked-out status.

Despite the fact that she is having second, third, even fourth misgivings over what is increasingly feeling like a foolhardy plan, some unknown determination is persistently nudging Willa into motion, and she is now on Omega Pearl's rickety bike, rapidly peddling toward town. She tries not to fixate on the sporadic bolts of panicked thoughts splintering through her head like lightning strikes, but instead strives to recall something Father Michael had said during one of his more notable sermons at Saint Cecelia's—something about fear having power over someone only when they open the door and allow it in. And as he talked she'd imagined all the times she'd not only opened the door, but also the windows, told fear to come on in and make itself comfortable while she sets it a place at the table. "Your favorite meal," she assures it, as she wrings her hands. She only wishes now that she'd made more of an effort to banish fear for good.

The streets are empty and still, quiet in a way that feels anything other than comforting, like riding into an ambush—a multitude of horrors alive and waiting behind every shadow.

The blackened crater where the house once stood yawns wide before her, dark and seemingly bottomless, where a dropped pebble or misplaced footstep has no chance to land, but will instead tumble into eternity.

She feels the press of fear returned, climbing her spine to cling at the base of her skull as she walks the bike along the sidewalk with purposeful intent. The complete absence of ordinary life—other than the weak glow of a late night television program showing in a neighboring house, a bedside lamp clicking on in an upstairs room as someone prepares for bed—feels not so much a relief, as it does distinctly threatening.

It makes little difference how many times Willa has passed the building's charred carcass over the past several days as she acclimates a scheme; because now, standing closer than she's ever dared in daylight, it is an unimaginable sight. Even the proviso of night fails to soften the sharp edges of fiery devastation; and the acrid smell of burnt timbers that is still here, hangs in the air like a grounded fog.

It is the odor of ruined, dead things that wafts up from the black and twisted beams haphazardly piled and leaning together in a grotesque monument of the gracious structure no longer in existence here.

Willa clicks on the flashlight she carries in her hand, sweeping the quaking beam along the perimeter of the burned house, her former hopefulness taking an immediate plummet; by all appearances, there is nothing left to claim that isn't charred, melted, ruined, or wholly unidentifiable.

She takes a step closer and the flashlight beam catches the briefest glimmer of something reflective at her feet. She bends and picks up a jagged triangle of broken glass filmed with black soot, turning it over in her hand. There is certainly nothing exceptional about a plain piece of broken glass other than in consideration of where it's come from. Although it is not quite what she is hoping for, she doesn't toss the shard back into the rubble, on the chance she fails to find something better suited to her idea of a memento.

She slides one foot closer, tipping forward to peer into the blackened pit, her spine instantly stiffening when she hears the distinct sound of something moving nearby. Her breathing clings to the inside of her throat as she sweeps the flashlight in the direction of the disturbance—hoping, praying, praying harder, that the beam will not land on a sinister pair of eyes looking back at her.

Willa's stare widens, saucer eyes all but exploding off her face as they follow the weak beam jumping and bobbing over the contents of the black hole open wide at her feet. Her lungs are prepared to take an immediate leap into screaming terror should the quivering light reveal so much as a moth rising from the ash.

And yet the light unveils nothing other than what she's already seen, blackened remains dead and still as a petrified cadaver. Apparently the sound she's heard is nothing but a shifting beam within the charred wreck, a fatally injured limb further surrendering to mortal injuries and buckling as the weight of the collapsed building settles deeper into itself.

Willa slowly releases a tightly held fist of air from her lungs, setting it loose on a heavy breath of relief.

But again, she hears it. The distinct sound of something moving. An approach that is neither brief nor sudden, but which advances with slow deliberation. Willa flicks off the light, gripping the metal cylinder tight against her thigh like a weapon. Despite every internal inclination now urging her to tear off at a sprint—run like hell, before hell has a chance to reach out and catch her—Willa remains anchored to the ground, held immobile by the colossal weight of her fear. She passionately wills her limbs and organs to perfect stillness, even as she feels the palms of her hands quaking violently against her legs.

She senses the unknown entity moving closer, and her heartbeat races off at a wildly leaping crescendo—her limbs poised for flight, but incapable of motion. Any previous empathy she's felt toward Norman Hitchcock and the curious workings of his felonious mind have altogether vaporized in the terrifying light of his actual presence. *He's here. Right here. And if he wants to, he can kill her and no one would ever know.*

Her jaw unhinges in preparation of a scream, her finger sliding along the flashlight cylinder until it bumps against the switch. *If she catches him off-guard—shines the light into his hollow black eyes and momentarily blinds him at the same instant she unleashes a gut-wrenching scream—there's a chance she might startle him long enough to get away.*

But it isn't a man she finds caught motionless in the beam when she flicks the switch and swings the light up into the space pressing toward her. The intended shriek dies in her mouth as she stares into the startled eyes of a skinny black dog, the animal returning Willa's wide-eyed gaze for barely an instant, before all at once turning and chasing off into the dark.

If she weren't so thoroughly shaken, she might have laughed at herself. But her insides are still rolling like tumbleweed caught by wind when she straddles Omega's bike a short while later and heads back to The Moonglow, a soot-covered doorknob clutched in her hand. *Only a dog—a pitiful, half-starved stray. A dog and not a crazed madman.* Yet even as she repeats the mantra, out loud and inside her head, the uneasiness remains hard and tight inside her chest.

Until now, Willa has easily considered Norman Hitchcock a face in a newspaper, but otherwise invisible, an enigma that belongs solely to Harriet's Bluff. His crimes, though curious, are not destined to hold anything beyond passing interest in her own life. After all, she will be gone, back on the road with Stella long before any of it has the chance to matter.

And such logic was all so easy to believe at first glance, back when it still seemed as if it could be true.

Nine

It's not as though she is all at once desirous of Stella's attentions or has grown newly sentimental. It's just that Willa thinks her mother might at least make something of an effort to acknowledge her only child's birthday—even if only to remark that she does in fact recall giving birth to a daughter fifteen years previous.

Instead, "I swear, Willa, but if you don't quit feeding those damn strays I'm gonna start poisoning the filthy things. They're crapping all over the yard and in the flower beds. It smells like a toilet out there," is the context of her birthday greeting.

Willa swallows another spoonful of soggy cornflakes without answering, seeing little point in challenging Stella to recount precisely what flowerbeds she's referring to. As far as Willa can tell, the only blooms she's noticed growing in the entire vicinity of The Moonglow are dandelions, scraggly bunches of Queen Anne's lace, and the occasional patch of clover. Besides which, it isn't Willa who's responsible for the arrival of the cats in question, something Stella might've calculated on her own, had she paused long enough from issuing threats to consider that such a sizable community of feral cats suggested long-term occupancy at The Moonglow, several generations longer than Willa has been here setting out the occasional slice of stale bread soaked with the leftover milk from her cereal.

"That's right, you go right ahead and ignore me. Just don't whine that you weren't warned when you see the nasty things dropping like flies. The last thing we need is Bertha the Beluga throwing us out of this dump before we're ready."

Willa swallows hard against her immediate impulse to fire back a retort. She doesn't so much care about the crude reference to Omega Pearl; but what does needle her irritation is Stella's inference that she actually has a plan, a scheme of some sort. Because if Willa was placing bets, she'd wager that no such design exists.

It is a disappointing, but thoroughly expected, pattern Willa immediately recognizes and thoroughly dislikes, inasmuch as it is precisely how Stella has always done things—haphazard and irrational, just as it was when Martin left, staying when she should have gone, leaving when she probably should've stayed.

Don't you ever look close enough at your own life to see the details? is the question Willa wants to shriek at top volume. Then maybe, just maybe, Stella might pause and shake the clouds from her head, and for once get a clear view of the way things really are.

But, as it has always been, little of what Stella does makes sense, and her reasoning rarely makes it to the surface. She plays her cards close to the chest, preferring to bluff, ever careful not to reveal her hand.

It is this side of Stella that Willa most recognizes and least understands. The one assuring her how far removed she is from ever understanding her mother's inner workings. An assimilation not so much startling, as it has always been this way. Frustratingly so.

As pointless an exercise as hindsight may be, there are still occasions when Willa surrenders to the temptation of wondering how different things might have turned out if her mother had said or done something that very first time Martin lost half his paycheck on a single bet at the horse track.

Willa had been in third grade, on her way to fourth, old enough to remember being surprised by Stella's failure to react. She guessed that Stella's lack of hysterics had to do with an assumption that Martin was so ashamed and disgusted with himself over the idiotic nature of his loss, that there would be little chance of him repeating such a foolish mistake. And yet, if her mother had been thinking as much, she'd been stone dead wrong, considering that the only notable difference between Martin's first disastrous experience at the track and the next was in losing his entire paycheck and not just a portion.

And then somehow it was a ritual, the most peculiar of family outings, Willa and her mother accompanying Martin on his twice monthly pilgrimages to the horse track—both ready and waiting when he pulled into the driveway on the first and last Friday of the month. The tires of his big grey Pontiac, lifting the dust with his impatient arrival, would summon them outside with a chafing chorus from the car's horn even before he braked the behemoth to a full stop.

As eagerly as Willa grasped any opportunity to escape the dreary little house and the mediocrity of her largely uneventful life in Hoosick Falls (the destination and purpose for leaving of far less importance than was the actual going), she couldn't quite figure Stella's motivation or the puzzling contradiction of her continued accompaniment to the track week after week when it was becoming obvious how much the routine infuriated her. The grim set of her lips alluding to the legion of angry phrases armed and amassed for battle just on the other side of her teeth.

Stella rarely spoke on the now familiar drive out to the track. Not a word before the money was lost and nothing afterwards when Martin slowly trailed back out to the parking lot where he'd left them sitting in the car, the tight set of his jaw and stiff-legged shuffle assuring that he was once again empty-handed. His only absolute success having been to gamble away another week's salary.

Willa wasn't long in learning to keep her inevitable complaints of boredom, thirst, and hunger to herself, since opening her mouth resulted in little other than to bring her discomforts flying back like a razor-edged boomerang.

"And just what do you expect me to do about it?" was the inevitable reply from Stella. "You think I'm not thirsty? You think I'm not bored out of my skull with this crap? Well there's not a damn thing I can do about it so you might just as well knock off the whining. I've got my own problems. I sure as hell don't need to hear about yours."

With Stella sitting stiff-spined in the front seat chain-smoking her indignation, Willa curled herself into a corner of the stiff vinyl backseat, working her fingers into a tear in the plastic. After a while she would squeeze her eyes shut against the dull ache of boredom, attempting to sleep away even a portion of the slow stretch of another heat-drenched afternoon.

Striving to force a nap with the full glint of sunlight pressing in from every corner of the sky proved an impossible undertaking, and it was never long before Willa abandoned the endeavor altogether. Once again, she would find herself sitting with her damp bangs pressed against the glass of the partially downed window, scanning the parking lot for other families, in the hope of locating a mutually bored and restless prisoner in the back seat of another parked car, someone equally anxious to pass the time making faces or exchange some other universally understood form of mute communication.

And always Willa was disappointed, though not especially surprised, to discover that there were never any other families in evidence, the array of vehicles aligned in the parking lot consistently empty aside from a jaunty pair of red furry dice or a looped string of rosary beads hanging from a rearview mirror.

The excursions to the track were of little variance, and the return to Hoosick Falls of assumable results, considering Martin Burkett's lack of either luck or skill in selecting a horse with a penchant for running hard and fast enough to win. It was a pitiable pattern that left them with little more to live on from week to week other than the hollow calories of his continuing frustrations and failures.

Once the sore press of unpaid bills and threatening calls from a growing list of creditors at last worked to harden Stella's features into a stony cast, Willa knew to tuck herself within the shadows of her own careful silence, ever expectant of the impending eruption that would eventually succeed in breaking the weakening seal from her mother's tightly held repose.

It is like moving through the thickest, blackest cloud—this ominous mood that has shuddered and collapsed overtop her—that is hard to look past and even harder to breathe. All morning at The Moonglow, as she trudges along behind Stella, wordlessly moving from one cottage to the next, changing rumpled linens and cleaning the accustomed disorder without actually seeing any of it, Willa finds herself fighting against the threat of babyish tears. She feels increasingly sorry for herself as the day wears on, taking pains to pause and remind herself every so often that she is simply another forgotten person existing in a world that clearly has no real place or purpose for her.

It is still early in the day when Willa catches herself watching for Jesse's truck to pull into the dusty parking lot, anxious for even a glimpse of someone who isn't Stella, if only to alleviate the dreaded sense of isolation piling up around her like a cinder block mountain.

But as the hours crawl past with still no sign of him, Willa now turns her mind to Omega Pearl, waiting for her imminent return from her weekly hair appointment. She doesn't care how immature or juvenile it may be, she has every intention of eliciting sympathy from Omega by telling her that her inconsiderate and selfish her mother has completely forgotten her birthday, simply because Willa knows how much it will anger Stella.

The morning is long past, and Willa is scrubbing the bathtub in cottage six when she at last hears the familiar rattle and hiss of Jesse's truck swinging into the parking lot, tires spewing a ground storm of dust and gravel.

She rushes to finish, making quick work of vacuuming the eternally molting rugs that lead from bed to bath, before darting outside into the sunlight without a word, and leaving a clearly agitated Stella to grudgingly make up the bed on her own.

Willa swipes her damp palms against the seat of her shorts, suddenly blank as to what she'll even say to him. The very reasoning of why she's been watching for him all morning yanked from her head like a hooked trout the moment she'd heard his arrival. *Maybe if she bumps into him accidentally on purpose...asks what Omega has had him doing all morning.* Whatever she says, it won't have anything to do with this thing she's been grousing over in her head—as if Jesse Truman would care even a smidgen about a forgotten birthday.

Only now, she finds herself staring, dumbfounded, at the vacant stretch of the parking lot, a tangle of confused disappointment see-sawing in her head, back and forth like an unlatched door caught by the wind. *He's not here. Only stayed a moment and gone. Maybe, hasn't even been here at all.*

Nothing moves in the heat. The cottages, the trees, even the air hovering over it, are eerily suspended in an unnatural web of quiet. The lake lies silently shimmering beneath the hard orb of a brilliant sun, its surface impossibly smooth and unblemished as though pressed under glass. There are no twittering sounds of summer insects or croaking frogs, not even the occasional drone of a car speeding past on the highway, not a single sound or movement spilling in to dispute the sensation of complete and utter abandonment.

"Done already, honey?"

Willa nearly drops her insides along with the ring of keys she is returning to the hook behind the desk when Omega's booming voice comes up behind her. She spins around, at once recognizing the tell-tale indications of Omega's visit to the beauty parlor; the pyramid of tight curls molded and sprayed into a lacquered monument atop her round head—plump sausage fingers winging the air as if her candy pink nail polish has only just been brushed on, and not painted hours earlier.

"Holy mackerel, but it's hot as Hades," she says, reaching for a torn envelope lying on the desk, her madly flapping arm jiggling like the jowls of a bloodhound as she fans her face, her perfect helmet remaining undisturbed by her frenzied stirring. "Norma talked me into staying in town for lunch and I gave in like an idiot. I blew my whole blasted diet before I even finished the salad," Omega moans, dropping into her chair behind the desk and twisting the cap from the bottle of cola she's carried in with her.

The day has been long and disappointing enough that Willa's earlier desire for commiserating conversation is altogether dead, wrapped, tied, and buried, and she edges toward the door as Omega Pearl continues her chatter.

"I'd better get going," Willa injects quickly when Omega pauses to swig a mouthful of soda. "It's my birthday and Stella's planning something special."

"Huh! You're kidding me. Your birthday? Really? Your mother never said a peep about it when I ran into her this morning," Omega says, wrinkling her brow as if truly startled by the omission, and Willa pauses, decidedly warmed by the gesture. "But then—and pardon me for saying so—we both know your mother can be a very peculiar bird sometimes."

Willa swallows hard to force down the urge to laugh. Stella has said far worse about Omega, and without bothering to tack on any "pardon me" nicety when she does.

"Shoot, what's that word I'm thinking of? Intro... something... introspective, that's it—she's an introspective woman."

Willa nods. She'll have to look up the word to be certain of the meaning, but either way, if she is to choose a word to describe Stella, *introspective* isn't the one that comes to mind.

"Here, honey, buy yourself a soda on me," Omega says, sliding the ashtray of coins toward Willa. "It's not everyday a girl has something to celebrate."

It doesn't much matter that she has no destination in mind when she turns her heel onto the highway leading into Harriet's Bluff. She is thinking of everything and nothing, her thoughts winding off on random trails—rushing forward then turning back, darting out a sight. Without wanting to, she is back to considering over Stella and her potential reaction should her only child meet an unexpected and tragic end. Here, now, today. On what could very well be the occasion of her last birthday. *Flattened by a tractor trailer barreling along the highway at 90 mph. Her body shattering like glass on impact so that searchers will need to comb the area for days, possibly even weeks, in a determined effort to recover the jigsaw collection of her scattered remains; a finger, an elbow, a glassy staring eyeball.*

Of even greater importance than the gruesome details of her demise is the question of how such a horrendous tragedy will affect Stella. Will her guilt be so all-consuming that she'll lose all will to function? Will she collapse into a well of sorrow and grief so profoundly devastating that she will never again be capable of resurrecting her ruined spirit?

Even in the wholly fabricated context of daydream speculation, it seems unlikely. Stella, after all, has never been the sort of person to mourn what is gone. She's someone who has clearly learned a thing or two about subsisting through dark times. And while it's true there have been moments when her mother's resilience feels nearly admirable, on this particular day, Willa merely finds it irritating.

She wanders through the lingering shimmer of late afternoon with no purpose other than killing time, ignoring the lengthening shadows and softening edges of fading light that arrive with the suggestion that it's time she head back to The Moonglow.

Instead, she threads her way toward the river skirting Harriet's Bluff along its Eastern border. She picks up her pace as she strides past the used tire store on Chestnut Street, surprised to see that the grotesque mounds of melted black rubber continue to smolder even though it's been nearly two weeks since fire destroyed the garage.

By now Willa has all but forgotten the terrible sense of dread and fear that gripped her heart so tightly the night of her encounter with the black dog, her curious affinity for the crazed and destructive Norman Hitchcock once again resurfacing to overshadow reason. And she wonders if maybe the certain lunacy behind her fascination might in fact be an indication of her own secret longing for revenge—an urge for retaliation against injuries she hasn't yet identified but nevertheless recognizes herself to possess. Or is she, in fact, confusing revenge with the twining of something else? A juxtapose of emotion alive and breathing regardless of whether or not she can find the necessary words to describe them beyond disappointment, regret, worry …

An endless string of hot rainless days has greatly diminished the threat of swimming in the river, and yet people in Harriet's Bluff are nevertheless compelled to stay away from what has long been declared perilous. It doesn't seem to matter that the deadly current has slackened considerably as the things of the earth dry up and evaporate, because the barely moving water remains distinctly murky below the surface, assuredly concealing a horrifying menagerie of unknown evils lying in wait of anyone idiotic enough to disturb them.

The brittle grass crunches under Willa's feet like stale crumbs, and she slows her steps as she nears the shoreline, approaching with attentive caution as she scans the bank for a glimpse of sunning reptiles amongst the pickerelweed and needle rush.

But there is nothing here moving beneath the colorless sheen of a blank sky. Willa stands for several long moments, her gaze fanning out over the surface of the slowly twining river, watching the water even as she steps on the back of her heel and pries off one sneaker, then the other, and wades into the river just deep enough to skim her calves. She feels like the smallest, most insignificant particle of drifting molecules in the vastness of this quiet place—planted into the scene like a plastic figurine on the verge of toppling over and floating away. And she knows that even should she be carried away and churned out to sea, it will make little difference to the world at large, because a million others have already been popped from the mold and stand ready to replace her.

It is so quiet, *too quiet;* as if somewhere the master switch has been thrown, suspending the world in mid-cycle. The water feels unexpectedly cool given the heat of the day, and Willa moves several steps deeper, halting where the water tickles just below her knees.

She closes her eyes against the brilliant whiteness of late afternoon sunlight shimmering across the water. An engine guns far off in the distance—then a screech as the unseen vehicle takes a curve and accelerates out of earshot. Willa tips her face upward without opening her eyes, watching the swirls of orangey white light behind her closed lids. *How incredible that she's even here in this place. Standing in a brown river. A million miles from Hoosick Falls and the pitiful little house—long past the days of listening for the sound of Martin's car to pull into the driveway.*

"Tell me as soon as you hear him," Stella would say, reaching across the kitchen table and covertly helping herself to a cigarette from Dee's open pack before her friend returned from the bathroom.

"Uh huh," Willa answered without taking her eyes from the *Good Housekeeping* magazine Dee has brought for Stella, engrossed in several full-color pages depicting *Grandma's Best Ever Cakes.*

She knows Stella won't bother with even a cursory flip through the glossy pages; will in fact handle the magazine only long enough to drop it unread on the coffee table with all the others her well-intentioned friend has gifted upon her over the years.

It's Willa's guess that Dee insists on holding to her misplaced optimism toward Stella's yet-to-be-seen domestic talents on account of their years of friendship. At least it's the only explanation she's ever arrived at to explain Dee's apparent belief that something as simple as a magazine will eventually succeed in inspiring Stella to attempt something of the domestic; tempt her to cook a meal that didn't originate from a box, push around a vacuum once in awhile, plant geranium seeds in pretty pots artfully arranged on the front porch, sew a set of "gaily matched throw pillows and bring new life to a shabby living room sofa."

"You'd think there'd be some sort of odds—you know, guaranteed odds," she heard Stella say, once Dee emerged from the bathroom swiping her wet fingers across the seat of her baggy jeans, apparently having washed her hands only to find that the hand towel draped over the edge of the tub still held the same sour odor reminiscent of aged vomit as it had the last time she'd attempted to use it.

"Odds of what?"

"Odds that he's lost enough times now that he *has* to win something."

Dee shook her head, tapping her cigarette pack on the edge of the table, poking a long acrylic nail into the opening when nothing came out. "You've got to be kidding me, Stel. If there was such a thing as *guaranteed odds,* don't you think every one of us would be standing right there next to him waiting for our turn to be a millionaire?"

Dee struck a match, dragging deep as she touched the flame to the end of her cigarette. "I hate to be the one to say it, sweetie, but some people are just born losers."

"Yeah, and some of us just marry them."

Willa feels the gentle brush of something feathering past her submerged ankle. A fleeting sensation that instantly works to snap open her lids—eyes wide and full with the immediate vision of some hideous thing circling within the dark tinted waters, pointed jaws opening wide to reveal a row of fine tipped snaggle teeth.

She spins around and scrambles to the safety of the embankment, watching the spot she's only just vacated for some telltale sign of the evil thing. And yet the water lies still. Quiet. Dark.

She knows she should head back now, but staring out across the river, she is just as certain that she isn't ready to face The Moonglow just yet. She bends to retrieve a flat grey stone at her feet, absently running it back and forth between her fingers, until a pensive flick of her wrist sends it skipping along the water's flat surface.

She crouches to select several more stones, each smooth and flat. Then, holding the collection in one hand, she skims them one-by-one across the top of the water, each dimpling the grey satin surface for only an instant before vanishing from sight.

"I wish Stella's piece of junk car didn't break down in this lousy damn town," she says out loud, expertly ricocheting a stone into an impressive triple skip along the water's dark skin before it is swallowed into the river.

She wings another. "I wish—" she hesitates, leaving the rest unsaid, knowing she sounds foolish and whiney and babyish, but then continuing a moment later when she decides that it feels strangely satisfying.

"I wish Norman Hitchcock was burning down The Moonglow at this very instant so I wouldn't have to sleep one more damn night in that crappy bed." She pauses, bending to select several more stones.

"I wish I was leaving this place right now—driving down the road in a shiny red sports car with a convertible top."

"I wish this stupid town didn't even exist."

"...that Stella would take two minutes out of her selfish life to remember she has a kid whose lousy birthday happens to be today," Willa recites, finding it necessary to skip three stones consecutively in order to complete the sentence.

She sends another stone sailing from her fingers, but she is already losing interest, the throw uninspired that it skips only once before plopping into a tight clump of mallow hugging the riverbank.

"I wish there was something else to do in this ridiculous town besides skipping stupid, ugly stones into disgusting brown water."

"I wish it would rain..."

"You and everybody else," a voice comes up behind her, startling the last of the stones from her fingers as she swings around and finds herself staring into Jesse Truman's strange navy eyes; his lips nearly curving into a smile as he watches Willa struggle to relocate the voice that has just now sped off at a wild gallop.

While it's true they seem to cross paths at The Moonglow on something of a regular basis now, such frequency has had little effect on easing their typically stilted interactions. Willa still doesn't know what to say to Jesse Truman, and she has yet to find a safe place to turn her gaze when she does. Just as it has been from the first, her tongue turns to clay with a single glance from his deep colored eyes—eyes that appear to take everything in, but let little if anything out. Even his infrequent shy smile is an expression that fails to fully penetrate his features—a book thoroughly unreadable despite an intriguing cover. *Wholly unknowable*, has been Willa's immediate and currently held conclusion.

Like a curtain descended, the twilight sky is rapidly fading from deep indigo toward the darker shades of night.

"You weren't at The Moonglow today," she says, talking past the immediate rush of hot embarrassment flooding over her face like melting wax. *How long has he been standing here? How much has he heard of her ridiculous chanting?*

"Omega had me run some errands in town," he shrugs without elaborating.

Willa nods, relieved for even this rudimentary conversation, since it is at least something to hide behind now that every other seed of logical thought has rudely packed up and left her head.

"Are you going swimming?"

"*In there?* It looks ... so cloudy," she says, though *dirty* is really what she's thinking. *Dirty. Dirty and disgusting.*

"It's not as bad out toward the middle where the water's still moving," he says, sitting on the ground and loosening the laces on his sneakers.

"Oh ... umm, well I don't know ... I think I probably need to get back," Willa answers, and even as she mumbles and stumbles over the words she knows that she wants to stay here as much as she's ever wanted anything.

"It's pretty nice now. Not much of a current," he says, clearly misinterpreting her hesitation, apparently believing her reluctance is somehow related to the fact that every man, woman, and child in Harriet's Bluff has been raised to heed the cautionary caveat that this place is off limits. Tragic narratives of drowning (gruesome details escalating with each retelling), never-recovered bodies of disobedient children and foolish drunks who'd ignored common sense and dared to challenge the river's dangerous current.

And even as she wavers, knowing full well the impossibility of anything other than her walking away, an implausible image is there forming in her mind—a vision of herself diving into the river with Jesse Truman, their bodies slicing through the water with the precision and grace of an Olympic pair. Forgetting for one perfect instant, the absolute impossibility of any such scene.

"I can't swim," she blurts out, surprising herself. Staring at the hideous confession suspended in the air between them as if it belongs to someone else.

Jesse continues as though she hasn't spoken, pulling each sneaker off before lifting his face. A curve of dark hair falls against his forehead, his eyes nearly indecipherable above the wide stripe of shadow cutting across one cheekbone.

"That's all right," he says, standing. "I'll teach you."

"No … no, I can't," she says, intending a laugh; but instead the strained pitch leaving her mouth lands as something embarrassingly reminiscent of a hiccupping blackbird or a turkey buzzard choking on a bone.

"Stella always says I'm thick as a plank and pitiful at following instructions," she says, though the statement is wholly untrue. *Why can't she just say yes as easily as she does no?*

"It doesn't matter. You already know how to swim. You just don't realize it yet. Everybody's born with the instinct to keep their head above water."

"You clearly have no idea who you're dealing with."

"You'll see once you try."

"Omega's warned me a hundred times not to go in there. She said nobody does—it's too dangerous," Willa persists, pressing past the voice of her own immediate desire to forget anything Omega Pearl Bodie or any other human being has ever told her. The urge to follow Jesse Truman into the river, or anywhere else he might name, knocks hard to dislodge her fear of entering the opaque stretch of water lying ominous in the near darkness like an enormous crack in the floor of the earth.

"That's only because of the current, and right now it's barely strong enough to carry a leaf."

And still, Willa's head is nodding a refusal no other part of her has agreed upon, feeling like a betrayer of her own self.

She shifts her eyes as he pulls off his tee-shirt, declining to watch as he peels off his clothing, so that she isn't altogether certain as to what he keeps on and what he discards on the ground, glancing back only after she hears his body break the water.

Asleep Without Dreaming

She watches as his even strokes move him further from the shore, her breath catching in her throat when he all at once vanishes beneath the shimmering surface like a swallowed morsel—exhaling only after his head breaks up through the dark water. And more than anything, she longs at that moment to reach out and grasp a fistful of necessary courage strong enough to outweigh her fears, to summon whatever it will take for her to stride to the river's edge and glide into the water after him.

And maybe it is her certainty that such a moment will never again present itself which succeeds in towing her forward with the draw of an invisible line. That prompts her to step into the shallow water along the weed-choked embankment and ignore the slippery feel of unseen vegetation touching her bare soles, tickling her ankles and the backs of her legs as she wades deeper. Her eyes holding steady on Jesse Truman as his smooth strokes close the distance.

Ten

"**B**reathe. Don't think so hard. Just let it happen, okay? Relax ... just breathe," Jesse reminds her time and again, this simplest instruction proving the most difficult for Willa to grasp.

It isn't so much a plan or certain agreement as it simply happens, that for the next several days she meets Jesse at the river every afternoon after they finish their duties at The Moonglow. And for an hour, sometimes longer, he patiently coaxes Willa's stubborn arms and legs to comply with his deceptively simple instructions. Repeating the same suggestions he's offered her enough times by now that she should be able to read them like an instruction manual inside her head—*reach with your arms, kick your legs—no, at the same time—you want to try and synchronize your movements. Cup your hands. Imagine you're pulling the water back with every stroke. Breathe, Willa. You have to remember to breathe. Try and find a rhythm—imagine a ticking clock.*

It is with a certain sense of elation that she does learn to swim by week's end. Although it is not a skill she executes particularly well, but only adequately. She will in fact never be an especially strong swimmer, if only because she is unable to relinquish her incurable trepidation of losing the ability to breathe convinced that she will somehow become distracted and forget to fill her lungs with air should she ever attempt to test her strength or strive for distance.

And then there is this other thing—her increasing anxiety that she will inadvertently leave an open window, allowing

Jesse a glimpse inside her head where he will see all of what she has been piling up in there—thoughts and images shamefully revealing just how often she's been thinking about things other than the backstroke and the dead man's float.

His touch is disappointingly brief as he once again attempts to educate Willa in the simple techniques of staying afloat and moving through the water. Yet, still, it is enough to enable a certain palpable intimacy when they are alone in the river, where no one else cares to go. The parallel currents of closeness and euphoria, so vibrant at times that she wants to laugh out loud and remind him how wonderfully strange it is that they don't really know each other at all, and yet, have become so familiar.

Her senses are tuned and ever watchful for even the briefest glimpse of Jesse Truman as she trudges along behind Stella, distractedly tending to the tedious chore of cleaning cottages while her insides glow with remembered light.

She listens for the sound of his truck rattling over the gravel out front, as she changes rumpled sheets and damp towels; scrubs the perpetual scum from sinks, toilets, and tubs; hangs fresh washing out on the line to dry.

And always, her thoughts twine back toward the river, ardently recalling each perfect afternoon like the arrival of a long-awaited package, reopening it again and again, each time finding the perfect gift. *Jesse glides in close beside her, lifting her arm as he demonstrates the limb's essential purpose in stroking the water rhythmically, then mimicking the movement with her other arm. And even as she listens, focusing attentively on his instructions, her senses remain attuned to his hands—the warmth of his fingers on her skin despite the coolness of the water; his serious, navy eyes that crinkle at the corners when he attempts not to smile over her pitiful efforts.*

And there is the particular way the sunlight cuts across the water, turning his skin golden, polishing over his wet hair and making it gleam. And she knows with every ounce of certainty threaded through her being, that something, everything, is changing.

Waves of heat ripple along the concrete in front of Willa like silvery ribbons as she trudges along the highway heading into Harriet's Bluff. The last of afternoon sun sears across the treetops with an unwavering slice of eternal flame, an occasional car speeding past, offering the only hint of a breeze. Her sleeveless cotton blouse sticks to her skin in damp patches, and the bulk of her hair, tied into a messy ponytail with a broken shoestring, feels like a wet cat clinging to her neck.

She slows her steps as the low growl of an approaching vehicle climbs up behind her, insides instinctively bracing to receive the anticipated sweep of air that will come as the car barrels past. As a precaution, she trains her steps from the roadway onto the gravel shoulder, considering the chance that the oncoming vehicle may happen to be the same carload of pesky boys who have targeted her several times already this week as she walks along the highway on her way into town.

The first time they'd crossed paths had been nearly a month earlier, on her way back from picking up cigarettes for Stella. "Hey, doll face, need a ride somewhere?" a voice had called out the open window as the car slowed, rolling alongside her, instinct immediately inducing her to quicken her pace.

She had pulled-up her chin and glanced away quickly, though it had taken every molecule of willpower to deny the reflex to turn her head toward the voice. From the single fleeting glimpse she'd initially garnered, she was certain she recognized at least two of the leering faces in the battered green Ford as belonging to the troupe of no account delinquents she'd often seen fooling around outside the newspaper store on Main Street. Hanging from the handrail, the junior apes grunted stupid monkey noises at passersby until the owner appeared to chase them off with the threat of a swinging broom.

"No, thanks," she'd replied, holding her jaw so stiff in her determination to appear confident and unflustered, it felt as if the words might break her lips as they left her mouth.

"All right, so you just wanna give me a hand-job then? My dick's about to explode," said a blond crew-cut head poking out from the rear side window as the car continued to crawl alongside her. His companions rewarded the nasty remark with a chorus of guffaws and barnyard snorts.

She pretended not to feel the immediate flush of heat spilling under her skin, fanning up and turning her face to flame as she delivered a withering stare back across her shoulder. "How 'bout you just stick it in your boyfriend's mouth like you always do?"

"Whoa, looks like she told you, Jerry," someone snorted, followed by hoots of laughter. Then, "Hey, you're gonna have yourself some real nice titties once they get to growing," another called out seconds before the driver suddenly accelerated, laying out a track of rubber in an unimpressive bid at machismo.

There had since been several further encounters with the obnoxious carload, always on this same stretch of highway, suggesting they have come to expect her. And now, overshadowing even her disgust over what has clearly become their idiot sport, is her fear that once they tire of shouting rude comments from car windows , and surely they will, the band of criminals will set their depraved minds onto other things— kidnapping or worse.

Now, as she hears the approaching vehicle down-shifting behind her, slowing to a threatening crawl, Willa instinctively squares her shoulders, steeling her resolve to keep from glancing back, prepared to sprint past the ditch weeds and bristly grasses crowding the edges of the highway and into the safety of the woods. Out of sight and gone even before one of them has chanced to fling open a car door.

"Hey, I just heard there's a fire out on Barnwood Road and I'm on my way over to have a look. Want to come?" a familiar voice—*the voice*—calls out through the open window of the truck rolling up alongside her.

"Oh, hey, Jesse. Um … yeah, sure." Willa swings around on legs as light as spun sugar, an immediate smile curving her lips. Her hand reaches for the door handle even as Jesse leans across the seat and pops it open from the inside.

"I heard the siren a few minutes ago," Willa says, as she hops up onto the seat beside him. "I figured somebody's toaster must've caught fire or something since it's too early in the day for one of Norman's fires."

"Could be he's changing tactics," Jesse smiles. "Unless maybe it's just one of those ordinary, once in awhile, fires they used to have around here before Norman showed up to lend a helping hand."

"Yeah, maybe. But nobody really cares about that kind."

As often as they've met at the river, this is the first time Willa has ever been within Jesse's inner sanctum, and her gaze makes a rapid slide over the trucks interior. It is a surprisingly uncluttered space (no Rosary beads hanging from the rearview mirror, bobbing hula girl on the dash, or roadmaps tucked up under the visor), tempered by the lingering odors of oil and gasoline.

"Actually, I've been thinking about it lately and I don't think people around here realize just how ingenious he really is," Willa says, as Jesse accelerates, determined not to allow the constant threat of uncomfortable silence an opportunity to wedge itself into untended vacancies.

"*Ingenious?*" Jesse repeats, lifting an eyebrow. "That's definitely not a word I've heard linked in a sentence with the name Norman Hitchcock. More like dangerous, heinous, diabolical, evil …"

"Well, sure, he's all of that, but he's definitely not a raving idiot either. He hasn't been caught has he?"

Willa can now see fat mushrooms of billowing smoke rising in dirty clouds above the tree line up ahead.

"Maybe he's just lucky."

"After all these months? Nobody's luck lasts that long."

Willa's shoulder bounces hard against Jesse's arm as he turns the wheel sharply, swinging the truck onto a dirt road pocked with an inverted island chain of craters; the trucks tires unraveling the dust as they race to close the distance to the fire.

"I think it has more to do with him being so smart. Stella always says madness is just a step away from genius."

Jessie takes a moment to answer, swerving hard to miss yet another ocean-size cavity eroding the hard-packed earth.

"I don't know, maybe. I just never got the impression that Norman's much of a thinker, more like an angry guy with a Zippo." Then, "Damn, look at that," he says, low under his breath once they emerge past the final stand of trees bordering the road—a flaming barn all at once exploding into view.

"It doesn't look like they're even trying to save it," Willa says, as Jesse noses the truck behind the last car in a line of vehicles parked along the weedy embankment hemming the dirt road.

Several firemen mill around their trucks, arms crossed, eyes trained on the wall of flame devouring the broad structure; others nodding their heads to punctuate aloof conversation.

"Probably too far gone," Jesse says, his expression turned darkly solemn in stark contrast to his relaxed demeanor of only a moment ago.

The clutch of spectators momentarily fall silent as the interior support beams give way, one wall, then another, collapsing with a shattering thud.

"Oh no ..." Willa breathes out between clenched teeth as an awful thought rushes into her head. She turns to Jesse. "Do you think there could be animals in there?" The horrifying image of trapped, burning creatures fills her stomach with the weight of stones.

"No, it's empty. If there were animals in there, you would've heard them by now."

"For certain?"

Jesse nods his head, his eyes holding to the flaming structure. "Besides, Hitchcock wouldn't set fire to a building with livestock inside. He's not a killer. He's just looking to get attention."

"But Omega told me he was a convicted murderer."

"Yeah, but this isn't the same thing. That was something else—this is about something completely different."

"How do you know that for sure?"

"I didn't say I did. It's just obvious. He's afraid of being forgotten. He's only doing this so people will remember who he is."

"Where were you?" Stella stands just inside the shadowed doorway, arms crossed tightly against her chest, as Willa comes up the steps and onto the porch.

"Nowhere," she answers, her mother's unexpected presence causing her to miss a step and stumble forward slightly.

"Oh really, is that so? *Nowhere?* Then that must've been *nobody* driving that truck that just let you off? Apparently I just witnessed a genuine miracle—*nowhere with nobody.*"

"Oh, you mean just now … oh well, yeah there was another fire. Didn't you hear the alarm?" Willa says, skirting past Stella and slipping into the cottage. "It was at this big farm out by the crossroads. The barn was enor—"

"You smell like smoke."

"The whole town smells like smoke."

"And what does *Mister Nobody* smell like?"

"There isn't any *Mr. Nobody*, but if there was then I guess he'd smell like smoke too," Willa says, trying hard to keep from flinching under Stella's pointed stare. "I just got a ride back from somebody who went to see the fire, too."

"Is that so? Then why the secrecy? Who exactly is this person driving you around to dangerous fires."

"There is no secrecy. He works for Omega—mowing the grass and stuff."

"Ah, that's it. Now I get it. Well I've seen that boy sniffing around here so don't bother trying to sell me that crap that there's nothing going on. Not when you take off for three hours without so much as a toodle-doo-see-you-later. Oh, I know his type. I can tell just from looking at him—hot pant's pretty boy. Well, let me tell you something, there isn't a good-looking man alive who doesn't know how to use it to his advantage. They're all cut from the same cloth. Just looking for—"

"Will you just stop it, please? We're friends. That's it," Willa says, watching Stella. Trying hard to appear unfazed by her line of questioning. "Actually, not even friends really. More like acquaintances. I just wanted to see where the fire was and he gave me a ride because he was on his way there, too. That's it. That's all there is to it. I don't know why you're being so crazy about it."

"I don't like this sneaky business," Stella says, tightening her arms against her chest in a shield hard enough to deflect bullets.

"There is no sneaky business."

"All right, then who is he?"

"What are you talking about? You just said you know who he is. You said you've seen him working around here. We say hello and goodbye and that's pretty much it. If you want to know anything else about him, you'll have to ask Omega," Willa says, even as she offers up an immediate prayer that considering how much Stella dislikes Omega, no such conversation will ever take place.

Willa picks up the glass she keeps on the lid of the toilet tank for brushing her teeth, wrinkling her nose at the coffee cups Stella has left in the tiny sink without even taking a second to rinse them free of their gritty dregs, but saying nothing that will provoke her mother further.

"You have no business riding around with strange men."

"I'd hardly call him a strange man, but that's not even the point because I'm not riding around with him or anybody else."

Why has Stella chosen this moment of all moments to be angry? It makes little sense considering all the afternoons Willa has spent out at the river with Jesse. Occasions when she's returned home at twilight braced for a foot-stomping, fist-shaking, tongue-lashing confrontation with Stella, only to find that apparently, her mother hasn't even noticed her absence. Up until tonight there have been no questions. No accusations or admonishments. So why then has Stella chosen this time to care?

"We just happen to work at the same place. That's all there is to it. We're sort've, but not actually, friends.*"*

"Don't be so damned naïve, Willa. Males and females have never, and will never, be friends. You're fooling yourself if you don't think human nature is a hell of a lot stronger than good intentions. When it comes to men and woman, boys and girls, males and females, whatever terminology you prefer, it's all about sex and the potential for having it."

"That's disgusting," Willa says, feeling her face flush with the heat of unwarranted shame. She truly hates that Stella is always so quick to draw her weapons, so ready to fire her crudities.

"Maybe so, but it's still true."

"No, it isn't!"

"You better believe it is, Cupcake. And you can either wise-up or keep on behaving like every other foolish girl who thinks she has it all figured out. Go ahead and learn the hard way."

"Like you did when you thought it was such a great idea to make a living arranging dead things in cracked pots—or was it, arranging dead things for crackpots?"

"The success of which proves my point exactly."

"All it proves is your knack for finding miserable people."

Stella glares at her without answering, but there's no need. It is after all, the truth.

Asleep Without Dreaming

Even now, the details remain clear in her mind. It had been raining all day and Willa recalls that she'd forgotten to bring an umbrella to school. She had her head down as she hurried across the patchy grass sprouting in handfuls over the front yard like weak follicles on an aging scalp, and it was only when she lifted her face to take the steps onto the porch that she caught sight of the newly placed sign. *NO REGRETS*. Each letter a neat block printed in black magic marker on a rectangle of cardboard tacked to the front railing and precisely angled in such a way to make it clearly visible from the street.

The dull cargo of restless boredom she ordinarily dragged home every afternoon was momentarily forgotten as she studied the words. Curiosity raking her brows into slanted windrows of deepening puzzlement as her gaze drifted toward the peculiar arrangements displayed in the two long windows bordering either side of the front door, a bizarre still life that dispelled each potential description tripping into her mind.

Dried floral arrangements had been placed on pedestals constructed of stacked milk crates and cardboard boxes piled and draped with floral print fabric that Willa at once recognized as being the set of sheets from her bed. She'd stared for several long moments at what in some ways struck her as familiar, but which she nevertheless failed to comprehend. Because, unlike the attractive varieties of dried plants and flowers purposely selected and preserved to retain shape, color, and beauty, these arrangements were *hideously* dead, dull, withered, and drooping. Dead and rotted by neglectful decomposition, rather than the result of any conscientious plan or design.

Sharp pinpricks of disbelief needled at the back of her neck as she shifted her gaze to land on a tall slender vase holding a collection of long-stemmed roses and sporting a crack long and deep as the Mississippi. The long deceased and blackened buds, dried into hardened knobs, offered little hint as to their former shadings. Placed alongside this Frankenstein masterpiece, artfully positioned on yet another makeshift pedestal was an enormous potted plant—leaves curled and dead blooms molting desiccated petals onto the floor below like a wash of ashy rain.

Her stare drifted back to the sign. *No Regrets. What was it about? What was it even supposed to mean? It made no sense. Absolutely no sense at all.*

"I'm only setting up here until business takes off and I can afford something better. This whole lousy town is either for sale or for rent so I won't have any problem finding an empty storefront when I'm ready," Stella said, intent as a surgeon as she poked through the stiff brown stems strewn across the kitchen table—withered carnations, molting roses, brittle fern leaves—remains of once beautiful blooms, curled and dried to that of the unrecognizable.

"No, come on, seriously, what are you doing with all this stuff?"

Stella didn't immediately answer, the corners of her mouth curling just enough to offer the hint of a smile as she continued separating the crumbling assortment spread out before her into various piles.

"I told you, I'm starting a business."

"What business? A business doing what?"

"I think it's obvious, Willa. I'm selling flower arrangements."

"But they're *dead.*"

"Great observation."

"You're selling dead flowers?"

"All cut flowers are dead."

"Well, yeah, but these are *really* dead."

"Dead flowers to you—something quite different to someone else. Like maybe a little peace of mind after being thrown down and stomped on like a piece of garbage," Stella said, her gaze holding to her task. "On the chance you haven't figured it out, that's pretty much what life is about—people dumping on each other. Nobody gets away from missing that boat. There's not a living soul who hasn't been sucker-punched some time or another. It's how people treat each other in this crappy world. So I've just invented a creative way for the wronged to give a little something back."

"But I don't get it. You think people are actually gonna come here and ask to buy flowers that look like that?"

"Anybody who's ever been a victim learns pretty quick there's no satisfaction in sitting around bleeding tears. The problem is they have no idea what else to do and that's where I come in with tasteful revenge for the injured soul."

"This is crazy."

"There's nothing crazy about wanting satisfaction when you've been wronged, and enjoying a taste of revenge is one of the nicest gifts you can give yourself. Getting even heals wounds and this is a hell of a lot more civilized than trying to run over some deadbeat with your car," Stella said, smiling as she snapped the shriveled head of something spidery and grey from its brittle stem.

"And if dumping a basket of dried-up junk on some lousy bastard's doorstep is gonna make some broken-hearted woman feel better about herself, I'm more than happy to make the delivery."

As ridiculous as it sounded, there was some small part of Stella's outlandish plan to peddle dead flowers to angry people that actually made a certain amount of sense. Maybe it really was harmless. Even kind of funny when Willa considered the absurdity of dead flowers being hand-delivered to the door of some callous good-for-nothing, or left on a heartless creep's desk for everyone to point and whisper about. And then there would be the likely reactions of the stunned recipients that would be a sight to see.

Even so, elbowing potential entertainment value aside, it seemed unlikely that anyone in Hoosick Falls would seriously take to such a peculiar idea. Worse, was Willa's certain conviction that once word of Stella's odd venture was set off in racing circulation around town, not only would her mother be deemed a monumental fool, but Willa, too, would surely be labeled loony by association.

"Dee thinks it's a brilliant idea, too. She's mad as hell she didn't come up with it herself."

"That's because Dee doesn't have to go to school here."

"Enough with the drama, Willa. Would it kill you to stop thinking about yourself for a minute? It's nobody's business what I do in the privacy of my own damn house."

Honestly, but Willa couldn't understand how Stella managed to remain so thoroughly ignorant of the people living around her in this hard little town. Because if she had any idea whatsoever as to the gossipy habits of her neighbors and countrymen, she wouldn't be making statements that included such erroneous concepts as *in the privacy of my own home.*

Maybe it was partially Willa's fault since she'd never told Stella how often she'd stumbled within hearing distance of some barely whispered conversation speculating over the *real reasons* behind Martin Burkett's disappearance. Mean and catty references compiled into a catalogue of Stella's offenses and peculiarities, all of which pointedly suggested justification of her husband's behavior.

"But what about your real job?" Willa ventured to ask.

"This is my real job."

"No, I mean the—"

"You know damn well I quit that place. I told you weeks ago."

"No you didn't. All you said was something about dry-cleaning chemicals might be linked to—"

"What I *said*, is that dry-cleaning chemicals *cause* cancer."

"But that article only mentioned how they still need to do research and see if—"

"Look, Willa—"

"You never said you were just gonna quit."

Stella ceased fumbling through the tangle of brittle flowers, lifting her head to reveal an expression altogether reminiscent of a dragon revving its engines in preparation of releasing a belching spear of flame from its mouth.

"*You're kidding me, right?* Or is this just some test to see how far you can push me toward the edge before I give up and jump?" Her eyes narrowed. The twin points of her stare hard enough to splinter granite. "For shit's sake, Willa, you mean to tell me if someone throws you a lit stick of dynamite, you're just gonna stand there holding it like an idiot until it explodes and blows your arm off?"

An uncomfortable silence squeezed the air like a closing fist. "I just don't think anyone is gonna want to buy dead flowers, is all," Willa says, taking a step backward. "Even if you find someone who thinks the idea is kind of funny or different, it doesn't mean they'll want to pay money for it. It's weird. Someone would have to be nuts, and even Hoosick Falls doesn't have that many crackpots."

"Then get ready to be surprised," Stella smirked, carefully separating the thorny stem of a rose from the molting head of a carnation. "Because if there's one thing this town has in abundance, it's crackpots."

Although it did take some time for Stella's *angry bouquets* to garner positive interest—several weeks before a single inquiry arrived to question what it was that she was selling—her unorthodox business slowly began to gather momentum. Apparently, there were more than just a handful of trounced-upon souls eager to deliver final insult to an unfaithful lover, rude neighbor, or double-crossing relative; though there was no way of knowing just yet how many of Stella's newfound customers reflected the heartbroken, as opposed to those who were simply ordering the hideous arrangements for the novelty or fleeting amusement of it.

Willa pretended not to notice, or otherwise care, when Stella left the house in the early hours at a time when, generally, only alley cats and raccoons could be found roaming about, well before the fringes of gray dawn melted away into the pinky pale light of morning. In truth, she was all too horribly aware of her mother's forays through the back alleys and trash cans of every florist, church, and funeral home within walking distance, gathering the deteriorated remains of discarded plants and cut flowers and loading them into the rusty metal wagon she pulled along to transport her rotting treasures.

Had she not felt so humiliated by her mother's very public misbehavior, Willa might've better appreciated the way Stella's ideas continued to swell and multiply with each new order. But as it stood, she saw no reason to be impressed when Stella began offering to scribe an insulting poem or nasty limerick personalized for the recipient, or congratulate her on expanding her inventory to include handsomely arranged platters of discarded cookies and candies turned to stone (stale and discolored by age, petrified goodies she'd retrieved from the dumpster behind the A & P grocery store). Nor did she comment on the baskets Stella artfully composed with a selection of grotesquely rotting fruit: oranges gone brown, deeply bruised apples turned swarthy and mushy, black-skinned bananas oozing thick dark snot where their decayed skins had split at the seams.

And while Stella glowed with smug satisfaction over her peculiar success like the first place winner of a coveted prize, Willa clung to the shadows, just as she'd done every other time her mother spontaneously slipped inside the skin of a new life, hoping to avoid guilt by association.

It wasn't that she hated her mother or even disliked her all that much. For all Stella's varied metamorphoses, she was what she was; remaining much the same person she'd always been beneath her chameleon's skin. And while true that person happened to be a mostly terrible and selfish mother, Willa hadn't gotten to the point where she felt compelled to step across the threshold and make the announcement to the room at large. For the time being at least, it was simply enough for her to think it.

"Stella says males and females can't be friends."

Jesse tips his head back, takes a long swallow from the bottle of cola in his hand. He brushes his forehead against the sleeve of his tee-shirt, a swath of perspiration instantly darkening the fabric.

"This being the same mother that used to sell rotting flowers?" he grins in his slow hesitant way, an expression that suggests he knows a joke the rest of the world has never heard and isn't likely to share.

"Um hum. That would be her."

"Is she angry, or maybe just disillusioned?"

"Well, actually, I come from a long line of angry, disillusioned people so how would I tell the difference?" Willa shoots a nervous glance toward the motel office, prepared to spring to her feet at the mere suggestion of Omega Pearl's peeping eyes, considering that both she and Stella have so thoroughly succeeded with their warnings and innuendos in making Willa feel as if her budding friendship with Jesse Truman is somehow comparable to building a hydrogen bomb in someone's basement.

"So, you're saying that one day you'll be in the business of arranging mummified petunias yourself?"

"Very funny. Stella and I have nothing in common and that includes ideas."

"I don't know, her ideas seem kind of interesting," he says, the smile gone from his mouth though the ghost of it remains.

"What's interesting is that there were actually enough angry people around to keep her in business until she got tired of it."

He shrugs. "It's not so surprising. Isn't everybody's angry about something? Sending dried-up flowers seems relatively civilized when you consider some of the other things people do to each other," Jesse says, his eyes shifting to stare after something in the distance. Though, when Willa follows his gaze, she can see nothing but the heat and dust that are always there.

"Yeah, maybe," Willa twitches her elbow to discourage a bothersome fly attempting to land. She grounds a pebble into the dirt with the toe of her sneaker.

"I'd better get back to work before Omega comes chasing after me with her stick," Jesse says, stifling a yawn as he pushes to his feet. "She wants me to dig out the cover for the septic tank before the guy comes in the morning."

"Again? Didn't you just do that a couple weeks ago?"

"Yep, but it's still backing up."

"It's a million degrees out. You're gonna get heat stroke."

"Yeah, well if there's one thing that can't be ignored, it's shit—your own or anybody else's," his lips slant toward something of a grin. "Especially like now when it declines to be flushed, or if it does, it's only because it's leaking into the lake. Granted she's prone to exaggerate, but Omega might be right this time when she says that having the whole place smelling like a sewer is bad for business."

Willa still hasn't decided whether he's serious or joking as he walks away.

Eleven

He's as much a phantom as he is a criminal, a unanimous conclusion that's only served to multiply the height and close the distance of the town's already skyrocketing fears.

That Norman Hitchcock somehow remains impregnable behind his cloak of invisibility as countless eyes peer down rabbit holes and under rocks, anxious to discover some minute evidence which will prove the essential clue that's eluded them for months, seems impossible at best. And yet he does, as evidenced by fires that continue to rage even as all ears remain assiduously tuned for the sound of a match head dragging across a friction strip.

From the very beginning there have been suspicions in circulation, suggestions that someone in Harriet's Bluff may very well be aiding Norman in his successful bid to remain comfortably elusive. Only now, this mistrust has swollen to the proportions of imminent overflow. *Someone has to be hiding him.* Keeping him fed and protected for either the thrill or dread of him. Some cowardly lion who is now equally guilty of Norman Hitchcock's ongoing spree. It's the only plausible explanation considering that every pebble has been shuffled aside, every crack and crevice frisked and combed for miles, with still no clue to indicate where he's been or where he intends to go next.

People who've lived in Harriet's Bluff their entire lives insist that the fire at Wicker's hardware store is the worst catastrophe ever visited upon their town.

A sturdy, three-story brick emporium erected nearly a century ago, its uninspired design is that of an enormous refrigerator box. But it is the store's vast and diverse inventory—a dizzying array of items ranging from thread, to chewing gum, to lawn mowers—that now provides the necessary fuel to feed an uncontrollable fire, enabling the inferno to burn and smolder over the course of several days. Exploding cans of kerosene, paint, and assorted chemicals, supplying the insatiable blaze until there is simply nothing left to consume.

Yet, even more staggering than the destruction is the sobering recognition that Norman Hitchcock has apparently grown bored with the ruination of vacant buildings and is now changing lanes on his criminal joyride, realigning former boundaries so that a building can no more be assumed safe by reason of inhabitation. The unexpected demise of Wicker's store, serves to assure that this particular rule no longer applies.

"It wouldn't surprise me if they never catch him," Willa says, watching Jesse as he winds a length of shiny black tape around a chain of pinholes in Omega's garden hose.

"The whole town is looking for him. He has to slip up sometime."

"Not necessarily. A million people could be looking for him and it wouldn't matter. He's like a superhero, except with evil powers. That's why they haven't found him—he's too smart," she says, sifting through the assortment of oak leaves she's gathered into a pile near her thigh, intent on lengthening the leaf chain draped across her lap.

Jesse tips his head, glancing at her, a smile darting across his lips. "I've heard about that before."

"Heard what?"

"About some girls having a thing for criminals."

"Very funny," she says, making a weak attempt to sound offended, even as she returns his smile. "I'm serious. People around here should stop assuming he's an idiot when it's pretty obvious by now that he's anything but."

"Mad genius, or not, he'll mess up eventually and that's when they'll get him."

"Interesting…I seem to recall you saying he was lucky. Like maybe he was born with a rabbit's foot in his mouth."

"He might be for now, but nobody's luck lasts forever."

"Maybe he'll be the first."

They watch each other. Everyone does. And there's no person living in or passing through Harriet's Bluff that's above suspicion. The hard, gritty, variety of mistrust that causes even the innocent to feel as if they are guilty of something.

And while opposing theories abound like weeds, the one opinion everyone does seem to agree on is the belief that Norman Hitchcock should've been found by now, and not still here, drifting amongst them like a lethal vapor.

Willa can think of no legitimate rationale as to why she holds such a fascination for Norman Hitchcock, other than to think it is somehow similar to the strange admiration others might have for outlaws such as Butch Cassidy or Jesse James. The brand of affinity born of legend rather than gleaned from the actual person, cultivating a false image artfully crafted with the rosy hues of myth and imagination.

For the most part, the detailed reconstruction of Norman Hitchcock that Willa has composed in her head is of little similarity to the sharp-angled, cold-eyed visage perpetually featured on the front page corner of the daily newspaper. Just as the fear and excitement generated by his unrelenting assaults on Harriet's Bluff loom before her as curiously surreal and impersonal, in such a way that keeps her all to easily disconnected from the events of this peculiar drama unraveling in a dying town where nothing really seems to happen at all.

Willa leans forward over her bent knees and reaches to tug a scraggly knot of dandelion from a crack splintering the wooden step. Stella has been in bed since right after lunch, claiming herself the victim of some undefined *summer complaint* as she motions Willa to draw the limp cotton curtains in a bid to exile the painfully bright afternoon light.

Willa will, of course, need to finish the day's work. There are only two more cottages left to clean and then she'll be finished; but even so, she has yet to pull to her feet and return to the waiting tasks. Instead, she effortlessly allows her thoughts to slowly slide into blank, as she tears the plant's leggy stem and pointed leaves into miniscule pieces, then sprinkles them over her feet in a flurry of green snow.

Omega Pearl is gone, taking off for parts unknown shortly before lunch. Willa had been lugging out a pail of dirty mop water from one of the cottages when she'd caught sight of Omega limping out from the office, and she'd paused to watch the woman's comical maneuverings, the way she angled her stout round body into the front seat of her car like a sow backing into its stall.

It wasn't until Omega yanked the door shut and turned the key that she'd finally glanced up and spotted Willa staring from the steps. She'd stuck her head out through the open window, shouting something that Willa failed to comprehend over the grunting complaints of the engine. Willa had responded with a puzzled stare, at which Omega merely shook her head, flipping an impatient wave of farewell as she accelerated past the cloud of dust churned up by her tires before heading out onto the highway.

Now, Willa fights the temptation to sit and do nothing. She sees the dreaded path laid out before her like stepping stones—idleness, boredom, melancholy—each step coaxing her deeper into an abyss of darker, gloomier thoughts.

She makes something of a floundering attempt to pull herself loose from the strong pull of lethargy, feeling like a helpless fish hooked on an unbreakable line. Again she reminds herself for the thousandth time that the monotonous chores she trudges through day after day at The Moonglow are in essence taking her one, two, three miles closer to California: every remade bed, vacuumed carpet, and scrubbed toilet, an essential part of the journey that will eventually lead to the Promised Land.

The sun is right now burning a hole through the top of her head and yet she lacks either the strength or motivation to stand and move into the shade. Instead she tips her face forward, envisioning a charred crater widening at the apex of her skull, singeing the thick waves of her honey-colored hair into blackened toast, melting her brains into scrambled goo. *What am I doing here? How did we ever end up in a place like this? We're like rats. Rats in a trap, only without the cheese...*

"Hey."

Willa's head snaps upward at the sound of Jesse Truman's voice and she watches him cross the ruined grass, her eyes following his gaze to the sprinkling of green crumbs peppering the step.

"I'll sweep it up before Omega sees it," she says, feeling oddly dazed as the fog in her head dissipates.

"Why bother? I doubt she notices half as much as she pretends she does around here," he shrugs.

"I'm not so sure. She's like an alien with twenty sets of eyes. It wouldn't surprise me if she can see things happening on Jupiter," Willa says, attempting to brush the shredded green bits from the steps with the toe of her sneaker. "And now that she's convinced someone's been prowling around here at night she's watching this place like it's on a slide under a microscope."

"Seriously? She never said anything about a prowler to me," Jesse says, setting down the toolbox he is holding, shoving his hands into the front pockets of his jeans. It's a wonder he can fix anything more complicated than a loose screw considering the pitiful collection of tools contained in the dented box

Omega keeps out in the shed; stone age implements—bent, rusted, or missing critical components—others splinted and bandaged with a peeling cast of black electrical tape.

"I dunno, maybe she just figures I'm a gullible idiot. I wouldn't be surprised if she's just trying the story out on me to see how well it goes over before she takes it for a spin around town," Willa says, sweeping the damp fringe of her bangs from her forehead. *Is it going to be this god-awful hot forever? She can't even remember the last time she went through a day without feeling like something dropped and left to waterlog in a puddle of perspiration.*

"Stella says Omega is just trying to get people to believe Norman's out here sneaking around so she can draw attention to herself, like that time before when found him hiding out here."

"Maybe, but it's a strange way to try and promote a business. 'Welcome to The Moonglow, lodgings preferred by criminals.'"

Willa grins. "Well it does fit in nicely with that story about him breaking her leg."

"Norman Hitchcock broke her leg?"

"Don't look so shocked," she grins. "It wasn't with his bare hands—more like his bare eyes. Apparently he took a night off from fire-play to come out here and stare into Omega's bedroom window," Willa smiles, brushing a wandering ant from the hem of her shorts. "It just doesn't make sense that she wouldn't call the police if she really believes Norman is nosing around. I mean, he *is* a killer, right? She shouldn't be fooling around like this if she's honestly suspicious."

Jesse shrugs. "Just because she's suspicious doesn't make her convinced. Could be she's just throwing it out there to see what comes back."

"Well, neither me or Stella have seen or heard anything unusual and we're around here just as much as Omega," Willa says, watching his face, surprised that he hasn't immediately determined Omega to be an attention-seeking crazy person.

"And besides, wouldn't it be pretty stupid for Norman Hitchcock to come here? It's not exactly an ideal hideout."

Jesse shrugs, "I've never heard anyone accuse him of being predictable."

"Maybe not, but still, it doesn't make much sense that he'd risk coming back to the same place where he was caught before. You'd figure he'd think this place is jinxed for him and cross it off the list. But then Omega on the other hand, I mean, she does like to exaggerate."

Jesse turns his eyes on Willa, surprising her with the pointed directness of his indigo stare.

"What if she's telling the truth? What if Norman Hitchcock really has been out here poking around?"

"I don't know … I mean, I guess it's possible. But still, with everyone on the lookout it doesn't make sense that he'd take a chance lurking around a place where people come and go fairly regular."

"It's a small town, there aren't that many accommodations to choose from."

Willa shrugs. "Yeah, but the fact the story came from Omega is the thing that makes me wonder. Sure she's had some good ones, but it's not like I believe many of them." Willa leans back on her palms, staring up at the cloudless white sky. "I just wonder how she'd react if I made an anonymous call to the police and the whole fleet came flying out here with guns drawn."

Willa tucks several tendrils of hair drifted loose from her ponytail behind her ear. *If she doesn't get back to work, it's unlikely she'll be finished by the time Omega returns, and Stella will be furious.*

"I'd appreciate if you don't." His words come quietly, without inflection, yet the statement falls like a blinding meteorite, slamming down to fill the space between them with a deadly thud.

It takes Willa a moment to react. Her stare swings to his face, at once knowing that she has not imagined the implication in his words. Yet she searches for some hint that maybe she is wrong, even as the somber expression staring back assures her that, *no,* there's been no mistake.

Twelve

Willa holds her fingers under the bathroom faucet, waiting for the water to run cold, even while knowing the temperature will drop no cooler than tepid. It has in fact been weeks since the water in Harriet's Bluff flowed cold—assuming that it ever has.

She soaks a washcloth and presses it against her face, squeezing her eyes tightly shut as she rubs her skin roughly to clear away the confusion of questions swarming behind the veil of her closed eyelids like a horde of angry gnats.

Again she holds the cloth beneath the running faucet, alternately rinsing and wringing, rubbing it brusquely along her neck and chest, the hollows of her armpits. Thinking ... trying not to think ... a corner of her senses sharpened to a fine point of expectancy, knowing that at any moment she will hear the sharp rap of Stella's knuckles against the door, admonishing her for wasting water.

"For craps sakes, Willa, this whole godforsaken place is dry as a cracker. You think I need that woman charging me extra for water? She's been looking for any excuse she can find to keep me trapped like an indentured servant in this hell-hole, and that's just one more thing she'd love to dump on me."

But Willa doesn't care. She's heard the litany of Stella's reprimands enough times that she no longer hears any of it, especially now when there is this other thing careening through her mind like a runaway train.

He says he has nowhere else to go. He'd slept in his truck for nearly two weeks before allowing himself to consider how easy it would be to slip into one of the vacant cabins for a quick shower and a few hours of sleep before dawn. He'd been careful to cover his tracks so that no one would be the wiser—or so he'd believed. And his sense of shame and guilt are apparent in every word.

It was impossible to watch his face as he talked, and so Willa deliberately settled her gaze on the neck of his tee-shirt, glancing up briefly to focus on the side of his face when his voice momentarily faltered. Then dropping to stare at the fingers of his left hand nervously picking at a piece of wood splintered loose from the step where they sat.

Even as he spoke, there were a dozen impatient questions rocketing to the surface, zippering across her mind like lightning strikes. *Why? Why is he sleeping in his truck? Where is his family? Does he have one? Why isn't he with them? Are they gone? Is that why everything about him always seems so solitary—so isolated?*

And yet she sensed the importance of leaving the deluge of her oncoming inquiries side-lined, at least for now. To press further when he was already so clearly embarrassed, was to become Omega Pearl. And while she was curious, an interrogation wasn't necessary for Willa to arrive at the conclusion she already had, that Jesse Truman's life away from The Moonglow resided on fragile ground.

"Maybe Omega would rent you—"

"I can't. I can't afford it on what she pays me. Not if I want to save enough to get out of here in a few months."

Willa required no further details to comprehend his dilemma. It is the same vexing quandary she and Stella remained bound by themselves; with nearly every dollar earned going toward hanging-on at The Moonglow when the thing they want most is to leave it.

After a long wordless pause, when nothing seemed the right thing to say, Jesse lifted his head, tilting his chin toward her. "Look, I'm sorry about all this. Apparently I don't have Norman Hitchcock's talent for invisibility. I never wanted or expected to drag anyone else into this."

Willa imagined her hand reaching out—touching his arm in a reassurance that even without knowing the details, she understands. *Your secret is safe with me,* is the thing she wants to say. And yet when she turns to look at him, she just as quickly allows her hand to fall back into her lap, unwilling that he see her quaking fingers, or otherwise misinterpret the words she can't quite manage to speak.

"What will you do if you get caught?"

"*If?* I'd say I already have been."

"I mean by Omega. You know I'd never say anything, don't you? You know I wouldn't," she said, meeting his dark eyes, then quickly looking away, pretending she hasn't seen the flickering light of uncertainty wavering in their depths.

"I'm just thinking it could be dangerous creeping around here when everyone for miles is hunting for an escaped criminal," Willa said, floundering past the landslide of disappointment threatening to suffocate her. *He doesn't trust her with his secret.* His reluctance to elaborate is an all too painful assurance of the truth that as often as they've talked, or laughed, swum in the river, and raced to fires, Jesse Truman has never actually told her much of anything about himself with regard to the life he returns to everyday once he climbs into his truck and drives away from The Moonglow. Certainly nothing that would explain why he wasn't at home tucked into his own bed, or why he would risk being caught breaking and entering by an increasingly over-zealous Omega.

"Well, no, I never learned to shoot it, but that's not so important. All I really need to do is point in the right direction and that should blow a nice big hole in the bastard. Don't much matter to me whichever of his parts turn-up missing afterwards," Omega said, after announcing she'd taken her daddy's shotgun out from under the bed where it had lain in state since his passing twenty-five years earlier with the intention of sleeping side-by-side with the thing.

Willa had waited for Jesse to say something more, hopeful for some hint of the direction to take, but there was only the colossal weight of silence. And when Willa at last heard her own voice leaving her mouth, giving an extra push to get the words past her lips, she was altogether surprised by the strange sense of calm determination that carried it. "Maybe there's something I can—"

"No. Thanks, but no. This is my mess."

She's left it at that, not telling him how she is already sketching out a plan to smuggle away one of the extra keys Omega keeps in the left-hand corner of her top desk drawer, just as she doesn't linger over her own purpose in taking such a risk for someone she knows so little about. Because while the cords of logic stretch taut inside her head with the insistence there are no certain answers to the question of her motivations, she knows it isn't true. Somewhere in her mind the true purpose behind her designs stands luminous and clear...patiently waiting until she is ready to see it.

Thirteen

Of the four rowboats overturned on the lake's weedy shore, there is none amongst the quartet that doesn't require some painstaking degree of first-aid if there's to be a prayer of staying afloat upon launching.

Willa has extended spare interest in the sorry fleet's moldering state ever since Jesse's initial disclosure of the lake's grossly polluted condition. And while his revelation is more than effective at keeping her on dry land, she does occasionally climb into the lone boat she's managed to overturn, finding it a suitable sanctuary for reading or daydreaming. Of even greater importance, the beached craft at water's edge has proven an ideal hiding place, or at least until Stella or Omega Pearl eventually sniff it out.

Now, as she trudges between cabins, carrying bucket, broom, and an armload of damp towels, Willa is startled to catch a glimpse of Jesse down at water's edge, struggling to remove a broken oarlock from one of the decrepit vessels.

She pauses to watch, at once curious as to why he's fooling around with the boats at all. Several moments tick past before she drops her cargo alongside the steps and quickly strides toward the cover of trees dotting the lakeshore, hoping that neither Omega nor her mother will chance to look out and catch sight of her before she has a chance to safely clear their eagle-eye line of vision.

"What's the point of fixing them if the lake's polluted?"

"She didn't say," Jesse answers without glancing up, by every indication, holding to the cavernous distance opened up between them ever since his reluctant admission days earlier.

Even now Willa feels compelled to reassure him that it doesn't matter—that she understands his embarrassment, or humiliation, or whatever else is crowding his thoughts—because she needs to convince him that she will never utter a word to another soul, and that holding his secret is a burden she gladly accepts.

"Does she actually intend to rent them out? Doesn't everyone around here know what's going on with the water?"

He doesn't answer.

Willa shoots a quick glance over her shoulder, briefly scanning the row of windows facing the lake for any indication that Omega is right now watching—a telltale bend in the wide slats of the aluminum blinds to indicate telescopic eyes—but detects nothing amiss.

She cuts her gaze to the place where Omega routinely parks her dull green Pontiac, a portion of the left bumper and one headlight all that is visible. Nothing quivers in the bright white sunlight other than the heat itself. And although two of the cottages have been rented since yesterday afternoon, there is a sense of absolute isolation pressing over everything here.

Willa slides her hand into the front pocket of her shorts, wrapping her fingers around the warm metal shape poking into a corner of the fabric. Jesse is now bending over the side of the boat and she watches his hands, the fingers working something that looks like putty into a long, narrow crack in the underside of the vessel.

The key presses against her palm. She will hold out her hand. Take it, she will say. Number eight. It's the furthest one from Omega's office and is hardly ever rented out because of consistent complaints over the lumpy mattress and creaky springs. Take it. Please, take it.

But even as she culls over her wording, willing Jesse to lift his head and meet her eyes, she sees that his fingers have taken on an added determination to keep his attentions purposely detached, pressing the putty into a crack, smoothing it with his fingertips before adding more. And as she watches him, intently focused on his task as though he's already forgotten her presence, she all at once understands the unlikelihood of his accepting her offering.

Maybe his certain refusal is something to be expected in light of their unseasoned friendship, their fledgling state of companionship not yet grown to the depths required for extending or receiving such considerable favors. Or maybe the simpler, harsher truth is that Willa has no business presuming that it does.

It is late in the afternoon when Willa steals her hundredth glance toward the parking lot to be certain that Jesse is gone for the day. The spot where he habitually parks is empty—a rectangle *enormously, glaringly, screamingly vacant,* in comparison to everything around it—the dust long settled. She strides purposely toward the lake, saying a quick prayer that Omega Pearl remains on the telephone berating her sister for giving up on her diet, as per her weekly ritual *(...you've always been a quitter...it's the truth, Dottie, you might as well go ahead and admit it. You'd sell your soul for a candy kiss and you know it. Fine, you like being fat—be fat. Stick a flag in your mouth and call yourself an ocean liner for all I care.).*

Willa carefully places the key beneath the narrow wood seat straddling the inside curve of the boat next in line for repairs, the jagged edge exposed just enough that he will be certain to see it.

That night Willa dreams of the river. The barely moving water that wanes closer toward death as summer whines past without rain; each cloudless day further diminishing the hope of restoring the current and replenishing its depths.

She dreams she is struggling to swim, awkward and clumsy in her attempts to crawl through water turned heavy and dark. Panic presses hard against the back of her ribs. It is just as she's always feared. She's forgotten how to breathe, rancid water rising to fill her nose and mouth like an ever-thickening molasses.

Stella appears, blowing in from nowhere, hands on hips, eyes glaring, chiding Willa for going into the river when *you damn well know you can't swim a stroke*. So self-absorbed in her angry tirade and the sound of her own voice, it takes several minutes before Stella comprehends that Willa is drowning and reluctantly reaches to pick up something at her feet, tossing it out like a life ring. Willa's blank eyes stare in stunned disbelief as the object—a diaphanous blue nightgown—flutters gracefully through the air to land on the surface of the dirty water like an injured parachute. The filmy garment barely quivers as the cloth absorbs the weight of water and slowly slides down into the dark cave of the river and out of sight, Stella's face settling into a scowl when Willa fails to grasp it.

For all its disjointed randomness, it is a vision that nevertheless speaks clearly to Willa's waking mind. The images still here spread across her thoughts even once the dream has broken apart and dissolved into a melting fog.

She lacks necessary faith. Maybe she always has. She doesn't trust. She doesn't believe. And Stella will not be the one to save her—not from her fears or her growing uncertainties. Because, even though she might make something of an attempt to lend aid should Willa ever be in critical need, Stella's weak exertions will never be enough. Her efforts only ever touch the surface of impending crisis for a brief shining moment, before sinking out of sight.

It is a dreary assessment, but altogether true. Willa knows this for certain, if only for the fact that it has always been this way.

Willa pulls the door of the cottage shut behind her and bends to pick-up the bucket of cleaning implements Stella has abandoned halfway through the morning's work with a complaint that her head is throbbing with the beat of a hundred piece marching band; a rhythm she claims to be so horrendous, it's impossible to see straight, let alone endeavor to push a vacuum or scrub a toilet.

"I swear it feels like my whole damn head is about to snap off my neck," Stella moans, flopping back onto the bed where Willa has just finished smoothing wrinkles from the spread.

She's been on her own for several days already, excepting for this morning's brief reprieve when Stella at last crawled out from her tangled nest of stale smelling sheets and proclaimed herself well enough to return to work. Her mother's recovery, though brief, comes not a moment too soon, since Willa has had more than enough of carrying the daily load by herself, and at the same time, keeping up with Stella's constant admonishments that Willa not allow Omega Pearl to discover she's been working on her own.

"You can believe she's the type that'll make a big mumbo jumbo deal about a kid working by herself just so she has an excuse to hold back on the salary."

And while Willa is careful to cover her mother's absence, the truth is Willa doesn't believe Stella or her inventory of ailments for an instant. *She's just bored. Lazy and bored. Selfish enough to keep the charade going for as long as she can get away with it.* Unfortunately, whether or not she's judged Stella's deception correctly is of little consequence. Unless Willa intends to haul her mother out from the covers and shove a mop in her hands, there's not all that much she can do other than grumble and continue doing the work herself.

Now, as Willa trudges off to the next cottage, her steps slow, then come to a full stop when she catches a glimpse of Jesse striding across the parking lot, one hand holding a wooden stepladder balanced on his shoulder, the other clutching Omega's toolbox. She waits expectantly for him to feel the weight of her stare; anxious to receive the responding glance he will turn in her direction at any moment, her mouth poised to produce an immediate smile when he does.

And yet, crushingly, impossibly, he ignores her silent plea, continuing toward the office without bothering to shift his gaze for even an instant, holding his focus to the closed tunnel of air and space laid out directly in front of him. Just as quickly as Willa has spotted him, he is gone, passing through Omega's open door and out of sight.

She shifts the bucket to her opposite hand, only then remembering to breathe. She exhales her disappointment on an achingly spilled sigh, her heartbeat sinking several notches below its accustomed rhythm as she trudges off to the next cabin.

As much as Willa strives to pretend it away, there is a perceivable distance in Jesse's outward demeanor that hasn't existed before now, an isolated air effectively apprising her that the decision to gift him with the key has been the wrong one. His uninviting countenance more than adequately reminds her just how little she either knows or understands him.

Clearly her assumption that she and Jesse Truman are friends is as premature as it is erroneous. And by offering him the pilfered key, her greatest success has been in forcing him into scrutinizing not only her actions, but worse, her motivations. All of which have lead him to an apparent conclusion of disapproval or full-out rejection, though probably it is both.

She reminds herself that it is foolish to even care. He is only a boy she's met in a down-and-out town where she doesn't belong and doesn't intend to stay. There is nothing unique or especially magical about his having taught her to swim; nothing special about racing across town and along back roads in his truck, her insides flittering with the flurried confetti of excitement that consistently arrives in witness of another of Norman Hitchcock's fires; nothing particularly memorable about the occasional lunches they share within the curtained sanctuary of the willow tree.

And it's all too painfully apparent as she watches him walk away—the lone citizen in his solitary world—that she's imagined a great many things which are not, and never have been, real. Most especially the strange and unfamiliar sensations that fill her with giddy amazement whenever she finds herself thinking of someone other than herself—this boy she's only just met.

Clearly she's invented all of it. Felt and believed in things that simply do not exist. And there at the center of her fatuous assumptions is the stark humiliation and embarrassment that comes with discovering oneself a fool. Because, like a fool, she knows that she still wants it. Still wants every part of it.

Fourteen

"Oh, you can bet he's got a story. No question about that. It's the details I'm working on," Omega Pearl says, twisting the cap from her bottle of cola like she's wringing the neck of a chicken, squinting at the plastic insert inside the cap on the chance she's a five thousand dollar instant prize winner. The sharp ping, as she pitches it into the metal wastebasket, attests that she isn't.

Willa shrugs, affecting a show of disinterest even as her eyes make a sliding search for some crevice through which she can make her escape. She's altogether certain that Omega is wise to Stella's now regular habit of truancy, her questions and remarks increasingly taking on the pointed feel of an inquisition. Not that Omega's directly confronted Willa or come looking for Stella, it's more the brand of suspicion that can be seen blinking on and off behind watchful eyes; as though the pot is right now simmering and only moments away from rolling into a full boil.

"You know what they say, *still waters run deep*. Ever heard that? It's pretty worn-out as far as clichés go, but that's why it's still around. It makes sense."

Willa nods, her senses at once snapping awake when she hears the low crunch of tires popping over gravel. *He's finished for the day.* Her thoughts brush past the possible meaning inside Omega's remark as she listens to his truck swing around in the parking lot and head out to the highway. *Still waters run deep? What is that even supposed to mean? Stupid. It makes no sense.*

"He doesn't strike me as all that different from anybody else," Willa shrugs, turning away, packing the cleaning supplies back inside the utility closet behind the desk, knowing that Omega is anticipating a far more interesting reply. *Well, yes, he did tell me about the man he stabbed in prison; he's had an insatiable urge to torture small animals in his basement from the time he was in kindergarten; he carries Norman's picture in his wallet and—*

"Don't get me wrong, honey, I don't have any complaints. He does a good enough job around here. Punctual, works hard, respectful—all admirable qualities. But I can read a person like a gypsy reads tea leaves, and if there's one thing I can sense right down to my bones, it's when somebody's got a skeleton knocking around in their closet."

Willa nearly smiles, but quickly swallows the smirk that would otherwise come if she didn't recognize the underlying danger in Omega's statement. Not because she actually believes that the woman possesses some astute ability to read people, but rather it's the niggling fear of what she suspects is Omega's dogged determination to dig beyond tea leaves and straight to the heart of whatever it is she sets herself to uncover. Just as Willa guesses it isn't only Jesse Truman stirring Omega's curiosity, but Willa and Stella as well.

"He just seems a little shy is all."

"Uh, uh, he keeps to himself and that's not the same thing. Not that anyone could blame him all that much when you consider the family he comes from. A bona fide American tragedy—"

"Praise heaven! I think that green station wagon is pulling in here," Omega all at once squeals, interrupting herself to peer out through the front door screen.

Willa shifts her weight to one foot, then back to the other, torn between taking advantage of Omega's momentary distraction by making a quick exit, and the temptation to remain, shamefully interested in hearing whatever tarnished tale Omega is alluding to, regardless of the warning that common decency is right now whispering into Willa's ear.

Nevertheless, the details are instantly lost as Omega focuses on the travelers. "Darn, I can't tell if he's actually coming into the lot or just pulling off the road for something," she says. Visitors to The Moonglow have become sporadic enough over the past weeks that every arrival now carries the import of a red carpet event.

"It looks like someone's getting out," Willa reports, stepping aside so that Omega can lean her weight against the door jab and gain a better view through the open doorway.

They watch, mesmerized now, as a stocky man bolts from the driver's seat and quickly wings around to the passenger side door, jerking it open and roughly extracting a small sobbing boy.

"Eweeee—" Omega and Willa moan in unison when the child promptly vomits into the dust at the man's feet.

"What kind of moron lets a kid up-heave like that in front of someone's business establishment? A kid gets carsick you pull off the road and let 'em puke in the weeds. Damn fool better be renting a cabin, otherwise he's not getting out of here until he cleans up that mess," Omega swears, clutching her cane like a threat as she clumsily maneuvers her round trunk and plaster leg past Willa and pushes out through the door.

"Isn't it my turn to play sick?" Willa says without opening her eyes, stubbornly burrowing her face into the pillow when Stella rattles her shoulder.

"What the hell's that supposed to mean? You think it's some big joke to wake up feeling like your head's about to split wide open?"

"No, but I'm pretty sure that after all these weeks I must've caught whatever you have."

"Are you kidding me? I haven't been on a damn vacation. I'm in pain, you nasty little witch."

"Maybe you should go to a doctor," Willa grumbles, her words muffled by the pillow. She's had enough of Stella's ongoing convalescence and her vague and unexplained ailments, symptoms that don't sound genuine as much as contrived to suit her purpose of bypassing a job she clearly despises.

"Doctor's don't see patients for free."

"Maybe Omega knows someone who—"

"Maybe you can stop being so damned selfish and try thinking about someone other than yourself for once."

Willa rolls over, her eyes widening as though she's been struck. *Selfish? Selfish!* The word selfish shouldn't even be allowed in a sentence that has her name in it. *Selfish!* Has she been selfish all these weeks that she's had to shoulder the responsibilities of cleaning rank cottages, washing and hanging up sheets and towels—then having to fold it all and put it away at the end of the day—all the while making certain to keep an eye over her shoulder, prepared to spring forward like a panther and detour Omega the instant she shows signs of suspicion or curiosity over the absent Stella. And whether or not Willa has succeeded in her assignment, she's beginning to care less and less. She's had enough of carrying the load while her mother remains comfortably tucked inside the cottage, sleeping and smoking in the peaceable gloom afforded by labor-free days and perpetually drawn shades.

Weeks earlier, Willa had been genuinely frightened by the headlong arrival of Stella's illness, her mind immediately crowding with a swell of alarming questions: *Does she have something serious? Incurable? What will become of her if something happens to Stella? What will she do on her own? Where will she go?*

And yet the passage of days has gradually cleared a path through the jumble of piled-up worries and concerns, allowing Willa a closer look into the face of Stella's alleged "sickness." Of significant consideration is the fact that Stella has rarely even had a headache before now, let alone suffered debilitating pain lasting for weeks, certainly not the chronic agony that leaves her incapable of accomplishing anything beyond rolling over in bed and adjusting her pillow, striking a match, or crushing the final remains of a cigarette into the pyramid of nicotine carcasses overfilling the ashtray.

And now there are other ailments, a growing list of lethal complaints, but never anything remotely suggestive of improvement or recovery. Over the past weeks, Willa's mood has been carefully perched atop twin peaks of sympathy and worry. But considering that her mother's alleged expiration date has come and gone several times already, she's no longer feeling as compassionate as she is resentful. Her original seed of suspicion has now quadrupled in size from sapling to full-grown tree, along with Willa's increasing conviction that Stella's make-believe illnesses aren't so much deadly, as they are a return to habit, namely her ritual pattern of losing interest and moving onto greener pastures. Except that, unlike her life back in Hoosick Falls, Stella is stuck here, unable to change gears as she ordinarily would do whenever her life came slamming up against the walls of boredom and mental lassitude.

Customarily, Stella's announcements that a change is in the works have been purposeful and dramatic. "You know you've sure-as-hell cracked the bottom of the barrel when you can't even afford to live in a dump like this," had been one such announcement. This one coming as Stella stood in the dark little kitchen of their house in Hoosick Falls, accenting her words with the toss of her purse onto the cluttered kitchen countertop, the tempered force of her agitation sending a stack of plastic containers, old mail, and anonymous junk skittering across the dull green Formica and onto the floor.

Willa had glanced up briefly from the Geography book opened before her on the kitchen table.

"I don't know why the hell I even try. What could be any worse than this crap hole?" Stella swears, kicking a tube of lipstick that has escaped from her disemboweled purse and rolled across the floor.

Willa shrugged her shoulders, returning her attention to her homework as Stella pivots on her heel and skulks off into the living room.

If they'd had the sort of relationship that allowed for a sharing of opinions, they would surely have agreed that ordinary life in Hoosick Falls had taken an enormous leap off center and was leaning dangerously into the red. But they didn't. And Willa had been furious when Stella used the last of their rapidly dwindling funds to enroll in a hair-styling course, insisting that it was the perfect opportunity for launching herself into a "dignified and respectable career."

"I'll thank you very much to stop rolling your eyes like lost marbles in your head. This is just the ticket for getting us out of here. Mark my words. If there's one thing people respect it's beauty. I can't think of a single successful woman alive who doesn't depend on her hairstylist to keep her looking pulled together. We're the ones who work the magic so they can go parading around pretending like they're natural beauties."

But once again Stella's brief flash of exuberance had just as quickly come crashing to a premature death, all the assurances she'd made just weeks earlier, vaporizing once the initial non-refundable weeks of instruction had passed and she found herself in the less than glamorous position of applying permanent wave solution to the volunteer heads of residents at the *Sunshine Village Nursing Home*. Her complaints of mind-numbing headaches and violent stomach cramps arrived with the swiftness of a rumor, as did her conviction that the odorous hair tonics, sprays, and dyes, necessary for sculpting certain popular coifs, were nothing other than camouflaged poisons, regular exposure of which was a guaranteed promise of her own imminent sickness and painful death should she continue toiling over head and hair.

"You can't tell me something that smells that god-awful isn't deadly. It sure as hell explains why hairdressers are such crack-pots. It's the damn fumes they're always sucking into their lungs."

The whole idea of poisoned scalps and insane hairstylists struck Willa as more ridiculous than worrisome, but she knew not to offer her opinion. Arguing with Stella had rarely gotten Willa anything other than additional frustration, so she made a not always successful effort to hold back and defend only those convictions that struck her as life or sanity saving, nailing down her tongue when she most wanted to open the corral and turn it loose.

Not long after quitting the business of beauty, once the desperation that came from living in dire straights for an extended period loomed in close enough, Stella managed to dredge up the motivation necessary to take a job at the dry cleaner in town. And while it proved as yet another position she proclaimed dreadful from the first day, she nevertheless stuck with it for several weeks until she'd gleaned a legitimate excuse to quit.

Astonishingly, the essential reasoning she'd been trolling for arrived directly into her hands one particularly slow afternoon as she flipped through an out-of-date magazine abandoned on the toilet tank in the employee bathroom. Nothing short of giddy to come across a brief article speculating over a possible link between breast cancer and prolonged exposure to certain chemicals, including those customarily used in the dry-cleaning process.

"I knew it! I knew it! I damn well knew it," Stella blurted out even before she'd made it through the door, unfolding the pages she'd torn from the magazine and tucked inside her purse, smoothing them out on the table in front of Willa.

"But you work at the counter," Willa said, glancing disinterestedly over the article.

"And? What's that supposed to mean?"

"So, then you're not actually working with any chemicals," Willa said, watching Stella as she moved to the counter and began plucking withered flowers from a discarded altar arrangement she'd picked-up from behind the Methodist Church and carried home.

While she was becoming increasingly puzzled over Stella's strange new habit of gathering discarded floral arrangements and dead potted plants from the neighborhood trash and carting them home, Willa's immediate concerns remained locked on the essentials, basic survival for instance, and whether anything edible was likely to materialize on the table come supper time.

"They're very strong chemicals. *Deadly chemicals,*" Stella said, her impatient tone inferring that Willa was the worst breed of idiot for missing the obvious. "They don't just evaporate off the clothes after they've been cleaned. Every time I take something off the rack and hand it over to a customer I'm getting poison on my hands. So, then maybe I happen to scratch my nose or rub my eye, and just like that I've affected an entire colony of cells. That's how simple it is. You spread the deadly toxins to the sensitive parts of your skin and they make a beeline straight for your organs."

"That doesn't really make sense, though. How can—"

"What doesn't make sense is that you apparently need to see tumors growing out of my head or maybe my breasts hacked off once they're loaded with cancer, before you quit with the baloney questions and take this seriously."

And the only real surprise was that Stella went into the cleaners the next day and quit her job, rather than simply not showing up at all.

Now that they are stuck at the Moonglow, Stella has had to adjust her methods for leaving behind things the instant they lose their flavor, even though the end results are more or less destined to be the same; change lanes the moment the urge arises, no matter who or what gets run off the road in the process.

"I don't care. It's not fair," Willa says now, fully knowing that once again she'll be the one delegated to clean the dismal settlement of cottages. She's been too long immersed in her mother's obstinate methods to pretend not to know how she plays her game. Because with Stella it isn't simply a matter of building an ailment until it's the size of a prehistoric glacier, it's just as necessary that she grab on with both hands, clenching her knuckles and holding firm until Willa weakens and eventually surrenders. And yield she will, for the sole reason that Willa wants badly enough to leave behind The Moonglow and every hurting thing they've either carried here, or foolishly cultivated since their arrival.

Fifteen

Willa has only just slipped into bed and pushed the summer weight blanket down past her feet to lie in the hot dark, when the fire alarm sounds, its shrill scream breaking open the quiet night like a brutally halved walnut.

She rolls over and steals a glance toward Stella, but the room is too dark to decipher much of anything other than the sharp line of her mother's back turned toward her. As much as Willa appreciates Stella's dead man's sleep, it's nevertheless bizarre that her mother so rarely wakens for any of these late night summons. Quite unlike Willa, who ordinarily bolts upright like Frankenstein's corpse come to life the instant the siren's first wailing notes crack the air.

Her mind lies quiet on the lingering fringe of unclaimed sleep, listening to the familiar commotion without interest, certain that at any moment she will hear the steady parade of fire trucks racing off across town, en route to some cloistered spot on the outskirts of Harriet's Bluff. Indeed it is only minutes later when she hears the startled bleats of the approaching fleet—except that instead of coursing on through town, the congregation remains within earshot. Remarkably proximate, Willa is sure, to the very heartbeat of Harriet's Bluff.

She dresses quickly, holding her eyes to the line of Stella's back for telltale indications of her stirring. And she is zipping her shorts as she cautiously creeps toward the door, gently pulling the metal tongue tooth to jagged tooth. Moderating each step with a carefully placed toe before allowing an entire foot to land, she remains ever aware of the multiple hazards placed in lethal landmines along the floor: an ill-placed pair of shoes; heaps of unwashed clothing; a collection of outdated fashion magazines Stella promptly confiscated after Omega left them bundled out front for the trash man, and which are now piled on the floor in an island chain of glossy paper.

She eases the screen door open in an effort to minimize the squeak of eternally un-oiled hinges and slips out onto the porch, then quickly descends the stairs and dashes to collect Omega Pearl's bicycle from its hiding place behind the cottage.

By every indication it is the class of fire that will burn for days. An especially tenacious breed that will continue to smolder even after the timbers have been thoroughly drenched for hours by a half dozen fire hoses. The seeds of flame, reluctant to quit, will flare up again and again, lick by fiery lick, devouring anything possessing the components necessary to nourish a lingering spark.

The fire is near enough that Willa hears it even before she catches a glimpse; the forcible roar of rushing flame taking hold of ancient timbers, loud enough to obliterate the deafening throb of adrenaline sluicing through her limbs in a molten current. And she stands hypnotized, watching as the fire grows in proportions of fury, sporadically turning her head to take in the activity racing around her as though she hasn't witnessed this very scene a dozen times already, both awake and in her dreams.

An arriving pumper-truck grinds to a halt across the street from the burning building, its crew working quickly to attach a thick umbilical cord to a nearby hydrant; an assembly of trucks, hoses, and firemen in their slick, shiny gear shout directions and call out for assistance as the roiling flames continue to swell despite the tsunami-strength jets of water directed against the brick walls of the abandoned mannequin factory. And Willa already knows, is in fact certain considering all the other fires she's witnessed over the past months, that heroic efforts notwithstanding, the building is only hours away from gone.

Staring up at the enormous building dissolving behind heavy curtains of smoke and flame, Willa finds herself all at once struck by the thought of how very sad it all is, pitiful really, that yet another piece of this town has been lost. In truth, stolen. As unaffectionate as she feels toward Harriet's Bluff herself, she is reminded there must've been a time when this town had been a nice enough place to live, open a business, or raise a family. Boarded-up store fronts still show random evidences of their original interesting architecture; the horse head fountain on Main Street, currently neglected by everyone but pigeons and vandals, nevertheless holds to a suggestion of the grandiose beneath the frosting of bird poop and chipped marble. The cast iron street lamps stand at intervals along the streets, stately sentinels attesting to the allure of an earlier age.

Omega Pearl had taken the opportunity to tell Willa about the host of stores and businesses that once dotted the town's main street, the majority of which are long since gone. Waxing poetic over the now faltering fleet of magnificent homes built on the North side of town, a tract dating back to the time of Moses, or so it would seem the way Omega tells it. "All the rich people lived up there on account of the river. When you've got money it's all about having the best view of whatever happens to be around."

Prosperity … and then not. As if some cruel-hearted entity has reached out and turned a page in the town's history. Chapter finished. Pivotal scene concluded. Ending all but written.

No one in Harriet's Bluff honestly considered the possibility of the zinc mine one day closing, and certainly not that the company would so callously vanish like a one-night stand, pick up and walk away without a single, backward glance.

For the next several years, families and businesses continued to come and go, though mostly go, once enough time had passed to render optimism for recovery futile. And anyone passing through was likely to stay just long enough to gulp down a cup of coffee and slice of pie at the diner, while studying a roadmap for the quickest route to another town.

It was several years after the mining company pulled up stakes, that C.J. Preston rode in on his white stallion with a plan to renovate the long-closed shoe factory and reopen it as a manufacturing plant for plastic mannequins, so that Harriet's Bluff unexpectedly found itself possessed of an opportunity to shake loose from the grip of its own imminent demise.

Omega insists there are still plenty of people in Harriet's Bluff who remember the prosperous years when the factory was breeding entire populations of plastic bodies, but for most, memory fails to reach that far. The reigning assumption, as far as Willa can tell, is that the old building has simply always been what it is at present—a towering brick relic with a largely forgotten past, and now, a mournfully ended future.

Fragments of conversation pass through the gathered crowd, sporadically lifting, then just as quickly drifting away like motes of dust as they stand witness to the forsaken landmark's demise; the assembly apparently far more affected by the reality of Norman Hitchcock's boundless capacity for undeterred retribution than by the harrowing scope of the blaze itself.

Willa only half listens to the snippets of conversation dipping and rising around her, largely disinterested by grievances she's heard a dozen times before. *There's no limit to what he'll do. He won't be satisfied until he kills someone. He has blood on his hands and that's something he'll never lose. He's a killer and he's just—"*

A shrill cry ladders up behind her like cat claws climbing her spine. Willa swings around, straining for a glimpse at the center of the growing commotion, and catches sight of a woman gesturing wildly to a pair of policemen standing on the corner opposite.

"I SAW HIM," the woman is shouting now. I was right there across the street with Harvey—my dog, Harvey—just standing there waiting for Harvey to finish his business. And I—my God, I swear it—I saw him! There was a sudden flash of light in one of those windows up there. That must've been what caught my eye. And then just like that—there he was. Running to beat the band. I'll swear on my life. It was him. I saw him."

"Ellie," a gray haired woman says, settling a comforting arm around the excited women's shoulder. "It could've just been someone else out walking their dog. They probably saw the flames just like you did and they figured they'd better get the hell away from the place before it explodes."

"Uh, uh. No. It was him. It was definitely him. Tall, thin, dark hair, just like they described him. Just like that picture in the paper."

"It still might've—"

"I'm not the only one that saw him either," the woman's voice rises on a wave of renewed excitement, pointing to indicate a short, bald man ringed by a half-circle of policemen.

"They could've caught him this time. He was right here. They could've got their hands on him, but they'd rather waste valuable time standing around asking ridiculous questions."

A series of shattering explosions inside the building brings an immediate halt to conversation, all eyes turning to watch as black smoke pours from an opening in the roof. In the factory's wide front windows high above the street, life-sized plastic bodies can be seen writhing and melting within the blazing inferno, lending to the eerie illusion of a large-scale human tragedy. No question, it's the oddest thing Willa has ever seen.

The crowd is gradually breaking away. The ugly black smoke and heat roiling up with the flames has turned an already hot night sweltering, and still it will be several hours yet before the blaze is declared under control.

By now Willa is feeling the weight of her own exhaustion pressing down to her kneecaps. In a few more hours she will need to be up for work, a struggle on ordinary days, never mind on those mornings after she's stayed up late reading some paperback left behind in one of the cottages, or, like now, after she's spent hours immersed in the drama of another fire.

She lifts the bike from the sidewalk where she's carelessly dropped it hours earlier, then turns to throw one last sweeping glance across her shoulder at the dying building in a bid to commit the scene to memory for later viewing. But all at once her stare lands on the deep shadowed doorway of the drugstore directly opposite, and she feels herself turning into a pillar of salt. Because someone is standing there. Right there, just out of view.

Brief flickers of firelight sporadically illuminate the far pockets of darkness, but only enough to reveal the slice of a dark sleeve, the narrow stripe of one denim clad leg.

She pretends not to see him, returning her gaze to the burning building, shooting quick glimpses toward the doorway from the corner of her eye. *Is it him? What is she supposed to do? Should she tell someone? Doesn't anyone else see him there? Has he been there the whole time?* The police cars are gone, having left some time ago, but there are still several firemen milling about. She starts across the street, wheeling the bike alongside quivering legs, just as the figure darts from the shadows and is gone. Vanished around the corner and out of sight as though he himself is merely a wisp of smoke.

Can it be? Is it possible that he's been standing there alongside them this entire night? Watching Norman's fire with none other than Norman Hitchcock himself.

The minute Omega Pearl is gone (her tires lifting a gritty haze of dust as she peels rubber out onto the highway, late as always for her Thursday afternoon card game), Willa immediately goes in search of Jesse.

His truck has been parked out front for hours and yet his physical self appears to be nowhere. She scans the broken line of cottages, hoping to determine his whereabouts with the glimpse of an open front door, a ladder propped against an outside wall, his toolbox sitting on a porch. But the forlorn buildings lie quiet and eerily still like a cemetery of teetering headstones.

With her perplexity climbing another rung, Willa now walks around to the back of the cottages. But again, there is nothing to indicate or otherwise suggest whatever crack or crevice he's somehow melted into. *Weird.* There aren't that many places to disappear around here, at least none she hasn't already checked.

Willa is skulking back toward the office, alternately dragging her feet and kicking at withered patches of grass, when a swell of terrible suggestions come skidding into her mind. *What if he doesn't want to be found? What if he's purposely staying out of sight? What if he's avoiding her?*

It's become something of a regular habit now for Willa to seek him out as soon as Omega leaves for her appointed card game in the backroom of *Veleda's House of Hair.* He knows she'll be looking for him.

Has he grown bored with her? Tired of her attentions? Is it still about the key? The damned, stupid key?

She wrestles with the question of which line-crossing offense she's said or done to ruin things, and concludes that it could very well be everything. She's allowed him too much of a glimpse inside her head, has idiotically extended a look or word that in turn has alerted him to the prominent place he occupies in her thoughts. And it's clearly a revelation that has not only startled him, but planted an immediate urgency to back away and quickly retreat.

Turning around before she reaches the office building, she trudges across the grass toward an irregular patch of shade laid out beneath a heavy-limbed maple. She sits on the flattened hump of a root arched above the ground and spreads out her dejection like a carefully arranged picnic cloth, loading it with the dreadful meal she's prepared for herself. *One oversized platter of ice cold dejection, a large tin of congealed heartbreak, plastic tub of melancholy, a bowl of gloom, extra large thermos laced with a bitter brew of piping hot anguish.*

And she feels as if she is choking to death, though she hasn't swallowed a thing.

Lifting her chin, Willa catches the fluttering stir of something moving out beyond the trees. She twists her head hard to scan the water for another glimpse of whatever it is that has drawn her attention, and is rewarded a moment later when she catches sight of Jesse Truman smoothly rowing one of Omega's dilapidated boats back to shore.

Her heart bobs up from the gloomy depths, a glowing orb on the surface of instantly renewed hope, her gaze holding to the dark brown oars rhythmically dipping in and out of the water as he brings the boat closer to land. She waits a moment longer, purposely working to steady her breathing, then bounces to her feet and strides across the parched grass just as Jesse swings his leg out over the side of the boat.

He glances up as if sensing her approach, but looks away quickly before Willa has a chance to glean some indication of gladness or displeasure that might be contained within his expression.

"Hey ... what're you doing?" Willa asks the back of his head as he bends to remove the oars from their locks.

"Making some test runs to see if the plugs will hold up before Omega starts renting them out."

"I can't help but wonder how many people will want to row around on a lake o'crap," Willa smiles, but the expression rapidly fades when Jesse fails to meet her eyes, his gaze instead remaining purposely focused on his task as he settles the oars into the waiting locks of the next boat.

"I'm sure she'll just forget to mention that minor detail,' he answers in a monotone, declining to lift his head or otherwise face her in an impossible to ignore indication that her company is neither desired, nor especially welcome.

"There was another fire last night," Willa says as he continues fiddling with the oars, some unexamined sense of fortitude stubbornly refusing to allow her to give up and walk away.

"I heard the alarm."

"I think maybe it was the worst one yet," she continues, purposely holding him to conversation despite his every indication of wanting to be left alone. *She doesn't deserve this— though maybe she does. How is she supposed to know? She hasn't done anything wrong. At least she doesn't think she has. It doesn't count if he won't tell her. It shouldn't count.*

"Yeah, I guess I missed it." His perfunctory tone mirrors what is clearly his scant interest, his attentions holding to the task of easing the next boat into the water.

"That's not all you missed. Someone saw Norman Hitchcock. A couple of people actually," she says, and she doesn't mention that for a moment she'd believed herself a witness, too. Because now, in the far more logical light of day, the previous night feels like something composed of reality and invention, and she is no longer sure which portion falls to conviction or wishful thinking.

But still, her own confusion aside, two people *did* see him for certain and that in itself is the biggest news yet. "Two different people saw him running away from the place right before it went up in flames," she says, waiting for his reaction, then, when he doesn't offer one, "They both gave statements to the police."

"Yeah, I heard some people talking about it in town this morning. Sounds like pretty good news if it's true. Now all they have to do is stop watching and actually get him," he says, still stubbornly refusing to meet her eyes, as if by turning his head he will break his concentration in wishing her away.

He gives the boat a hard shove into the water, the abrupt action causing one of the oars to jerk forward unexpectedly and pop from the lock, then swinging outward and sliding over the side of the boat to lodge in the soft mud at waters edge. And it is as Jesse instinctively reaches to retrieve the errant tool that Willa catches sight of the dark shadow staining the side of his face.

"What—oh my, God—how did you—what happened?"

"Nothing." He turns away quickly.

"Your face—"

Willa circles to the opposite side of the boat. Her fingers press against her lips to hold back a cry as she stares at the purplish mask blotted in deep bruises across one side of his face. The unmarred portion of his skin instantly staining pink in response to her emphatic attentions. She attempts to look away in solicitude of his palpable discomfort, yet she cannot force her eyes to leave the terrible suggestion of everything she sees there—the angry gash slashed across the top of his cheekbone, one eye nearly obscured by the purplish black shadings of deeply bruised tissue swelled up around it.

"It's not a big deal. I just tripped over a stump—a log or something—when I went down to the river for a swim last night. It was pitch dark and I wasn't paying attention."

"But that cut—it looks awful—like you should've gone for stitches or—"

"It's okay."

"Jesse—" Willa protests as he brushes past, determinedly shoving the boat into the shallows and swinging his leg over the side.

"I'd appreciate if you don't say anything to Omega. You know how she dramatizes everything and I already feel like enough of an idiot without having to explain details to her," he says, grasping an oar in either hand, careful to avoid Willa's stare as he rows determinedly away, out toward the middle of the lake where eyes and voices can no longer reach him.

Sixteen

Omega Pearl stands propped in the doorway of the office, leaning her weight against the jamb, her injured leg sticking out in front of her like a cockeyed periscope. She watches Willa trudge across the parking lot, her round moon face glazed with a curious expression of anxiety and something else. The *something else* causing Willa's heartbeat to take a crazy skip behind her ribs.

"Have you seen Jesse Truman?" Omega calls out even before Willa reaches her. "HAVE YOU SEEN JESSE?" she tries again when Willa tips her head to indicate that she hasn't caught her words.

"Nope, uh uh," Willa shakes her head, at once confused by the urgency contained in the simple question, since it is by Omega's own specific instructions that Jesse doesn't start work before nine in the morning as a courtesy to any lodgers currently occupying the cottages.

"Why? What time is it?" Willa asks, throwing a glance over her shoulder on the unlikely chance she's somehow missed seeing his truck in the near empty lot: *two cars, a dull red truck, and Omega's own monstrous tank, but no sign of Jesse.*

Oddly enough, Omega's peculiar urgency feels altogether suited to this morning that has already started on a strange note. For starters, Stella has finally crawled out of bed and proclaimed herself recovered, or nearly, assuming Willa agrees to race into town and pick-up a bottle of aspirin and box of sanitary pads.

"I'd go myself if I wasn't bleeding like a stuck pig," Stella says, shaking Willa awake even before the filmy light of gray dawn has lifted beyond the windows.

But it isn't until she's fumbling with the buttons on her blouse, still groggy from unsatisfied sleep, that the full weight of Stella's announcement begins to steep its way into her head. Whatever the reasoning behind her mother's decision to end her questionable and seemingly endless convalescence, Willa makes no guesses. She doesn't really care. She's merely relieved to think that maybe the episode has passed, or at least for this immediate instant.

"Your mother said she sent you into town for female products," Omega says cutting her eyes to the bag clutched in Willa's hand. "You didn't see him out on the highway? Driving past? Pulled over anywhere?"

"No."

"What about yesterday? Did you see him yesterday?"

"Um—well, yeah, but just for a minute or two. He was messing around with the rowboats, checking them for leaks, I think," Willa says, fighting the urge to take a step back from the pointed intensity of Omega's stare.

"Was there anything *wrong*?"

"Wrong? No ... I don't think so. They seemed to be holding up pretty well."

"No, I mean with *him*. Was there anything wrong with him?"

"With Jesse? Like what?"

"Like anything," Omega presses, a rise of impatience cutting through her tone as she shifts her shoulder away from the door jamb and tilts toward Willa like a wayward drunk. "Did you notice anything *peculiar*?"

"No."

"He looked all right to you?"

"Yeah, sure. I mean he just looked like—well, like he always does," Willa replies evenly, clutching tightly to what she hopes is something resembling of nonchalance.

Only yesterday she'd considered Jesse's request that she make no mention of his injury to Omega uncharacteristically melodramatic and altogether unnecessary. Only now, as Omega interrogates her like the star witness in a criminal trial, Willa feels a tightening noose of confusion squeezing against her windpipe as she rapidly attempts to put together pieces of a puzzle not yet formed in order to deduce whatever it is that Omega is apparently searching for.

For Pete's sakes, Jesse Truman can't be the first person in Harriet's Bluff who ever tripped over a stick in the dark.

"Is something wrong?"

"Maybe ... well, I don't really know. It's just something I heard from Veleda while we were playing cards yesterday. Apparently somebody's got their stories mixed up."

Willa almost wishes that Stella hadn't chosen this day of all days to declare her miraculous recovery. Or at least that she didn't insist she doesn't need Willa's help.

Now, with no menial duties to start or finish, no chores to divert her thoughts from the clatter of unknowns cawing inside her head like a mad colony of blackbirds, or deter her eyes from staring obsessively over the dusty parking lot, she can only pray that she will catch Jesse before Omega Pearl has a chance to accost him. She is certain that his immediate assumption will be that she is the one who has betrayed his confidence, rather than some blabbermouth dealing cards in the backroom of a hair salon.

With so few cabins rented, Willa guesses that Stella will be finished fairly early, especially since when it comes to housekeeping, Stella is anything but thorough. Ordinarily Willa wouldn't care either way, but now, unless her mother declares herself drained from the unaccustomed activity and in need of a nap, there will be an additional pair of watchful eyes to consider if she hopes to intercept Jesse before someone else claims the opportunity.

Just as Willa fears, it is early afternoon when Stella concludes her work for the day. And with still no sign of Jesse, there is nothing to do but hold to her vigilant sentry, anxiously watching and waiting to catch a glimpse of whatever drama is primed to unfold.

It is easy as it is pointless to argue with herself over the reasons why she shouldn't care about someone like Jesse Truman, but they are arguments without conviction. The fact remains that she does care. For whatever reasons, she does.

The long shadows of late afternoon are beginning their languid stretch toward twilight when Stella tents the magazine she is paging through over her chest and shuts her eyes. She sighs deeply, causing the paper tent to dip and shift slightly. Her head drifts sideways on her pillow as if she is being tipped overboard.

Anxious as she is to dart outside, Willa nevertheless forces herself to wait until she is certain that Stella is fully asleep before drifting across the floorboards like a dispersing vapor. Releasing the latch with the slightest click, she slips out through the screen door.

Her guess is that he's gone to the river, and she hurries there now with the hopeful expectation of finding him stretched out on the bank like an indolent cat absorbing the dwindling rays of sunlight.

The grassy field that no one ever mows is high with thin scratchy blades gone too long without rain. Her hands swat at the long tendrils scribbling ticklish licks against her legs, as she presses toward the glint of water lying beyond the fringe of brambles and pickerelweed.

She rapidly scans the stretch of riverbank, her gaze lingering over the deep pockets of shade fanned out from trees reaching scabby arms out over the bank, even though she somehow knows that he isn't here.

But if not here, then where? She has no idea where he lives—though even if she did it's unlikely she possesses the necessary courage to show up uninvited. Maybe there is some private place he goes in pursuit of solitude (if such a location even exists in a town as close and watchful as Harriet's Bluff); and if this is true, he's never mentioned it.

Dead-ended. She pulls off her sneakers and tosses them back onto the dry grass sparsely combed up over the riverbank, then wiggles her bottom along the crook of a fallen branch jutting out over the water where she can easily dangle her bare feet into the river.

She stares down into the barely moving current, considering what color the water might be if not for the absence of rain and a constant sun that's slowed the current and turned the river the color of liquid rust.

The afternoon has visibly deepened, the tree shadows lengthening as the sun melts down behind the sky. Willa shifts her weight on the branch, stretching her toes to relieve the dull ache creeping up the backs of her legs from too long sitting.

She takes little notice of the danger of falling as her mood slips several notches deeper into melancholy, her thoughts winding back toward Stella, altogether certain that even before crawling out from her sickbed, a changing route and destination were fermenting in her mother's head.

Lately everything Stella does—regardless of how ordinary or accustomed—feels offensive. Loud, coarse, rude. Whether she's spreading butter on a slice of bread, tearing Jackie Kennedy pictures from her pile of magazines, or opening a can of soup, Willa finds her annoyance bristling with her mother's every action. She screams at Stella with a silent intensity. Her rage swells to near eruption as she imagines shaking her mother long and hard, forcing her arms and legs to swing back and forth like a fatally injured rag doll, then palming her like a football and hurling her a million miles away.

Willa assumes she should feel something of guilt for coveting such ugly thoughts inside her head; certain there must be something terribly wrong with a daughter who entertains such violent deliberations against her mother. But nevertheless, she is unable to keep the angry images from coming.

Quite simply, she's had enough of Stella's odd behaviors and peculiar brand of ideas. And not just this current frustrating limbo of waiting for her mother to stop faking illness and get to work on a plan to get them out of here, but all those schemes previous. In particular the one that landed them here. Namely, Stella's ridiculously conceived brainstorm to make a living peddling hideous monuments of ugly dead things.

It wasn't that being surrounded by decayed and rotten things had the disturbing effect on Willa that a similar inventory might've had on another child—one whose home wasn't already gloomy and morose without such props. Rather, it was Stella's boundless obsession to further accumulate, despite her already vast collection of wilted flowers and curling foliage that constantly served to needle Willa's irritation.

"Jeez, don't you have enough of this stuff already?" Willa complained once it became impossible to sit at the kitchen table and eat a bowl of cereal without first pushing aside a mountain of petrified carnations or a repugnant arrangement in progress.

"I'm running a damn business, in case you've forgotten."

"As if I could," Willa muttered under her breath, then, "I just don't get why you have to keep so much of this junk piled everywhere. It smells—old."

"Well, you might as well get used to it. This is the best idea I've ever had in my life and I'm not about to give it up just because you've suddenly decided to be Little Miss Royalty."

And it was at those times especially, just as it is now, when Stella makes so little effort to conceal the fact that she simply doesn't care, and has little concern for anything other than whatever she herself is enamored with at any particular moment—that Willa allows her thoughts to quietly tip-toe back to Martin. Wondering where he's gone and what explanation he has devised to explain to himself why it's been so easy to keep from coming back.

Asleep Without Dreaming

She imagines the details of the life he's most surely left them for, inventing and rearranging a myriad of details like an interior designer coordinating the perfect room, until she eventually grows bored with the art of pointless conjecture, reminding herself that it doesn't so much matter anymore what has become of him. Too much time has passed and he's been gone long enough now to render his abandonment complete. As it is, the mystery of his whereabouts is really only something to pull out at those times when Stella's eccentricities grow discomfortingly large and Willa finds it necessary to remind herself that she does in fact have another lifeline somewhere in the world.

A twig snaps somewhere nearby.

She sits perfectly still, her legs stalling in mid-swing. A terrifying vision of Norman Hitchcock creeping toward her through the woods instantly materializes behind the screen of her unblinking stare, her lungs tightly gripping her breath in an effort to suffocate the loud hammering of her heart.

Is he so bold? Would he really strut around Harriet's Bluff in broad daylight? Yes, of course. Why wouldn't he? If Norman Hitchcock has proven anything over the past months other than a talent for turning a spark into an inferno, it's that he's fearless.

The sound of footsteps snapping the dry grass draws closer, distinct in a way that at once chases off any fleeting hope or consideration that the sound might belong to a foraging animal.

Willa carefully eases her weight from the branch, struggling to cram her wet feet into dry sneakers as her brain scrambles wildly after an escape plan.

He's here. He's here ... right here.

"Oh...hey," Jesse stammers, halting in his steps, exchanging a startled expression as he steps from the trees and finds himself face to face with Willa's gaping stare.

"I was just—you scared me to death," she breathes in a deep exaggeration of relief, swallowing a knot of astonishment inside a nervous laugh.

"Sorry. There's never anyone here."

She hesitates a moment before answering, making an impossible effort to meet his eyes without seeing his injured face; the swelling and discoloration looking just as angry and garish as it had a day ago.

"Why didn't you show up at The Moonglow today?"

"I figured I wouldn't be able to avoid running into Omega."

"Except now she's mad because you didn't show up. You probably should've just gone in and told her what happened. I'm sure you're not the only person around here who ever had an accident."

He doesn't reply, moving only to anchor his fingers into the front pockets of his jeans.

"She asked me a bunch of questions when she saw me this morning, but I didn't tell her anything—just that I saw you working on the boats."

"What else did she say?"

She shifts her eyes from his face to focus on a small tear in the shoulder of his tee shirt, deliberately avoiding the discomforting intensity of his gaze.

"I don't know … just whether I saw you yesterday, how you looked, that sort of thing."

"How I looked?"

"Yeah. She said she heard something when she was at Veleda's."

"What did she hear?"

"She didn't say. Just that she heard something."

He doesn't answer.

"Jesse … what's going on?" Willa says, her voice careful and quiet in the same way she's learned to adjust her tone whenever she approaches the stray cats that come out from the woods behind the cabins looking for scraps, similarly afraid that he will immediately bolt should she speak too loudly or move too quickly.

"I probably shouldn't go back there is all."

Something dark and heavy breaks loose and plummets to the floor of her stomach. "Why? Why not? Because Omega Pearl Bodie listens to gossip?"

He looks away.

"What's the big deal anyway? Why don't you just tell her what happened? It seems pretty ridiculous to think you have to quit your job because you tripped over a stick." And even as she says it, Willa understands that it is more than that. That maybe the reason it sounds so absurd is because it isn't true.

He turns away and sits on the ground, slowly beginning to untie his sneakers.

"Jesse—"

"Do you want to go for a swim?" he says without lifting his eyes.

No, she doesn't. She doesn't like the water here. Doesn't like the weird, ominous color that so effectively conceals anything that might be here slithering just below the surface. Doesn't like the stagnant taste that leaks its way into her mouth and nose—the invisible but distinct residue it leaves in her hair and on her skin.

Neither speaks as Jesse stands to pull off his tee-shirt and moves to the river's edge. The water is no longer deep enough to dive from the shore and she watches as he wades in nearly to his waist, then tips forward and slices beneath the surface.

She holds her eyes on the dark skin of the barely rippled water, watching to see where he will resurface even as she bends to pull off one sneaker and then the other.

Willa emerges from the water several steps behind Jesse and quickly drops to a scraggly patch of grass combed over the river bank like the final stands of hair on a bald dome, purposeful to sit with her arms tightly wrapped around her bent knees. She always feels self-conscious rising from the water with wet clothes plastered to her skin in such a way as to accentuate embarrassing places, and she says a prayer that the last shimmers of sunlight are strong enough yet to dry her white cotton shirt—or at least to a point where the fabric is no longer transparent.

"Did you mean what you said about not going back to The Moonglow?"

"I don't know, maybe."

Willa shifts her gaze toward Jesse, now lying on his back, a bent arm draped across his eyes in a shield against the dying sun, the cut on his cheek and surrounding plum colored stain hauntingly visible on either side of his narrow wrist.

"Is it really just because of Omega?"

"I don't know. Maybe that's only part of it. Maybe it's just time for me to move on to something else."

Willa tightens the thin arms circling her knees. "It's just gossip, Jesse. It doesn't mean anything," she says, even while knowing that of course it does. It means something in the way he is attempting to hide his injured face; in the way he's purposely stayed away from The Moonglow and now talks about leaving altogether rather than simply explaining the accidental nature of his injury to Omega and so putting an end to it.

"It means something. It always means something."

"Is it true? About the branch—is that what really happened?" she says against her kneecap, so quietly she thinks it unlikely that he's even heard her.

"No," his reply comes at length, the single word tumbling inertly from his lips, but delivering the impact of a head-on collision.

"Jess—"

"I don't want to talk about it."

"Maybe if—"

"Not now—not ever."

And it isn't just the statement, but the way he says it that works so effectively to make her understand. Words that offer nothing, yet explain everything.

Does he feel her eyes studying him? She tries to look away but has forgotten the necessary mechanics. *One knee bent the other straight. His face still. One sun browned limb draped across his eyes like a wall intentionally placed to conceal his expression.*

She watches her hand reaching out to touch his wrist uncertainly, carefully sliding the arm away from his face. His navy eyes stare back, unblinking as her fingers feather across his bruised face—a hesitant breath of drifting air—her gaze traveling the ugly path of his injuries, willing him to tell her what has caused this, even while knowing that he won't. Either a sin or a secret he's chosen not to share.

He doesn't move away from her touch. His stare doesn't waver. The bottomless navy eyes stay with her as she presses her palm to his breastbone, holding firmly to the heartbeat racing beneath her fingers.

Seventeen

"I never said he wasn't a nice kid," Omega Pearl says, crossing her arms in a staunch barricade, fully outfitted to hold her ground. "I like him just fine, but I had no choice but to send him packing. That family has big problems and I sure as heck don't need that kind of trouble around here."

"My family has problems and you haven't fired us."

"You don't have problems, honey. You have a mother who happens to be a little eccentric and that's not the same thing."

"It's not fair to fire someone just because you don't like their relatives," Willa persists, losing the battle to keep the tones of growing desperation from leaking into her voice. "It's not like he did anything wrong. You can't just get rid of someone for having a stupid accident."

"Honey, you're fooling yourself if you think that business on his face had anything to do with an *accident*," Omega says, unfolding her arms and laying one thick limb along the sill, balancing her weight as she props a round magnifying mirror against the window screen and begins tweezing her wooly eyebrows, a shimmer of white sunlight reflecting from the silvery glass and shooting a wavering streak of ghostly light across the ceiling.

"Sometimes fairness just doesn't fit into the equation. All I know is that his old man is a hothead with a nasty attitude, and I sure as heck don't need to get myself mixed up in something I can't do anything about. Yes, I feel sorry for the boy, but that don't obligate me to involve myself in a mess that's none of my business."

How did this happen? The instant she heard Jesse's tires popping over the gravel in the lot outside the front office—grit and dust swirling up around his open windows like a dirty vapor—a flood of relief had swept in, settling her knotted insides and lifting her heart with the certainty that as long as he was here now, all the rest was destined to be sorted, repaired, and happily remedied.

Willa felt something tumble and roll inside when he stepped down from the cab: joy, exuberance, relief bouncing behind her ribs and against the walls of her chest like an avalanche of rubber balls. It had taken every workable atom to force herself to turn away on jelly legs and continue up the steps into the cabin where Stella was already in the midst of changing sheets. With an armload of fresh linens hugged tightly in her arms, Willa struggled to keep from turning back and racing after him.

But then all at once he was gone, the dust lifting around his tires even before the gritty particles have had the chance to settle from his arrival. An ominous cloud rolling out after him like plumes of smoke as he accelerated onto the highway.

"What happened? What did you say to him?"

"Not much of anything. He understands."

"Understands what? You can't just fire someone for no good reason. It's not right. His private life is no one's business. It's nobody's concern."

"It's not so private if the whole town knows about it. Don't tell me you people in California never heard of the term *common knowledge?*"

"Sure, only we call it *gossip*," Willa says, further losing the battle to pretend only minor interest.

Omega shakes her head, her tongue making a conciliatory clicking sound against the roof of her mouth. "Oh for Pete's sakes, girl, didn't I tell you? You've sweet on him, aren't you? Well, I warned you. I told you to watch out for yourself. Those quiet brooding types aren't that way by accident. They're hush-hush just so you won't hear the skeletons rattling around in the closet."

"I'm not sweet on anybody. I just don't think it's right to—
"

"Oh believe me, I know a thing or two about the lure of a pretty face. I'm a woman, not a eunuch. Why do you think I let him work here in the first place? I'd have to be dead, blind, or crazy not to notice a kisser like that. Not that I didn't feel sorry for him. That business with his mother was pretty dreadful as such things go."

Willa feels her eyes widen. *So that's the big secret.* "She's dead?"

"*Dead?* Is that what he told you?" Omega nearly smiles, pleased to think she's caught him in a lie, as if this in itself qualifies any lack of reasoning behind her monitions.

"No, I just thought when you said—he's never even mentioned her."

"Hum. Well I don't see how I'd blame him. It was plenty ugly. Makes sense he'd want to keep it under wraps," Omega breathes an exaggerated sigh as she turns her concentration from her brows and hobbles across the room, dropping into the chair behind the desk; the heavy wood frame groaning a complaint as she settles her weight.

"No question it was that father of his that drove her over the edge. Everybody knows it, but they wouldn't dare say it to his face. The last person you want to cross is Red Truman. That man's got a bite to rival a rattlesnake. Philandering hotshot with one hell of a nasty disposition. Far as I know he's still an office manager or something over at that insurance place on Elm Street, but it's hard to say, considering he spends most of his time down at the firehouse playing poker with his buddies. Fools all seem to think no one's figured out that the only reason they all signed-up as volunteers was so they'd have a place to congregate away from their wives. But it looks like the joke's on them now that they have real fires to contend with," Omega laughs, pulling open a drawer and rifling through the contents in search of her scratched plastic compact, flipping it open and tilting the mirror to examine her newly weeded brows.

Willa crosses her arms, pinching the insides of her elbows as she waits anxiously for Omega to continue.

"You'd just think that after what happened with the kid's mother—well it was just terrible. A hell of a mess. Sure, there are some around here that think she went too far, but that's easy to say when it's not your husband who's parking his shoes under another woman's bed."

"Wait, I don't get it. If she's not dead than what happened to her?"

Omega watches Willa's face, not quite successful in suppressing the inspired grin tickling the corners of her lips once she recognizes the opportunity to relay the details of a particularly shocking incident. "Well, no, she's not dead. She's alive and breathing just fine, though when you consider she's been in the state pen for the past ten years she might very well be wishing otherwise right now."

"She's in *jail?*" Willa's brows take a wild leap toward her hairline. It's true that Jesse's closed-book manner has grown an ocean of presumptions inside her head, as to some past injury or current wound existing in his life; but Omega's statement is altogether out in left field from anything Willa has jotted down on her own list of possibilities.

"If you ask me, it's Red Truman who should be in jail. He's the one that drove her to it. Just another good-looking son-of-a-bitch without a soul. Jerk messed around for years and that poor woman put up with it. If she turned the other cheek once, then she did a hundred times. Would probably still be if he didn't finally walk out and start another family not three blocks away. He never even bothered to divorce Marion before his little tramp started popping out the babies. She had the two little girls within a couple years of each other and then the next thing I heard she was expecting another.

"Of course Marion was devastated. She hardly ever left the house after he took off, and anytime I did happen to bump into her out at the market or the bank, she was wearing the same slacks and a wrinkled old shirt that looked like something Red must've left behind. That went on for quite some time, her falling apart all over the place, and then just like that—she seemed to snap out of it. Started combing her hair and wearing nice clothes again like nothing ever happened. It was as if she just woke-up one morning and decided she was done crying over that good-for-nothing. At least that's what everyone figured that morning she strode into town wearing a pretty new dress with matching shoes—would you believe I still remember those shoes. They were the cutest pumps. Prettiest shade of blue. Robin's egg, I guess you'd call it. You know the color I'm talking about? So pretty. Really the perfect shade for her coloring. Blondes just come to life when they wear blue.

"So anyways, she came strolling into Veleda's to have her hair done and was just thrilled over the moon when Veleda offered her a complimentary manicure. All us ladies were saying how wonderful it was that she was finally over that bum, straightening out her life and everything. At least that's what we thought when she walked out of Veleda's with her chin held high and a nice little spring in her step. I don't think it was even an hour later when the news came. I was still under the dryer in rollers."

"What news? What happened?"

"She walked into Red's office and tried to kill him, is what happened."

"For real? What did she do?"

"She had a handgun tucked right there inside her purse and she just waltzed up to his desk and pulled the thing out. She might've actually killed him, too, if it wasn't for the manicure. Veleda says if Marion hadn't been so concerned about smudging her polish Red never would've had the chance to dive across the desk and yank the gun out of her hand like he did."

Willa can only stare at Omega Pearl in disbelief. If not for the years of living alongside Stella's odd behaviors, she might think the bizarre tale more invention than truth; but as it is, the story seems wholly conceivable. *A woman scorned.* She's witnessed that same roiling anger in Stella, and she knows there are very few boundaries that such rage will not cross.

"The damnedest thing is the way the whole episode ended up turning Red into something of a celebrity around here. He actually—"

"But none of that has anything to do with Jesse. It's not about him. He didn't do anything wrong."

"Look, honey, you saw his face. Something's obviously going on over there. Something is definitely not right. Red Truman is a dangerous man."

"*Dangerous?* If that's what you really think why doesn't anyone do something?"

"Do what? What's anybody supposed to do? There aren't any heroes in Harriet's Bluff. Nobody wants to go up against a monster like Red Truman. That's a war that can't be won. The best thing for all of us is to just keep our noses out of places where they don't belong."

"Then why did you fire him? Why can't you just leave him alone to do his work and take care of himself?"

Willa waits for a response, but for once Omega doesn't have a ready answer.

"It's not as easy as all that. Nothing's ever so easy," Omega says at length.

Willa knows that if Stella happened to walk in right now and caught the way Willa is pressing Omega, she would be furious. Time and again she has warned Willa that she is not to say or do anything in Omega Pearl's presence that the woman might consider offensive.

"That big mouth cow is our bread and butter until we can blow out of this dump, so just smile, let her talk, and keep your mouth shut."

But, right now, Willa doesn't care, and she shoves the basket of cleaning supplies back inside the closet, slamming the door hard enough to make the contents rattle.

She watches for him everywhere, senses tuned in wait, anxious for even a glimpse of his battered truck parked along the streets of Harriet's Bluff or idling at a traffic light—his long fingers tapping the steering wheel, impatient for the color to change. But it is as though Jesse Truman has been swallowed into the unreachable infinity of space. There is no sign of him anywhere; no clue or teasing suggestion of his whereabouts.

And as another hollow day echoes long and lonely through her head, Willa feels her grip on hopeful expectation loosening, slipping through one finger, then another, until there is only her fear and the growing conviction that Jesse Truman has taken whatever treasure he's managed to amass over the past months and simply moved on.

Every afternoon, when Stella curls up like a cat and dozes, Willa slips away from The Moonglow and heads directly to the river. She trudges along the highway, cuts across the field of brittle grass, fervently prays that this will be the day when he will reappear. Like a delayed magician's trick, she will find him stroking across the dark tinted water or lying on the riverbank, wet, blue-jean-clad legs stretched out to dry in the sun, an arm protectively thrown across his eyes.

But just as it's been on every occasion since the afternoon of his expulsion from The Moonglow, the river lies before her, silent and undisturbed, the bank empty. Not so much as a single deteriorating footprint left behind to suggest that he's ever walked this corner of earth before. There is only the strange tale that Omega has so gleefully shared. The details of which continue to wind through Willa's head like a curse, even after she arrives at the decision not to accept what Omega has told her as absolute fact; resolved to skepticism until Jesse tells her otherwise. Because he will, she trusts, should they ever cross paths again, have to tell her the truth.

Eighteen

She doesn't understand how it is that people find it so effortless to leave her. To walk away as though they've never known her.

For a long time after Martin had gone off to live a new and improved life, Willa had let herself believe that his disappearance was somehow linked to those forces responsible for fulfilling the consequences of superstition. The burden of proof lying in the fact that he'd vanished thirteen days after her thirteenth birthday. (Although she later discovered that her math had in fact been incorrect, and it had actually been fourteen days after her birthday when he left.) She'd gone back to reviewing the particulars multiple times in her head, deciding that really, it was the simplicity of her father's actions on an otherwise unexceptional morning that so considerably added to the weight of his abandonment.

On the surface there was nothing unusual or notably premeditated in the way he skimmed through the newspaper between bites of buttered toast, or how he'd poured himself a second cup of coffee when he only ever drank one. No apparent significance that he forgot his paper bag lunch on the kitchen counter—a thick spread peanut butter sandwich and a bruised apple—since he remembered to kiss Stella on his way out the door as he always did when he left for work (the briefest grazing of his lips against the corner of her mouth), almost as if he hadn't already decided that he wasn't coming back.

Asleep Without Dreaming

It made no sense why he would simply drop his long-anticipated winnings in Stella's lap and disappear. What then had been the point of him shouldering the humiliation of losing for all those long months if in the end he had no intention of relishing his victory?

It had become customary, as much as expected, that when Martin at last emerged from the low slung building adjacent the track, his steps dragging like a man struggling to keep from collapsing under the weight of his own corpse, they'd known, even before he reached the car, that he'd once more lost everything he'd gone in with.

It had become a familiar pattern, the sort that felt destined to repeat unaltered for as long as there were horses to run and gamblers to dream. So that, even now, Willa can effortlessly retrieve the image of his jaunty stride that afternoon, the immediate indicator that something had changed.

Having caught only the briefest glimpse of Martin leaving the building, and so failing to witness his buoyant approach as Willa had, Stella purposely turned her grim stare to the window opposite, steeling herself for the accustomed ride home in angry silence. Even after the car door opened and closed behind him with a conquering thud, Stella made no acknowledgment of his return other than to offer him the back of her head and a granite-set slice of her profile.

"Here," he'd said, dropping a fat roll of bills into Stella's lap. She swung her face around to stare at him, no less incredulous than if he'd climbed into the car with two heads and a tail.

"YOU WON! You actually won something?" Willa squealed, bobbing up against the back of the seat like a cork on water, straining for a glimpse of his treasure.

"Sure as heck did," he grinned, smug satisfaction racing across his face like spilled liquid.

"How much is it?" Willa breathed, unable to coax her voice above an awed whisper as she stared at the thick roll in Stella's hand, holding her breath for fear of blowing the fragile winnings away through the open car window as her mother carefully uncoiled the bills with the particular care customarily afforded the handling of heirloom china or glass.

"One ... thousand ... dollars," Martin announced with slow deliberation even before Stella had finished counting.

"I can't believe you—" Stella began, recovering her voice.

"Believe it, baby. Maybe you just need to have a little trust in the old man once in awhile," he added, the enormous grin still there, stretched across his face as he backed from the parking spot, an expression Willa had so rarely seen on his person that she has never forgotten it.

It was impossible for Willa to think beyond what she expected would be Stella's top priority purchase with Martin's winnings—a trip to the big grocery store in Ephrata, where she would amass boxes and bags of extravagant treats that looked, smelled, and tasted like the delectable fare Willa was forever studying and invisibly digesting within the pages of Dee's hand-me-down magazines. Abundant goodies eons removed from the boring staples that had carried them through the months of famine (day-old bread, beans, peanut butter, bologna ...) while they waited for Martin to conquer his losses.

But instead of steak, potatoes, and the seven-layer chocolate cake vividly created and wondrously prepared in Willa's imagination, Stella returned home several hours after leaving the house conspicuously unencumbered by the anticipated groceries, and instead carting a sizable collection of large colorful bags, all apparently necessary for carrying her bounteous selection of new outfits and matching shoes.

"Oh, stop your whining," Stella said, pooh-poohing away the notion of something as uninspired as food when Willa complained that there wasn't a single grocery bag tucked in amongst the array of fancy department store bags. "Just sit down over there on the sofa and I'll show you everything," Stella instructed, right then stripping down to her underwear in the middle of the living room and proceeding to model each outfit, refusing to change into the next until Willa had dutifully admired each expertly matched ensemble to her mother's satisfaction.

As impossible as it had always been for Willa to comprehend the mind or madness behind her mother's erratic behaviors, she was nevertheless swift to arrive at the conclusion that the impromptu fashion show had nothing whatsoever to do with any particular need or desire to hear Willa's opinion. As always, Willa was merely the audience, the obliging spectator whose necessary role was to admire what Stella herself already did.

She tried to imagine just where her mother intended to wear the low-cut pink ruffled blouse, the snug-fitting peacock blue dress, the leopard print heels, or any of the other garish items Stella continued to pull from the bags, articles as copiously impractical as they were unnecessary for sitting on the sofa to paint her toenails or smoke at the kitchen table with Dee.

But then maybe that was the point. Maybe Stella's actual goal was to look like someone who belonged inside a life altogether different from the one she currently occupied.

The afternoon was long gone and put away by the time Stella eventually tired of prancing back and forth along her imaginary runway and concluded her production. Her arms filled with the various items she'd tossed over the arm of the chair and across the back of the couch while in the midst of repeated costume changes, she carried the collection down the hall to her room and closed the door behind her.

In the weeks after his leaving, once the full comprehension arrived that Martin wasn't merely a missing person, but rather a deliberate runaway, Willa chewed every one of her nails down to the tender quick, watching Stella for some elusive opening that would allow even a fleeting glimpse into the tightly nailed crux of her emotions. And yet there was nothing about Stella's countenance which proved readable. It was almost as if she'd climbed inside her skin and pulled whatever she was feeling in after her, purposeful in leaving nothing exposed for scrutiny.

"I'm taking the bus over to Ephrata," Stella announced one morning as Willa was leaving for school. "I'll be back this afternoon."

"What for?" Willa said, stuffing a hastily assembled cheese sandwich into her paper lunch bag and throwing a brief glance over her shoulder, noting Stella's plain tweed skirt and modest blouse and immediately wondering why she'd reverted to her old wardrobe rather than taking the opportunity to wear one of her colorful new costumes.

"There's something I need to take care of," was all she offered in place of an explanation as she brushed past Willa on her way out the door.

It was late in the afternoon when Willa stomped up the steps onto the back porch, awkwardly nudging the screen door open with her elbow. She didn't bother to brush her feet on the molting straw mat askew just within the threshold before tracking a dusty trail across the kitchen linoleum. Wiping her feet was an altogether pointless effort, she figured, since the floor hadn't been washed in months and wasn't likely to receive attention anytime soon. She dumped her school books on the table with a heavy thud, undecided whether the pile would sit undisturbed until morning when she gathered it all up again. Or would she make an effort to complete at least some of her assignments, silently grousing over the fact that the school day rarely ended with the dismissal bell, but instead carried long into the evenings in the form of chapter reviews, reports, projects, and reading assignments.

Mostly, Willa only did her school assignments out of boredom. On especially bleak evenings, when the only alternative to algebra problems and diagramming sentences was to stare at the peeling wallpaper and dusty sills, fervently wishing herself into life on another planet. It might've been different if the house wasn't always so dark and gloomy—like a funeral home minus the company of mourners—if walking through the door after school entailed finding Stella in the midst of meal preparation, instead of sorting dried-up flowers on sheets of newspaper spread out on the kitchen table.

And speaking of Stella, where was she? The house, Willa all at once noticed, was eerily silent, the sort of quiet that was so loud it felt like shouting. She turned her eyes to the doorway opening into the living room, her spine instantly stiffening when she caught sight of Stella sitting in a chair staring out at nothing. The blanched expression stretched taut across her mother's features speaking volumes of what she had yet to say out loud.

"The only reason I even put up with him going to that damn track was because I didn't trust him," Stella said, without shifting her eyes to where Willa stood silently in the doorway, her voice scratching over her teeth like bulk lead dragged on a chain. "I figured if he was gonna throw every dime we have down the toilet, I'd best be there to make sure he was at least blowing it on dumb-ass horses and not whores."

Willa held to the doorframe, at once afraid, certain that Stella's swelling agitation was in fact leading to some definite place, waiting silently as her mother lifted the near empty glass of amber liquid precariously nestled in her lap.

"A thousand dollars he throws at me—*A THOUSAND STINKING DOLLARS.* Big damn stinkin' deal. A thousand lousy dollars doesn't mean crap when he keeps ten for himself," she spat the words like a mouthful of poison darts aimed at some fatal target as her hand again carried the glass to her lips, but paused without drinking. The glass suddenly hurtled across the room, the liquid rising in a golden arc as it hit the wall.

"What're you—"

"Oh yeah, that's right, the rat bastard kept TEN for himself."

"But how? That's impossible. That can't be right. He handed you—"

"What's impossible is that I was such an idiot. He never willingly gave me a dollar in his life. That alone should've made me suspicious when he finally did. I had a feeling something wasn't right. I knew it. I damn well knew it, but I let myself play the part of the dimwit fool anyway."

Willa sees the molten flame of emotion building up behind Stella's eyes—hurt, anger, betrayal—all there knotted together like a fist ready to spring.

"ACCOUNT CLOSED, is what that witch at the bank said. Account freaking closed," she punched her fist hard against her thigh. "He opened an account just long enough to hide the money until he could beat it out of here."

"But …"

"He obviously didn't want me finding it under his pillow."

"How did you even know about the bank?"

"I'm not stupid. Not that kind of stupid."

"Maybe it's a mistake. When he comes back he'll probably—"

"For cripes sakes, Willa, get your head out of the sand and wake the hell up. He's GONE and he's not coming back. This isn't an accident, it's one million percent premeditated. All those years he wasted sitting at that damn machine making lousy pencils and it turns out the rat bastard was obviously scheming how to get out of here the whole time," she rages, pummeling the tops of her legs with her closed fists like someone making every effort not to cry. "Lousy bastard. Damn lousy bastard."

Over the next several days Stella's hurt and anger unfurled in a flux of wordless, yet deliberate actions. Her closed, but distinctly simmering rage, reaching out with both hands to yank the sparse wardrobe of limp cotton shirts left hanging in Martin's side of the closet from misshapen wire hangers and hurling them across the room to tent atop a tangle of mismatched socks she'd upended onto the floor from his dresser drawer.

Next, she'd rummaged through the coat closet in search of his winter jacket, gloves, hats, boots … anything previously overlooked in her determination to exorcise his traitorous existence. Books, glasses, keys, mail addressed to Martin that had accumulated in his absence, all tossed onto the growing monument rising up from her bedroom floor.

Willa watched Stella's frenetic ritual in careful silence, fearful of trespassing into the sphere of her mother's roiling anger and risking the enraged blackness being turned onto herself. Instead she held to her distance. Fully aware, but pretending not to notice days later when Stella settled cross-legged on the floor beside the pile she'd amassed, and proceeded to hack at the snarl of Martin's clothing and abandoned possessions with a pair of kitchen shears until no scrap remained that was larger than a postage stamp.

And not until Stella had completed her maniacal task did Willa see that it wasn't merely his leftover wardrobe and personal effects that lay shredded and destroyed in the trail of debris strewn across the dull wood floor. Also there, tangled amongst the plain cotton scraps of her father's massacred shirts, wooly bits of socks, and microscopic crumbs of paper, was a distinctly vivid collection of torn strips suspiciously reminiscent of the bright shades and florid prints of Stella's extravagant new wardrobe.

Barbara Forte Abate

Nineteen

The air outside feels stiff with the static of an unspent
storm, the atmosphere agonizingly still with the wait for
rain that is unlikely to come.
The cats are yowling, six or seven winding around Willa's
ankles in tight circles as she stands out behind the cottage,
shaking dry food into an eclectic assemblage of aluminum pie
plates and empty plastic food containers that she keeps hidden
in the narrow crawl space dug out beneath a rear outside wall.

For months Stella has berated her for feeding the strays that
scratch at the dust like farmyard chickens raking for bugs and
cry on the porch even after Stella has shooed them away with a
broom. Yet Willa pays little attention to her mother's
complaints.

"They're not doing any harm. They're just hungry. I don't
see why you even care."

"I care because that fatso in the office will have a canary if
she sees you enticing them to come around here. They're not
even real cats. They've been wild too long to be anything but
a nuisance."

"I don't care. I feel sorry for them. They're starving."

"For cripes sakes, Willa, would it kill you to listen to me
even once? It's always the same damn argument with you.
We'll see how you change your tune when one of the filthy
things bites you and gives you rabies."

Lately however, Stella hasn't bothered with her usual
complaints, her head apparently tuned to another channel and
focused on other things. Nevertheless, Willa takes the

precaution of feeding the animals only after her mother has gone to bed or leaves the cottage for any length of time, being sure to return the bag of dry pellets and the assortment of feeding dishes to their hiding spot once the cats have inhaled every last particle of food.

Now, sitting behind the cottage in a sadly listing lawn chair, watching the cats as they forcefully nudge faces and bodies in an effort to claim the last of the pellets, Willa stares out across the scruffy patches of dead and dying grasses scribbled around the buildings. The thunder continues to rumble in the distance, though further off now, the sound rolling away like an enormous boulder tumbling downhill. And still the rain doesn't come.

"If I'd stepped on the damn thing you'd be having a screaming fit," Stella swears, tossing a black transistor radio toward Willa as the screen door claps shut behind her.

"Where'd this come from?"

"You tell me."

"I dunno, it's not mine."

"Uh, huh, right. And I'm the Queen of England come for a cup of tea. Frankly, Willa, as long as I don't get a hysterical summons from that cow in the office screaming that someone's had their cabin robbed by the cleaning lady, I don't care where it came from. I'm just letting you know that if you're gonna leave your crap lying around on the steps where people are supposed to walk, then don't dare bitch about it when it turns up busted. Bad enough I have to dodge those damn cats every time I walk out the door."

Stella turns and blows off down the hallway to the bathroom, and a moment later the sound of water can be heard running in the sink. Willa studies the instrument in her hand, clicking the dial to switch it on and off. The scratchy fuzz of static assures that it's in working order. She's never owned a radio of any kind, yet this one looks strangely familiar. She runs her fingernail along a crack in the hard plastic casing, newly certain that she's seen it before.

"It's not mine," Willa says when Stella comes back into the room and flops onto her unmade bed like a deflating rag doll.

"Just like those diseased animals running around using the yard for a toilet aren't yours," Stella scoffs, reaching for her cigarettes and a magazine she's leafed through at least a dozen times already.

Willa continues to stare at the radio in her hand, as if expecting it to speak. She has definitely seen it before, or at least one very much like it. Whether or not it actually is one and the same, she can't absolutely say. After all, it isn't as if cracked black transistor radios are especially uncommon in the world, and surely there are plenty of people in Harriet's Bluff aside from Jesse Truman who own one.

Even so, that doesn't explain how or why it has landed on her doorstep. *Unless it is a gift.* Unless Jesse has been here and left this for her because ... because why? She can't really say.

It takes Willa nearly twice as long to walk into town if she follows the railroad tracks through the woods, but it's the only route affording any real relief from the press of unrelenting heat simmering over the landscape. Besides, it isn't as if there is anywhere she needs to get to in a hurry. With Jesse gone, there is no longer purpose in Willa keeping to the highway with the hope that he will pull up alongside her in his nervously chattering truck, calling out the window with an invitation to the river, or a wild chase after Norman's latest fire.

She's all but stopped caring about or even remembering the warnings that have previously worked to keep her decisively removed from the woods on her back-and-forth treks into town; namely Omega's frequent retelling of some long ago incident involving a mentally deficient drifter who'd walked the train tracks into Harriet's Bluff and come across a little boy playing alone in the woods—the particulars of which Omega thankfully left un-described. Although the heinous possibilities crowd into Willa's imagination every time she finds herself tempted to brush aside the barely concealed innuendos of gross depravity and tragedy punctuated by the exaggerated dance of Omega's heavy brows, and breaches the darkly poisonous sanctum contained beyond the tree line *just this once.*

Because now, with Willa's own concerns tightly ensnared in things far more real and closer in distance to the importance of her own life, Omega's caveats have lost potency in the way of those stories that have been delivered a time too many. No longer inspiring the consideration generally afforded tales of sobering caution, they have instead slipped several notches into the realms of intriguing fabrication—told and retold for no particular purpose other than as a sordid brand of entertainment.

It is nearly August and the months of hot and rainless days have turned even the simplest activities into impossible endeavors. And if not for the fact that everything about The Moonglow has become especially ugly and increasingly unbearable, Willa doubts she would so wantonly spend her flagging stores of energy trekking into town nearly every afternoon the way she does, in search of someone who is never there.

Except that now, ever since arriving at the conclusion that it is simply ridiculous to continue to heed Omega's assuredly overblown and unproven warnings to avoid the woods, the journey has become a good deal less sufferable. The leafy rooftop graciously buffering the glare of sunlight as she follows the railroad tracks laid through the trees along a crumbling bed that leads directly into Harriet's Bluff.

Yet even then, there is a certain hour, late in the day, with the shadows reaching long and deep, when the dense stand of woods feels particularly ominous and thick beneath its veil of weighty silence, stirring Willa to quicken her pace as she shuffles along the abandoned ties. A distinct chill sweeps across her hairline, a reminder that while the alleged transient of Omega's tale may indeed be long extinct, there is now the very real possibility that Norman Hitchcock is secreted here somewhere—is right now watching from behind a nearby tree like the Big Bad Wolf waiting for Little Red Riding Hood to come skipping along the path with her basket of goodies.

She knows it's ridiculous even as she allows the notion to spread inside her head, scoffing out loud at her irrational fears as she switches on the transistor radio she's carried with her ever since its appearance days earlier. Excepting that now, turning the dial with her thumb, there is only the faraway rise and fall of fading voices coming through the speaker. She clicks it off with an irritated sigh, guessing that the batteries are well on their way to being dead by now.

Sunlight filters down through the trees, speckling the ground in spilling yards of delicate golden lace. Willa pauses for an instant, hearing the sound of scuffling somewhere nearby—dry leaves and broken sticks shifting to suggest an animal rooting through the underbrush. She holds still a moment longer, then continues on, satisfied that a wild four-legged creature is responsible for the disturbance, rather than a domesticated two-legged one.

Back in Hoosick Falls, Willa had loved roaming the woods, spending entire afternoons wandering in her private world; making dandelion chains, peeling bark from broken sticks scattered on the forest floor until they were fully shorn and wonderfully smooth, all the while singing out-of-tune medleys of her favorite songs, anything other than gathering the ramp that Stella had sent her to gather for supper. Although Willa had never been particularly fond of the wild leeks, she'd quickly grown to despise them completely once Stella had taken to cooking the awful stuff nearly every night.

"I've pretty much had it with all the damn complaining, Willa. It's free and it's nutritious. The human body isn't designed to run on a diet of toast and hotdogs. A person has to put taste aside every once in awhile and force down some vegetables, too."

"There's no way those weeds are a vegetable. And besides, how can something that smells like cat pee even be edible?" Willa said time and again, wrinkling her nose against the dreadful odor rising from the pot boiling on the stove.

"If you don't like it, Miss High and Mighty, you're more than welcome to go out and find something more accommodating of your royal tastes."

And she had. Had in fact gone about finding something else all summer long—late at night as she crept through the neighboring gardens in search of ripening produce; filling first her pockets and then her hands with green beans, sweet peas, tomatoes, tender young carrots, baby cucumbers, and glossy green peppers.

Afterward, returning from yet another of her nighttime raids, she swore to both herself and God—on the chance that he was listening—that this was the end of it. This was the last time she'd cave to temptation and invade the fruit of another's labor. Promising that from that moment onward, she would fill herself with the horrible smelling ramp and never again resort to thievery.

And there was such immediate relief in her resolve to turn honest and sin no more, it was only with the deepest remorse that she would again find herself crouched between the lush rows of bushy tomato plants and green beans in a neighbor's garden, her fingers quaking as she filled the pockets of her blouse and silently promised that it *absolutely, positively, was the very last time*. But she'd been so hungry, so nearly starved, that she knew better than to trust herself when she once again vowed never to steal another tomato for as long as she lived.

Now, Willa slackens her pace, eyes drifting to her shuffling feet as she considers the dismal possibilities available for passing the remainder of the afternoon and coming evening. She can't remember a time when she's ever felt so lonesome and forlorn—an echo tumbling though space—though maybe it's just that the present stands out sharper in her mind than the past. Jesse's gone. Really truly gone. Even Stella has taken on distance. They barely speak to each other, chipping out a hole in their mutual shroud of silence only when absolutely necessary, though even then, it is all but impossible to execute a conversation that doesn't threaten to turn and bite them both.

Most afternoons, once she's finished with her housekeeping duties, Stella slams into the cabin and collapses onto her bed, spine propped against the headboard, taking quick drags on endless cigarettes as her eyes spit unspoken grievances into the air hovering around her. Occasionally she reaches for the slender notebook she now keeps propped against the lamp on her bedside table, scribbling furiously for several intense moments before slapping the paper cover shut.

Though curious as to what Stella is so diligently recording within the accumulating pages, Willa will not risk even the briefest glimpse. Long time experience assuring her that it is wiser to remain ignorant of the details pertaining to Stella's potential schemes and instead hope that whatever is germinating inside her head will eventually lose necessary oxygen and die away.

Her thoughts jerk back to the present as an easily recognizable odor wafts across her senses. *Cigarette smoke?*

She quickens her steps, eyes skimming the surroundings as the smell grows increasingly pungent. Burning. Something is definitely burning ... but where? There's nothing here. Nothing other than trees and the things they discard— branches, empty nut shells, curled brown leaves scattered along the ground like pages torn from an ancient book.

And all at once she sees it—a wispy curl of grey smoke snaking up from the forest floor just ahead. Her steps halt in mid-stride as she stares at the ghostly apparition, momentarily uncertain as to the full nature of what it is she is seeing. Her eyes swing away from the trees, sweeping the ground to land on a circle of newborn sparks shyly licking the forest bed of broken sticks and crumbled leaves. A knot of panic rockets up past her ribcage to lodge in her throat even as she sprints forward, a force she hasn't known she possessed propelling her jellied limbs into action.

The fire is freshly seeded, but swelling quickly, a neat wheel of ragged flames spilling outward and rapidly multiplying as they greedily consume the abundant wealth of natural fuel littering the forest floor.

"Oh my, god—oh my god ... " she breathes without taking in air, too frightened even to scream, frantic with a sense of necessary action, though having no concept of what that action should be. There is nothing here—nothing she can use to drown or smother the rapidly climbing flames. No light bulb blinks awake in her stalled thoughts other than the intuition to stamp the emerging blaze to immediate death.

The heat is everywhere, nipping at her legs and outstretched hands, snapping up behind her and breathing along her scalp, her lungs choking on the acrid smoke weeping into her eyes, nose, and mouth as she attempts to kick earth over the amplifying ring of fire.

And she knows it is hopeless. The flames are reproducing far too fast for her to conquer. Her antics serve little purpose other than to increase the risk of setting herself on fire.

A *whoosh* of scorched air sends flames running up the trunk of a nearby tree and out along the spindly arms of its lower branches. And it is impossible to move as she stares into the rapidly growing inferno with unblinking eyes, violently shaking her head to clear her vision of the horrifying scene exploding around her like warfare, unable to see or hear anything beyond the rush and roar of fire chasing hard on the tail of panicked fear racing inside her head.

Go. Run. Move. Don't stand here like an idiot. Run!

She struggles to scream, but her mouth refuses to unhinge. She is standing like a pillar of salt in the middle of a hundred acres of kindling, smothering inside the throbbing pulse of rapidly moving flame and yet she cannot make a sound.

There is another deep whooshing sound, louder than the last, as a living chain of fire sweeps up through the trees. Leaping tongues of flame crackle and spit along the forest floor in every direction. And still she can't force her legs to move as she frantically tries to remember the elusive code that will unlock her knees and propel her away from the steady rumblings of devouring fire.

She thinks she hears sirens screaming to cover the distance. And she knows that even if the sound is real, even if the cavalry is truly coming, they will not arrive in time to save her. Not from the fire and not from Norman Hitchcock. Because he's here. She can feel him watching. Watching her helpless entrapment inside the cage of his fire and making no attempt to save her.

And then somehow the trance is broken and she is in flight, spinning on her heel, running hard and fast, focusing beyond the smoke to the precise spot where the line of, as yet, untouched trees begins and ends. And she doesn't look back for fear of what she'll see there. Terrified of what she is certain to find in pursuit.

If she runs another step, her insides will implode. She can feel the smoke still trapped within her lungs, a sharp stab of pain searing her chest each time she reaches for breath. And if Norman Hitchcock has held to his pursuit, Willa knows she hasn't the strength to save herself.

She slows to an awkward lope which gradually slackens to an uneven walk, denying herself even a single backward glance, clenching her teeth against the terrifying certainty that she will feel Norman Hitchcock's fingers closing around her neck at any moment.

The wave of oncoming sirens sounds close enough now to suggest that they've reached the fire. She takes a hungry gulp of smokeless air, staggering forward when her knees attempt to buckle. Should she go back and explain what happened? Tell them what she saw, though really she hasn't seen anything but the fire. At least tell them how she tried to stifle the flames?

She folds nearly in half, pressing her hands against her knees to keep from collapsing, swallowing the air in exaggerated gasps for several minutes as she attempts to ease the sharp stitch stabbing into her side. She lifts her head slowly, instantly pausing. There is something there—partly obscured by a colony of thick tree trunks—a building of some sort? She throws a sweeping glance across her shoulder, and while there are no obvious signs of Norman Hitchcock creeping up to throttle her senseless, her heartbeat continues its steady canter inside her chest.

Straightening, Willa takes a teetering step forward, then another, fear and curiosity drawing her toward whatever is there hugged within the trees.

The entire wood frame structure has a definite tilt to the north and she wonders if it's even safe to enter. Holding to the threshold, her eyes scan the shack's single room, taking in the old mattress pushed into a corner, the three-legged table leaning drunkenly against one wall, three small windows with broken panes—the few remaining shards of splintered glass sticking up in a way that makes her think of monster teeth.

"What are you doing here?"

Willa presses a palm to her mouth, stifling a scream even as she feels her breath whoosh out past her lungs. She spins around, startled eyes landing abruptly on the figure partially obscured by the open door she's only just passed through, certain that her heart would've stopped altogether if not for the fact that it is pumping too frantically to cease so quickly.

"Jesse! You scared me to death," she says, attempting a weak smile, though she is still too shaken for the expression to succeed.

"Yeah, same here. How did you find me?"

The slight edge of hostility in his voice instantly tilts her off balance, her mood taking an immediate shift from relief to uncertainty.

"Find you? I wasn't looking for you," she says, the words feeling unexpectedly sharp in her mouth. "The woods are on fire—everything is burning. I tried to put it out, but it spread so fast ... it's just ... everything ... it's all burning. I heard sirens, but I couldn't just stand there and wait. He's here. Norman. He's here in the woods."

His face is obscured in partial shadow, yet Willa is certain she sees something resembling skepticism pass over his features. She remains rooted in the doorway as he strides across the creaky floor to sit on the edge of the mattress, leaning his back against the wall.

"You saw him?"

"Well, no, but it's obvious he only just lit it a minute before I got there. It was still kind of small. I thought I could stomp it out."

"Then you're lucky you didn't end up a piece of bacon."

She feels his eyes watching as she crosses to sit on the edge of the mattress. Can he sense her discomfort...her terrible uncertainty? She's catalogued dozens of questions over the past several days in her search for him, but she can no longer read them. Her mind is too densely clouded by the lingering terror of fire and smoke which has rendered everything previously relevant as wholly non-consequential.

"It's very strange how every empty building I've ever been in has had a dirty old mattress in the corner. Where do all these mattresses come from?" she says in a strained attempt at lightness, making a deliberate push past the crush of discomforting air circling in a dense flock between them.

He surprises her by flashing the fleeting curve of a smile. "I don't know, but you're right, it's weird," he says, his solemn expression quickly returning.

Willa pulls up her legs, resting her chin on her bent knees, the movement all at once making her aware of the a sharp ache throbbing a fiery trail along the scorched skin of her calves.

She swallows a wince, dropping her eyes to stare at her sneakers. What was previously dingy white canvas is now black with smoke and soot, the rubber soles permanently warped along the toe and instep, hideously disfigured from her frantic efforts to stomp out the flames.

"Jesse ..." she lifts her head. "What are you doing here? This isn't ... you don't live here do you?"

"No. I just like to come here sometimes to be by myself."

She tilts her chin, staring at the ceiling where a thin oblong of sky peeks through a hole in the roof, dusting the room with pale shimmery light. She waits a moment longer before shifting her gaze back to his face.

"This is why I haven't seen you around. You've been here." Statements, not questions.

"I have a lot of time on my hands since Omega sent me packing."

"Did you hear anything? Did you smell the smoke?" Willa says, tucking a drifting strand of hair behind one ear.

He lifts his shoulders in a disinterested shrug. "These woods are a couple hundred acres. I hear something every time I come here. There's always a woodchuck or some other animal scratching around under the stoop or shuffling in the leaves."

"It could've been Norman Hitchcock scratching around. He must've just set that fire when I came along. Maybe it wasn't even an accident how I came across it like that. Maybe he was just sitting there waiting for someone to walk by so he could tease them."

"You think this is about teasing people?"

"Maybe," Willa bristles at the note of incredulity in his tone. "You don't think it's a big tease to start a fire right under someone's nose?"

"No. I think it's insane."

"Right. And insane people love games don't they?"

"Maybe no one started it. Maybe it just happened."

"I thought the spontaneous combustion theory was dead."

"It does happen sometimes."

"Not in Harriet's Bluff."

"Why wouldn't it?"

"Because this town has its very own homicidal maniac named Norman Hitchcock to do the job nature never intended."

"He isn't crazy—he's angry."

"Same difference."

"I've been around angry people my whole life. Angry and crazy are not the same things."

"Are you?"

"What?"

"Angry or crazy?"

"I don't know," he answers, his voice all at once quiet.

"Do you trust me, Jesse?" she says after a moment, the question barreling past her general penchant for caution, because it is altogether impossible not to think of all those things Omega has told her, especially when he has never cared to share anything of such importance himself.

She waits for his answer in the murky gloom of the crooked old shack, her mind holding to the incredible verity that he is even here, barely an arm's length spanned between them where they sit like castaways adrift on the island of a musty old mattress. And she knows that in another place at some other time she would surely lack the necessary courage to ask the question. But now, alone in the lengthening shadows of a place that feels distinctly intimate despite his distance, her words lay before him like a newly opened invitation.

"I don't know ... should I?" If he senses her crushing disappointment in his responses he gives no indication.

Willa straightens her legs in front of her, then quickly folds them back, the brief movement chasing the throbbing lope of her singed flesh from a trot to a gallop. She knots her fingers tightly around her bent knees, biting down hard on the wince of pain immediately rising to her lips.

"If you have to ask, then I guess you just answered the question," Willa says, stung by his words and making no attempt to hide it. "Is that why you lied that day when I asked you what happened to your face? You're not honest because you don't think I can be trusted?"

"It has nothing to do with trust. Some things are just better left alone," he pauses, staring up at the ceiling for a long moment before continuing. "Some things just feel worse when you talk about them, so you don't. It's no more complicated than that."

"That might be true when you're dealing with someone like Omega Pearl, but it's supposed to be different with your friends."

"Friends? Are we? Are we friends?"

"I thought … I guess I thought we were. If not friends, then *something.*"

"Something what?"

Heat rushes over her face, melting deep into the roots of her hair. The far-off notes of a bird's innocent trilling loop through the grey silence, the sound strangely mocking in the harsh wake of his pointed question.

"What am I doing here? Why did I even come to this place?" she says, though she hasn't intended to speak her thoughts out loud. The words, stiff and tight, crash against the brittle quiet, scattering it around them like shards of splintered glass.

Again, he hesitates before answering. Always the hesitation.

"I don't know."

"Yeah, okay, well look, I have to go. I should tell someone what happened. At least what I saw," she says, unwilling as she is ill-prepared to sit through another span of stilted conversation and awkward silence.

"They might think you started it yourself."

"*Me?* That's crazy. I'll tell them exactly what happened. How I was walking through the woods and saw the fire."

"What makes you think they'll believe you?"

She stares at him incredulous. "Why wouldn't they?"

"Why should they?"

"Because it's the truth, that's why."

"No one around here really knows you. You're a stranger."

Willa doesn't answer. What can she say? Maybe he's right.

"I have to go," she utters, deliberately avoiding his eyes. There are certain things she wants to say, but won't. Because, somehow, no matter how carefully she phrases her words to Jesse Truman, there remains a certain neediness that she consistently fails to conceal.

"Willa ..." he says, so quiet she might not have heard him had she not been listening so hard for his voice. "I don't know if it's such a good idea to be my friend."

And even before his fingers reach out to touch her wrist, she feels them on her skin. Lightly at first, then tightening, so that all at once she is folding into him—feels his mouth fall against her ear.

Something else then ... if not friends ... then something.

His kiss is neither sudden nor unexpected, just necessary. And even before he presses his lips against her mouth, his very closeness sends her senses madly spiraling like a vortex caught inside a blue and silver dream. His touch intensifies when she doesn't pull away. His kiss bringing words like *eternity* and *forever* rocketing through her mind.

She tastes the pungent odor of wood smoke that clings to her skin and hair, and is now on his lips; the burnt aroma absorbed into the soft fibers of his tee-shirt pressing against her. His very essence wraps around her like the fingers of a closing fist.

There are things she needs to ask him, and she senses that he knows this. But not now. Her queries can wait. But this, all of this, cannot—the sweet river of kisses that goes on and on—because nothing is more important. Nothing more urgent or essential. The rest of the world vanishes like a melting fog. The whole of existence blessedly extinct beyond the crooked door and broken windows.

Twenty

It is sinister in a way that makes looking at it thoroughly unnerving, even as it draws the eye and holds it steady. Acre upon acre of blackened skeletal remains—silent and dead beneath an unflinching paper white sky, once enormous tree trunks whittled away by the flames to the improbable thinness of charred toothpicks, lush plant life and living creatures gone as if they've never been.

"Looks like they'll have to come up with a new theory to explain where Norman's been hiding since it apparently isn't in the woods," Jesse says, downshifting, swerving to avoid hitting a displaced and confused-looking woodchuck sitting in the road ahead.

Willa nods, stealing a glance at the long fingers loosely wrapped around the knob of the stick shift, wrestling against the urge to reach out and lay her hand over his, still too shy with the newness of all that is opened up between them to lend action to the unexpected crush of impulses alighting in her mind with the regularity of breathing.

Incredibly, wonderfully, the afternoon in the burning woods has changed everything. No longer does she feel inclined to drag through her work at The Moonglow nurturing her heartache like an open wound, dejectedly wondering where Jesse is and whether he is thinking of her even a fraction of how she unceasingly thinks of him.

While she hoped for it, she hadn't dared expect that the very next day would find him here waiting, his truck pulled over and idling just down the road from The Moonglow. Her heartbeat leaps forward to keep pace with her quickening steps as she all but skips toward the truck loitering on the shoulder of the highway.

"Hey," he says, his voice endearingly shy and uncertain when Willa pauses beside the open passenger window.

"Hey."

"Want a ride?"

"Sure. Thanks," she says. Polite. Proper.

"So, where are you headed?" he asks as she settles herself onto the seat beside him and pulls the door shut.

"Nowhere really," Willa answers, wanting to smile easily, maybe even a bit flirtatiously as she says it. Yet she hesitates to follow through, unsure in the way of someone wholly inexperienced with the behaviors of love and romance. Her only true confidence rests in the surety of how much she longs to possess every portion of this newfound something.

Mostly they go to the river. There's never anyone there. Though one time they are surprised to spy an old man fishing from the far bank. They'd felt decidedly uneasy beneath the man's wary stare in this place where they are so accustomed to solitude, and neither Willa nor Jesse care to venture into the water that day. Both are vastly relieved when the intruder fails to return on subsequent days…grateful that no one does.

The end of summer is fast approaching. By now the river has taken on the appearance of something scarcely alive; its flat dark stillness lending to the illusion of a bottomless crevice where water bleeds up from the earth rather than down from the sky.

Even then, Willa readily follows Jesse into the water on those occasions when they come to swim, settled in the knowledge that afterwards they will lie on the bank, eyes closed and fingers touching, linked together in a ligature of companionable silence.

More often than she would dare to admit, Willa finds her desires spilling backwards to the decrepit little shanty in the woods—some newly shimmering part of her wanting him to take her there. Yet she says nothing, aware of the stark implication in such a request, and not especially certain if she is prepared to claim that which she is silently coveting.

"Jesse … do you believe in God?" she asks instead, sitting beside him on the riverbank, staring up at the blank page of a sky that has forgotten how to rain.

"I don't know. I guess I'm not so sure either way." He pauses, then, "Do you?"

"I think so—though maybe it's more that I'm afraid not to. I mean, if God doesn't exist, then all of this is pretty much for nothing. There would be no point to any of it."

Jesse smiles, his eyes focused on the river. "You have an interesting way of looking at things."

"It's from all the years of living with Stella and her crazy ideas."

"If you're talking about her selling dead flowers, that isn't as crazy as it is ingenious. It's the people who buy them that're nuts," he says, picking up a twig near his feet and methodically snapping it into miniscule pieces.

His face is nearly healed now. The deep purple bruises reminiscent of rotting plums have turned a yolky umbra of paling yellow. The angry gash along his cheekbone is a more permanent memento, but even that is notably faded now. Willa glances away, unable to keep her eyes turned to the shadows of his private abuse for any length of time. She knows not to push for explanations and yet she silently wills him to tell her something of what is already so visible.

The sun slides deeper into the tree tops as evening creeps closer.

"Selling trash is just the half of it. Very little of what Stella does makes sense. It's not enough for her to be different. She prefers to do things no one in their right mind would even think of."

"Like what?"

"Like everything. She just … she just doesn't make sense."

"Maybe you try too hard to figure everything out. Some things aren't supposed to make sense. They're just want they are," he says, and she can't help but think that maybe he isn't so much talking about Stella as he is referring to himself.

Willa closes her eyes. A pleasurable warmth spills over her insides as his fingers reach to encircle her hand—neither of them finding cause to speak as the sun slides down and leaves the sky altogether.

Odd as it is, it's nevertheless true that Willa has never given a gift to anyone other than her mother and father; and even then her presentations have been of the variety manufactured in grade school—projects created in art class: clay ashtrays, tissue paper bouquets, construction paper valentines pasted with glitter, and lopsided hearts crayoned in rainbow colors.

The giving and receiving of gifts is simply another of those customs that have passed into oblivion along with Martin, until now, as Willa comes to the conclusion that she needs something for Jesse. Something he will immediately recognize as special, but that isn't presumptuous or discomfortingly sentimental. Something that will forever prompt him into thinking of her. Not only now, but later, once time has inevitably passed and whatever it is that currently exists between them has potentially changed.

She is already certain of what she intends to buy, as she fingers through the knot of bills Stella has stowed in the back corner of her dresser drawer, nervously slipping several dollars into the front pocket of her denim shorts and quickly sliding the drawer shut on her act of thievery.

Only grudgingly has Stella allowed Willa an occasional dollar as compensation for her help cleaning the cabins and managing the laundry—now and again offered as an enticement to walk into town when Stella is alarmingly low on cigarettes. Her mother claims it as an absolute necessity that they skimp on all things non-essential if they ever hope to break away from Harriet's Bluff. And while Stella is adamant that there be no allowances for frivolous purchases such as ice cream bars from the corner market or pop from the vending machine outside Omega's office, she does make an exception in allowing for cigarettes and movie magazines, declaring these items imperative to her well-being and mental health.

And it is because of Stella's lopsided sense of fairness that Willa feels no particular sense of guilt now, as she helps herself to what is surely only a fraction of her entitled share of earnings. She is only taking what belongs to her.

Willa's foremost impression of Harriet's Bluff remains unchanged from first sight all those months earlier, and there are few notable alterations that might possibly sway her opinions from red light to green. In fact, she is certain that if roads somehow possessed capabilities for speech, every single stretch of pavement leading into town would be vehemently shouting *DEAD END, TURN AROUND, GO BACK,* to any traveler passing over them.

Everything about the place appears on the verge of shutting down, folding up and blowing away like a scrap of litter on the wind. As it is, every time she finds herself striding along the main street edged with ancient brick buildings, it is with the expectation of finding yet another business newly folded. She can't imagine why the people residing here appear content to live amongst the dust of old things. Or why someone doesn't make something of an effort to breathe a visage of renewed life into this town rather than leaving it as it is—a relic indelibly marked by the lonely and abandoned character of a phantom town just one step removed from full-on death.

There is only one store in Harriet's Bluff where Willa thinks she might find what she is looking for, and she wanders through Vincent's Pharmacy for ten … fifteen … twenty minutes, loitering in narrow aisles abundantly stocked with shampoo, hair color, comic books and toilet paper. All the while, aggressively pretending lack of interest in the revolving rack displayed on the front counter, on the chance that the blond teenager filing her nails and occasionally glancing over at Willa from behind the register possesses an ability to read minds and will so deduce the highly personal nature of Willa's intended purchase.

She moves toward a neatly aligned tier of magazines, picking up a copy of Field and Stream, feigning curiosity over an article detailing the best pole for fly fishing. Sheepishly returning it to the shelf when her gaze lands on the sheet of paper taped above the shelf, admonishing customers for thumbing through magazines they don't intend to purchase.

Summoning her courage, she approaches the counter, pausing to thoughtfully consider the assortment of gum and candy arranged in colorful rows on parallel shelves. She reaches for a pack of Double Mint, but quickly replaces it and picks Juicy Fruit instead, frowning uncertainly as her eyes track the selections a moment longer before lifting her head like an afterthought and nervously sliding her attentions over to the very item she's come for.

Under the not-so-discreet gaze of the cashier hovering behind the counter—a short thin girl not much older than Willa who is seemingly intent upon trying to recall whether she knows Willa from school, church, or maybe some defunct bowling league—Willa self-consciously fingers the heavy silver links of the various ID bracelets laddering the display rack.

She pretends not to feel the irritating prod of the girl's silent curiosity, fervently wishing there was some other store where she might have gone to make her selection, some quietly obscure shop where the cashier doesn't stare in nosey anticipation of a purchase.

"Engraving costs extra. You have to pay by the letter," the girl says as Willa continues examining the bracelets.

She doesn't respond to the girl's announcement beyond a barely discernible nod. Immediately calculating the numbers in her head, she makes a purposeful effort not to smile her relief once she concludes that the money folded in her pocket will be enough.

And yet impossibly, he is once again gone. Two … three … five days … gone.

Every afternoon Willa impatiently waits for an opportunity to slip away from The Moonglow and hurry out to the river, anxiously watching the road for Jesse's pickup, assuring herself that if not today, then certainly tomorrow, he will reappear like a rabbit pulled from a magician's hat—sheepishly grinning with some crazy explanation as to why he hasn't been here waiting in his usual place.

In Jesse's absence, the trek into town feels impossibly long and tiresome. A hundred miles across a concrete wasteland. She swings her head hopefully in the direction of every approaching vehicle on the chance that one will be Jesse Truman, disappointed, but not especially surprised when none of them are.

It requires an ever-increasing effort to ignore the pressing weight of the small flat jewelry box she consistently carries with her in a bid to keep even the weakest spark of optimism alive. Yet the burden of the gift swells with each day it remains un-given. And it has come to feel as if she is dragging a rotting cadaver, all the more odorous the longer she holds it.

How foolish she is. So stupid and naïve. So quick to believe he cares for her. So eager to accept all these things she's invented in her head.

For several days she continues to trek out to the river, carrying a prayer that she will find him there, holding as best she can to her dwindling faith that he can't possibly have left Harriet's Bluff. Not without telling her … not after the things they've said to each other. Not after the way he's looked at her. After the way he's touched her … kissed her.

Still, the days pass with neither sight nor sound of him. And now, sitting alone on the desiccated riverbank, Willa considers even the temporary satisfaction to be had from hurling the bright shiny gift hard and high above the water—watching it slam against the murky surface to disappear like a shameful secret.

But even as she holds the box in her hand on the verge of release, Willa is unable to wing it away, hating the thought of his name forever lost to the shadowy depths, slowly deteriorating at the bottom of the river, unseen and forgotten in the murk.

With twilight curling out along the lingering edges of late afternoon, Willa trudges back to The Moonglow, dragging the uncompromising burden of frustration that comes with the hollow emptiness of not knowing.

Twenty-one

Willa opens her eyes. Beyond the open window she hears the dull, steady drone of a distant lawn mower, the monotonous hum tranquilizing in a way that only such ordinary sounds can be.

The cabin lies quiet around her and she wonders if Stella has gone off again without bothering to tell her. Although her mother's short-term desertions have become something of a habit over the past weeks, the immediate sense of anxiety that crashes over her like a piano dropped from the clouds the instant she recognizes she's been left alone again, remains undiminished.

The badly creased paperback Willa has been reading just before dozing-off has fallen to the floor, losing her place. She leans over the edge of the bed to retrieve the book, thumbing through the yellowed pages in search of the last recognizable passage.

No longer groggy from sleep, merely bored with the prospect of waking to another afternoon with nothing to do, Willa re-closes her eyes. Her senses drift loosely on the verge of dropping back into sleep when the sound of the closet door closing immediately jars her awake—the hollow thud followed by the rhythmic tap of hard soles clicking across the wood floor on their way down the hall to the bathroom.

She rolls onto her back; shifts her head on the pillow and for the first time notices the suitcase lying open on her mother's bed. "Running away?" Willa says, sitting up when Stella reappears carrying a can of hairspray.

"That's a lovely thought, but no, it's only for the weekend."

"Huh? You mean you *really are* going somewhere?" Willa straightens her spine from a slouch, staring after Stella as she flits back and forth like a distracted moth gathering her assorted inventory—nightgown, shiny red pumps, nylon stockings—carelessly stuffing each item into the case before snapping it shut.

"There's still some peanut butter and jelly left and here's a couple dollars if you need anything else," Stella says, rifling through her purse for the elusive bills.

"But I don't get it, what're you doing? Where are you going?"

"Nowhere important. I'll be back Sunday night. I just need to get the hell out of here for a little while. Think of this as a nice little vacation for you, too. Just be damn sure you don't let anything slip to Miss Nosey."

"*A vacation?* Are you kidding? Sitting around this dump by myself is a vacation?"

"Someone your age shouldn't be so negative."

"Someone your age shouldn't—"

"Okay, Willa, I get it. You're obviously looking for an argument, but it'll have to wait till I get back. Then we can go at it tooth and nail. Right now I have to get moving before Nosey Nellie gets back from her hair appointment."

"This isn't fair. I can't believe you're just taking off and making me stay here by myself.'

"Enough with the drama, all right. It's just one damn weekend."

"That's not what this is about. It's that you don't care. You just don't care," Willa shouts, turning from the disinterested reflection in Stella's blank gaze and storming down the hall to the bathroom for lack of anywhere else to go. And she slams the door as hard as she can behind her; though there's no point, Stella is already gone.

Willa reminds herself that it doesn't matter. That she simply doesn't care what her mother does. Still, her thoughts continue marching back in search of Stella, wondering where she's gone and why. Her conflicted emotions swinging back and forth between twin points of anger and anxiety, even as she reminds herself again and again that she really, truly doesn't care.

She passes the time scheming through intricate layers of ideas for taking off herself. Plans that envision Stella coming home from her weekend excursion to find the same dismal and empty room she left—only without Willa still here in it. Even then, she wonders if such a scenario will leave her mother distressed or simply relieved.

Willa is increasingly certain that Stella is brewing together the details of some newly hatched idea. Past experience, rather than any particular hint, leading her to the conviction. Stella rarely, if ever, explains her intentions; and Willa has most often had to find things out for herself—either by inadvertently tripping over something, or having it come crashing down on her head.

Just as there are those seeds Stella plants, but then fails to consistently water or feed. As it had been with her initial stab at leaving Hoosick Falls months earlier, that, too, one more plan she'd failed to disclose.

Although Stella had made no mention of going anywhere, it was easy enough for Willa to conclude that something was likely in the works, when over the course of several weeks she came home from school every day to find another closet mysteriously empty; a shelf in a kitchen cupboard all at once bare; nick-knacks vanished from a tabletop or windowsill, leaving only a dust rimmed shadow of whatever was formerly settled there.

"What's going on?" she'd at last felt compelled to ask once the wall of cardboard boxes stacked in a corner of the living room had grown too mountainous to ignore or otherwise rationalize.

"We're getting the hell out of here," Stella answered without looking up, haphazardly wrapping mismatched coffee cups with torn sheets of newspaper before carelessly bundling them into a cardboard box advertising saltine crackers.

"Why? Where are we going?"

"Does it matter? We're just going, that's all."

"But what if Martin comes back and we're gone? How will he—"

"*Comes back?*" Stella laughed. "You've got a lot to learn about men, toots. Once a man goes, he's gone for good. Especially one with ten-thousand bills in his pocket."

Willa didn't answer, less disturbed by the prospect of being uprooted from a place that had never seen to offer anything of particular value or comfort, than she was of going off into the unknown with someone as reckless as her mother. Otherwise, when it came to her sentiments toward the town where she'd lived her entire life, there was little she could think to say about Hoosick Falls other than the truth that it existed. Mostly it was the kind of place impossible to describe inasmuch as it defied description. A worn out settlement thoroughly lacking the charm of some rural places, it was the sort of town where people passing through felt relieved when they had no reason to stay.

To Willa, it had always seemed something of a shadow town, murky edges with nothing inside, no real depth or particular feature that might've otherwise rendered it memorable or even remotely interesting beyond its bland ugliness. Although Willa seldom had occasion to see or experience much of the world beyond Hoosick Falls, she nevertheless puzzled why anyone would ever consider settling here as long as there was even just one other parcel in the world to be chosen instead. Because, surely, any place had to be better than this.

The house where Willa had lived her entire life was small, notably plain and rundown, a 1920's bungalow propped at the end of a street lined on either side by similar structures, the majority of which had not weathered the past forty or more years with any observable visage of grace.

As far as Willa was concerned, the only enviable quality about the house she shared with her parents was that it boasted two porches—one attached in front and another in back—unlike the other houses dotting the street, each of which only had a front porch just wide and deep enough to allow for two aluminum lawn chairs and a small table barely adequate for holding a bottle of pop and the essential ashtray.

The backyards of each shabby bungalow were all but identical, near barren scratches of earth that failed to grow much of anything other than a few scattered tufts of sickly crabgrass and hardy dandelion.

A handful of old timers yet remained—ancient men who religiously nodded their white thatched heads in wistful recollection of "the old days." Yet Willa had serious doubts as to whether such times ever truly existed in Hoosick Falls. It simply felt too far a stretch for the imagination.

The single movie theatre—shut down in the late 1950's, its insides stripped, gutted, and hauled away—now served as a feed storage warehouse for the hardware store adjacent. The Village Department Store, Charlotte's Dress Shop, and Robert's Haberdashery, were likewise gone, dark and empty for at least as long as Willa could remember.

Un-patronized businesses continued to fail as unemployed men moved away with, or from, their families; their abandoned homes eventually boarded up for lack of tenants or interested buyers. All that remained merely added credence to the mournful essence of a town deeply entwined in the irretrievable stages of decay, as it continued to die its quiet, steady death. Not the sort of place a person left and afterward missed.

Yet, they still hadn't left. Not then. And over the next several weeks which easily stretched into months, the towers of packed boxes remained more or less untouched. Until gradually, as certain items were needed—the deep iron skillet, toaster, bath towels, heating pad—the waiting cargo began to find its way back into cupboards, drawers, and closets, item by item, where it would remain. There was simply no point in repacking what was apparently going nowhere.

The sound of the fire alarm drills a widening tunnel through the fog of her sleep. Willa rolls onto her side, hugging the sheet up under her neck and holding it there with the crook of her bent elbow.

A month ago she would have leapt out of bed the moment the alarm summoned her awake. But by now there have been too many fires. Enough sad, old buildings and dilapidated structures now destroyed to effectively dilute the interest of even the most curious, especially in the middle of a deep, moonless night.

Nevertheless, she cannot hold her imagination from wondering over the potential location of Norman Hitchcock's latest victim, as she closes her eyes and patiently waits for sleep to resettle. Certain in the knowledge that the details will be in circulation all over town by morning, aided and abetted in continuous rotation by Omega Pearl Bodie herself.

Willa carries little expectation of relocating the shack in the woods, but she is determined to at least make an attempt to find it. There is always a chance that once in the vicinity, she will recollect enough necessary landmarks along the path she'd taken with Jesse, that she will eventually stumble upon the building again.

She feels as if she is walking in circles—certain trees and boulders looking familiar, and then not. Layers of light fall down through outstretched limbs, the sky that particular shade of faded blue—so light it gives the appearance of unending blank space rolling into eternity, rather than an actual firmament curved above the earth.

Slowing her pace, Willa drags her feet through the litter of some previous year's offal, dead limbs and brittle leaves scattered along the ground like ancient corpses rudely desecrated by nature. She pauses, pressing a hand into the pocket of her shorts to touch the shiny silver box containing Jesse's gift, though she can't say why she continues to carry it with her like a talisman when it's proven to be anything but.

Increasingly frustrated with her failure to recall direction, Willa is on the verge of turning back and returning to The Moonglow, dragging the burden of her disappointment like an unfixable wound, when she all at once spots the dead and leafless tree—crazily twisted branches at once familiar. *She knows this tree.* That day with Jesse—they'd passed it as they walked away from the shack. He'd laughed at her insistence that the strange gnarly trunk reminded her of a sinister talking tree from a favorite childhood cartoon. This tree was nearly identical to the animated version with its deep, soot-colored bark and twining witch-like arms; the only missing ingredients were a large gaping mouth and dark, glaring eyes.

"You're sure it was a cartoon and not a crazy kid nightmare," Jesse said, grinning at her vivid description.

"Yes, I'm serious! It was a cartoon with Casper the Friendly Ghost," she says, laughing with him, tipping her head to the last traces of sunlight tumbling down through the naked branches.

It is impossible to gage with any certainty whether Jesse has been back to the shanty since the day of the forest fire, the meager collection of furnishings apparently undisturbed since that afternoon. The mottled mattress and crippled table remain as the solitary furnishings. No crushed soda cans or discarded candy wrappers dropped on the floor to indicate trespass.

For several long moments, she stands in the doorway surveying the gloomy space, her eyes darting from one far corner to the next, until satisfied (or disappointed) that she is alone. She cautiously inches her way into the dingy vacuity of the shack, a sobering press of mournfulness rushing over her in a black tide.

Nothing … she feels nothing reminiscent of that day, merely the yawning emptiness characteristic of forlorn places. She's made an enormous mistake in coming back here. The remembered sweetness of that afternoon is thoroughly gone, leaving only a sobering sense of loss and yearning for the person whose absence now echoes so loudly.

It's true she's come to understand something of the grim nature and suggested complications in Jesse's life, but what of those other things? There have been genuine moments passed between them: conversations, laughter, touching, kissing … Can't he feel her reaching out to grasp hold of all these incredible things unfolding between them? Doesn't he want and welcome it himself? And if he does, then where is he now? How can he vanish so easily if he is feeling even a portion of what she herself is?

Even Stella's mysterious weekend vanishing act doesn't matter in the same way that Jesse's abandonment does. With Stella there are no true surprises. Willa has grown to expect her mother's self-centered and unexplained behaviors, occurrences that appear not so much spontaneous as inscrutable schemes a long time premeditated and simply in wait of execution.

Over the past weeks, she has fallen even further out of touch with Stella, mutually wary of each other even before they've decided why they should be, neither making an effort to repair or reclaim a relationship that has likely never existed. And while Stella hasn't taken it upon herself to say so, it is, and has always been, abundantly clear that her mother's aspirations are hers alone in the sense that they make no allowances for Willa beyond that of a reluctant mother saddled with the care and feeding of a tag-a-long child.

Willa tucks her legs up against her chest, closes her eyes and leans her forehead against her bent knees. She hasn't thought to drop a trail of breadcrumbs as assurance for finding her way back out of the woods, which means she'll need to head back soon—before night descends to obscure any potential clues that might assist in her navigation back to The Moonglow.

Yet she can't quite manage to shake herself loose from the lethargic sense of emptiness pressing in around her; her thoughts twining back to the afternoon when she first happened upon the shack and found Jesse Truman. The terrible surprise of discovering the newly lit fire in the woods, and her helplessness to stop or otherwise contain the blaze, feel faraway and unimportant, unequivocally overshadowed by everything else unfolded here afterward.

All at once the memory of his touch is alive and pulsing inside her head; and she can feel the warm glow rising up from the depths of her insides as she recalls the feel of his fingers against the back of her neck beneath her hair—drawing her to him until she is close enough that they are sharing breath—the recollection wrenching something loose inside her chest and dropping it like an anchor into a sea of unquenchable longing.

She awakens with a jolt, her eyes darting across the gloom as she frantically struggles to recall where she is and how she's come to be here, even as she hears the sound that has doubtless awakened her—footsteps shuffling through the litter of dead leaves just beyond the door. She listens as the steps move away, only to return an instant later, her immediate instincts urging her to do something—move, hide—but finding that she can't.

A crippling knot of fear holds her immobile as the flow of blood coursing through her veins turns frigid, her mind spinning through a heinous lineup of homicidal creatures potentially lurking on the other side of the door.

Norman Hitchcock ...

Her mouth unhinges in preparation of a scream as a stick snaps beneath the phantom tread now paused outside. The door slowly yawns open.

"Jesse ..."

He hangs in the doorway, his expression mirroring her own stunned surprise.

"How did you—"

"I thought you left. I thought you were gone," she interrupts, not so much wanting to speak or hear any of it just now, as to leap forward and throw her arms around him.

"No, I've been around," he answers slowly, holding to the doorway.

"No, you haven't. You haven't been anywhere ..." she begins, then hesitates, and all at once the words are tumbling out.

"It's not fair. You can't keep doing this. You can't make me believe you care, that you feel something—and then just disappear."

She watches him for a response, but there is only the dull blank expression staring back at her. She feels the beginning pricks of anger along her scalp, or maybe it is frustration; she doesn't know. So often they feel like the same things. She is only certain that she needs him to say something, to tell her he is sorry, even if it doesn't come with an explanation. Because he's been gone long enough now, that to have him standing here feels far more relevant than accounts of where he's been.

"I don't want you to be part of this."

"Part of what?"

He pushes his hands into the front pockets of his jeans. "My family ... my life."

Something snaps behind her eyes and she struggles to hold her expression steady, her face hovering on the verge of crumbling beneath his terrible, dismissive words.

"Okay. Fine. I get it," she mumbles, rising to her feet, careful to keep her eyes safely removed from his.

"I don't mean—"

"Forget it. You don't have to explain anything. It's okay."

His hand shoots out to catch her arm when she attempts to brush past.

"Look, I'm sorry, Willa. That's not how I meant it."

She pulls back, forcing him to release her arm. "Things happen. Things happen to everyone. But you can say something instead of just vanishing like you fell off the earth. Even if it's just goodbye. You can say goodbye."

"It's not that simple."

"I didn't say simple—just not impossible."

"Some things are."

"Only because you make them that way," her voice swells like a bundle of sticks in her throat as she stares into the wall of his closed expression.

"You don't understand what this is about."

"Oh? Really? Am I supposed to? Isn't that why you keep running away every time something happens? So you can keep it all to yourself?"

"Maybe you just need to trust me when I say you don't want to be part of this."

"It's not about trusting you, Jesse. It's more about you trusting me. Because if you did, you'd tell me what's going on, and why you keep doing this vanishing act."

He turns away deliberately, and for an instant she is certain he will leave. But when he looks back there is something desperately complicated in his eyes, etched into the sharp angles and curves of his face, a depth of raw emotion so starkly shattering that her immediate instinct is to take a backward step away from it.

"Okay, I'll tell you. I'll tell you if you really want to know—just not now."

Why not now? She wants to shout. Why, if he is at last conceding to tell her something of what she's been so long asking for, can't he just tell her? But she only nods, grateful for the descending veil of grey shadow leaking through the broken windows and into the shack, cloaking the remains of afternoon light and somehow softening the dangerous edge of everything he hasn't said.

"I have to go. I'm not really sure of the way back and it'll be dark soon."

"I'll show you."

Willa follows him through the trees. Neither of them makes any real attempt at conversation, almost as if the things left unspoken between them have in actuality been uttered, leaving them both shamefully exposed.

She considers telling him about Stella, how her mother has gone off without explanation and not yet returned. Yet she recognizes that it is only a temporary diversion for pretending away the mound of disappointment and anxiety she's piled up around Jesse's own vacancy over the past several days.

In the end she holds to the silence, reasoning that any discussion of Stella's runaway weekend will only come out sounding like an intentionally placed parallel to his own disappearance. Instead, she continues after him without speaking, her mind swirling with the possibilities of how different things might be between them had they been ordinary people rather than the ones they are—societal misfits spinning in separate, though equally uncertain, orbits.

"I know the rest of the way from here," she says, once they reach the line of towering pines bordering the meadow lying beyond the edge of woods. In fact, she'd begun to recognize the surroundings some ways back—about the time they crossed the dry creek bed. Yet, reluctant to release him until he's given her something to carry away with her—a word, a look, a touch—she doesn't admit it until now.

"You're sure you'll be all right from here?"

She nods, watching his face, relieved that the stormy expression he'd greeted her with earlier is now gone.

He drops his gaze, at once shy, staring hard at the toe of his sneaker for a moment before lifting his head.

"I'm not sure what I should say."

"You don't have to say anything," she shrugs, not because she means it, but because it seems the thing he most needs to hear at this moment.

Asleep Without Dreaming

He doesn't answer as he reaches for her hand, his fingers briefly grazing across her wrist before turning away and striding off into the trees.

It is the sound of a quickened tread moving across the porch and pausing at the front door of the cottage that rattles Willa awake, her senses not yet fully aroused as the door creaks open then hastily closes with greater force than would be deemed considerate in a sleeping house.

Stella drops her suitcase on the bed before heading down the hall to the bathroom and Willa waits for the sound of the closing door before turning her head, straining for a glimpse of the clock on the dresser across the room. It takes a moment to decipher the position of the hands glowing weakly on the clock's face from behind the gritty web of sleep clouding her eyes. *Just past midnight.*

Willa rolls onto her side, staring at the shadowed expanse of the wall opposite her bed. From behind the closed bathroom door she hears the toilet flush, the sound followed by a familiar squeak as Stella turns the faucet handles on the sink.

The water runs for what seems an abnormally long time. Willa lies still, listening to the quiet rhythm of her own breathing as she waits for Stella to emerge, or sleep to return, whichever comes first.

Her thoughts slowly melt into the drifting space of limbo, her shifting consciousness breaking away into random pieces as the weight of drowsiness presses firmly against her eyelids. She slides her fingers beneath her pillow as she remembers Jesse's bracelet, thinking to hold it in her hand as she falls back to sleep.

But there is nothing—the box is gone.

She springs upright, feeling for the switch on the bedside lamp, intent on searching the tangle of sheets, the clutter littering the floor, every crack or crevice large enough to have swallowed Jesse's gift ... even as it dawns on her that she won't find it here. Because she knows where it is. Knows with absolute conviction the place where she's left it. She clearly envisions it, almost as if she is still there sitting in the crooked little shanty, running her finger along the neat block letters engraved on the bracelet's rectangular face, as she worries over Jesse Truman. Using a corner of her blouse to polish the cloudy prints from the shiny surface before returning it to the box, and setting it next to her on the dingy mattress, where it remains.

Twenty-two

There is something decidedly changed about Stella, though Willa can't say precisely what that is. She only knows that some intrinsic component is no longer the same. Not that Stella has ever been anything other than difficult to read or understand. It's just that now, a day after her prodigal return, accurately guessing what is skidding around inside her mother's head feels as likely as Willa solving the mystery of the Bermuda triangle.

"Where did you go?" Willa asks, watching Stella fill a cup with hot water from the bathroom tap then stir in a heaping tablespoon of instant coffee.

"On a rocket trip to the moon."

"Very funny. Where were you?"

"How about this—how about we drop the question and answer part of the program for the time being? Just believe me when I say it's gonna take a little more creative maneuvering than originally thought to get us the hell out of this place."

Willa lifts an eyebrow, but says nothing. There's never been a time when she hasn't been wary of Stella's brand of schemes, especially now that they require disappearances to unexplained destinations and sketchy details afterwards.

"Okay," Willa says, brushing a sprinkling of cracker crumbs from the top of her bedspread and into her palm. It seems the safest, easiest response in the face of Stella's fluctuating mood, buoyant one moment, and then diving deep, bobbing back to the surface in anticipation of the next plummet.

"You see, right there. That's what I'm talking about. If you really gave a damn about this damn mess, you wouldn't be so willing to ignore it."

Willa lifts her head, shoots a scorching glare in Stella's direction, but says nothing. She's played this game one too many times already.

From the moment she'd first known in her heart that Martin wasn't coming back, Willa had turned her thoughts to devising a plan that would convince Stella to pack up their sorry lives in Hoosick Falls and disappear themselves—leaving behind nothing other than the space they'd occupied should anyone be foolish enough to come along and wish to claim it.

It made little difference where they went. The destination was of far less consequence than the actual leaving. Yet, as often as Willa silently blueprinted both logical designs and outlandish ideas, she could never quite bring herself to reveal anything of what she was thinking, quite possibly afraid that Stella would actually listen.

She'd assumed it was a definite lack of courage that kept her holding so firmly to the belief that it was safer to dream without expectation than it was to think she might eventually achieve anything other than what had become accustomed. Dreams, she suspected, were actually a ploy of nature—extravagant episodes churned into a person's head for the sole purpose of keeping an otherwise empty mind from fading to blank. Just as she knew that to pursue every crazy thought that popped into her head was in effect to become Stella. It was an affliction, Willa promised herself, that she would never allow a foothold.

She had long ago grasped the understanding that there is less disappointment to be had in fiercely wanting things than there is in claiming something highly coveted, only to find out that it is the wrong thing. The sole exception to her edict—a single, muted concept that lives in the deepest depths of her mind—is that one perfect something that promises to seal lasting happiness and eternal contentment onto the entire broadcloth of her future. That one essential something, that unfortunately, is a notion yet to come.

She's convinced herself that this Holy Grail will simply one day arrive, careening crazily into her head like an attack from an unseen assailant. And she will, right then, know the direction she needs to follow in order to claim the elusive prize of her heart's desire.

While this treasure has so far not revealed itself, what has, is the certainty of those things she quite definitely doesn't want: the grey, lonely life in Hoosick Falls; living in an ugly little house with a mother who sells dead flowers to miserable people; or the one she has now—each day opening her eyes to find she's still in Harriet's Bluff, West Virginia, a place where all dreams unequivocally come to die.

Oddly enough, Willa doesn't see it. She doesn't yet recognize that her ambition to reject these things is an entirely prodigious aspiration all on its own.

She can hear the men's voices coming through the trees even before she is close enough to see them standing in a half-circle outside the shack.

"… just a few clothes and …"

She freezes—quickly ducks down out of sight.

"I'd swear on my dead granny that he's been here. Few days, it looks like. I'd just like to know where he stashed all the stuff he's been using to start the fires. There isn't even a book of matches in there," one of the men says, crooking his thumb toward the shanty.

"Willa …" a voice whispers just behind her shoulder.

"Wh—" she spins around, an unformed cry clinging to the walls of her mouth, heartbeat skipping like stones across water.

"Shh," Jesse grabs her arm, pulling her behind a dense tangle of knotted brambles.

"What's going on?"

"They think they've found Norman's hideout," he says, his voice a tight whisper as they watch Sheriff Belcher enter the shack, closely followed by the cluster of men, several of whom Willa recognizes from around town.

Panic knots her insides as she instantly recalls her purpose in coming here. Her face flames with the terrible certainty that one of the men is right now plucking the bracelet from the dingy mattress where she forgot it. She pictures him studying the engraving before handing it to the sheriff who will cock his head and smirk knowingly, as he examines the five etched letters for an intense moment before dropping it into his front shirt pocket.

And what if the bracelet proves somehow consequential to the search party combing the shack? Because they are desperate to find something—anything or anyone—that might lead them to capturing the elusive Norman Hitchcock. She knows she has to tell Jesse why she's come here, yet the admission is hesitant in coming. How exactly is she supposed to go about explaining that, despite her appeals and insistence on trust, she may very well have implicated him in whatever it is the men think they've discovered?

Jesse remains focused on the men now filing from the building. Willa holds to her crouched position behind the fortress of prickly shrubs until no longer able to ignore the cramps shooting along the backs of her legs in flaming arrows. She rocks her weight back to sit on the ground.

"Shit," Jesse swears under his breath when Sheriff Belcher holds up a red, plaid shirt and utters something they are unable to hear, the remark earning a hearty guffaw from his companions.

"Now what?" Willa's voice squeaks without finishing the question—*now that they have a shiny, new, silver bracelet in their possession, boldly pronouncing a trespasser named JESSE as the owner.*

"I don't know," he says, dropping back beside Willa, his eyes staying on the men as they stride away. The red shirt and what appears to be a balled-up piece of cloth, clutched under Sheriff Belcher's heavy arm.

They know to wait until the men are fully gone before chancing even the slightest movement. But even then, they remain silent and still for several moments longer before Jesse turns his head to stare at Willa, as if only just now recalling her presence.

"Those were your things they took?"

He nods.

"They must think they've finally found Norman's hideout. I'll bet as soon as they get back to town they'll be running the evidence up the flagpole."

Jesse doesn't answer, watching her face as if he is waiting for something—something she hasn't yet said.

"But if they think this is where he's been hiding, shouldn't somebody have stayed behind just in case he comes back?" she says, brushing past the expectancy in his expression.

"That would explain why they haven't caught him yet. Nobody read the chapter about setting up a stakeout," Jesse says, the suggestion of a grin teasing at the corners of his mouth.

Willa attempts a smile but the expression doesn't come. "I ... it seems ... well, there is something else ..." She ducks her head, biting the corner of her lip, taking a moment to gather necessary courage before lifting her face. "I think I forgot something when I was here yesterday."

"What?"

"It was just something—a present for someone—a little box. I'm pretty sure I left it in there which means they would've found it when they were poking around."

"A present for who?"

"It was just a—just a gift."

"For who?" The whole of his mouth appears on the verge of a grin, an amused glint winking back at her from deep within his eyes.

"It was—I'm sorry. I'm really sorry, Jesse. If I've made trouble for you—" she stumbles over the words, her voice crumbling in her mouth as she drops her gaze and all at once takes notice of the wrist casually draped over one bent knee.

"I found it last night after you left. Sat on it actually," he smiles sheepishly as she stares at the heavy silver links drooped over the top of his hand.

She feels him waiting for her to say something, and yet all she can think is how distant this moment is from the perfect scene she's orchestrated dozens of times in her head.

"I don't know what to say, Willa. This is the nicest … it's the nicest thing anyone's ever …," he says without finishing, and the look he gives her is deep and complicated.

Can he see the waves of heat flooding up under her skin and spilling out behind her eyes?

"Maybe if we hadn't just witnessed the sheriff stealing your shirt, this wouldn't feel so strange," she says, managing something of a laugh.

"Don't get me wrong. I really liked that shirt," he grins, "but compared to this …" He reaches out and touches her hand, gently, carefully even, his fingers quaking ever so slightly in a betrayal of things he hasn't said.

She makes no attempt to tell herself that she hasn't seen it coming or otherwise pretend that the feeling has only just arrived—enormous and screaming—the certainty that she is crazy in love with Jesse Truman. Because she knows that it's been here all along, even if she hasn't fully recognized what it means until now. Almost as if she's just this instant gone racing around a corner in her heart, careening headlong into him, looking up in stunned surprise to see the shy grin planted on his boyishly handsome face. Deep navy eyes silently asking what's taken her so long to get here.

Twenty-three

She likes the way the chain hangs against his wrist. The way it droops over the top of his hand or dips in an arch to touch the base of his palm. Just as it thrills her how he wears it all the time. Never takes it off. Never. Not when they go swimming in the river or even when he works on the engine of his chronically ailing pickup, the silver links gleaming above the shiny black grease staining his fingers.

Willa truly believes that he is not merely offering polite words of meaningless flattery when he tells her that he's never been given anything so special. Just as it isn't so much a warm flush of pride that she feels upon receiving his sincere thanks, rather, something far more resembling of gratitude. The sort that comes from knowing that someone cares enough for her to want to belong to her—possibly even as much as she longs to belong to him.

Most often it is his tired old truck parked alongside the garage at the Texaco station that Willa sees before chancing a glimpse of Jesse himself, putting air in someone's tires, washing a windshield, partially obscured from view by an upraised hood as he checks the oil in a waiting customer's engine.

Willa fairly bubbles with excitement when he tells her about his new job, happy because she knows how much he needs the work, relieved to know where to find him most days. She is elated that the station is not so far from The Moonglow that she can't walk here most afternoons, if only for a brief exchange of silent smiles and meaningful glances.

Poised on the bench like a waiting passenger, she watches him now from the empty bus shelter across the street from the station. She studies his expression. His eyes are cast downward as if earnestly contemplating the nozzle running fuel into the tank of a bright blue sedan pulled up alongside the pumps, though his thoughts will, in fact, be a million miles away.

A passing breeze lightly feathers the dark hair drifted across his forehead as the car pulls away; and he glances up, their gazes instantly locking so that they both forget to smile. It is only with the greatest effort that Willa rises to her feet several moments later, continuing along the sidewalk on rubbery legs.

They are in mutual agreement over the necessity of keeping their feelings for each other private, and thus hopefully undiscovered, should such a thing be possible in a town that prides itself on knowing everything about everyone. For Willa, who has neither ties to nor interest in anyone in Harriet's Bluff other than Jesse, her bid for secrecy is more than just a determination to shield the particulars of her life from the ever-meddling Omega Pearl Bodie. Mostly it is Stella who concerns her. Because more than any other person that Willa has ever known, it is her mother who possesses an unparalleled talent for ruination, effectively poisoning everything she touches and with barely an effort.

Willa catches a whiff of nail polish even before she pulls open the screen door to find Stella sitting on the bed, one foot propped on the edge of the mattress as she paints her toenails a violent shade of *Dragon Lady Red*.

"You end up in trouble and you're on your own," Stella says without looking up.

"Um ... well, okay, thank you, I guess," Willa replies lightly, pausing in the doorway as she makes a rapid effort to gauge something of an accurate reading of Stella's mood: silly, sarcastic, annoyed, angry?

"Yeah, that's right, everything's a joke with you." Stella dips the miniature brush into the bottle of polish, hesitating for a moment to study her toes before continuing to lacquer the color over her nails. "But this happens to be serious."

"Serious what? Gossip? Fairytales? A news bulletin?"

"You're denying it?" Stella lifts her head, eyes narrowing like a viper scoping its prey.

"Yes. Definitely. Whatever *it* is."

"Let's not play that game, Willa. I'm not in the mood. *It* happens to be that boy you're running around with."

"I have no idea what you're talking about?" Willa says, trying to pretend away the flash flood of stunned surprise that arrives with her mother's stark pronouncement. *How is it possible that Stella knows anything about Jesse?* "Where do you even get this stuff from? Oh, yeah, of course, Omega Pearl, right? Apparently she thinks I—"

"Nobody has to tell me what I can see just fine with my own two eyes, especially when you're making a spectacle of yourself in a place where we both happen to live."

"A spectacle?" Willa repeats, genuinely startled.

"You have no business chasing after that kind of boy."

"*Chasing?* What kind of boy? What kind of boy is he?"

"Don't play stupid. I'm warning you, Willa, you'd better stop this now."

"He's just my friend."

"That's the point. The only person you're fooling with that line is yourself. Boys *are not* and *cannot* be your friends and that's the damn truth whether you want to believe it or not."

"Friendships aren't about gender, they're about people."

"*Friendship?* Well then I've got a news flash for you. Granted you might very well be naïve enough to actually think you're playing the friendship card, but I'll guarantee he's not shuffling the same deck. You may not want to hear it, and you may not want to see it, but if he's a male and he's got a dick in his pants, then he's thinking about sex. And that, Willa, is a cold, hard fact of life."

She thinks she might easily kill Stella right now—reach with both hands and choke the filthy words from her horrible ugly mouth. All she has to do is take a step forward. She can do it. She knows she can do it. And yet somehow she forces herself to turn away from her frothing black rage before murder is committed, spinning on her heel and slamming out the door through which she's only just come.

She knows better than to react to Stella's crudities and ignorance. And yet the acidic taste of her mother's words remains with her regardless. The vulgarities of her statements successful in making Willa feel cheap and dirty simply from having heard them.

That she is crazy about Jesse Truman feels as absolute as any truth can possibly be. No question, merely fact. Just as she holds no serious doubts that he cares for her in return. And it makes no real difference in Willa's mind as to the degree of his affections, or the reasoning as to why they exist, as it simply matters that they do.

Only now there is this other thing. This crude, ugly accusation that Stella has thrown out to hang in the air like a bad odor. And although she deliberately fails to mention her mother's perverse vow to Jesse, the words are there regardless, endlessly playing their crude taunt inside her head.

"Why did you drop out of school if you only had a year left 'til graduation?" Willa asks, leaning over the side of the boat just far enough to trail her fingertips through the cool water as Jesse rows out toward the middle of the lake. Instantly, she yanks her hand back, recalling the alleged ingredients in this particular body of water.

With Omega gone to visit her ailing sister out of town, and Stella taking the opportunity to ignore her cleaning duties and cocoon herself in the cottage (napping, smoking, and clipping pictures from a newly acquired stack of Omega's discarded magazine), Willa receives only minimal resistance from Jesse when she suggests he drive out to The Moonglow so they can enjoy a row around the lake.

"Damn, do you see that? This tub's sprung a new leak," Jesse tips his chin, indicating the plump droplets sprouting from an otherwise undetectable hole in the bow of the boat.

Willa stares at the trail of tears slowly trickling below the gunwale as he continues rowing.

"Shouldn't we go back?" Although she's become an adequate enough swimmer by now, and she can probably stay afloat should the boat suddenly abandon them in the middle of the lake, Willa is nevertheless horrified at the prospect of stroking her way back to shore through turd-infested waters.

"No. It's a slow leak, and we're not going out far enough to worry about it."

She allows him a moment to return to her question before concluding that he has no intention of doing so.

"Why did you drop out, Jesse?"

"That's when my mother got sick," he says without meeting her gaze, his stare focusing on an invisible spot far off on the water. "There was nobody else to help—just me."

"What about your father?"

"What about him?" he answers, his tone darkening with the eclipse that all at once passes over his expression, rendering his mood unreadable in the space of an instant.

"I don't know, I just thought—I"

"He's not interested. He's never been interested."

"But why does—"

"Just leave it alone, okay," he says, slicing off her question before she can finish. An immediate wave of coldness floods into his eyes—an expression so brittle, Willa has to look away for an instant to keep from shattering into a million pieces.

She shifts her gaze, carefully studying him through lowered lashes: the hard set of his jaw, deep-colored eyes gone so dark they appear nearly black, hard straight shoulders rolling with machine-like precision.

"There's a lot we don't know about each other," she says at length.

"There's a lot we don't need to know. There's no point."

Willa looks away as the weight of silence rushes in to fill the empty space broken open between them. Now, there is only the sound of water lapping hollow through the wood as the boat cuts smoothly through the water. And it isn't so much the words, but rather the way he says them, that makes her want to cry.

Twenty-four

By some miracle Willa doesn't right then die of fright. Stella's voice cuts through the dark, startling her like a slap, nearly tumbling her down the very steps she's just so carefully navigated.

"Where have you been?" Stella repeats from the other side of the closed screen door, the weight of her words falling like stones as she slams her palm against the wood frame. The high shine of anger is visible in her eyes.

"There was a fire down at—"

"It's the middle of the night."

"Well, yeah, but that's when they always are," Willa says, swallowing hard, working to level her tone.

"I'm not an idiot," Stella hisses. "This isn't about some damned fire."

"Didn't you hear the whistle?"

"That whistle means nothing."

"It means there's a fire," Willa says evenly, rapidly contemplating some probable means of turning invisible and pressing her way past Stella into the cottage. A plan she just as quickly abandons for the fact that such an impulse can only prove fruitless, considering that once inside, her sole achievement will be in trapping herself in the room with Stella.

"Another freaking' fire. Big deal. They'll be a dozen more before they catch that fool. It's like watching the same damn movie a hundred times."

"You're wrong. They're all different," Willa says. And it's true. Each fire has its own personality—its own visage and particular fingerprint—the only parallels being smoke and flame.

"Actually, Willa, they're not. Not at all. That's just another one of those lies you keep telling yourself because the truth is so disappointing. It's really all the same brand of baloney. All of it. Fires. Men. Marriage. Money … it doesn't matter, it's all the same crap," she says, meaningless words continuing to trail from her lips even as she melts backward into the gloomy depths of the cottage.

Willa has the distinct feeling that she's somehow dodged a bullet, but there's little relief in finding herself momentarily spared. She can still feel the barrel pressed against her temple, steady, cocked, ready to re-fire.

She'd known how big a chance she was taking when she slipped out this time, more so because she hadn't even tried to be as careful sneaking away as she usually is. Stella had only been asleep for a short time when the fire alarm sounded, not long enough to assure she'd reached the necessary place of unconscious dreams. But Willa's expectation of finding Jesse waiting for her amongst the crowd she knows will be gathered to witness this newest blaze is greater than her sense of caution.

It proved an unnecessary risk. Willa had scanned the dozen or so slightly dazed and silent spectators, likewise pulled from sleep by the lure of fire and the hope of another Norman Hitchcock sighting, disappointed, then crushed, to find he isn't there after all. Not Jesse, or Norman either. And although Willa stood for a long time watching the derelict bungalow burn, she isn't actually present, her gaze held to the fire, but not seeing any of it.

As the flaming roof weakened and eventually collapsed inside the bungalow's four supporting walls with a thunderous clap, followed by an enormous shattering roar, her thoughts remained on Jesse, wondering where he was and why that place wasn't here. Because he must've known that she would come. That she would always come.

Her hair is the only thing about herself that anyone has ever referred to as beautiful, despite the fact that she doesn't often take the time to fuss over it. Most often she impatiently runs a brush through the untamed mass of waves, pulling it back into a heavy ponytail on hot days, leaving it to tumble over her shoulders and down her back when it isn't. And while Willa has never considered any element of her looks of the caliber to warrant vanity, she does understand the value of her soft, butter-shaded strands. She knows from the fawning compliments that have come from the time her hair was long enough to hold a plastic baby barrette. It is this single feature that makes her noticeable, potentially beautiful when every other component of her person seems altogether ordinary. It makes Stella's suggestion all the more horrifying.

"You seem to forget I'm a *professional hair dresser*," Stella says, lifting a skein of Willa's hair.

"I don't care. I'm not cutting it. I like it just fine the way it is."

"For Pete's sake, Willa, you never even comb that mess. A skinny little twig like you doesn't need all that hair anyway. You need a nice little bob—maybe even a pixie. That would be cute."

Willa glares at her mother, too annoyed even to speak. Stella's attentions have always been front and center on her own looks, consistently, thankfully, distant from concerns or interest in Willa's. She has certainly never cared about Willa's hair. Never. Not her hair, her eyes, her clothes—no single particle of Willa's appearance has ever held particular interest.

"I don't want my hair cut," Willa repeats, jerking her head, forcing Stella to release the thick strand she holds in her fingers. "I like it the way it is."

"Okay, fine, this is the deal," Stella says, dropping onto her bed, reaching for the open pack of cigarettes on her night table. "I wasn't gonna say anything until afterward because I knew you'd get all excited, but, well, it just so happens I met someone who will buy it."

"*Buy—my hair?* You want to sell my hair?" Willa stares at Stella sitting on the bed smoking calmly. Her insides clenched, not with excitement, but in horror.

"It's big business, Willa. They make beautiful wigs from human hair. People are willing to pay big dollars for the real thing."

"I don't care. There's no way I'm selling my hair."

"Oh course not," Stella crosses her arms, eyes narrowing. "Because you're selfish. You're a damn, selfish, little brat."

"What's selfish about not wanting—"

"We can use that money, Willa. It's the only way we're ever gonna get the hell out of here. You expect me to just take care of everything, don't you? Pull money off the trees while you run all over town with that boy."

Sell your own damn hair, is what she wants to scream at Stella, even as she glares at her mother's short and tidy coif—the style she faithfully cultivates in an as-close-as-she-can-get-without-actually-resorting-to-a-head-transplant-replica   of Jackie Kennedy's. She won't do this, she won't. She can't. Her hair is the only thing that makes her different. That keeps her from fading into the background. That causes anyone to even notice her. Even Jesse. Especially Jesse.

She won't do it. She'll never do it. They'll have to find some other way. Stella is being ridiculous. Or just mean. Because she's always been envious of what she doesn't have herself.

She thinks it must be a dream ... A dream inside a dream maybe. Because she is watching it happen. Watching herself from somewhere far off. She is flying—her arms spread like wings, legs stretched out behind her, the thick waves of her hair lifting behind her in a fanning cape. She is soaring above the earth, dipping, gliding .... laughter winding from her lips like an endless spiraling ribbon. And she feels so light, it's as if she has no body, a feather, drifting, twining down gently ... But then all at once her sense of exhilaration snaps like a breaking limb and is gone—now something else altogether. She is no longer flying, but struggling to break free—to break free from something—to get away.

It is still dark when she opens her eyes. The air inside the cottage is thick from the previous day's heat, heavy with the hot morning to come. Even so there is a definite lightness. It's as if her head has not yet settled, remains aloft, floating within the strange nonsensical dream. She lifts her head from the pillow, reaching to push a damp tendril of hair from her cheek. And it is right then that she understands. *Understands that it is gone.*

She can't imagine seeing Jesse, she can't imagine seeing anyone. She hasn't spoken a word to Stella for the entire week and it's not as much a surprise as a relief when her mother takes off again on one of her mystery excursions.

As Willa has now come to expect, her mother offers neither explanation nor detail as to where she is going or why, but this time Willa doesn't care. She has no desire for details. In fact she thinks maybe she prefers never to hear her mother's voice again.

Stella sits on the unmade bed, legs tightly crossed, impatiently smoking as she waits for the cover of darkness to drop before carrying her single suitcase out the door and down the steps, saying she will be back Sunday night.

"You'd best make sure and behave yourself while I'm gone," Stella says, digging through her purse for a few bills, tossing them on top of the dresser.

Willa doesn't give a fig where Stella's going. It's enough to know what she's carrying inside her suitcase. What does it matter where she's taking it? The only thing of consequence is that it is no longer Willa's.

Twenty-five

"**G**OOD LORD! WHAT IN THE WORLD?"
"It was too hot having all that hair. Stella cut it for me. She used to be a hair stylist."
"Humph...What'd she use, a chain saw?"

Willa shrugs. There isn't much to say. Nothing actually. *Only that she hates Stella. She hates her. She hates her.*

"Well, not to insult your mother, but you should've had Veleda do it for you. She wouldn't have been so *radical*," Omega says, then shaking her head, "I've got be honest, I don't love it. All that beautiful hair—"

"Was that the siren I heard last night," Willa interrupts, unable to bear another second of Omega's rather offending sympathy. As if she doesn't already know she's now the world's ugliest duckling.

"I'll tell you this, they'd better get their hands on him soon or I'm boarding this place up and moving down to my sister's place in Decatur," Omega says, folding a stick of Juicy Fruit into her mouth.

Willa slips the ring of keys back onto the designated hook, turning her head to steal a glance over Omega's shoulder at the newspaper lying open on her desk. Glaring from its long held station in the left hand corner of the front page is Norman Hitchcock's hard edged stare, a large photo of the recently charred bungalow printed beneath it.

"Aren't you afraid that if you leave he'll come and burn this place down, too?"

"Don't kid yourself, honey. It's just a matter of time before he runs out of empties and starts lighting up whatever's left. Occupied or not. It's pretty clear they haven't a clue how to stop him, and if that's the case, I don't intend to sit around waiting for my turn to get toasted-up like a marshmallow. That's how the criminal mind works. He'll just keep going until someone stops him—getting bolder and bolder until he gets caught or hits the wall."

"Do you ever wonder if maybe he doesn't really exist?"

"*Doesn't exist?* You've gotta be kidding," Omega snorts in disbelief. "That the crazy fool exists is about the only thing anybody does know for sure."

"Then where is he? They've turned the whole town upside down looking for him. How can there even be anyplace left to hide?"

"Well, they did find that shack in the woods, but really, honey, anybody who wants to stay hidden bad enough can do it. Even if it means digging out an ant hole. And don't forget he's been spotted at the scene of the crime—though you'd think one of those idiots would've chased after him or at least screamed for help. If I'd been there I would've hit him in the head with a brick and stopped the bastard cold."

Willa shrugs, seeing no point in pursuing what Omega apparently doesn't understand. For any number of reasons the fires no longer feel as urgent as they did at the beginning of the summer. Just as the sinister visage of Norman Hitchcock that's been printed in newspapers, posted in windows, and nailed on telephone poles over the span of months has become familiar enough that it's lost much of its original potency, his phantom-like invisibility has taken on the proportions of someone not so much criminal as near mythical.

"Is everything okay?" Willa says watching the side of Jesse's face as he stands pumping gas into a battered old Chevy pickup pulled up alongside the pumps; the driver drums his thumbs against the steering wheel as though this obvious show of impatience will somehow serve to hurry the fuel into his tank.

"Yeah, fine," Jesse answers without turning his head.

He doesn't even see her. Hasn't glanced at her long enough to notice the horror of her stolen hair. For days she's been sick with anxiety worrying over his certain stunned reaction to her ruined looks; and yet here he stands, without once turning his head to look at her.

"It's just that you haven't been around for a few days and I—"

"I had to take a couple days off."

Willa waits, allowing him space to elaborate, and yet he ignores the invitation.

"Omega said she's thinking about closing up The Moonglow and moving down south to stay with her sister," Willa says in an attempt to draw him into conversation.

"Why's that?"

"She thinks it's just a matter of time before Norman Hitchcock gets bored with burning vacant buildings and starts incinerating people in their beds," Willa says, smiling. Hopeful that her lighthearted poke at Omega's paranoia will serve to lessen the palpable discomfort circling the air between them in preparation of a solid landing.

Ordinarily Willa understands not to approach Jesse at the station; but he's been absent for several days. So when she chances by and sees him stacking a pile of used tires against the outside garage wall, she approaches without hesitation.

"I just can't decide if she really believes that or is only saying it for dramatic purposes."

He releases the trigger on the gas nozzle, returning it to its cradle on the pump with unnecessary force. "I don't really have time to talk now," Jesse says, throwing a glance over his shoulder to where the station owner, Mr. Sepe, is sprinkling a shower of kitty litter over a puddle of dark liquid pooled on the cement floor inside one of the open garage bays.

"I just thought ... I don't know, that maybe you were sick or something," she tells him, when what she really wants to say is that his random disappearances confuse and even frighten her.

"I have to finish stacking the tires." He lifts his hand, pushing back a curve of dark hair drifted against his forehead. While the movement is fleeting, Willa nevertheless detects a discernable trembling in his slender fingers.

"Why won't you tell me what's going on, Jesse? Why can't you tell me what this is about?" Willa says quietly, her eyes pleading in such a way as to make it impossible for him to turn and walk away. And yet, somehow, he does.

She can only hope that the day will eventually arrive when he will trust her enough to tell her of this thing shadowing his life, even while she understands not to expect it.

But she knows she will wait, maybe not patiently, but wait, nevertheless. Coveting every little piece he either gives her voluntarily or accidentally reveals, carefully fitting them together to create something of a real and actual portrait of this person, Jesse Truman.

Twenty-six

His truck is here, waiting just down the road from The Moonglow when Willa finishes for the afternoon.

"Hey," he says when she pauses outside the open passenger side window, his easy smile nearly effective in convincing her that she's imagined the look of immediate shock sprinting across his features once he registers her changed looks.

A surge of words and emotion instantly scramble for bearing inside her head. Love, anger, confusion, arriving hard on the heels of shame over her wrecked appearance.

"Need a ride?"

No, she doesn't need a ride. She'll never need a ride from him or anyone else ever again. That's it. She isn't doing this anymore. She's done with crazy people and their crazy people games. Tired of feeling worried and afraid, not knowing who will be the next to vanish without explanation—to reappear or not. She doesn't expect him to tell her everything, just something. Enough so that she can understand. Because once you let someone care for you, it isn't just about you anymore.

But, "okay," is what she says, and he leans across the seat and yanks hard on the door handle to open it from the inside.

"You all right?" he says, throwing Willa a quick glance as he swings the truck back onto the highway.

"Um, hum." She moves her lips to form a portion of a smile she doesn't quite feel. She's reluctantly come to believe that this is how it will always be with Jesse Truman. That to push or complain or admonish is to forfeit. That to care for him requires that she endure his absences, silences, and mysteries.

"Your hair ..."

She dares a glimpse at herself through his eyes—the hideous, ugly picture he assuredly sees—and she turns her head away, fighting against the urge to open the door and leap from the moving truck, tumbling down the embankment into oblivion.

"I cut it. It was too hot," she says, trying not to remember how Jesse has touched her hair; wrapped thick tendrils around his hand and gently tugged her head to rest against his chest as they lay on the riverbank; loosened her perpetually messy ponytail to lay a butter shaded curtain across her face, parting the strands to kiss her lips.

He takes a moment to answer, and his voice is quietly serious when it comes. "It looks nice."

"Liar," she finds herself smiling despite her grief. Happy for the lie. Happy for his effort.

She presses her face against his neck, touching her lips to the pulse beating there. "You taste like summer," she whispers against his skin.

"That doesn't make sense. Summer doesn't taste like anything," he says, and Willa can hear the smile in his voice.

"Yes it does, it tastes like sunshine and clover and puffy white clouds," she laughs, rolling onto her back and staring up at the dappled light sprinkling through the tree tops.

"You're a kook."

It is nearly the end of summer and the river is now barely moving. They've come here with the intention to swim, but in the end they remain on the bank, the river's eerie stillness and murky color increasingly foreign and unappealing.

"It's looking pretty gross," Jesse says, staring out at the water.

"If you go in there now, you're likely to come out a different color," Willa says, disappointed, because this is all there is. There is nowhere else in Harriet's Bluff where they can go for a swim and cool off.

"I'm pretty sure this is the driest it's ever been around here. It's even starting to make The Moonglow's lake-of-crap look tempting."

They kick off their sneakers and sit side-by-side on the bank, grateful for the shade of an enormous spreading maple. After a while Jesse lies back on the dry grass and closes his eyes. He is so quiet and still Willa believes he's fallen asleep, until he suddenly reaches for her hand, tugging gently with an invitation to stretch out beside him.

It's impossible to think that summer is nearly gone. So much has happened, so many things changed, and yet oddly, Harriet's Bluff feels more or less the same. Impossible—but nevertheless true.

If not for Jesse Truman ... if not for Jesse ... Willa thinks, then stops, unable to step past that single introduction and over the threshold into imagination. Because if not for Jesse, she can't conceive of where she would be, or even *how* she would be. Every other ingredient comprising the whole of this summer has felt volatile and altogether wrong. Like a windowless train blindly hurtling over tracks in the wrong direction—a horrifying collision imminent, but no one capable of throwing the switch to stop it.

She can feel the threat of change breathing hard overtop them; and she thinks it wholly unlikely that Stella will care to wait out the winter at The Moonglow. Just as it's unlikely that Omega Pearl will even want them around, considering she's already made it known that the place pretty much shuts down once the summer months come to a close.

It's likely that only a matter of weeks, possibly days, remain before Stella makes the announcement that the time has come to move on. Willa is certain of it, more so since the theft of her hair and subsequent discovery of the thickening roll of bills Stella has been growing at the back of her dresser drawer like a fledgling miracle garden. An especially startling accumulation, considering the sorry state of their affairs, multiplied by the fact that Willa has never for an instant believed Stella's story about selling her hair. Even now, she remains convinced that her crowning glory was simply a victim of her mother's willful rage. Stella's method of punishing her for possessing something she doesn't have herself.

And at the center of it all, is this boy of a dozen mysteries, who, despite his frustrating penchant for secrecy, appeals to her as the only entity in the whole of Harriet's Bluff that feels genuine.

Jesse sits up, squeezing Willa's fingers before releasing her hand and beginning to pull on his sneakers. "Damn-it," he swears under his breath when the shoelace breaks in his hand.

Willa silently watches his attempts to tie the severed ends together.

"Stella left again," she says at length.

His dark hair sweeps forward, grazing the top of one eyebrow as he glances up. "Where did she go?"

"She never says." Willa wiggles her heel into her sneaker. "If I didn't know better I'd say she's found herself a boyfriend, but that can't be it because where would she ever meet anyone around here? Definitely not at The Moonglow. Besides, she's always saying how men are worthless and can't be trusted."

"Then what makes you think she met someone?"

"I can't explain it. There's just something about the way she's been acting. Something about the way she looks. Like, I don't know … Like a woman who's advertising something, is what she thinks, but is too embarrassed to say it out loud. "I mean, I've seen this all before. It's as if she's building up to something," Willa says, pausing briefly before blurting out the question she's been inking back and forth in her mind all afternoon. "Will you stay with me?"

He lifts his head, navy eyes deep and questioning.

"I know I sound like a baby, but it's a little scary being alone with a murderous arsonist on the loose." And she knows how foolish she sounds because she isn't alone. Not really. Not with Omega Pearl forever on the lookout for all things suspicious. And then there is the handful of guests currently occupying several of the cottages. Surely enough live bodies on hand to deter a visit from Norman Hitchcock.

"There's nothing for you to be afraid of. He's not after someone like you."

"Maybe … but I just thought…"

"What if your mother comes back early?"

"She never does."

"You said she's unpredictable."

Willa drops her eyes, concentrating on jamming her other foot into the remaining sneaker as a flood of humiliation pounds up around her ears and blurs her vision. *He knows precisely what she's asking and he's looking for the kindest way to say, no.*

"Alright, so okay, maybe I'll see you tomorrow then," she says, quickly rising to her feet before he's finished lacing his high-tops.

"Hold on, I'll drive you."

"No, I'm fine. I feel like walking," she says, turning away before she all out succeeds in decimating the few remaining crumbs of her self-respect.

Twenty-seven

The sound comes again, low and soft through the simmering night, carrying through the dark like a warm breath exhaled from the trees.

Willa sits up in bed, then drops her feet to the floor, cautiously snaking her way to the window adjacent Stella's vacant bed. She scans the darkness beyond the sill, her gaze traveling slowly ... hesitant ... terrified to find the shine of eyes staring back. But there is nothing hovering within the deep shadows clinging to the cabin that doesn't appear altogether ordinary.

The sharp ping of something small and hard hits the edge of the window screen, startling her backwards into the protective shroud of darkness.

"*Willa.*"

Instantly recognizing the whispered voice, Willa lifts her face to peer out through the screen. He has moved closer to the window, and though she can now make out the outline of his slender frame, his features remain blurred in shadow.

"What're you doing here?"

"Were you asleep?" he asks, as if he hasn't heard her question.

"Sort of ... well, no."

Somewhere nearby a door squeaks on its hinges. A bulb blinks awake on the porch of a neighboring cottage, breaking the darkness with a spill of weak yellow light.

"So, do you think maybe you could come out here before the National Guard arrives?"

"What're you talking about? Come where?" she whispers back.

"With me," he says and she isn't certain if she's heard the shy hesitation in his voice or simply imagined it.

She takes a moment to answer. "Wait there. I'll be out in a minute."

She dresses quickly in the dark, yanking up her shorts even before she pulls her nightgown over her head and tosses it toward the bed, not caring whether it lands on mattress or floor. She doesn't pause to turn on a light as she reaches into the closet and jerks a sleeveless cotton blouse from its bent wire hanger, buttoning up the placket with trembling fingers as she tries to recall where she's left her sneakers.

Willa doesn't ask where he's parked his truck or what it is he's carrying in the tight bundle clutched under his arm as they walk in silence.

The moon is high and white against the dark sky, nearly full if not for a thin slice of missing light. Following Jesse as he walks just slightly ahead of her, Willa feels as though she is trailing a mirage—her body passing through an illusion. And only once they reach the fringe of trees at the edge of woods does he pause, turning to face Willa with his quietly serious question, "Are you sure?"

She nods, not trusting herself to speak. Glad for the darkness. Grateful that she can't read whatever expression is there behind the grey shadows obscuring his face.

The night is full of sound, insects and unseen creatures shrill and throbbing within the cover of dark woods.

"Can you see okay?" Jesse says when the path narrows and they are forced to walk in a tight single file.

"Yes," she answers, though the canopy of treetops webbed together overhead has all but eclipsed the moon's bright light, and she can no longer see the clear outlines of the path. She focuses her eyes on the vague silhouette of Jesse's back as they continue through the woods, concentrating her stare on his narrow shoulders, the back of his head where the dark hair grazes the neck of his white tee shirt.

Jesse Truman, she imagines herself saying out loud, her senses savoring the taste of his name on her tongue. And she smiles, right then in her mind's eye seeing the glimmer of moonlight reflected in his gaze as his head turns back toward the sound of her voice.

Someone has tacked up a bright yellow NO TRESPASSING sign on the outside of the shack, but Jesse ignores it. Silently lifting a hand and signaling Willa to wait while he pushes open the door and steps inside to check for scavenging rodents and wandering skunks, though the possibility of face-to-face contact with meandering wildlife feels far less frightening than the ever present threat of finding Norman Hitchcock himself camped out across the dirty mattress.

But there is nothing inside other than what has been here each time previous, an injured collection of forlorn furnishings draped in stale air.

Willa can feel his hesitation, as if he is waiting for her to say something, anything maybe. But she declines the opening, unsure of the particular words that belong here and fearful of choosing the wrong ones.

She watches Jesse take the bundle from under his arm, unfurling what she now sees is a blanket, overtop the mattress. It would be a simple enough thing for her to cross the room and offer assistance, smooth the folds and tuck the edges. And yet she is powerless to move, wholly unequipped to command her body to follow the logical and uncomplicated instructions directed by her head.

The incredible white light of the moon shining directly overhead leaks its dreamlike luminance through the ceiling cracks and pane-less windows, striping across one long edge of the mattress and spilling onto the floor in a radiant gossamer puddle.

Finished with his task, Jesse turns and sits on a corner of the mattress. She feels the weight of his eyes. *We're here. The stage is set.* His expectant stare stirs together the thoughts that never seem to leave her head. Still, her tongue lies like a lump of unformed clay inside her mouth, held still by the fear that the sound of her voice is far too heavy for the frailty of moonlight and silvery air drifting out between them.

She moves toward him on hollow legs and perches on the edge of the mattress, barely an arm's length from where he sits, close enough to reach out and touch her if he chooses, yet far enough removed to avoid the suggestion that he must.

A long moment passes, infinitely loud and blaring in the silence. Willa bends and pulls off her sneakers, pretending herself oblivious to the wild hammering of her heart and the quaking of her hands. She lies back on the scratchy wool blanket, her breath catching in her throat as she focuses on the stiff line of his back, squeezing her eyes tight and concentrating in an effort to reclaim the accustomed rhythm of her breathing. *Slow, easy... tick tock, tick tock ... steady, even. Smooth, calm, easy.*

The night pressing in around them has ceased to move. Willa rolls onto her side, seconds piling into minutes that pile into eternities before Jesse at last bends to untie his sneakers. He stretches out on his back beside her, his face turned toward the ceiling.

"Willa ..." he begins, faltering when she reaches out and lays a hand on his arm.

"It's okay if we don't talk."

He shifts and turns onto his side, facing her, Willa's uncertain gaze instantly caught and held by the glimmer in his deep navy eyes. And suddenly she is tumbling forward, falling into a hole that spills directly into eternity, losing her bearings even as his arms wrap around her.

She tucks her face against his neck and closes her eyes, breathing in his scent—the lingering odor of engines and gasoline, but also something else. Summer. Hair and skin that smell of sunlight and warm breezes.

His chin rests against the top of her head where she lies folded within his embrace. And there has never been a time, not ever in her life, when she's felt anything like she does now—as safe as she is thoroughly cherished.

Willa reluctantly stirs, drawing back just enough to tip her head away from his neck, fully expectant of feeling the softness of his lips touching against her face. But his eyes are closed, his breathing moving in and out with a steady cadence. Their faces are only inches apart. Willa studies the dark curve of lashes laid against the smooth crest of his cheeks like fairy wings, the sharp line of his nose, the soft arc of his lips, striving to memorize every curve and angle of his face as he sleeps.

Her eyelids snap open. It is still dark, but the night has unequivocally changed, the room now softly washed in the murky light that comes with approaching dawn.

Jesse mumbles in his sleep—a low groan rumbling in his throat as he flips onto his back. And it is only as the fog of sleep melts away behind her eyes that Willa suddenly comprehends that it's his fitful tossing that's awoken her.

"Jess ..." she shakes his arm as another distressed groan gathers into his mouth. "Jesse, wake up. You're having a dream," she says, tightening her grip, again shaking his arm, harder now.

"Wh ... what? What's wrong?"

"You were having a bad dream."

"Oh ... I ... I don't know what ... I'm sorry," he says, running a hand through his hair, pushing a fringe of stray locks back from his forehead.

"It's all right," Willa says feeling the immediate flush of his embarrassment. "Show me someone who says they've never dreamed of being chased by a hideous green monster with huge pointy teeth and I'll show you a liar."

He doesn't reply, lying still and straight. His eyes wide and staring.

"Hey," she touches his arm. "It's no big deal," then, when he still doesn't respond, "What was it? What where you dreaming about?"

"I don't know."

And somehow she knows that it's a lie. Because the dream hasn't left him. It is still right here, filling the room like a poisonous fog.

Still holding his arm, Willa moves her other hand against the thin cotton fabric of his tee-shirt, gently tracing her fingers across his chest, the parallel curves of his ribs, his stomach, until finally, he shifts his shoulders and turns to face her.

"This blanket is itchy," she whispers, trying a smile.

"It's an army blanket. One-hundred percent wool," he says, and his eyes are full and dark.

Willa watches him, offering no resistance as she feels herself swallowed into the very depths of his stare. She lifts her hand to his chin, touching his jaw, his ear, slowly moving her fingers through his soft dark hair to the back of his neck.

They don't speak, the air grown heavy and thick in such a way to negate the intrusion of speech. And now there is his touch—his hand on her arm, her shoulder, trailing along her back. His mouth close enough to share her breathing. He kisses her, softly, carefully, his lips grazing along her lips, cheek, touching her ear … then again trailing to her mouth.

"Willa," he says her name, only once, as if to remind her that she is still here tethered to the earth. Though it makes little difference. All sense of time, and space, and reason, gone as if none have ever existed.

His lips never leave her mouth. Not when she feels his fingers unbuttoning her blouse, or when he slips his hand inside the loosened fabric to cup her small breast—all the time kissing her. And even when she pushes away his tee-shirt, her hands flat against the smooth heat of his skin, their lips break apart for only the instant it takes for him to pull the shirt over his head.

Pressing against him, Willa feels his heartbeat pumping through her own skin; the pulse of their internal organs separated only by skin and bone—molecules and cells, absorbed into each other like poured liquid—the dizzying sensation of skin against skin, swelling up large and full in her head to eclipse every particle of thought formerly in existence there.

And it no longer matters that her glorious honeyed mass of hair is gone, because he makes her believe she is beautiful. The most beautiful perfect creature. She hears herself telling him that she loves him. And although she is uncertain if the actual words leave her mouth, they are there everywhere inside her head, beaming out through her fingertips, her lips, her breath, exploding beneath her ribs as he wraps his arms around her and makes her forget every other person in the world who isn't him.

And not until much later will she allow her memory to recall what she persistently forces away in the milky soft light of rising dawn—the telltale implications of grievous injury that she feels along his back as she holds him—her fingers unconsciously tracing the distinct threads of heavy welts spanning the breadth of his shoulders.

Twenty-eight

So, let me guess—you figured you'd better get your sneaky little ass home before *your mother* shows up," Stella's voice assails her like a slap even before Willa steps into the cottage and the screen door snaps shut behind her.

Willa freezes in mid-step, her blood instantly draining to form icy pools in the soles of her feet. Her eyes sweep the room, all at once impaled by the pointed spires of Stella's black stare glaring at her from the decrepit chair pulled up near the window, legs slung over one threadbare arm, feet tapping the air in an agitated cadence.

"*You're home,*" is all Willa can think to say.

"Why, yes, as a matter of fact I am. And I can see from your expression what a big, fat surprise that is for you," Stella answers, her voice dripping with an artificial sweetness far more disconcerting than the more deliberate bite so readily apparent in her follow-up question. "So how about you tell me where the hell you've been?"

"I couldn't sleep, so I just figured I'd walk around for—"

"Baloney. You don't seriously expect me to believe you were just strolling around all night sightseeing."

"It's the truth," Willa says, rushing her words past the quaver in her voice.

"If you're gonna lie at least put some effort into it."

"I'm not lying."

"Like hell." Stella's tone is low and dangerous. She swings her legs to the floor and rises in one fluid movement. "You're scared of the dark."

Willa takes an instinctive step backwards. "Maybe when I was five," she says, though in truth she can't remember when she's stopped being afraid—or if she even has.

"Do you honestly think I'm such an idiot I don't recognize a bold-faced lie when I hear it?"

A darkening knot of indignation clenches the muscles of Stella's face like a closing fist, alerting Willa to the futility of attempting an answer. She well knows the unpredictable patterns of her mother's moods, the ranting that carries her to the very edge of a certain short-circuit, but then just as quickly disperses into the invisible particles comprising thin air.

"Because, I know what you're doing. I know exactly what's going on. You're doing every damn thing I told you not to. You're no better than those whorish strays of yours."

Willa stares without looking, determined not to hear, refusing to allow the poisonous words to take root inside her head. Holding firm to the lingering essence of Jesse Truman steeped into her skin and anchored in her heart, even as Stella strives to wrench it away and stomp it like rubbish at her feet.

"Well, you know what?" Stella suddenly snickers, her poisonous rage edging away in a blink. "I don't give a damn! I really don't care. I was just making conversation."

"What's wrong with you?" Willa stares, fear and disbelief wrestling for immediate possession of her face. *What is going on? She feels like someone pushed into the path of a barreling tractor trailer, only to have the massive thing evaporate like mist seconds before impact.*

"Not a damn thing, actually. As far as I'm concerned I'm just about finished with all this anyway. It's right about time for my life to get better, so you can go right ahead and run with the gypsies if that's what lights your fire. It's your business. Be my guest."

Willa makes a move to brush past her.

"That's right, run away and hide. You've always been the kind who needs to find out the hard way. Just remember this conversation five years from now when you're living in a trailer with your brood of dirty, starving brats and deadbeat boyfriend. Waking up every day for the rest of your life hating the world and everything in it because you chose to stick your nose in the air and walk away instead of listening to good advice when it was being offered."

Willa doesn't answer. Doesn't open her mouth for fear of what awful things might come out.

From the time she was old enough to comprehend Stella's particular set of rules and ironclad edicts, Willa has known to steer clear of her mother's private space and all those articles occupying it.

Back in Hoosick Falls, Stella had always been diligent in keeping her bedroom door closed. Even on those infrequent occasions when the door was inadvertently left ajar and Willa could see her mother standing in front of her dressing table dabbing her throat and wrists with perfume, or sitting on the edge of her bed pulling on nylons, she'd known not to venture into the room—obediently holding to the doorway regardless of whether she had something to tell, ask, or show her mother.

It is a rule so long established that Willa has never thought to consider whether there might be some peculiarity in her mother's obsessive insistence on privacy. As it is, she simply accepts it as yet another of Stella's concrete and not-to-be questioned regulations. And if not for a cause as provoking and unpardonable as imminent starvation, it is altogether doubtful that Willa would dare venture into her mother's currently established boundaries now.

Even before she opens Stella's dresser drawer for what is only the second time in her life, Willa feels a definite sense of fear and dread violently churning inside her stomach. And when she carefully inches it open just wide enough to slip her hand inside, panic surges upward to clench tight fingers around her madly thumping heart.

Asleep Without Dreaming

Ordinarily she has little interest in anything that Stella might be concealing amongst the jumble of wardrobe articles crammed into her dresser drawers. But it's been several days now since Stella has sent her to the market in town, days since there's been anything to eat other than handfuls of dry cornflakes and plastic spoonfuls of peanut butter.

When Willa can no long hold back from complaining that human beings can't be expected to survive on dry cereal, Stella's disinterested response is to shrug and announce that the money she's managed to put away from the days of her dead flower business has dried up weeks ago and that as far as she can tell money has yet to start budding on the trees. She makes no mention of the money supposedly acquired from stealing and selling Willa's hair, and still, there is the weekly salary from Omega to consider. True, it is a meager stipend, but at the very least it is *something*, and Willa has every intention of finding the hiding spot where Stella has tucked it away.

For the past several days, Willa has waited with anxious impatience for the chance to be alone inside the cottage; and at last Stella is gone, having risen uncharacteristically early that morning with the announcement that she was going into town to *attend to a few things.*

Willa watched from behind the front screen door until Stella's bright yellow dress appeared as a faraway dot of yolk, moving briskly along the highway, before shutting the heavy inside door and turning the deadbolt. The wide aluminum blinds have earlier been drawn tight against the bright rays of morning light, leaving the room oppressively shrouded within a veil of grainy gloom and stale heat.

There's no telling how long Stella will be gone, but Willa guesses she'll have ample time to gather the handful of coins she expects to find dotting the clutter spilled across the top of the dresser and lay claim to a dollar or two tucked away at the back of a drawer before her mother's return.

She rapidly skims the surface of Stella's night table, pocketing the two dimes she finds there before crossing to the dresser and scanning the accumulation for an additional glimmer of loose change. But there is nothing of use scattered amongst the dusty collection of magazines, papers, and crumpled cigarette packs, other than a handful of bobby pins and the stub of a black eyebrow pencil.

She eases open the same drawer she had invaded weeks earlier on her quest for the necessary funds to buy Jesse's bracelet. Weeding through the tangle of nylons and underwear and feeling along the sides and bottom of the compartment, she impatiently shoves it closed, finding nothing of what's she's hoped for. She yanks another drawer open, rapidly combing her fingers through the contents, but once more finding nothing aside from the ordinary inventory of clothing and accessories.

Willa moves quickly, ignoring her swelling sense of criminality as she rifles briefly through the remaining drawers, expectant that her fingertips will, at any moment, touch upon the telltale smoothness of paper bills folded together. And yet, still—nothing.

Deliberately avoiding the tangle of clothes heaped in a pile in front of the open closet door, she peers into the dim recess. Her gaze skims the clutter: shoes, bags, magazines jumbled together on the floor below the hemline of hanging garments, then lifts to where Stella's collection of saucy little hats and their matching purses are tossed together on an upper shelf— fashionable items that have little purpose in the life they are currently living

Hopeless. There are dozens of potential hiding places within the disheveled room that might prove adequate for concealing Stella's nest egg, but there isn't enough time to examine every seam, poke fingers into the toe of every shoe and frisk every pocket. And considering the fact that Stella can't have all that much to accomplish in a town as barely there as this one, it's altogether likely she's on her way back to The Moonglow at this very moment.

Asleep Without Dreaming

Willa returns the closet door to its previous half-open position, eyeballing the dresser to assure that no drawer has been left askew. She shoots a glance toward her mother's unmade bed, the tangle of sheets drifted over the edge of the mattress and onto the floor, pausing to listen for any sound indicative of Stella's return, shoes crunching over gravel, heels tapping across the porch.

She lifts a single blind with her finger, stealing a quick peek at the dusty slice of parking lot visible from the window before cutting her eyes toward the road in search of a bright glimpse of yellow in motion. But there is nothing stirring in the high summer heat, the cottage itself quiet as a box shut tight around her. She hurries to the bed, lifting both pillows then bending to push her hands between mattress and box spring, disappointed but not especially surprised when she fails to discover the elusive treasure. *Because of course, Stella is far more clever than that.*

She ducks her head to survey the dusty space under the bed, but the tightly drawn blinds have left the room too dark to see anything other than the outline of several cardboard shoeboxes and some empty bottles lying on their sides and rolled against the wall. She selects the nearest box and yanks off the lid, peering inside at a collection of receipts, scraps of paper, and canceled checks—*Stella's idea of bookkeeping.*

Replacing the lid, Willa shoves the box back into the shadowy depths beneath the bed, her fingers chasing amongst an abundant garden of dust-balls before landing on another box. She draws it out and hastily flips off the lid.

Her blood races cold in her veins. A horrified scream climbs her throat, and her hand flies to her mouth in a shield holding back the ineludible sounds of immediate horror.

Inside the box, staring back from the sinister twin slashes of its dead black eyes, is a doll. An ugly, frightening, hideous little doll.

A scrap of floral print fabric twines the primitive body in a crudely fashioned dress; the color and pattern of the cloth strangely familiar. Several strands of yellowy gold hair are glued to the top of the doll's head, real hair Willa guesses, considering the creator's apparent intent to replicate an actual person as authentically as possible. But most chilling are the pins stuck into the vile creature's cloth body, dozens of shiny silver points cruelly drilled into the arms, legs, torso, and head. Bloodless wounds nevertheless lethal in their definite purpose and unmistakable intent.

It is as if everything around her has ceased to move—the seconds no longer ticking past—her frozen stare unable to leave the thing in the box.

What is this ugly thing? Who is it? Who is this meant to be?

And gradually, like a light steadily gaining strength as it closes the distance, Willa sees what she's failed to recognize at first glance, all at once aware of what it is laid out neatly in the bottom of the box—stacks of fives, tens, and twenty-dollar bills. A pretty, green mattress for an ugly little doll.

Asleep Without Dreaming

Twenty-nine

Look, honey, if you want me to be honest, I have to say your mother struck me as the type right from the start. She's one of those women that like people doing for her, but not the other way around," Omega Pearl says as she flips through an old issue of *Ladies Home Journal* in search of previously overlooked coupons.

"Hum … I wonder if this *Spam* stuff is any good. I've never been crazy about meat in a can, but it looks interesting. There's a nice recipe here, too."

"It's just that she isn't used to this kind of work," Willa says, attempting to ignore how much she dislikes the taste of her lie. After all, when it comes to Stella, Omega's observations are nothing if not dead-on accurate.

"What's to get used to? I need help and she needs money. It doesn't get much simpler than that."

Nothing involving Stella is simple, is what Willa wants to say. *She keeps a hideous doll stuck with pins inside a box of money under her bed. What about that? Just how simple is that?* Willa can hardly imagine which expression would win the battle for immediate appearance on Omega's face should she dare tell her what she's found—shock and horror for certain, fear pushing in hard.

"She has what under her bed?" Omega would say, looking up, scissors poised over a coupon for marshmallow fluff.

"I don't really know for sure. A doll of some sort with pins—"

"A Voodoo doll? If it has pins stuck in it, that's what it is. But who is it? Who does it look like?"

"I don't know, I can't really tell."

"I sure as hell hope it isn't supposed to be me."

"It's just an ugly doll with hair—real hair—glued on it head."

"Maybe it's a joke."

"Yes, of course it is. How can anything so ridiculous be anything but hilarious?"

"Is that all? Is there anything else in the box?"

"MONEY, it's full of money. That's really the joke. All that dough, and yet we're still here in this dump without a cracker to eat for breakfast."

"I don't know what happened with the sheets," Willa says instead. "She just must've gotten mixed-up and put the dirty ones back on instead of the clean ones."

"Um hum," Omega narrows her eyes. "And the dirty towels? Mixed those up too? Soap scum in the tub? Hair in the sink?"

"She doesn't have much experience with cleaning."

"Any idiot can clean, honey. Now I'm not blaming you, but I'm just telling you I know what she's up to. She figures I'm some dumb hick bumpkin she can take advantage of, but you can believe me when I say that my Mama didn't raise no fools. I'll explain it to her myself if that's what she needs to get the message loud and clear."

"Yes ma'am."

While there is some relief to be had from Omega's intention to confront Stella, Willa doesn't expect there's any brand of interference that will prove effective in exorcising whatever demon it is now churning to life inside her mother's head.

And though she knows it's impossible, Willa secretly wishes for someone to see what she herself has, even if it results in immediate expulsion from The Moonglow. Just one rational soul to examine the hideous little doll and assure her that she is mistaken. Dead wrong in her conviction that it's her own hair glued on the tortured creature's head, and that Stella has not created the crude object to represent none other than Willa herself.

She wonders if it's possible for a mother to truly hate her daughter. The very notion seems to scream against anything designed by God or intended by nature, and yet there have been definite times in Willa's life when she's felt the certain hate, or at least the strong dislike, of her mother. And always the recognition has rocked her senses hard enough that she refuses to look at it even at those times when it is inches away—glaring into her eyes hard enough to scorch her soul.

It is a strange and terrible game that Stella loves to play—the theft of her hair, the dreadful little doll, and of course the letters. The hurtful, sickening letters.

She remembers the lightning spiking off in the distance as she hurried home from school that day, the deepening shades of indigo overhead lending to the illusion that the sky was closing in on the earth with rapid precision.

Shifting her armload of books, Willa reached past the unhinged door of the mailbox, feeling along the cool metal walls, expecting nothing, but instead finding a thick envelope. She rarely received mail of her own and so had been instantly thrilled to see that the name printed on the thick parcel was her own. Clutching the treasure to her chest, she sped up the driveway and into the house, haphazardly dropping her books on the table and caring little when the teetering pile promptly tumbled to the floor.

Willa flipped over the envelope in her hand, once again scanning its face to assure that it was indeed addressed to her, that in her haste she hadn't inadvertently torn into someone else's mail. But no, there had been no mistake. It was her own name staring back in bold black ink: **MISS. WILLA BURKETT.**

The bulging manila envelope held at least two dozen sealed envelopes of varying shapes and sizes, all of them blank, unmarked on the outside other than for an identical number written in the left hand corner of each.

She unfolded the single sheet of paper tucked inside the first envelope she opened—disbelief, shock, and annoyance piling together as she attempted to digest the tight scrawl of unfamiliar handwriting. She slid her fingers inside the torn edge of the envelope and retrieved the accompanying photograph of a middle-aged man, his face grinning at her like a demented Jack-O-Lantern from his awkward perch on the arm of a bright green upholstered chair, wearing nothing but an obscenely tight pair of bright red briefs that are just barely visible below his full and extravagantly furry chest.

Who was this? Did she know him? Should she?

Willa dropped the photograph as if scorched and rapidly tore through the remaining envelopes at random, the contents of each letter disturbingly similar in their unfamiliarity, creepily intimate letters and their accompanying photographs lending to the jarring implication that Willa had somehow done something to solicit their common attentions.

But then all at once she understood—*a joke*. Of course, it was a joke. Someone's idea of a sick, stupid joke. But who? Who disliked her enough to target her in such crude fashion? Because it wasn't funny. Nothing even remotely funny.

She took a frantic run through her thoughts, compiling a mental list of potential suspects, but nevertheless unable to conceive of whoever it was that apparently disliked her enough to go through the trouble of humiliating her in private.

Mostly she wanted to pretend that it didn't matter, that it was just an ignorant prank having no effect on her whatsoever. Except that it did. Just as the recognition that she apparently possessed an enemy she hadn't even suspected the existence of until now was nothing, if not jarring.

In school Willa had been careful to remain more or less nondescript. She'd never felt confident in pursuing or accepting friendships for the very reason that nearly everything about her life felt too odd for sharing, peculiar in a way that she preferred to keep herself separate even from kids she'd known her entire life. She was friendly, but without friends. Safely invisible she'd believed, at least until now.

With no certain place to turn her anger, Willa furiously ripped the pile of letters and their accompanying photographs into microscopic bits before pushing the shredded crumbs of paper down behind an empty cereal box crushed into the kitchen garbage bin.

But even then, after she'd gone to her room and closed the door, flopped across her bed and dropped an arm over the edge to reach the library book she'd left open on the floor, Willa was unable to keep her thoughts from wandering back to the collection of startling letters. Her mind endlessly churning over the possible identity of whomever it was that had chosen her to be the butt of their idiotic joke.

Although she made every attempt to swallow the acrid taste of anger swelling into her mouth, the unease of knowing that the offending letters were still there inside the house remained loud and blaring in her head, infinite particles no less threatening in miniscule pieces than they'd been while whole.

Closing her book with a sharp snap, Willa returned to the kitchen and yanked the bag of garbage from the bin. She tied the top of the bag into a tight knot, and then carried it out to the metal trash can parked behind the tumbledown garden shed.

Someone had gone to a lot of trouble for nothing because she had no intention of letting it annoy her one second longer. It was stupid and ignorant, but it wasn't her problem. Over, done, forgotten.

She stuffed the bag deep into the can, slamming the lid overtop her rage.

For days afterwards, even though she steadfastly refused to allow thoughts of the nauseating letters to settle, Willa nevertheless found it impossible to shake loose from the feeling that she'd been shamefully soiled and stripped of all armor.

The second bulging envelope arrived a week later, this one heavier and thicker than the one previous. Willa tore open the large brown envelope and briefly shuffled through the new collection of letters, noting that just as it had been with the first batch, the envelopes were blank, except for the matched numbers printed in the top corner of each.

She plucked a dull steak knife from the mound of unwashed dishes in the sink and sliced open several of the envelopes, tearing out the letters folded inside. Her eyes skimmed the words, the messages much like those she'd read days earlier. Only now she wasn't so much stunned as she was decidedly irked.

As horrifying as it was to see her own name printed in distinct black letters on the front of the large envelope by the faceless mockery of a stranger's hand, knowing the ugliness secreted inside, Willa couldn't force her eyes to look away any more than she could command her fingers to drop the offending pages. Because there was something there— something glaring back at her, urging her to see; some recognition that her mind stubbornly refused to comprehend, even as she watched its steady formation inside her head— large chunks of reasoning circled by an ever-tightening lasso of suspicion—spinning her thoughts faster and faster as she began adding it all together.

These men knew things about her. Private things. Things that strangers had no business knowing. What she looked like, *I've always had a special appreciation for long-haired blondes.* Things she liked to do, *Ever since I was a kid I've enjoyed bike riding … reading mysteries is a particular passion of mine.* Her favorite food, *I never would've expected to find another person in this pretentious world who, like me, would choose a hotdog smothered in beans and coleslaw with a side of macaroni and cheese over a four star meal any day of the week.* Traits and preferences not so much extraordinary inasmuch as they belonged to Willa.

Assuredly, there was little about her personal self that warranted perusal by the collection of faces and bodies laid out before her in glossy snapshots and poorly lit Polaroid's, and yet that was precisely what had happened. Each letter contained a piece of her that she'd never willingly offered or otherwise agreed to share.

And just like that she'd known—the revelation arriving like a stick aimed at her head to deliver the identity of the one person all too capable of such crude intent.

Over a span of several months Stella had managed to amass an astonishingly diverse inventory of items in various stages of decay, so that the collection not only far exceeded her original selection of withered flowers and petrified brown stems, but also the boundaries of the small sun porch housing her fledgling business.

Stepping into the cluttered space that her mother used as her workroom, Willa found herself instantly surrounded by a tight settlement of cardboard boxes, plastic tubs, paper bags, and wooden produce crates stamped with the name of the grocery store in town. Each was filled and carefully labeled with Stella's unorthodox inventory: crumbling cut flowers, skeletal remains of house plants, leggy clumps of yard weeds (dirt-encrusted roots still intact) boxes of candies and cookies long past expiration, hard nuggets of something that bore a suspicious resemblance to petrified dog poop.

"Don't tell me you're interested in ordering an arrangement?" Stella said from the doorway.

Willa swung around, her indignation flaring to extinguish any momentary interest she'd had in studying the peculiar assortment crowded around her. "Yes, actually, I am. I'd like the most hideous and disgusting thing you have available and I'd like it sent to Stella Burkett."

Stella opened her mouth, but her lips just as quickly snapped shut when her gaze dropped to take in the bulging brown envelope tucked under Willa's arm.

"What's that?"

"I can't believe you're even my mother. You're horrible. Horrible and wicked and awful."

Willa took a step closer, shoving the envelope against Stella's tightly crossed arms, forcing her to take hold of it.

"Why would you even do such a thing? Is this supposed to be funny? Because it's not. There's nothing funny about it. It's disgusting," Willa said, the words rolling out in a quavering hiss. "And don't say you had nothing to do with it, because that's a lie. I know you did. I know it."

"What the hell's gotten into you?" Stella scowls. "I have no idea what you're carrying on about, but whatever it is I don't have time for it. I've got a dozen—"

A river of heat flooded over Willa's face, singeing a swath across her skin like a newly laid highway. "Oh yes you do! Don't even try to deny it. You gave out my name to strangers. You told them personal, private, things about me," Willa felt the immediate peppering of molten tears burning holes behind her lids, threatening to spill, and she snatched back the offending envelope from Stella's hands only to slam it down at her feet, sending a trail of escaping letters skittering across the lusterless floorboards.

Stella's eyes instantly widened as she stared at the letters, squatting quickly to retrieve them. "What are you doing with these?"

"They're all from men. *Strange, nasty men.*"

"This isn't yours. These aren't for you," Stella snapped, grabbing at the runaway letters and stuffing them back into the envelope.

"That happens to be MY name if you haven't noticed."

"You should've shown it to me before you just ripped it open. You know damn well you never get mail."

"What the—that's ridiculous. If something has my name on it then it's for me."

"Not everything. And you sure as hell knew that when you went meddling through it. It's my personal business."

"There's pictures of men in there wearing nothing but their under—"

"It's none of your business. It's none of your damn business and I don't appreciate having you snooping through my belongings."

"*Snooping?* It's addressed to ME."

"The minute you saw those letters you knew damn well they weren't for you."

"How was I supposed to know that? You can't go around stealing someone's name without asking. It's mine. It's MY name."

Stella turned and stuffed the envelope into a box beneath her work table, an old varnished door supported by two saw horses. She pretended that she didn't notice or otherwise care about the storm swelling up behind Willa's eyes as she peeled several sheets of newspaper from a pile at her feet, spreading them across the top of the table like a hobo's tablecloth before emptying a box of withered marigolds.

"Why would you want mail like this? Why is it even coming here?" Willa said, her insides quaking like shifting earth as she watched Stella casually sorting through the petrified stems.

"Okay, since you've already stuck your nose where it doesn't belong, it so happens, Dee was the one who suggested it. She said it didn't seem such a bad way to meet someone nice," Stella said, deliberately tilting her face to shield her expression from the flared points of Willa's disbelieving stare as she combed through the mess of brown twigs and stems strewn out before her like a slaughtered stick army. "It was only a few dollars to run an ad for two weeks and—"

"*An ad?* An ad for what?"

"Cut the naïve act, Willa. You're not such a blooming idiot that you've never heard of a personals ad. People do it all the time. It's a good way to see what's out there. And there's always the chance of meeting—"

"Why are you meeting anyone? You're still *married*, aren't you?" Willa said, her eyes narrowing even before the next thought was fully formed inside her head. "*That's why you used my name.* So you can stay anonymous and just wait to see what shows up in the mail. Then all you have to do is sort through and claim your big prize." She glared at Stella, her eyes aimed like weapons, fighting the urge to wrench her mother's slender neck until it snapped and severing the infuriating expression of complacency from her face.

"Don't be so damned melodramatic, Willa. It just struck me as an interesting idea. None of those fools know who I—who you are. It's all done by a special number code so everyone's identity is protected."

"I don't care if it's done by sign language, I don't want any part of it. It gives me the creeps."

"Well, let me tell you something, Miss Priss, if you ever expect to get the hell out of this dump then you'd better start to care. Because the last time I looked there wasn't a pile of resumes stacked up outside the door waiting for either one of us to point a finger and make a selection."

And thankfully, that was the end of it. There were no more letters. No more talk of leaving. Almost as if none of it had ever happened.

Asleep Without Dreaming

Thirty

Willa has been gone all afternoon, joyously riding a dozen country roads with Jesse in his pickup, allowing herself the temporary illusion that this is the totality of her existence. Nothing else, just this. Gold and blue light float above the treetops; gossamer wings spread overtop like a force field holding back everything else that has no place in the company of such perfection.

"I should probably drive you back before they send out the fleet to look for you," Jesse says.

Willa nods, aware of the long shadows stretching out to indicate late afternoon, hating the thought of going back to The Moonglow as much as she dislikes actually being there.

She drags her feet across the dirt and gravel parking lot like twin brick loaves, her dejected limbs too heavy even to lift against the dust.

She misses him already. She's been apart from him for less then ten minutes and she misses him so hard it hurts.

Willa lifts her head, immediately pausing at the impossible sight of Omega Pearl and Stella sitting together on the front step outside the office, several bottles of pop and a box of Lorna Doones set in the space between them.

The low murmur of their conversation drifts toward Willa across the grass, dry blades crunching under her feet like a lawn spread with cornflakes as she approaches. The women's quiet voices all at once break loose with a shriek of riotous laughter as Willa nears, and she eyes them warily, scanning their faces for some exterior sign that might clue her to the import of whatever it is passing between them.

"Good gracious, honey, you look parched. Here, have a cola," Omega Pearl says, holding out a bottle to Willa.

"Thank you," Willa takes the drink and Omega shifts her body sideways in an awkward attempt at repositioning her leg in its cumbersome cast.

"So anyway, listen to this, Stel, he comes into the office and says he wants to rent a cottage, but only for a *couple hours*. Don't get me wrong, I'm in no position to turn down cash paying customers right now, but this arrogant fool was far too cocky for his own good. I knew I didn't like him from the minute I laid eyes on him. So I tell him, 'I'm not running *that* sort of place' and he makes a big show of being insulted and says how he doesn't appreciate the insinuation. So I say, 'This is a small town, *Mister Brown,*' that's the name he signed on the register—how original, right? 'If you don't *appreciate the insinuation,* then you'd best find some other way to spend your afternoon. Like maybe you could take your *daughter* out there shopping for a new Barbie doll.' "

Stella chuckles, lifting the bottle of cola to her lips. "I'll bet that put a pinch in his shorts."

"No ma'am, not that nasty pig. He just pulled out his wallet and made a show of paying the overnight rate."

"What'd you say then?"

"Not a darn thing. I just took his money of course. It's not my business to be the morals police, is it?" Omega snorts, laughing longer and louder than seems necessary for a story that doesn't strike Willa as all that amusing.

In fact, Willa's pretty certain that had they been back in Hoosick Falls, Stella would right now be slipping into her carefully versed role of commiserating supporter of all sisterhood, and consoling Mister Brown's wife with her cultured and gentle Jackie voice, convincing the betrayed wife (because, of course, there is always a betrayed wife) that ordering the perfect rotten arrangement and having it promptly delivered to her husband's office was just the thing for letting him know that she was onto him, and his little party was now over.

Squeezing the neck of the cola bottle she still holds in her hand, Willa skulks around the corner and out of sight to sit in a lengthening stripe of shade spilling out from the back of the cottage.

She actually recalls the man and girl that Omega is right now attempting to spin into an entertaining anecdote. Willa had been cleaning a recently vacated cottage with Stella, when her attention was immediately piqued by the sound of tires rolling in too fast over the unpaved parking lot. Her arms overflowing with the bundle of sheets and towels Stella had stripped from the rumpled bed and gathered from the bathroom floor, Willa had paused, clumsily parting the curtain with her free hand just as a dark-haired girl alighted from a green sedan convertible parked at the far end of the dusty lot. She'd watched as the paunchy middle-aged man sauntered into the office and the girl walked around to lean against the fender, tugging the hem of her pink cotton shorts as if to readjust an uncomfortably creeping seam, nervously (or impatiently) combing her fingers through her long dark hair while she waited for him to return. And when he at last reappeared, a key dangling from one chubby finger like a prize, the girl followed him into a cottage without so much as a single backward glance, a calf resigned to its own imminent slaughter.

It had been a simple enough deduction that the two were not father and daughter; screamingly obvious in the girl's overdrawn affectations and fidgety poses as she waited for the man to return with the key like someone auditioning for a part. And Willa had deliberately steered her immediate curiosity away from the temptation to wonder over the wrongly paired twosome's purpose in coming to The Moonglow. Feeling the guilt and shame of an accomplice, simply for having witnessed their arrival, she was sorry for the wife she somehow knew existed, and disgusted by the deceiving husband. But even more so, she was angered by the girl's selfish ignorance in allowing him to cast her in what is clearly a grown-up's game.

Now, as she listens to the frivolous laughter rolling out from the front steps like spilled marbles, it strikes Willa as altogether remarkable that the two women have actually managed to land on common ground, garnering such ill-placed amusement from an episode that does little but serve to highlight the grossly criminal behaviors of strangers.

Still groggy with sleep, it takes several moments for Willa to recall where she is as her eyes adjust to the absence of light, another instant to comprehend that someone is here staring at her in the dark.

She lies perfectly still, feigning sleep, all at once certain that the hard stare boring holes through the gloom to pin her to the mattress in helpless terror belongs to no one other than Stella.

"What right do you have telling anyone my business?" Stella growls, her voice hard-edged and ominous, a thunderhead seconds away from splitting open to unleash a deluge.

Immediate fear striking her mute, Willa doesn't answer, clutching the sheet with fingers gone to rigor mortis, holding tightly to the protection of darkness.

"You think I'm some television show for everybody to watch? Some gossip column for people to snicker over?"

Willa squeezes her eyes shut, momentarily eclipsing the ominous threat of doom stretching toward her, but only for an instant, her lids jerking open of their own accord when she feels the icy chill of Stella's presence skulking closer.

"I don't know what you're talking about," Willa manages a squeak. *Stupid, Omega. She must've said something to Stella; though really, Willa can't imagine what. It isn't as if Willa doesn't know not to tell Omega anything of consequence about her mother. Certainly nothing that would clue her to Stella's disappearances, the box of money, or the crazy doll—the only immediate topics she can think of to explain her mother's enflamed of devil-eyed anger.*

"You think I need that nosey gossip poking around here looking for baloney piled stories she can repeat all over town?"

"Are you talking about this afternoon? I thought you were just talking—that maybe she was just being friendly. I mean she did say something a couple days ago about the rooms not being cleaned properly but I—"

"*Friendly?* There's no such thing. Friendly is a made-up word. It's nonsense. There's no such thing as *friendly.* It's a myth—a dumb-ass fairytale word for stupid gullible people."

Willa slides herself upright, wiggling backward on the mattress to prop her back against the wobbly headboard.

"And too damn bad if she doesn't like the job I'm doing. As if anyone would even notice in this rat-hole," Stella says, the shine in her eyes flaring back at Willa like twin rattlers poised to strike.

"I just—"

"You think you've got it all figured out, but you don't know a damn thing. It's nobody's figgin' business what I keep under my bed. I don't care if you find somebody's hand in a jar or a human head rolling around in a hat box, you'd better keep your mouth shut. What I do is my business. MY OWN DAMN BUSINESS."

"I never said anything about—"

"You think I don't know what you've been up to? Oh, that's right, I know damn well you've been poking around. You even helped yourself once, didn't you? You think I'm so stupid I can't count?" And all at once Stella is laughing, a sound low and deep like a rumbling engine. "So tell me, what did you think when you opened the box? Scared the bejeebees out of you, I'll bet."

But Willa doesn't answer, because for once Stella's words are dead-on accurate. It had scared her and still does. Even more so now in the face of her mother's erratic swing between anger and unreasonable hilarity. Just as it frightens her that her own secrets clearly aren't secrets at all, considering how one way or another Stella eventually comes to know everything she does. Even what she's thinking. In such a way that Willa has the feeling she's been invaded, her every thought ransacked, and subsequently dissected.

No less sobering is Stella's full-blown confidence that the hideous voodoo doll she's arranged in the box will frighten Willa far more than any angry confrontation should she ever again consider going in search of Stella's treasure, because it does, and she won't.

And hovering over everything is the unshakable sensation that the end of something is coming, is right now staring at her hard enough to make her flesh ache. It is an entity that she cannot see, yet vigorously feels. Hears it screaming louder than any sound she's ever heard. And it leaves her more afraid than she's ever been of anything.

Asleep Without Dreaming

Thirty-one

She's never believed until now that such depth of emotion even exists. Before Jesse Truman, Willa is of the definite opinion that sentiments such as love and devotion are merely inventions created to fill space on greeting cards. Common, meaningless expressions hauled out time and again by ladies like Omega Pearl Bodie and her gaggle of friends at the beauty parlor, where they routinely launch into all-knowing discussions detailing these long-extinct qualities so sadly lacking in the modern male. Fairytale words abundant in over-wrought literature and the private diaries of naïve females, but far from representative of anything bordering on the genuine or factual.

It isn't until her own floundering life takes a sharp turn and makes a head-on collision into Jesse Truman—with his bottomless navy eyes and quiet mystery—that the comprehension springs forth and Willa at last understands what it's all about.

And yet despite her significant awakening, no matter how familiar or emotionally connected she believes they have become, confused moments remain when she has the distinct sense that he is taking a step inside himself, drifting deep enough that she can see nothing of him beyond his skin, his thoughts as far away and inaccessible as some distant planet.

The end of summer is no longer running alongside them, but is now sprinting past at full throttle. And it isn't merely the as-yet unscripted conclusion of a strange and wonderful season winding to a close that presses heavily over the days. There is something else—a sense of finality that bears down like a threat—as if the entire peculiar chronicle unfolding into the present history of Harriet's Bluff is, in fact, methodically plotting its way toward some ultimate collision of impossible proportions.

The light beyond the shack's broken windows is already slipping, beginning a slow, hazy melt into the artificial gold of late afternoon and signaling that Willa needs to be heading back to The Moonglow if she hopes to avoid another confrontation with Stella.

But where is he? Why hasn't he come? Something has happened. Too many days have passed.

Willa wants to be angry with him, but always the blame boomerangs back to rest on herself. After all, she has no doubts that she's aided in the construction of this fluctuating wall of separation, if only because she's never looked hard enough to find an opening to admit what Omega has told her months ago—the ugly tale of his not-so-personal life. If he was to understand that she is aware of those things he is so diligently attempting to conceal—not only aware, but wholly commiserating of—then there would no longer be a need for him to work so hard at secrecy.

Just as she has no explanation for her failure to seriously attempt formulating even a potential plan that might somehow help him to change things. No honest reason why she has never wrestled with designs to acknowledge the unmistakable hardness of his life, other than the fear of sabotaging his pride. It's the same brand of cowardice that keeps her from offering anything that, in effect, might ultimately serve to heal him.

"We don't get along and that's never going to change. My old man doesn't want anything or anyone around to remind him of what he obviously wants to forget. If it wasn't for my brother, I'd just leave, but he's only a little kid and I can't run out on him like that," Jessie had said days earlier, the last afternoon they'd been at the shack together.

Her eyes sprung wide in surprise. "You have a brother?" *A notable fact that Omega hasn't mentioned.*

"He's my half brother. Red doesn't want me around him, but he's only five and he needs someone to watch out for him. I'd never forgive myself if someone ... I don't want anything to happen to him."

"What about his mother?"

He smiled, but there was sparse amusement contained in the expression. "She's long gone. She was messing around with one of Red's friend's and by the time he figured out what was going on she was halfway to Texas. Luke was only two at the time and she just left him," Jesse said, dropping his gaze. "I can't just take off now and leave him alone with someone like Red—not after everything he's been through already."

"Jesse," she said, and when he didn't respond, "Are you saying your father's dangerous? Do you think he'd—are you afraid he'll hurt him?"

He takes a moment to answer, declining to meet Willa's eyes. "He'll hurt him, but he won't touch him if that's what you're asking. His kind of hurt will be to ignore him. He won't hear and he won't see. Not when it means having to look at things he doesn't want to believe."

Willa could feel him waiting, expectant, wanting or maybe just needing her to say something, but his cryptic words had riddled her head with confusion. *What is he really telling her?* His statements lay in her mind like a puzzle, and she'd sensed a prerequisite for caution.

She watched the side of his face where they lay on their backs, side-by-side on the scratchy army blanket covering the mattress, silently urging him to say something more.

He sat up and leaned against the wall.

"What does he need to see?" Willa said carefully, the quiet growing between them now taking on conspicuous weight.

She pulled herself upright, bracing her determination to press forward. "Is this only about Luke? Or do you—"

"It's got nothing to do with me. I can take care of myself. He can't," he'd said, his expression snapping shut with his oath.

Silence fell with the finality of closed pages and Willa caught her lower lip with her teeth to keep her frustrated sigh from escaping. A crumb is all she ever gets. A single crumb to toss together with the handful of others he sprinkles out like random ingredients.

The air hung so tight it might have suffocated them, yet Jesse surprised her a few minutes later, reaching out to touch her hand lying on the blanket between them. Tracing his fingers along the outstretched length of her own, the dangling links of the chain circling his wrist tickling against her skin, as he covered the top of her hand with his palm. Neither speaking as late afternoon closed in around them.

And now, just as she's done for the past several days, Willa finds herself waiting, internally pacing within the purgatory of expectation, her longings and concerns rushing up against a widening wall of emotion that feels distinctly like anger. *It's been too many days. If he cares anything for her—and doesn't he?—he would find a way to be here. If only for a little while. He would come. He would know that she is here today, had come yesterday, and will come again tomorrow. He'd know and he would come. If he cared at all, he would have.*

Willa trudges across the straw-colored grass, the basket of cleaning implements cumbersome in her arms. Something flutters along the blurred edge of her vision; and she turns to see Omega lumbering out through the front door of the office, propelling her weight forward with awkward half-circle swings of her healing limb.

Curious, Willa pauses, watching Omega where she stands staring out toward the road. A cloud of gritty dust hangs heavy in the air as a lone vehicle just beyond Willa's field of vision accelerates from the parking lot and onto the highway.

The car gone, Omega turns, excitedly pumping the air with her arm in a vigorous effort to garner Willa's attention. Willa's immediate impulse is to pretend spontaneous blindness; but she knows it will only lead to the inevitable conclusion of having Omega track her down later, her injured leg slowing the process, but not stopping it. In a dull haze of slow-motion reluctance, Willa drops the basket in a far more careless manner than she intends, sending powdered cleansers, balled-up dusting rags, and cans of furniture polish rolling out across the parched grass.

Even before Willa reaches her, the peculiar expression on Omega Pearl's face has brought the metallic taste of dread flooding up to fill her mouth.

"Is she in some kind of trouble?" is the first thing Omega says.

"Trouble? Uh uh, there's no trouble. She's just feeling a little sick again. Some sort of female ailment. Nothing serious."

"Female problems are always serious. I'd better check on her and see if there's something I can do."

"She doesn't like anyone to see her when she's sick," Willa answers too quickly. "She's okay, really. It's just—she gets real cranky. She only ever wants to be by herself when she's not feeling right."

Willa has the distinct feeling that Omega isn't so much asking questions as she is searching for weak links and pinholes in Willa's explanation, an interrogation that leaves her newly fearful and enraged with Stella for leaving her in such a position in the first place. As it is, Stella has been gone all weekend and now here it is Tuesday, and she still hasn't returned from wherever it is she's waltzed off to this time.

"Well that's all well and fine, but she has to realize the work around here still needs—"

"I can take care of everything until she's better. I know what needs to be done."

Omega studies her as if contemplating an especially grave decision, though, in fact, she well knows that Willa has carried the bulk of the required duties over the past months, since it's easy enough to determine when Stella has helped if only because of how badly the work is done.

"Hum ... well, I suppose that'll be all right for a couple days," Omega says, holding her stare to Willa's face should some telltale indication of the lie she strongly suspects chance a fleeting appearance. "But you'd better tell her I said she needs to get to a doctor. I can't afford having to worry about a sickly housekeeper, and God forbid she's got something contagious."

"She'll be okay. She's had this same thing before," Willa answers, making only a tepid effort to hide her annoyance at Omega's pitiless assessment. *What should the woman care as long as the work's getting done? And for Pete's sakes, what if Stella really was laid up in bed suffering some horrific female agony? Would it kill Omega to be a little more sensitive?*

"Um, hum. Let's hope so. You just be sure and tell her that female troubles are not something to ignore. My cousin Theda had her whole uterus chopped out last winter because of a tumor. They took the whole darn thing and she's still not right."

Good Lord, what a horrible thing to tell a kid, Willa seethes behind a cardboard smile as she gathers up the runaway cleaning supplies and returns them to the upturned basket she's dropped on the grass.

Stella has never been late in returning on Sunday. She knows that Omega will be gone visiting one of her sister's in Elksboro, thus lessening the chance of being caught when she returns with suitcase in hand. Not that Stella is required to make explanations to Omega. She merely claims that the purpose behind her secrecy is more in keeping with her distaste for gossip, namely herself offered up as a topic by Omega Pearl during her weekly appointment at Veleda's House of Hair.

Only now it's Tuesday, and despite Willa's continuous internal assurances that Stella's failure to reappear on the designated day doesn't necessarily mean anything serious or alarming, she can't quite squelch the acrid taste of panic sporadically rising from her stomach to fill her mouth. *This is bad. Whatever this is, it's definitely bad. It must be bad.*

It's why she can't bring herself to look under Stella's bed for the box of money. Maybe later, but not now. Because then she'll know. She'd know for certain whether Stella is even coming back at all.

Thirty-two

She goes to motels with men. She knocks 'em out and rolls 'em for cash. It's all right here—read it for yourself," Omega pants, wild-eyed and flushed, as she waves the newspaper in front of Willa like a flag.

"This is stupid. It's got nothing to do with Stella. She might act a little kooky sometimes, but she's not a criminal," Willa says, her voice so tight it hurts her teeth to speak. For all her mother's tumultuous moods and sporadic twists of behavior, she certainly isn't capable of doing anything as deviant as this thing Omega Pearl is suggesting.

"Knock someone out? That's crazy—it's impossible." How would a woman as fussy and delicate as Stella ever find the strength to knock someone out? Especially a man. This detail alone makes the suggestion positively infeasible.

It's been three days since the earlier confrontation with Omega Pearl, and Stella still hasn't returned. And although the earlier pinpricks of dread and anxiety have since swelled to the proportions of enormous, Willa can think of no alternative other than to continue pretending Stella's presence, and hope she'll surface before long. And she knows it's nothing less than a blessed stroke of luck and timing that she's spotted Omega half-limping, half-dragging, her way across the grass on a determined beeline to the cottage Willa shares with Stella.

"The cops say this woman put some sort of drug or weird herbal concoction in her victims' drinks, and it knocked 'em out cold," Omega continues, the words tumbling forth in rapid-fire succession as her eyes dart over the article in search of startling passages, alternately shifting her gaze sideways, watching Willa's expression as she details the specifics.

"They say she's been showing up in towns all over the state and someone finally came up with a detail that points the finger in this direction. Apparently one of her victims remembers her mentioning a fugitive arsonist burning up the town where she—"

"Well they're wrong," Willa shouts, tightening her hands into a single fist at her waist. "This has nothing to do with Stella. This isn't her. This isn't something she'd do. You're just accusing her because you don't like her."

"Now, honey, you've got to—"

"NO! I don't care what you think," Willa screams. But rather than a shrill cry to mimic the one inside her head, the voice crawling past her lips is harsh and deep. And she right then sees herself spinning away from Omega's stunned expression—imagines her legs pumping hard and fast—even as she remains frozen, staring back at her motionless reflection in Omega's small, round eyes.

"All right fine. But look, you'd better let me talk to her then."

"You can't. Not right now. She doesn't like being bothered. I told you how she is when she's sick," Willa says; and she can hear the immediate fear and uncertainty flooding into her voice and across her face like a poisonous bile, all of it right there where Omega can see it.

"She's not here, is she?" Omega says, her eyes growing rounder, twin marbles about to pop from their sockets. "There's no female troubles, no sickness … she's not here. You're alone." And then, as if the full portrait has only just materialized in living color, "She just took off and left you here by yourself."

Willa doesn't answer. She can't. Her throat has swelled shut, her tongue solidified in her mouth like hardened clay. The impossibility of everything Omega has said echoes in her head with the snarling sounds of a thousand voices. And suddenly she is tearing away, fleeing from the terrible insinuations, sprinting through the tall grass and ditch weeds alongside the road, down the embankment, and along the blackened edge of the charred forest.

Even when her legs begin to throb and her breathing shortens into sharp, painful gasps, she is unable to shake herself loose from the burden of lies. All of the awful things Omega has said are still here, clinging against the back of her skull with talons sunk deep into the bone—words that twist through her brain like a curse.

Willa doesn't know why the memory resurfaces now, flying back like a returning boomerang to suggest some possible connection strung out between two otherwise unrelated incidents: this awful mess now, and an all but forgotten afternoon back in Hoosick Falls shortly before they left for good.

Had Willa cut across the front yard as was oftentimes her habit, she wouldn't have failed to notice the car parked in the driveway. But that day she'd come across the dirt yard in back and bounded up the steps onto the rear porch, attempting to shoo away the cats with her foot before Stella chanced to spot the feral colony and launched into another of her tirades. And it wasn't until she pulled the screen door open and skipped into the kitchen that she heard Stella speaking to someone in the front room.

The responding voice was wholly unfamiliar, and Willa slid across the gritty linoleum to steal a tentative peek into the living room where Stella and the visitor stood talking. Catching sight of what could only mean trouble, Willa felt her blood instantly flush away to pool behind her knees. Her insides at once rubbery, even as she held herself stiffly within the threshold, waiting for Stella to shift her eyes the necessary fraction and detect her presence.

Police… what did Stella do, was Willa's first thought. Did his being there have something to do with the letters? Had someone found out about Stella placing a personal ad using her kid as a decoy? Was that illegal? Or maybe it had something to do with Stella's business. Was it against the law to sell dead flowers? Or at least those that had been picked from trash piles all over town.

"Well, no, I don't have a description. I told you I haven't seen anyone face-to-face, but a person knows when they're being watched," Stella says, her voice indignant.

"So then you didn't actually *see* anyone?"

"No, I'm saying that I *did* see someone. There was a shadow right there outside," Stella pointed to indicate one of the room's double windows, the yellow-stained shades tightly drawn.

"This your daughter, ma'am?" the officer said, turning his attentions on Willa, pen poised over a small notepad open in his hand.

"Yes, but she doesn't know anything about this," Stella interrupted, attempting to steer the man's focus back onto herself. "What kind of idiot tells a fifteen year old girl there's a pervert out in the bushes staring in the windows?"

"Your name?" he says, ignoring Stella as he tips his chin in Willa's direction.

Willa stared at the shiny metal bar pinned above the pocket of his shirt. *Schmitt.* She'd seen him patrolling around town, an overweight cop with the comical swagger of a cartoon character, his salt and pepper hair combed back from an expression of perpetual boredom (though maybe a certain state of disinterest, Willa wasn't sure how to tell the difference.)

"Willa Burkett."

His pen remained poised above the notepad cupped in his hand. "Wilma Bur—"

"WILLA. Willa Burkett."

He lifted one bushy brow, but otherwise failed to comment as his pen scratched across the paper.

"Have you been aware of any suspicious or unusual activity around the house? Seen anyone wandering around that you don't recognize? Someone you don't think belongs in the neighborhood?"

"Um … well, I don't—"

"For crap sake! No wonder people get so damned annoyed with you cops," Stella interrupted, stepping close enough to Officer Schmitt that he was forced to take a step backward. "I just told you I didn't want her scared to death over this, and you immediately start firing a string of ridiculous questions at her anyway. We're two females alone here. Just how damn terrified do we need to be for you to take this seriously?"

"Look, ma'am, I have to—"

"NO, YOU LOOK! It's pretty straight forward, just like I told you. Some weirdo's been creeping around my house staring in the windows and scaring the hell out of me. Isn't that considered a crime anymore? I bet you'd take it pretty damned serious if it was your wife or mother who was being leered at."

Officer Schmitt returned her glare, a twitch along his jaw-line hinting at the response he knew well enough not to voice. He snapped the notebook shut and moved toward the door.

"I'll have a look around outside," he said on his way out, closing the door behind him with a force just short of a slam.

"What's going on?" Willa demanded as soon as he was gone. "How come you never told me there's someone's sneaking around the house?

"I didn't want you to—"

"And don't try and tell me that baloney about not wanting to scare me. Finding a cop standing in the living room is just as scary as hearing there's a pervert hiding in the bushes."

"Shh—" Stella hisses. They could hear the branches of the rhododendron scratching against the clapboards outside the window as Officer Schmitt examined the foliage for telltale signs of an intruder. The sharp snap of a branch, then another, attesting to either his ungainly bulk or careless movements. "There's nothing for you to be concerned about."

"If someone's staring in our house I—"

"I didn't actually say there was—I said there *could be.*"

"What's that supposed to mean? Did you see someone or not?"

"Shh—" she hissed again, both falling silent at the sound of impatient knuckles rapping against the front door.

Stella strode to the door, pulling it open with an abruptness that left Officer Schmitt momentarily startled.

"I didn't find anything unusual," he said, instantly regaining his composure. "We'll keep an eye on the house for a few days, but in the meantime if you see or hear anything else, call the station right away."

Stella nodded, a satisfied smile settling over her mouth as she closed the door, an expression Willa had seen often enough to render it instantly readable.

"What? Are you kidding? You made this whole thing up, didn't you?"

"In case you haven't noticed, Willa, this is a wicked world we live in. All I'm looking for is a little protection. Without some incentive the cops in this town wouldn't so much as throw a stick at this place, let alone an occasional glance. It wouldn't matter if we were being attacked by aliens, they don't see people like us. We don't exist."

"Protection from what?"

"Protection, Willa. Just protection. I might've fallen behind on my religion, but even a heathen knows that God helps those who help themselves."

They'd taken very little with them when they left. Nothing beyond the bare essentials. They'd simply gone.

Considering that Stella had always been prone to secrecy and unexplained impulses, Willa wasn't especially surprised when her mother shook her awake in the middle of full darkness to announce that they were leaving.

"Don't turn on the light," Stella admonished when Willa instinctively reached for the lamp. "It'll draw attention."

Bewildered, but nevertheless compliant in her state of fogged grogginess, Willa pulled open drawers and pushed unseen clothes into the suitcase laid open across the end of her bed, hoping she was at least taking a goodly portion of those things she would've chosen had it been daylight or if she were fully awake.

Neither spoke as they stuffed their cases into the cavernous trunk of Stella's battered old car. Willa was fully awake by then, her mind tangled with immediate questions, yet she knew to hold back her inquiries in the face of her mother's distinct urgency to get away.

Stella rolled the car backward in the driveway without starting the engine, turning the key in the ignition only once the tires hit the curb and the bulky tank unceremoniously halted. She pumped the gas pedal with an impatient effort to crank the engine to life, emitting a string of curses barely contained under her breath as ancient components struggled to catch.

The loud grunts and creaks coming from under the hood rolled away up the street in a rude assault on the quiet night, announcing the approaching car even before its arrival. With any further pretense of remaining noiseless effectively shattered, Stella trounced her foot hard on the gas pedal, launching the car onto the slumbering street with a jarring hiccup.

At the end of the block, Stella jerked the wheel sharply and headed away from the center of town. Willa sat rigid in the back seat, as if her spine had been fused to the vinyl, trying not to focus on the rather harrowing complication that her mother had never bothered to procure a driver's license, had in fact, never properly learned to drive. Stella herself saw no problem with this minor detail, considering that from the moment the car moved into the driveway months earlier, it had simply been her habit to slide behind the wheel and drive off whenever she had somewhere to go.

A habit that apparently hasn't changed, regardless of whether or not she has a car.

Willa creeps through the unlatched screen door. The cottage lies eerie and silent around her. Dread and fear collide with the suggestion that the police have already been here collecting an unsuspecting Stella, at last returned, only to find herself promptly hauled away under lock and key courtesy of the ever-watchful eyes of Omega Pearl Bodie.

And yet when Willa throws a sweeping glance past the open closet door with its drooping wardrobe, across the unmade beds, down the hall to where she can see the untouched line of toiletries arranged on the toilet tank, she knows that no one has been here in her absence. Not the police, nor the persistently curious Omega, not the alleged criminal herself.

How could you do this? How could you do something so awful? Willa's breathing feels suddenly painful, clawing up from her chest and scratching over her lips in a spill across the empty room, her voice a harsh whisper as the words tear open inside her head. *You don't even care. You don't. When have you ever cared about anything but yourself?*

She pictures Stella stretched across the bed, imagines her mother's calm disinterest as she half-heartedly listens to Willa's accusations. The invisible scene strong enough to turn Willa's insides hot with rage.

It's disgusting. What you've done is disgusting. They know about you. They know and they're looking for you. It's over. You've ruined it. You've ruined everything.

The money, of course, is Stella's coveted prize, an illicit treasure she's easily protected with the ugly doll. Willa knows that the roster of accusations steadily piling in her head is of little consequence to her mother, and she is more than certain what Stella would say if she were standing here now, face-to-face with her laundry list of crimes.

What the hell's the big deal? It's not like I killed anybody for cripe sake. How about all those married men going off with a strange woman they picked up in a bar? Don't any of those idiots think maybe they had it coming? Because they did. They got what they deserved. Maybe the dirty cheats will think twice next time. Maybe—though I wouldn't bet on it.

Willa's knees quake violently, her limbs no longer capable of supporting her weight. She drops to sit on the edge of Stella's bed, bending forward until her forehead touches her knees.

What is she supposed to do with this mess—this god-awful catastrophe? It's ragingly clear that Stella is in deep, and Willa can only hope that her mother has some miracle plan for getting out of this colossal disaster she's orchestrated.

Yet she knows that if she sinks to her knees right now and sticks her hand under the bed in search of the box, she will find nothing other than the empty space it once occupied. Just as she knows that Stella isn't coming back. Not now. Probably not ever.

Thirty-three

There is nothing left. Willa has taken it all, every hat and matching pair of shoes, every nightgown, flower patterned dress and slim-fitting pencil skirt Stella has left hanging in the closet or stuffed into her allotment of dresser drawers. Every shred of her former presence once here is now gone. Dead things tossed into a dead river.

Afterward, Willa sits on the bank and watches the last armload of her mother's visible life drift away, ever so slowly, stubbornly refusing to sink. She fervently prays that the dark tinted water will relent, yawn its once mighty mouth to swallow these final remnants into the hidden depths of its watery insides. Yet she is fearful that the brittle trove will instead continue to float away like a crippled fleet bound for parts unknown.

It is some time later when she returns to the cottage and sweeps the accumulated dust from the vacant closet and out from under the bed. Now, should the police eventually find their way to The Moonglow, there is nothing here to see. Nothing incriminating to prove that Stella has ever been here. Nothing even to prove that Willa has ever had a mother.

Throughout the afternoon, as Willa works to obliterate all signs of Stella from the cottage, her senses remain tuned in alert expectation of an enraged outburst from Omega Pearl Bodie. That the woman is right now diligently posed behind the slightly upturned blinds watching her comings and goings, Willa is certain. Yet despite the clear indications of Willa's activities, as she carries away several armloads of Stella's clothing and accessories, Omega remains out of sight; the office door firmly closed against Willa's determined extinction of all tangible links to her vanished mother.

It is long past dark when Willa's task is at last complete. She tumbles into bed without supper, far too weary in heart and soul to care about something as pointless and insignificant as pushing food into her mouth.

But sleep will not come as a troupe of demons bearing hideous fears crowd inside her head, running back and forth in an erratic dance, slamming up against the walls of her skull so that every cell moans in a single throbbing ache.

Her apprehensions will neither leave nor settle, piling one on top of another in a pyramid so high as to obliterate even the strongest glimmer of hopeful light. They taunt her with the truth that this has been only one day that she's managed to put behind her. There is still tomorrow to navigate, and the day after … and then all the days to follow.

Tomorrow she will talk to Omega. She'll admit only what feels necessary, though even then it will be more than she cares to share. Yet Willa understands it's a necessary hurdle if she intends to ask Omega to let her stay in the cottage a while longer. She'll take on Stella's cleaning job, reminding Omega, if necessary, that yes, absolutely she can handle it. Has in fact been handling it for a goodly portion of their time here.

Willa will stay only until she's sorted things through and figured out what to do, however long that is. Because right now she doesn't know. Hasn't a clue. And all she can see when she wakes in the morning and goes to sleep at night is the colossal wall of fearful unknowns piling up around her like an infernal curse.

How often she's wished, prayed, begged to be alone. Doing what she wants, going where she wants, away from Stella. A normal person at last living a normal life. And now here she is alone, not so much liberated as terrified. Fiercely wanting to take her foolish pleas back, even as she promises never to think or utter them again.

And she can't say right now whether she loves her mother or hates her. Whether she wants to protect or condemn her. Because the more Willa wrestles against the avalanche of confusion meshed together inside her head, the more it seems that love and hate feel pretty much the same.

The days pass, but Willa doesn't keep track. It is several nights later when she hears something of the familiar winding toward her through the dense layers of a dreamless sleep—the same sound she's heard often enough over the course of this summer that it barely causes her to stir beyond the brief movement required to roll over onto her opposite side.

A fire. Just another fire.

As is now the pattern, sleep has been a long time in coming, and she clings to the murky edges of unconsciousness, willing the night to return to quiet. But even after several minutes have passed—then several more—the sirens continue to rattle the dark with an urgent scream.

Another big one. The kind that will require assistance from fire companies in every nearby town. Apparently Norman Hitchcock has once again succeeded—slipped through the cracks in his insatiable quest to win his terrible game.

Willa swings one leg over the edge of the mattress, feeling with her toes for the shorts she's dropped on the floor hours earlier.

Surely she's witnessed enough fires over the past months that she never has need of seeing another. Yet, it is that same sense of fevered excitement and curiosity she's felt nearly every time previous that once again works to peel through the layers of groggy sleep and propel her to wakefulness, carrying her down the creaky cottage steps and into the yard.

The moon rides high and full in a bed of slowly drifting clouds. Fat and round—bright in a way that turns the night alive with shadows. Shadows that move, whisper and sigh in response to the far-off clamor, even as they remain perfectly still and impossibly silent.

She races along the highway, Omega's bicycle bumping and shimmying beneath her like a reluctant stallion as she wings her way toward the telltale sounds of fire and its accompanying commotion. And while she hasn't yet deduced the precise location of the blaze, she is certain that as long as she remains alert to sound and smell, she will eventually find it just as she always has.

Her knees lock instinctively and she jerks the handle bars, wildly swerving to avoid an enormous black cat that darts into her path from nowhere. The animal turns its head to glare at her with ominous yellow eyes, then vanishes into a clustered nest of honeysuckle bushes as Willa resumes peddling and barrels past.

Fully awake with renewed charges of adrenaline, any lingering sense of drowsiness she's carried with her into the night is altogether gone as her legs slide up and down like mechanical pistons pumping the pedals, beads of perspiration dotting the skin along her hairline and dampening the armpits of her sleeveless blouse in half-moon crescents.

A wailing hook and ladder truck whizzes past in a red, shining blur just as Willa nears the invisible line where the highway ends and the placid streets of Harriet's Bluff begin. In the bright white moonlight she can easily make out the name, *Burnsville,* painted on the side of the truck in elegant black scroll. A pumper truck sails by mere seconds later, both vehicles swerving sharply to accommodate the turn into a narrow dirt lane just beyond the trees up ahead.

For no reason she can explain, Willa suddenly feels it—the distinct sense of something wholly apparent, yet nevertheless impossible to comprehend. An eerie chill prickles a discomforting trail along the back of her neck like the inscription of a bony finger, lending to the terrible assurance that despite its assumed familiarity, everything about this night is in fact unmistakably different.

Even from a distance, certain details of the flaming house are clearly visible—the peeling paint and boarded-up windows effectively suited to the aura of lonesome abandonment shrouding the sad dwelling like a widow's dirge.

By all appearances the house is a long time forgotten and thoroughly ignored, the former residents gone for lack of interest, or possibly died off to extinction years earlier, neither condition an unusual occurrence in such a thoroughly forgettable place as Harriet's Bluff.

With her legs still straddling the bike, Willa pauses to watch the assembled crews struggle to maneuver the thick ropes of heavy black hose laid out over the grass, strategically aiming nozzles to blow powerful jets of water against one side of the house. Despite their inspired intent, the effort nevertheless proves ineffective in drowning the black smoke billowing up from acid-tongued flames spiking the heavens through large portions of the roof.

Willa swings her leg over the seat, quickly wheeling the wobbly bike to the edge of the yard where it's less likely to be underfoot. Releasing her grip on the handlebars, she allows the vehicle to drop on its side like a handful of carelessly discarded wrappers, leaving it there with the expectation of retrieving it later. The furthest thought from her mind right then is the suggestion that she may never care to see it again.

"BACK—EVERYBODY BACK," a fireman shouts to the handful of spectators clustered at the base of the hill as chunks of burning shingles shoot upward and outward.

The moon is almost directly overhead, moving in and out of the drifting clouds teasingly, as the flames stretch skyward in a determined effort to burn the brilliant white orb from the sky.

While the attending audience quickly swells, the collected throng stands uncharacteristically silent. An eerie quiet drops like a weighted curtain to eclipse the usual chatter and accustomed exchanges of curious speculation. All faces remain focused on the unfolding scene—a sea of unblinking eyes watching as the firemen wrestle cumbersome equipment and shout directions back and forth. The company of onlookers willingly surrender their attentions to the mesmerizing sounds of the burning house itself: its wretched cries of agony as the fire rapidly devours both skin and bones; the splintering crash of something collapsing within the walls; the unearthly wail of a lifeless thing dying a tragic death.

Despite valiant efforts to quell the inferno, the flames appear to grow increasingly furious, at once louder and more distinct. And is not merely the crack and hiss of all-consuming fire, but something else entirely. Something Willa can't recall hearing at any blaze previous—a sound so distinctly human that hearing it now turns her blood icy cold even as it sweeps the air from her lungs.

"OH MY, GOD," someone screams, and Willa knows then that it isn't her imagination—someone else has felt it, too.

An immediate swell of commotion sweeps its way along the crowd—a collective gasp followed by a frenzied rush of excitement. A flood of confusion arrives on the tail of a certain sense of immediacy, yet it is still another instant before Willa sees what those standing in front already have. A figure, just emerged from the wide open front door of the house, runs across the yard, one outstretched arm completely engulfed in flames.

The fire rapidly fans out across his chest, wicking up into his hair as he runs across the grass screaming in agony, the horrible reel continuing to play even after two firemen rush forward and grab the frantic burning man, wrestling him to the ground—rolling him back and forth to smother the flames.

"IT'S HIM. THEY'VE GOT HIM. THEY'VE GOT HITCHCOCK."

"OH, SWEET JESUS … THEY'VE FINALLY GOT HIM. THEY CAUGHT HIM."

"THEY SHOULD THROW HIM RIGHT BACK IN THERE. HE LIKES FIRE, GIVE HIM FIRE."

Norman Hitchcock. Is it possible?

"She's still in there ... inside ... she's in there. I can't get to her ... I can't find her," the burned man wails. And the crowd instantly falls silent, unwilling to miss even a syllable of Norman Hitchcock's potential confession.

"There's too much smoke," the man continues to cry, choking, gasping as he struggles to speak. "I can't get to her ... I can't find her."

Then again, the screaming, only now they aren't the sounds of a dying house or a burning man, but someone in the crowd—a woman staring in wide-eyed horror at the flaming house.

"OH, MY, GOD—SWEET JESUS—OH MY, GOD," the woman cries over and over in a wrenching litany. And Willa instinctively lifts her gaze to follow the heightening screams and sees the very cause of the woman's broken repetition—a small, dark face in an upstairs window. *A child. Her mouth wide in silent terror. No sound she can possibly make that is capable of reaching past the sound of crashing beams and splintering wood.*

Suddenly, someone bolts loose from the crowd, running toward the house with frantic determination—the tall slender body at once recognizable as a handful of men rush forward to subdue him, grappling to pull him back even as he fights to free himself. "LET ME GO! LET ME GO. I'VE GOT TO HELP HER. I'VE GOT TO HELP!"

Willa shouts to him over the commotion, but if he hears her, he gives no indication.

"THERE'S A KID IN THERE. PLEASE. DON'T YOU SEE? I HAVE TO HELP HER. SHE'LL DIE. I'VE GOT TO GO IN THERE," he pleads, frantically struggling to pull himself loose from the persistent restraint of multiple hands.

And he is still shouting, begging them to release him, when the face in the window vanishes, melting like an illusion behind a curtain of fire and smoke.

Thirty-four

Willa pushes her way through the crowd calling his name, but no one moves aside or otherwise turns to acknowledge her. The immediate memory of the terrifying scene is still freshly alive and bleeding. The crush of pale waxen faces holds in mute horror as they stare into the inferno, all eyes searching for some hopeful glimpse of what is so obviously gone.

"JESSE—" she shouts again, reaching the place where the men had been holding him only to find he is gone. She spins around, eyes frantically raking the crowd, the clusters of firemen, the line of trucks and the night itself. Calling his name ... all the while calling his name.

She runs without destination. Runs to escape the image of the small, dark face framed within the burning window. Runs from the lingering sound of a child's terrified screams, cries that had no chance of reaching the watching crowd, but which Willa nevertheless continues to hear over and over, like a howling wind threshing her on all sides. She feels the wetness on her face though she doesn't consciously know when the tears have started leaking from her eyes. *Dead. A living, breathing child is dead. But not for nothing, because they've got him. They've caught the murderous madman. It's finished. Over.*

Low growing briars and rangy branches reach out to snare her, scratching against her arms and legs as she tears through the thicket fringing the woods, then plunges between the trees into the dark abyss of unlit forest.

Asleep Without Dreaming

Her breathing feels raspy and tight in her chest and she gasps in a hungry effort to collect even a single mouthful of air. Her lungs are close to bursting as the night comes crashing down.

Unseen brambles slice her skin like broken glass as she moves through the darkness like someone possessed of an urgent destination, though in truth she has nowhere to go. No place to hide herself away from the terrible images racing through her head.

An occasional glimmer of bright white moonlight winks through the leafy canopy lifted against the sky on heavy branches. Ordinarily a welcoming comfort, all at once the assurance of light is nearly as frightening as the sinister threat of darkness. The moonlight somehow serving to illuminate the horrible pictures inscribed within her eyes; things she refuses to look at but can plainly see—the burning house, a flaming man, the terrified face in an unreachable window at the top of a rapidly disintegrating house.

She doesn't believe she is consciously looking for the gnarled tree, yet she feels distinctly relieved once she's found it; its crooked arms, at once recognizable, draw her forward like a beckoning hand, assuring her that the shack is here—just ahead. The place she's been heading to all along.

The door is slightly ajar and she feels Jesse's presence even before she reaches out her hand to push it open, the dull ache of rusty hinges unable to mask the muffled sounds of quiet agony leaking from within.

"Jesse ..." Willa says so quietly that if she's truly spoken, it is less than a whisper.

"Jesse?" she repeats, peering into the heavy gloom in search of the response that has failed to come.

"No—" he says as she steps inside, his voice coming in deep, ragged breaths. "Go. Please—just go." The voice, frighteningly unfamiliar, sends her heartbeat racing forward with a surge of uncertain fear.

"It's all right," she says, pausing in the doorway. "I was there. I know what happened."

A lacy dusting of silvery moonlight leaks through the pane-less windows from the night outside, and Willa can see him sitting on the dingy mattress, his lanky frame folded tight into the corner, head bowed against his bent knees.

"I saw everything ..." she begins, and then pauses. She wholly believes that she understands something of what he is feeling—looking at him now and still seeing his frantic distress as the men held him back from his heroic attempt to save the dying child. And yet she feels herself stumble, unsure if adequate words even exist to phrase such emotions.

"You're a hero. Don't you understand? Everyone saw you. Everyone saw how you tried to save her," she says quietly, moving to kneel on the mattress beside him, leaning forward to press her face into the smoky curve of his neck, surprised to feel the wetness on his face, her emotions at once unhinged by the unexpected presence of his tears.

He shoves her away roughly, causing her to fall backward on the mattress, and she stares at him in stunned surprise.

"Hero? Can't you see what this is about?" he stares at her with unreadable eyes, dark and deep and wholly unfamiliar. "I'm anything but a hero."

"You tried to help, Jesse. You tried and that's the same thing. It counts for something." Willa hesitates, forcing herself not to look away from the overwhelming crux of emotion mirrored in his eyes. The magnitude of everything she sees there rushes at her like a mortal landslide carrying the burden of things far too terrible to comprehend.

"They couldn't let you go in there. It was too late. You've got to see that. There was nothing you could do."

He doesn't answer.

"They caught him, Jesse. Did you see that? They caught him. They got Norman Hitchcock."

A plat of dark hair falls across one eye, but he doesn't reach to push it away. "No, they didn't. They didn't catch anyone.

He has nothing to do with it. He isn't the one they're looking for."

"But he—"

"It's me. I'm the one," he says, his voice cracking, shattering like glass. "I did it. I'm the one. I thought it was empty. I didn't know anyone was in there. I swear I didn't know. It was all boarded up. It was supposed to be empty."

Tears streak his soot-darkened cheeks like rain across a dirty windshield. And when he lifts a hand to sweep the wetness from his cheek, Willa sees the angry blisters of charcoaled skin bubbled along his fingers.

"Oh my, God—your hands—"

He stares at her without answering, the silence behind his tortured expression speaking louder and clearer than any response he might offer—the immediate understanding of what he's said and what he fails to say, hurtling toward her with the force of a runaway train.

"*You?*" The single word slices over her lips in what feels like a blade sharpened with cruel intent. "You? All this time it's been you?" she repeats, unable even to feel her tongue forming the words.

She tries to move but can't. Tries to stand, but can't recall her legs. The air pressing in around her all at once turns silvery black and impossible to breathe. An entire lifetime ticks past before he finally speaks, his broken voice winding in from a place far off.

"I never wanted to hurt anyone. That's not what any of this is about. None of it was ever about hurting innocent people. I wouldn't've done it. I never would've done it if I'd known someone was in there."

"But, why, Jesse? Why did you do it at all?"

"Because I'm no good. I've never done a good thing in my life," his voice snags and breaks—drops away out of reach.

There is a steady hammering inside her head, the noise echoing loud enough to obliterate the quiet. *How is this possible? What is he telling her? What does he mean? Because she doesn't ...*

can't … understand. This is Jesse, not a madman … this isn't real. It isn't real. This can't be real.

His voice crawls back from a distance, traveling across miles, and Willa leans forward over her bent knees, struggling to comprehend his words. "Everyone will think this has something to do with what happened to my mother, but none of it was ever about her. I barely even know her. I haven't seen her since they put her away. She wanted to ruin his life because of how he just threw her away when he lost interest; but the way it worked out, she went to prison and he became a hero.

"People around here still ask him about it. Apparently they haven't lost their fascination for hearing how he wrestled a loaded gun away from a madwoman. He never gets tired of telling how he 'looked her straight in the eyes and told her to give him the gun. How he didn't even blink—just reached and took it out of her hand," Jesse says, his voice stumbling with the quiet hesitation of someone surprised to hear himself speaking.

"Having her go to prison was the perfect convenience for him. He had an entire new life away from us already, so the only real problem was finding himself stuck with a son he didn't want. His girlfriend wasn't having any part of raising a kid that wasn't hers, so he jumped at the offer when one of his buddies down at the firehouse said I could hang around on days off from school and summer vacations. He said I could help out at the station by doing little chores and that it was never too early to learn how to be one of them—to be a fireman," His voice swells against some unseen obstacle lodged in the back of his throat, an obstruction too large for his words to easily move past.

He wipes at his cheek with a damaged hand and Willa waits for him to continue. She makes no move to speak. There is nothing she can say that will ever fit here.

"The first time he … the first time he touched me … I didn't understand what it was about. I didn't know … just that it must be wrong. *Bad.* Worse than bad, but I didn't know what to do. Him and Red grew up together. Lifelong friends. I was supposed to trust him.

"His name's Joel. Him and my old man lost their fathers in an explosion at the zinc mine. They were little kids when it happened, and being fatherless was the thing that brought them together.

"Maybe that's why I thought I had to believe him when he told me not to be a sissy, that it was all part of the special bond between men and boys ... but I didn't ... I wouldn't. I wouldn't do what he wanted me to. I said no. I said no ... I said NO."

Again he pauses, grasping for the necessary courage to continue.

"The more I cried the madder he got. He warned me I'd better not tell anyone. He said no one would believe a kid with a jailbird mother anyway. He threatened me every time, but he didn't really have to. I had nobody I could tell, and even if I did, how was I supposed to? How do you say something like that out loud?

"I promised myself that if I tried hard enough, I could block it out. Just pretend that none of it ever happened. That it wasn't really me. But I started having nightmares and failing in school. It wasn't just about being ashamed, it was something else—like I was being eaten alive. I knew I had to tell Red—but I was afraid—sick and afraid.

"I'd just turned ten when I finally got the nerve to tell him, and I knew the instant I said it that I'd made a mistake. He called me a liar. A sick pervert ... a lot of things. He grabbed my arm when I tried to run, shouting how he'd known Joel his whole life and that I was a liar. A filthy disgusting liar," his voice falls to a near whisper, the pause going on for so long that Willa is certain he's said all that he intends.

"He dragged me down to the fire station. Made me stand in front of Joel and tell him to his face everything I'd accused him of. My old man apologized for my *sick, perverted lies* and promised Joel that he'd take care of the situation. They shook hands and patted each other on the back, but I saw the look in Joel's eyes—a promise he'd get even.

"The fires were just, maybe a way to … I don't know. I can't even remember when I thought of starting the first one. It was just this thing that was always there in my mind—some angry, evil thing waiting for a chance to come alive.

"Being around the other guys when they were playing their weekly card games and listening to them bragging about the fires they'd been to made it easy enough to learn what I needed to know. Not just about putting them out, but the best ways to start one—what a fire needs to live and breathe. I saw how my old man thrived on the adrenaline. Saw the way it kicked in every time the alarm went off, and I knew I had to use that somehow. Even if it was just to get his attention. Let him know he can't just erase the people he brought into the world because he'd lost interest. He can't just turn his back on what he doesn't want to see—can't throw his kid into a place worse than hell and walk away.

"Once I was old enough that he couldn't push me around so easily, he started throwing punches. The only thing that's ever kept him away is the fires. The alarm goes off and he's gone—even when it means dropping his fists. Not because he's some kind of hero, he just figures it's another chance to show-off. He's been bragging to his buddies all summer that he'll be the one to nail Norman Hitchcock.

"Every time he went off running after another fire, I chalked one up for me, because here he thinks he knows everything when he obviously doesn't know shit.

"I prayed every time I did it that it would be the last. That it would be the one that finished them and neither would be coming back. It was the only way—the only way to stop a monster is to kill it.

"I hated doing it at first. I'd get the shakes and throw-up. I swore I'd never do it again. I knew people were scared and that was never my intention, especially when I thought about the other guys at the firehouse. I was afraid one of them would get hurt and it wasn't supposed to be about anyone else—just him and Joel. They're the only ones any of this was meant for.

"But after a while I stopped feeling sorry. Stopped thinking how despicable I was and started believing that maybe it wasn't just about the two of them. Maybe they were all just as guilty for refusing to see what was right there in front of them—for looking the other way because it was too ugly to accuse one of their own. They must've suspected. They must've known, but they didn't care. Nobody did.

"I was just a little boy, for God's sake. Just a kid," he chokes, lowering his head and touching his forehead against his bent knee, his narrow shoulders quaking.

A span as wide and deep as decades passes before he lifts his head to continue, his voice splintering, breaking, so that Willa has to lean forward in order to catch his words.

"I couldn't just wait around for the same thing to happen to Luke. I'm not a kid anymore, I can fight back, but he can't.

"I figured if I just kept doing this thing I started without letting myself think about it, it wasn't so bad. I told myself they're only fires—just fires. And after awhile it felt okay. It felt okay in the very worst way."

Willa feels her tears leaking past her lashes, tears so hot they burn holes in her skin as they trail down her face; yet she hasn't the necessary strength to brush them away.

"Everything changed when I met you. You made me believe that maybe I didn't have to do this anymore. That I could stop and forget about everything—about them. I didn't have to be that kind of person anymore because ... because of how you cared for me ... really cared.

"But I was just fooling myself. I thought I could burn the ugliness out of me, but it's still here—it's still here and I can't get rid of it. *I can't get rid of it.*"

Willa gathers his injured words like scattered petals, holding them tightly in her fist. And although she can still detect an occasional quaver, she senses a gathering of strength—hesitant but otherwise steady—as if he is resolved to the necessity of confession. And as she waits, listens, hears the very things she's been asking for all along, it is nevertheless impossible to fully comprehend the entirety of what he is saying.

Does she even know Jesse Truman? Has she ever known him at all? All the fires. An entire summer in flames. All the times they've raced in his truck to witness fire after fire—all the time speculating over Norman Hitchcock's ongoing appetite for revenge. How can any of what Jesse is now saying even be possible—or honest? She's known all along that something is wrong, but not this. Never this. And now there are a dozen hideous pictures forming inside her head. Ugly, perverse images he has opened up and laid out before her; two wicked men she has never known, but who she clearly sees. Each of them repulsive in the very worst way.

She understands he is waiting for something, senses his need for some solacing word or gesture in exchange for his terrible secrets. Yet the broad scope of her feelings lie quiet and still, shrouded beneath a barrier of stunned disbelief and uncertainty.

"But what about Norman Hitchcock? He really did escape from prison, didn't he? There are all those newspaper stories, it's—"

"Coincidence," he says. "When he broke out, everyone just assumed he came back here for revenge. The reason they've never found him is because he isn't here. I doubt he ever had any intention of coming back. This town isn't the sort of place you come back to once you've had the chance to leave it."

Why, why, why has he done this? He's ruined everything. For the first time in her life she's truly felt connected to another person. She would've helped him. Somehow. She would've figured out some other way. There had to be something else. They could've run away. Taken the little boy with them and never looked back. She would've done that. He'd only had to ask. She would've done anything.

A million words spin through her mind, utterances instantly caught within a vortex of emotion, keeping them from leaving her mouth. Assurances, accusations, promises—all remain unspoken. And she wraps her arms around her bent knees, holding tight as the world splinters and crashes down around her in a million unmendable shards, ducking her face when she can no longer bear to see.

He asks her to forgive him. To please, if nothing else, to please forgive him. To say something. To just say something. To please say something. And in her heart, she tells him she simply can't think about it yet because she still needs to pretend for a time that none of it has happened. It is too much to grasp so soon. Too much to take in at one time. Time. That is the thing she needs. *Time.* Time to think. Time to sort it out and make herself understand. She explains it to him calmly, rationally, without accusation—except that she can't make herself speak the words where he can hear them.

She listens as he rises to his feet, but she doesn't lift her head, still welded to her kneecaps. Her confusion and uncertainty feel too much like rejection for either of them to ignore it away; just as the necessary strength that would allow her to raise her face and offer even the most minimal reassurance is altogether gone.

He moves toward the door. He says he is going to the river.

To swim, she believes. *To wash away the ugly stain of what he's done and of what has been done to him. To clear his mind of the tortured images of a dying child and all those other visions this terrible night has unquestionably seeded in his head.*

And she might have gone with him. She might have followed so he isn't left to shoulder the deepest darkest agony of this night alone. But she doesn't. She isn't prepared to share the burden of his guilt and suffering, so she squeezes her eyes shut and listens to him go.

Thirty-five

They find him on a Tuesday afternoon nearly two weeks after his disappearance, and the men struggle to pull his body from the murky depths of the scarcely moving river.

Later, they will deem it probable that he's been here all along; through all the days they've searched and found nothing. Right here—imprisoned within the dense tangle of slimy vegetation spilling into the water from the profusion of brambles and undergrowth crowding the water line where the river sluggishly rubs against the land.

Slimy tendrils and whip-like stems stubbornly cling to the soiled tee-shirt molded to his chest with a slick glue of muddy water. Intertwining fingers of plant life reluctant to release him, trail from his limp dangling arms and wind around his blue-jean-clad legs as if determined to hold the sodden denim from leaving his lifeless limbs. Others droop from his neck like the eerily dismembered tentacles of some deep river creature as they lift him from the water and carry him across the field to the line of dust-lacquered pick-ups that have brought them here.

Willa hears an urgent voice screaming frantically inside her head, commanding her not to watch, fervently warning her not to look. But even then, her eyes bypass her resolve, deceive her into seeing everything. Her unblinking stare holds tightly to his ruined face, transfixed by the fine threads of feathery river weeds drawn across his water-bloated features in crazed lines to suggest a piece of broken china—shattered, then carelessly repaired.

She presses the heels of her palms hard against the sockets of her eyes, determined to flatten the images before they have engraved themselves inside her brain. Yet, in the wink of one brief instant, the grotesque portrait has already been etched too finely to ever be extinguished. Disconcertingly intact. Preserved in every horrific detail.

For a long time afterward—likely forever—she knows she will continue to see him here in this place where they've found him, submerged beneath the dark tinted water, held still within a cave of quiet gloom as the bright, hot days fold into deep moist nights. His flesh untouched even by moonlight. Unable to speak, or breathe, or see. Forever powerless to break free from the twining green arms holding him. Eternally asleep in a place without dreams.

She doesn't cry—as if she's all but forgotten the basic operating instructions wiring her emotions. Foolishly persistent in her determination to convince herself that it is some other unfortunate dead boy that the men now carry away mournfully, each man holding to the solemn stony silence that customarily accompanies the receipt of such tragedies.

Her gaze instinctively lands on the bracelet drooping from his wrist to lie against the inside curve of his hand. Her stare purposely drifts to the foot clad in a mud-colored sneaker, its dangling shoelace broken once and tied together, his other foot bare. And she frantically strives to assure herself that there is nothing remarkably similar in any of that which is immediately familiar.

The weight of her anguish holds her to the ground like an anchor.

"Oh, God, no—please no," she hears someone cry. Each syllable unwinding with the passionate wail that carries all desperate prayers. Uncertain as to who it is that has mimicked the very plea twisting within her mouth, even as she feels the words crushing over her lips like stones.

Now bolting forward, she flees across the field ahead of the men, refusing herself even a single backward glance as she frantically lumbers through the tall grass to reach the wide dirt road that has brought her here.

Thirty-six

She lifts the mug of beer and swallows deeply, certain from the way he watches her—discreet at first, lowering his gaze when she tips her head in his direction, instantly growing bolder when she doesn't look away—that by the time she is ready to leave the bar, he will have told her his name and asked for hers.

Just as she knows that before the balmy fabric of dawn has fragmented and melted into morning, before she's walked the three blocks back to her motel room across from the bus depot, she will have let him kiss her. And if not this night, then definitely the next, before she boards the bus back to Harriet's Bluff, she will have slept with him. Once for sure, but no more than twice.

She is neither naïve nor ignorant of the crude phrases and ugly words passed back and forth in gossipy whispers to describe women who do what she does. Along with everyone else, she's learned such coarse designations back in grade school. Heard them cruelly snarled from behind mean expressions in the lunchroom or shouted on the playground. Has uttered them herself on occasion, even once she understands the contemptible nature of their meanings.

The changes unfolding in other corners of the world—an era of women's liberation and free love—have not yet reached this far. Even so, despite whatever ignoble references people might use to describe the doings in her life, she's never stopped to care. Because for Willa there is something of far more importance than popular opinion or expected morals. Something achingly real. A mortal stake driven deep into the very core of her soul. Some essential part of herself which desperately strives to recapture what she once held so close to her heart that it felt like her own breathing; continuing to seek what is lost despite having long ago arrived at the conviction that she will never again feel anything like it—will in fact never again feel anything at all.

And it is always the same string of emotions that flood over her when someone touches her who isn't Jesse. From the first kiss, a stranger's hand cupping her breast, unfamiliar hands trailing along her back and touching her hair ... she will immediately know that she wants nothing more than to have it over. Even as her nameless paramours lose themselves to a fleeting moment of unfurled lust, her thoughts will have purposefully flown away to focus on a slice of artificial brilliance winking through a part in the pale curtains of some cheaply furnished hotel room—a neon light assuring the availability of *Rheingold* beer just across the street in yet another nondescript bar. All the while wanting whoever it is she's allowed to seduce her to be finished with what they've come for. Wishing him spent and still beside her so that she might pretend both him and herself away.

She understands that should she ever fully allow herself to examine this secret and shameful piece of her life, she might very well find herself irretrievably disturbed by the overt simplicity of giving herself away unconditionally. Eternally broken by the disconsolate truth that there's never been a need to explain anything about herself to any of these men, because she's never been with anyone who doesn't understand that all of this is temporary. Each brief coupling has no real meaning or durability beyond the fleeting here and now.

There is merely the sense of relief that comes from her knowing that none of them will ever care enough to express curiosity over the tiny scar dimpled in the skin just above her left eyebrow (an incident with a slingshot when she was eight);

or ask if she'd care to see a movie some Friday night; whether she prefers pepperoni or extra cheese on her pizza. None of what she does is intended for permanence. Each is a meaningless interlude made all the more inconsequential because none of the men that Willa Burkett allows to touch her will ever know or care anything about her or her reasoning for being here. There is no requirement to reveal where she's come from. No question as to her purpose in traveling to yet another distant town that has little to offer, other than the transitory juncture of a one-night stand.

She assures herself that this is all she wants. Tells herself time and again that it is enough. There is no one left she needs to think about, least of all herself.

It's been several years now since Omega Pearl Bodie left behind The Moonglow and moved down to Georgia to live with her sister. She's tried to sell the place, but there have been no takers. The FOR SALE sign is still there—tilting crazily where it's been hammered into a barren patch of earth out in front of the dark and empty office—as is Willa. She lives in one of the boarded-up cottages for the simple fact that she has no where to go and little money to get there. Though mostly she stays because she doesn't know how to leave.

It's been eight years since Jesse's drowning. Yet the why and how of it remains a mystery. It is true he hadn't known about the father and child living in the empty house, no one in Harriet's Bluff had. The pair were in fact strangers, hapless vagrants passing through on their way to someplace better. Their doomed role in that final blaze chiefly recalled as the concluding stroke of misfortune in the midst of events already deemed hopelessly tragic.

Only recently has Norman Hitchcock at last surfaced, found living in a small town in Texas. People are almost sad to see him ferried back to prison. He is, after all, something of a legend; and most consider it regrettable that he'd never been aware of his absentee role during that fearful summer in Harriet's Bluff.

Not until he is back behind bars does he learn the details of his near mythical run of infamy, and the crimes he knew nothing about. And he's genuinely disappointed that he's missed it all—the fear, the fires, and the fame.

Stella has never come back. Vanished in much the same deceitful way Martin had gone all those years earlier—premeditated abandonment, deceptively executed in the context of an otherwise unexceptional act. Except with Stella there'd been no misplaced kiss as she'd gone out the door for the last time, once more lending Willa to question what it is about herself that makes it so easy for people to leave her. She still finds herself occasionally wondering if Stella has indeed succeeded in outrunning either her crimes or her demons. Whether she's self-destructed or remarkably survived.

Despite the necessary lies she is forever feeding herself, Willa has never successfully convinced herself that all of this is not entirely about Jesse and the hollow place he's left yawning wide and deep inside her, the place where her heart has long ago cracked open and been swallowed by her soul.

She knows the most dangerous untruths are the ones you tell yourself. They are the ones that crash the hardest. Splinter the deepest. Wound the greatest. She understands, too, the danger of living within the walls of memory, as if there is nothing else beyond that which has already gone.

Yet the passage of time has done little to hinder the perilous chunks of remembrance that continue to break loose and rise up behind her eyes, reviving the very essence of Jesse Truman and the way he'd loved her. Even though she forces herself to look away the very moment they appear, the gauzy images are still there everywhere inside her head. Her days with him have taken on the deceptively hazy shadings of shimmering blue and gold. Carefully selected recollections of laughing and teasing that imply a tangible warmth and closeness, even while she recognizes that little of it can actually be true. Such intimacy could never have been as perfect as memory claims for the glaring truth of how it all ended.

Yet she remembers the details of moments she's rarely trusted herself to revive: lying on the riverbank ... the way he'd reached out and touched her arm before taking her hand that first time, wrapping her fingers into his palm when she failed to pull away. Even now she vividly recalls how much the moment had surprised her—surprised them both.

And there are still times when she can close her eyes and almost feel the warmth of his lips brushing against the back of her neck as she bends to re-tie a shoelace that has come undone. Can again hear those things he whispered in her ear as she clung to his shoulders in the dark river. His words and their meanings glowing through her insides like an enormous bright light.

Her senses readily reclaim even the smell of him—freshly soaped and showered—hair and skin that tasted of summer. And always she remembers his hands—the unexpected gentleness of his touch. Hands that said so much more than words and held as much emotion as a heart. And his eyes. His incredible navy eyes.

And she knows that these memories are purposely incomplete in that they recall only the sweetness of days and little of those other things. The way that everything had gone so horribly wrong never figures as prominently as the tender and hopeful promises dreamed inside her head. Because she'd so roundly believed in Jesse Truman before the truth came crashing down. Had loved and cherished everything about him in such a way that even now, she doesn't know how to let him go.

Despite everything that's transpired, she's never quite succeeded in convincing herself that his love for her was anything less than genuine. As real and true as someone so fatally flawed and tragically wounded could offer.

Only as the true portrait emerges, indubitably rising with the suggestion that quite possibly she'd had the power to change things if only she'd lifted her head—if only she'd said the necessary words when he'd most needed to hear them—that she rushes to slam the lid on what is still too ugly to see. Hindsight, after all, is nothing if not futile. Just as truth has no means for reversing what is already done. It is over. Over in a way that can never be repaired or rewritten, regardless of anything she's come to understand or otherwise believe.

One day she'll leave. Maybe follow Stella's one time dream to California. Maybe she will. She hasn't quite decided. But there's no one here to talk to and she's stopped listening to herself long ago.

The End

Made in the USA
Lexington, KY
13 September 2012